The closer Mac got to the water, the more he sensed another presence. A shiver of anticipation inched its way up his spine when he closed in on a quarry or if someone tried to ambush him. That shiver, in full force now, made him hope the noise of the falls would muffle the sound of his approach. He took no chances as he placed each footstep carefully, moving through the trees as silently as an Indian. *Why not?* he thought. *After all, I am half-Indian.* He saw a flash of white just as he reached the tree line at the edge of the pool. Peering through the trees at the waterfall, he saw what had triggered his senses. The ghostly apparition turned into a woman bathing.

A white flash of bare skin shimmered through the sluicing water. A curtain of dark hair shielded all but her long legs and saucy derrière. Struck immediately by the sight of her gorgeous body, his jaw dropped open, and he had to consciously shut it. He licked his dry lips and tried to compose himself. She wasn't a ghost. She was an angel.

A surreal scene of flashing refractions of light from the sun on the spray of water surrounded her. A rainbow formed an arch, framing her exquisite body. He became mesmerized by the heavenly vision.

What They Are Saying About

Rising Star Rosina LaFata

In AVENGING ANGEL, Rosina LaFata repeats her specialty of creating a strong, delightfully human heroine, a hero you long to have in your own life, enjoyable supporting characters—and one whale of an exciting adventure for them. I look forward to her future books, and hope there will be many of them to enjoy.

—Fran Priddy
Granny's Ghost

Chocolate's good for you. It makes you feel better. So, too, does SWEET TEMPTATIONS, with its heroine who raises cake decoration to a creative art, a great new neighbor to swoon over, and "the other woman" to detest—the action takes place on The Hill, St. Louis's delightful traditional Italian neighborhood, and will keep you turning the pages.

—Fran Priddy
Spider In The Christmas Tree

SWEET TEMPTATIONS kept me turning the pages until the wee hours of the morning. I couldn't put it down. I loved the action between a hero to die for and the heroine every woman wants to be. A book you can really enjoy reading.

—Sharon Sandvoss

Wings

Avenging Angel

by

Rosina LaFata

A Wings ePress, Inc.

Historical Romance Novel

For Kathy: Thank you for being such a great friend. I hope you enjoy Angel's Story. Love Rosina

Wings ePress, Inc.

Edited by: Crystal Laver
Copy Edited by: Ann K. Oortman
Senior Editor: Crystal Laver
Executive Editor: Lorraine Stephens
Cover Artist: Crystal Laver

Wings ePress Books
http://www.wings-press.com

ISBN 1-59088-887-1

Published In the United States Of America

March 2003

Wings ePress Inc.
403 Wallace Court
Richmond, KY 40475

Dedication

For my children,

Linda, Bob, and Cynthia,

who never lost faith in me.

I love you.

Acknowledgements

I would like to thank my critique group, Sue and Amy Harms, Carey Krieger, and Debbie Hull for their patience as I went through three re-writes of this manuscript. Without their belief in me, I would have given up a long time ago. Thanks, girls, you are the best.

I also want to thank my friend and teacher Bob Menchhofer for helping me edit my original manuscript. Bob, thank you for your precious time and generosity.

You all played a part of getting this manuscript to print. I couldn't have done it without you.

One

Pearly gray tendrils of dawn tinted the darkness with their first attempt to push the night sky into oblivion. Samantha leaned her elbows on the ledge of her open bedroom window and watched the sky brighten to gold. Night shadows still clung to the earth around bushes and trees, reluctant to give way to the light.

Stretching, she leaned farther out the upstairs window into the fresh morning. For now, while the sun still hid its face from the world, the air remained cool. She lifted the heavy mass of chestnut hair away from her neck to allow the breeze to caress her hot body. Soon the radiant sphere would cook the day with its blistering August heat.

She breathed in the familiar pungency of her surroundings—the smell of livestock, the fragrance of wildflowers, and the aroma of Ma's bread baking. She listened to the sounds of cattle lowing, horses nickering, and the usual murmur of voices telling her that her three older brothers and father were already busy with morning chores. Nothing unusual was going on outside.

Her Pa had chosen well when he settled in the fertile valley along the Missouri River. The land grew lush crops and fat cattle. Situated some fifty miles west of the old Missouri

Capital in St. Charles and about one hundred miles east of the new capital in Jefferson City, they were far enough away from the city to suit him.

Ducking to avoid the sash, Sammy pulled her head back into her room. She hurried to dress, still trying to capture the illusive memory of what woke her earlier than usual this morning. In concession to her Ma, she donned a calico skirt and matching shirtwaist. Once her indoor chores were finished, she could change into the leather split skirt Ma allowed her to wear when she helped her brother with the horses.

As Sammy opened her door and bounced down the narrow steps with all the exuberance of her seventeen years, she let her hand glide over the smooth worn wood of the stair railing. Carving the railing for Ma had been Da's special pride. He'd rubbed it until it was as smooth as butter, and his gift of love for her turned into a treasure for Sammy as well.

Nearing the bottom of the stairs, she recognized the sound that had awakened her. Lordy, it must be her brother Ryan. She remembered he'd rode into town last night. It served him right for drinking too much, not that he did it that often. Sammy chuckled to herself as she planned the heckling she would give him. She relished the thought of getting back at him for all the teasing he'd heaped on her.

The steps ended in the corner of the room that served as kitchen and parlor. Adjusting her eyes to the shadows still lurking around the furniture, she saw her mother bent over a bucket, retching. *Lord, have mercy! It wasn't Ryan.* Sammy nearly tripped on her skirts as she rushed to help. Snatching a cloth from the table, she hurried to wipe her mother's face.

"Ma, what's wrong?"

"Sorry, Sammy Luv, I feel terrible this morning. I think the smell of breakfast cookin is getting' to me."

"But Ma, it smells wonderful. How can it make you sick? Is the bacon rancid, or the milk spoiled from all the heat?"

"Ach, you know everything has been kept in the cellar where it's nice and cool. The food is not spoiled. Leave off the questions and just help me back to bed. I'm afraid you'll have to see to feeding Pa and your brothers." The sound of her mother's impatience alerted Sammy to the fact that all was not well. Her mother had remarkable self control and never spoke harshly to anyone. Besides that, Sammy could not remember a time that her mother had gone back to bed. This must be serious.

Sammy fussed over her, trying to adjust the sheet and plump her pillow, but only succeeded in causing more disarray. Catching her lower lip between her teeth, she nibbled at the tender skin as she contemplated her mother's condition.

"Stop your fidgeting, Lass. I know you hate to cook, but do you think you can manage to finish breakfast? I moved the pan from the fire, but the bacon isn't quite done."

"Oh, Ma, you know it's only the hot kitchen that I hate. I don't mind cooking over an open fire when I'm hunting wild horses and camping with J.R."

"I know." Her mother's voice registered resignation. "You never were one for inside chores. All you want to do is tag along with your brothers. You'd rather be target shootin' and messin' with the horses than learnin' what you need to know to run a house. And I suspect you hate cookin' over an open fire as much as you hate cookin' in the kitchen, but you pretend to like it so you can go with J.R."

Seeing the halfhearted grin on her mother's face assured Sammy that the old gripes weren't all that serious. Laughing heartily in her ever-teasing manner, she sassed back, "Yeah, but just think, Ma. If the Indians ever do attack, I'll be able to save you all with my superior marksmanship. And don't you dare tell J.R. how much I hate to cook."

"Go on with you, Sammy Luv. Pa and your brothers will be in for breakfast soon, and nothing will be ready. I'll deal with your more gentile training when I'm feelin' better." Her ma tried to laugh, but instead groaned and clutched her stomach as another wave of nausea hit her.

Stopping at the doorway, Sammy turned and gently coaxed, "Can I fix you a cuppa hot tea? Maybe you have some herbs in your basket for an upset stomach. You're always nursing the neighbors, is there anything in there that's good for what ails you?"

"Stop with your questions! The only thing good for me now is some peace and quiet. Don't fuss over me!" As Sammy turned to leave the room, her mother stopped her. "And Sammy Luv, stop biting your lip. There's nothin' to worry about. I won't die from feeling a bit off this morning."

As Samantha finished the breakfast, she dreaded the thought of telling her father that Ma was sick. He doted on the woman. They would all be fetching and carrying for the next month. Samantha knew Pa wouldn't let Ma lift a finger until he made certain she'd recovered. Mentally shrugging, she figured maybe now was as good a time as any to put some effort into learning the things Ma always insisted she master.

She set the table, then walked to the door to strike the iron triangle hanging on the porch. The resounding clang received an answering whoop of welcome from her three brothers as they dropped their chores to race to the yard pump. Laughing at their antics, Sammy looked up and saw the dust from a rider coming in at a fast pace. Her father's training had her reaching inside the doorway for her Hawkin rifle. Then she made out the buckboard. Realizing it wasn't Indians, she squinted to identify the visitor.

Standing with arms akimbo, she laughed at Dennis O'Brien as he awkwardly jumped from the buckboard in such a hurry that he stumbled and almost fell at her feet.

"If you're that hungry, Dennis me boy, you better slow down. You won't get to eat if you kill yourself jumping from a moving buckboard. There's plenty for everyone. Come on in if you're not afraid to eat my cooking."

Her laughter died as she caught a second look at Dennis' face when he righted himself. She knew instantly this was no social call. A pained expression of desperation replaced his usual grin, and his normally pale complexion glowed dark red. Sammy waited while he slapped his hat against his thigh and tried to bring some semblance of order to his unruly red hair. His fingers shook noticeably. This looked more serious than the usual shyness her presence caused him every time he saw her. As he blurted out his problem, Sammy barely noticed her Pa and brothers stopping behind Dennis to listen.

"Samantha, Ma's real sick, and so are the five youngest kids. We need your ma quick. Can she come over now and help? Ma's real worried about the twins. They haven't been able to keep anything down since dinner last night."

Sammy's thoughts fleetingly associated her mother's illness with the O'Brien's. Was this some epidemic starting? Her heart pounded in fear. Before she could open her mouth to explain why her Ma couldn't help this time, her Pa clapped Dennis on the back.

"Don't worry, Dennis, my Elizabeth will be right over. You know she's always glad to give your ma a hand. Didn't she help deliver those twins six months back? She wouldn't take a chance on those babies not makin' it. You'd think they were her own the way she's always braggin' about how smart they are. Come on in and eat while she packs what she needs. You can escort her back to your place after breakfast."

"Pa!" Sammy pulled on her father's sleeve, trying to get his attention while he continued talking.

As he finished, he turned to Samantha, put his arm around her shoulder, and patiently asked, "What is it, Sammy? Can't you see Dennis is a nervous wreck? Stop your jawin'. Times a'wastin'. Get in there and help your ma get her things together so she can be on her way."

"But Pa, Ma can't go. She must have the same sickness as Mrs. O'Brien and the children." Sammy watched his expression turn to one of shock and knew she'd better explain quickly.

"She's sick. I've put her back to bed to rest. She said she'll be fine, but she was retchin' in the bucket when I got up."

Sammy saw the blood drain from her father's face. She could see the panic and disbelief dull his eyes. She'd been afraid this would happen.

"Oh, my God! Elizabeth!" He boomed.

His voice frightened Sammy with its heart-wrenching anguish. As she watched in stunned silence, her father thundered up the steps into the cabin. She heard his boots pounding the wooden plank floor as he raced through the kitchen toward the back bedroom, her three brothers and Dennis right on his heels. The five men left Sammy standing dumbfounded outside.

Shaking her head, she entered the cabin and tried to listen to the murmuring in her parent's bedroom. Her three brothers crowded the doorway with Dennis behind them. Suddenly her father gave a great whoop, then her brothers started laughing, hugging, and slapping each other on the back. Dennis started shaking everyone's hand, while Sammy stood rooted in shocked, wondering what could be so wonderful about Ma being sick.

Tired of being ignored, she stamped her foot and yelled to be heard over the noise. "Will someone tell me what is going on? Ma's sick, and you all are raisin' enough ruckus to send her to an early grave."

The men parted to allow Sammy's father by as he stepped out of the bedroom. The look on his face stunned her. Joy radiated from his eyes, even as tears wet his cheeks. Never before had she seen such a look of love and happiness. As he explained to Sammy that her mother was going to present her with a new brother or sister in about seven months, she sank into a chair.

After seventeen years and at the age of forty-three, how could this be? Her father continued, explaining that he realized Elizabeth didn't have the same illness as the O'Brien family because the only time she ever got sick was when she was breeding.

Shock and impatience caused Sammy to yell at her father. "How can you be so happy? Don't you know how dangerous this is for her to have a baby at her age?"

"Sammy, Luv, calm down." Her father lifted her from the chair and wrapped his arms around her. The compassion she saw on his face told her he realized how much this upset her. Besides, she never raised her voice to her parents. She knew he could always read her moods like a book, and holding her tight, he stroked her hair and softly comforted her.

"Listen to me, Lass. Your ma and I didn't plan this, but it is a gift from God that we welcome, just as we welcomed each of you. None of us know His design for us. We just take what He sends, and we make the best of it. It's called life, child. You live it day to day, and you deal with the trials and the blessings and thank the Almighty that He gives you the opportunity to handle each experience wisely."

"Oh, Pa, I'm sorry. It's just that I'm so worried about Ma."

"I know, luv, but don't let your worrying spoil the joy. Your ma's a healthy woman, and I believe she and the baby will be fine. Now, I think we all forgot about Dennis and his problem. Someone has to go help Nancy O'Brien with those sick babies. Let's get these boys fed so you can take your ma's place."

"Pa, I don't know anythin' about nursin'!" Sammy squealed.

"Your ma will tell you what to do." Not one to take no for an answer, he turned to the others with a grin and gestured to the table. "Come on, lads, time to eat."

Breakfast disappeared with haste. Confusion reigned while Sammy's oldest brother J.R. hitched her horse Sassy to the buckboard. Sammy used that time to pack a basket of food and check her mother's supply of herbs. She had to listen carefully to her mother's instructions because she was not skilled with their different uses.

Sammy hated to leave her mother in bed, but she'd insisted that she already felt better, and promised Sammy she would take it easy the rest of the day. With no reason to delay, Sammy turned to go. Leaving the cabin, she began loading the baskets into the back of the buckboard. She noticed Dennis had unhitched his horse and was leading him to the corral. Her father stopped a minute to speak to Dennis, then continued toward Sammy.

"Sammy, I want you to take your gun. Dennis is staying to help J.R. with the horses this morning. You shouldn't have any trouble. You've been back and forth between the two farms a hundred times by yourself. Just keep your eyes open and don't dally."

"Da, you know I'm capable of takin' care of myself. I don't need Dennis O'Brien to protect me."

"I know, lass. You're a better shot than any of us, but don't get over confident. Watch out for snakes, you know how Sassy spooks every time she sees one, so stay on the road. No short cuts barrelin' over the hills. I don't want you to lose a wheel and have to walk through the tall grass. Dennis will start back before the evening meal. If you plan on comin' home tonight, wait for him to escort you back. I don't want you on the road after dark by yourself."

Sammy dashed up the steps, stopped on the porch, and turned to her father to give him a saucy answer. "It's not me you have to worry about today, Da, it's Ma. You better stick close to the house and see that she doesn't do any heavy work while I'm gone."

With that off her chest, Sammy snatched her gun belt from the hook by the door. Her father had given her the Colt Patterson No. 3 for her birthday when she turned fifteen. The small gun was perfect for her. Its weight easy enough to handle, and if she got within fifty yards of her target, her aim was deadly. Throwing the strap over her shoulder, she called a last goodbye to her mother and ran out to the buckboard. She gave her Pa a hug, and he laughed at her impudence.

Giving her a hand up into the buckboard, he couldn't seem to resist the urge to give her a playful swat on the behind. "You behave yourself, lass. No sassy back talk to sweet Mrs. O'Brien. She's not used to your blabber."

"Oh, Pa, you raised me better than that. Besides, she knows me well enough not to take anythin' I say seriously." Waving a jaunty goodbye, Sammy left on her mission of mercy.

As she passed the corral, she lifted a reluctant hand to her brothers and Dennis. *Just like a man,* Sammy thought with resentment. *How like Dennis to forget his ma might need help when J.R. presented him with an alternative.*

Sammy thought she was more capable of helping J.R. with the horses than nursing the O'Briens, but she had no choice. Ma was too sick to go, so that left only her. She knew it was the neighborly thing to do, but she would much rather be working the stock. *Lordy,* she thought, *I almost forgot my intention of learning everything Ma wants to teach me. I guess I better forget horses today and start with nursing the O'Briens.*

With a longing look back at the corral, she set off to help their neighbors through one more crisis. With twelve children, their farm was a continual infirmary. However, this time with Nancy O'Brien and the five youngest all sick at the same time, it really was a disaster.

As she rounded a curve in the road, she lost sight of her farm. Turning east, she marveled at the morning sky. Once, she laughingly coined the phrase, "sky blue pink". That's how it looked this morning. The pale blue was streaked with variegated pink, so she almost couldn't tell where the blue ended and the pink began. It was glorious to behold. It made her feel good to be alive and ready to meet whatever life had in store for her. It was the kind of morning she loved best when she was riding with J.R. The earthy smells of wheat in the fields and the teasing hints of wild violets blooming in the woods sharpened her senses, adding to her exhilaration.

Her thoughts returned to her family farm, and she began to give serious consideration to her ma and how having another baby would change their lives. She couldn't help worrying about her mother in childbirth at her age. Selfishly, she worried that she wouldn't be able to go on any more trips with J.R. to round up wild horses. Her ma would surely need her around more.

Her scattered reflections returned to the O'Briens. What would happen if Dennis asked her to marry him? Could she really leave her family in a time of need? Did she want to leave them just yet? She knew Dennis was eager to start a life for himself. Maybe it was too stifling living with eleven siblings.

He hadn't even tried to kiss her yet. Sometimes he would shyly hold her hand, but she always twirled away from him. He invariably hurried to help her dismount as if he couldn't wait to touch her. His large hands easily spanned her waist, and he would slowly lower her as though he hated to let her go. Sammy teased him a lot about how slow he was, chiding him that she was perfectly capable of dismounting without his help. Dennis always blushed as if she'd caught him doing something he shouldn't, and she delighted in watching his face turn red. It was so much fun to tease him; he easily fell for her jokes. Sometimes he was just too serious.

Musing about Dennis prompted her to analyze her feelings. She certainly felt comfortable with him, and they always had fun together. Sammy supposed she loved him. However, she was just as content when they weren't together. She hadn't met anyone else she wanted to be with more, so she assumed if she married him, she'd be happy. They did enjoy each other's company without friction, much like her easy relationship with her brothers. Well, what else was there?

Sammy stopped daydreaming as she neared the O'Brien farm. She needed to go over in her mind the instructions her mother had given her. Right now, she had no time for her bouncing thoughts. Like pulling petals from a daisy, "I love him—I love him not." She didn't have time to think about Dennis this morning.

Cantering down the hill, she detected the acrid smell of smoke. She looked up and saw the O'Brien farm and screamed a mindless, keening, "No! What's happened? Noooo... Dear God, nooo...! How did the house catch fire? Please, don't let it be true."

She raced the buckboard into the yard screaming a denial. Her heart pounded like a herd of stampeding cattle. Goose bumps raised the fine hairs on the back of her neck as she frantically stared around the grisly sight, only to find everyone lying still, frozen in death. The bodies were strewn around the yard like so many rag dolls.

What happened here? Who did this? The O'Briens didn't have any enemies. They were the closest friends her family had. Everyone she knew liked and respected them. Sawing on the reins, Sammy jumped from the still-rocking buckboard. Tears streamed down her face. Stumbling and choking, her mind reeled with possibilities as she ran from body to body, looking for any sign of life. Everyone had been shot to death. They must have been caught by surprise. Mr. O'Brien wasn't even armed. Sammy felt close to hysteria. Her loud sobs and denials drowned out the crackling of the fire. Of the fourteen O'Briens, she only found eight bodies. Thank God Dennis was safe at her farm!

"The babies. Where are the babies?" she screamed. She looked at the house. Flames engulfed the structure. She buried her head in her lap as she doubled over into the soft earth. "God, no! Please, not all five of them, too."

Her stomach threatened to rebel. She wanted to erase the scene and bring back the usual O'Brien confusion and constant chatter. Staggering to her feet, she yelled out her rage.

"Lord, let me shoot at something. I want to kill whoever did this."

Shaking violently, Sammy didn't know what to do first. This was as close to panic as she had ever felt, and losing her breakfast was imminent. She compelled herself to harden her mind to her own discomfort. Home, Sammy needed to get home. How could she tell Dennis? Pa and the boys would have to come back with him and help bury his family.

Forcing herself to get a grip on her emotions, she tried to compose poor Nancy O'Brien's body, but her outrage exploded again. "God, how could you let this happen? This woman never hurt anyone."

Dennis couldn't see this. He would go crazy. Thank God, the revolting beast that raped Mrs. O'Brien spared nine-year-old Margaret and eleven-year-old Jennifer. Sammy didn't think she could bear it if he'd molested the children, too.

With a heavy heart, Samantha took a last look around the yard. Smoke obscured most of the area, and it looked like there was nothing left. The black curtain parted with the shifting breeze, and she caught a glimpse of the corral. A saddle hung over the fence, and she immediately thought about Dennis driving the buckboard. He'd want to ride so he could get back here faster. Her eyes glazed over as she walked trance-like to the fence.

When she reached up to lift the saddle down, she saw it was the same one Mr. O'Brien had given Dennis for his sixteenth birthday. Dennis had carved his name into the leather in bold block letters. In the three years he had used the saddle, the letters were worn down to a shadow of what they were when new. Sammy's shaking fingers traced his name with the reverence of a caress. Dennis' saddlebags still hung around the saddle horn. He never did pick up after himself. She was thankful he didn't bring them into the barn this morning. At least he would have something from his family left to treasure.

Flinging the saddle and saddle bags into the buckboard, she released a shuddering sigh and wearily climbed onto the seat. Her body felt as if she'd suddenly turned into an old woman. She had no energy left. Using the sleeve of her blouse, she wiped her tears and turned Sassy away from the gruesome scene.

Samantha couldn't get back to her home fast enough. Ignoring her father's warning, she took the short cut across the hills. She couldn't waste time returning by road. Her hands still shook with reaction, and her sympathy for Dennis grew so profound she felt as if she'd lost her own family.

As she neared the familiar bent oak tree that marked the boundary of their farm, she could smell the nauseous odor of something burning and thought her pa must be getting rid of the old stuff he cleaned out of the shed yesterday. Then rounding the bend at the bottom of the hill, she saw the smoke, thick and black. A premonition of disaster hit her like a mule kick to the midriff. Her heart skipped to a stop, and her blood raced through her body. She felt it pounding in her head with enough force to burst. Her stomach rolled as she slapped the reins.

"Giddy-up, go, Sassy. Run! Hurry! Please hurry. Faster, faster!" she shouted. This was more than a trash fire. Her mind refused to accept what she saw.

Reaching the yard, Sammy jumped from the buckboard and started running before Sassy came to a full stop. The house was a burning skeleton. Her three brothers and her father were lying in the front yard, all four of them unmoving. Dennis lay crumpled in the corral. Blood soaked the ground around each body. "No! Pa, don't be dead. J.R, Tim, Ryan. No, it can't be. God, how could you let this happen?"

Sobbing and screaming, she ran from her father to each of her brothers. She checked Dennis last, but she already knew what she would find. The awkward positions and stiffness of each body proclaimed their death.

"*Ma*!" She didn't see her mother. As she struggled to regain control of her breathing, she saw the fluttering of some white cloth at the grassy edge of the woods. Stumbling over the rough ground, she ran crying to where her mother lay with her skirts up around her hips. Blood streamed down her legs and her sightless eyes stared up at the blue sky she would never see again. Her mother's mouth gaped open, a look of shock frozen on her face. Her hands clutched around the open wound in her chest as if trying to stem the flow of her life's blood.

The sight of her mother was more than Sammy could handle, and this time she couldn't control the revolt of her stomach. Turning abruptly, she collapsed in a retching, sobbing heap. It took her a few minutes to stop choking and crawl back to her mother's body. Shaking uncontrollably, she tried to close her mother's mouth. However, all muscle control had left with her ma's last breath, and Sammy could not keep her jaw from falling open. After several failed attempts, she gave up trying to close her mother's mouth and gently pressed her fingers over her mother's eyes to close the lids. Then, she gave in to the grief that tore her insides apart and wrapped her arms around her mother, cradled her head to her chest, and sobbed. Rooted to the spot, she knelt, rocking the now lifeless body.

Sammy wasn't sure how long she clutched her mother before she realized whoever had killed her family and the O'Briens might still be around. Reacting in a near frenzy of panic, her rage exploded. "I'll kill you. So help me God, I'll kill you, whoever you are! I won't let you get away with this."

Coughing and sputtering through the smoke, she began to ready the bodies for burial. Working in a trance, not even stopping to think about getting help, she channeled her rage into the necessary task.

It took Sammy most of the day to dig a grave and bury her family. She made their bodies as decent as possible, regretting she had no clean clothes to dress them in and hating that she had to make it one mass grave. She did the hard work automatically in a state of shock, not really aware of how she was able to accomplish it or why she was doing this alone.

It was a compulsion. She didn't want anyone to see the degradation of her mother's body. "Oh, Pa, I hope you and the boys died before this happened to Ma." She hated to think that her father and brothers might have witnessed her mother's rape and murder.

Indians were always a nuisance, but as far as she knew, they had never done this kind of ruthless killing. She saw arrows scattered carelessly around the yard, but they looked distinctively different from the ones her brothers had shown her. These almost looked like crudely made toys. The ones she remembered seeing were works of art.

Anger built resentment in her heart when she thought that she hadn't been there to help defend their farm. She could out shoot all three of her brothers. If she had been home maybe her gun would have made the difference in the lives of her family. Sammy had a keen eye. Neither tin cans nor wild game ever eluded her shot. Her brother J.R. wasn't dumb. He'd told her often enough he'd rather have her on a hunting trip than any cowhand. Thinking about her brother caused fresh tears to stream down her dirty cheeks.

Reality set in as she pushed her resentment aside. She had to get out of there. Slumped in total defeat, using the shovel as a crutch to hold up her empty body, Sammy bowed her head and said a prayer over the grave of her family. She thought of the O'Briens. There was no one to bury them now that Dennis was gone. Swallowing the lump in her throat, she wondered if she should take the chance of staying in the area another day. Shuddering with regret, she decided she couldn't risk the chance of discovery.

Then, as she had at the O'Briens, she looked around the farmstead to see what she could salvage. There was nothing left. The barn and the house were still smoldering. She could see the chimney would be the only evidence that a farm once occupied this ground. Time would allow the wilderness to encroach over the cleared land, returning it to its natural state. Sammy didn't think time would ever erase the pain of this day. Somehow, someway, she would avenge her family.

Hardening her heart, she took a last look around the yard. She saw no indication of any livestock, not even the barn cats. The only thing left standing was the broken corral. A few oddly twisted tools lay about, the handles burned beyond use. Only a rake and the old shovel she'd used to dig the graves were recognizable.

Glancing back to where she'd found her mother's body, she saw her ma's antique cedar chest lying at the edge of the yard. Someone had pulled it from the fire, then deserted it. If she took the time to wait until the ashes cooled, maybe she could sift through the debris and find more. For now though, she had to get away.

Hearing a nicker, she turned to see Sassy tossing her head. It seemed she had suffered the constraints of the buckboard harness long enough. The events of the day had forced all thoughts of her horse from Sammy's mind. Throwing the shovel into the back of the buckboard, she trudged to the well to get the mare some water. After she rinsed her face and took a drink for herself, she tried to think.

With all the emotions of the past several hours she'd even forgotten to strap on her gun for self-protection. Glancing at the weapon, lying on the floorboards under the buckboard seat, she reassured herself it was within reach, then turned to the task of loading ma's cedar chest. She needed to feel comforting arms wrapped around her before she fell to pieces. The thought finally penetrated her whirling brain. There was no where to go and no one to give her comfort.

Anger at the senseless slaughter overcame Samantha again as she screamed aloud in the pain of her loss. Yelling at the top of her voice, hoping the killers could hear her, she shouted her vengeful vow. "I'll get the man that did this to you, Ma. I swear, I'll make him pay. Whoever did this will die by my hand, and I'll make damn sure he knows the reason I'm pulling the trigger!"

Two

It didn't matter how fast Sammy urged her horse to run. She couldn't escape the fear that chased her shadow, kept pace with her buckboard, or seemed ready to pounce around the next bend.

The day had turned picture perfect and Sammy resented it. "Why can't it rain?" she screamed. "It shouldn't be so pretty. I'd rather see the sky shrouded with black clouds." That would better reflect her mood and give her the feeling that God in his mercy cried with her. But Sammy couldn't change the weather any more than she could change the nightmare she tried to escape as she raced her buckboard through the thick woodland.

How could her life change so fast? Her family and all the people she knew and loved would no longer share her world. Blood raced through her veins, agitating her heart to pound a litany of grief and panic. One minute she'd been a happy seventeen year old, walking out with Dennis O'Brien, who'd been sure to ask her to marry him as soon as she turned eighteen. Then today's events had transformed her into a frightened young woman, alone in the world.

Soon she'd have to stop and think. She hadn't had a clear thought all day. Gut instinct and raw emotions were all that kept her moving. As she forded a small stream, she heard the roar of water upstream to her left. Suddenly alert, she recognized the area. She'd entered the dense woods surrounding Devils Den. The place was well-named for its wild uninhabitable forest. A creek twisted through the area, forming a series of waterfalls. She remembered J.R. had said it was called Lost Creek.

Tears streamed down her face as she recalled all the good times she would never know again. If she remembered right, one of the falls dropped twenty feet into a small pool. *Just what I need,* she thought. *I'll stop at the pool to wash away the smell and grime from the fire. Then I'll plan what I should do next.* Her mind careened from grief and panic to relief as she spotted the source of refreshment. It would be perfect. She would feel better if she could eliminate the odor clinging to her clothes and rest for just a few minutes. Her tired body told her it had to be suppertime. The rumbling in her stomach reminded her she hadn't eaten since morning. Somewhere during her mad rush across the hills, she'd lost the provisions she'd so carefully packed that morning. If she had used half her brain, she'd have secured the food basket a little better.

It was too late now, and she regretted the lack of food, but she would manage. Her pa and her brothers had seen to that. Poor Ma, she'd always gotten upset when they had taken her hunting and fishing. Nothing could have matched her Irish temper when they'd taught her how to shoot. Ma argued her place was in the kitchen and not on the range, but Pa had insisted!

"If we're going to live in the wilds, I want all of my family to be able to survive and that includes you, Nellie!" So, Sammy had learned how to cook, clean, and sew enough to get by. But she could hunt, fish, and shoot well enough to rival her brothers.

She'd begun the lessons about guns before she could even lift one. Pa made sure she and the boys knew how dangerous they were and the safe way to handle one. Sammy had a good eye, and by the time her pa had given her the Colt for her fifteenth birthday, she won every target contest her brothers could devise. True to her father's word, even Sammy's mother practiced until she could nail the cans propped on the fence post with some regularity.

Once again thoughts of her family caused tears to pour from her tired eyes, clouding her vision. She had to get control of herself. Ah! There was the pool. Now, she could wash away the soot and smell from the fire. Then, she would decide what to do next.

Her possessions included her horse Sassy, the buckboard, and Ma's cedar chest. She didn't even know what Ma kept in the chest. She hoped there were some clean clothes. Patches of dried blood and dirt covered her torn, soot-blackened dress. She compelled herself not to look at the condition of her outfit. It only served to remind her of the reality of this morning's nightmare.

She pushed a damp, stringy clump of hair off her face. The neat coil she'd started out with that morning no longer existed. She lifted a strand from her shoulder and looked at it in a detached way. Was this the beautiful chestnut hair Pa had loved? Tears burned their way down her face, and angrily she lifted a hand to wipe them away. Dirt smeared her fingers, and she knew her face must be streaked. Her eyes felt swollen and dull. She hated crying. It always made her nose run. Touching her nose, Sammy wondered if it was as red as it felt. Her fingers traced her full lips and came away smeared with blood from where she'd bitten through the bottom one to stifle her grief. All in all, she knew she didn't look anything like her old self, but she didn't care. Her looks were never important to her, least of all today.

Sammy pulled the buckboard to a stop beside the waterfall, ignoring the danger of what she meant to do. She'd been told often enough that she was impulsive, so this obsession to get clean and hang the consequence didn't phase her. Besides, no one ventured into Devils Den. It was too spooky.

Her tired brain registered the beauty of the setting. The slanting sun sparkled off the water and made dancing diamonds of the spray that rebounded from the surface of the pool. "Damn! Nothing should be beautiful today. Go away! Hide behind some clouds or something!" she screamed, cursing the sun again.

Turning her back to a scene that she would normally take pleasure in, she took care of Sassy first. After she unhitched her and let her get a drink, she crooned soft words into the horse's ear. "Ah, Sassy Luv. At least I still have you. I'm sorry I ignored you all day. I'll make it up to you, baby."

She felt guilty for neglecting the mare and pushing her much harder then she ever had. Hugging Sassy and rubbing her face against the coarse hair on the horse's neck, she took some comfort from the soft nickering. It felt as if Sassy had tried to communicate her condolences.

Then, Sammy couldn't wait any longer. Steeling her heart against the pain of her loss, and without even a glance to ascertain her privacy, she stripped out of her soiled clothes. After she tore a small piece from her petticoat to use as a wash cloth, she released the rest of her hair and dove into the cool water.

She swam to the falls and struggled through the spray to search for a hold on the slippery rocks. Finally she reached the ledge. Battling against the force of the water, she found a solid handhold and climbed up the sheer granite face. As she knelt on the natural platform beneath the cascading water, she fought to maintain her balance. At last she was able to stand inside the hollowed out cliff behind the water.

It felt wonderful as it crashed over her body and pounded the aches away. The water cooled her heated body and sighing with gratification, she tipped her head back to let it scour her hair. The last twelve hours began to replay themselves through her head again, and she had no way to control or stop her tumbling thoughts.

~ * ~

Nicholas MacNamee had been riding hard all day. Although hot and tired, he knew he had to continue. He'd been in the saddle since dawn. As he followed Lost Creek through the thick underbrush, he realized he could encounter Indians at any time. He stayed cautious, as well as alert to the signs, as he hurried along. Mac, as most of his army buddies called him, let his recent past play through his thoughts as he rode.

He'd been a scout for the army for four years now. At the age of twenty-five, he felt he wasn't ready to settle down yet. He loved the wild, free life he led. The adventure of tracking the enemy and outsmarting them was something he enjoyed.

He watched the trail closely. It was a habit. Even though he wasn't trailing anyone, he didn't forget his lessons in survival. He had grown up on the fringe of civilization and handling horses and guns was second nature to him. Except for his time spent back east at college, he'd always lived on the edge of danger. Why did he get these niggling doubts about his purpose in life?

When Indian trouble had started up again, he'd approached his father's friend, Commander Williams, and volunteered as a scout. City life was stifling his adventurous nature. He knew he could track a cold trail better than most, and he had a nose for trouble ahead. The instinct must have come from his ancestors.

He enjoyed his assignment, and he'd been invaluable in saving the troops from several ambushes. He couldn't understand his restlessness.

Just the thought of his talent made the hair on the back of his neck stand at attention. Was it working now? His body tensed as he cautiously slid from the back of his big, gray stallion and quietly led him through the woods until he heard the roar of a waterfall.

The closer Mac got to the water, the more he sensed another presence. A shiver of anticipation inched its way up his spine when he closed in on a quarry or if someone tried to ambush him. That shiver, in full force now, made him hope the noise of the falls would muffle the sound of his approach. He took no chances as he placed each footstep carefully, moving through the trees as silently as an Indian. *Why not?* he thought. *After all, I am half-Indian.* He saw a flash of white just as he reached the tree line at the edge of the pool. Peering through the trees at the waterfall, he saw what had triggered his senses. The ghostly apparition turned into a woman bathing.

A white flash of bare skin shimmered through the sluicing water. A curtain of dark hair shielded all but her long legs and saucy derrière. Struck immediately by the sight of her gorgeous body, his jaw dropped open, and he had to consciously shut it. He licked his dry lips and tried to compose himself. She wasn't a ghost. She was an angel.

A surreal scene of flashing refractions of light from the sun on the spray of water surrounding her. The rainbow formed an arch, framing her exquisite body. He became mesmerized by the heavenly vision.

A quick appraisal of the surrounding area told him the girl was alone. As unlikely as that appeared, he prepared himself for anything unexpected. There was sure to be a husband or family of some sort to defend the lady, and he didn't relish being shot for invading her privacy. He knew, however, that no lady ever ventured alone in this neck of the woods. Without someone close by to protect her, she'd placed herself in mortal danger.

Peering through the trees to determine the situation, he spotted her filly grazing on the other side of the pond. Quickly he placed his hand over Renegade's nose and mouth before his horse could signal the mare. A buckboard and one horse were the only occupants of the clearing. How could anyone be foolish enough to leave the woman alone?

As he pondered all of this, she emerged from under the falls and dove into the pool to swim to the opposite bank where she climbed out of the water.

He gasped. Her hair streamed long, past her hips and rivulets of water ran from her shapely body in shimmering iridescence. The miniature perfection of her stature awed him. She seemed so tiny! It would surprise him if the top of her head reached his shoulders. He envisioned his large hands spanning her tiny waist, caressing her slim hips only to move up to cup her shapely bosom.

Her breasts weren't huge and pendulous from child bearing, nor were they the tiny buds of an adolescent. Everything about her looked in proportion. She appeared young, but he couldn't tell her exact age from this distance.

The sight of her drying her body with an old petticoat enchanted Mac. Erotic visions continued to flash through his mind as he watched her innocently attend her torso. Even her movement to the old cedar chest seemed to be an exotic dance for his personal pleasure.

Mac shook his head to regain his composure and watched as she opened the chest and began to rummage through it. It seemed that all it contained were men's clothes. No, there, she found a dress. God! Mac found his heart breaking as he watched her fall to her knees and sob convulsively into the white dress clutched to her bosom. He became agitated and indecisive.

Struck by her sadness, he felt a need to comfort her, but didn't want to embarrass her by announcing his presence before she dressed. He decided to wait till she finished dressing then pretend to happen by. He watched while she seemed to regain her composure then determinedly set about choosing some clothing.

Puzzled, he saw her take a piece of cloth and use a Bowie knife, that looked too large for her to handle, to cut off a strip and begin to bind those beautiful breasts. When she finished, she pulled out some long johns, looked at them in disgust, and climbed into them. He had to smile. Next she put on a pair of men's pants and a brown cotton shirt that was obviously several sizes too large. She seemed to have difficulty holding up the huge pants and long trailing ends of the shirt as she walked over to the buckboard. Again welding the Bowie knife, she deftly cut a piece of leather harness to use as a belt.

Mac grew more intrigued by the scene unfolding before him. He watched with amusement to see what she would do next. His grin vanished instantly when she knelt on the ground and grabbed a fist of her hair right at the neckline and whacked it off with that deadly knife. It happened so fast that her action startled him into betraying his position.

Without realizing his own intentions, he yelled a guttural denial aloud. His reaction startled Renegade. The huge horse snapped his head up and caused the harness to jingle. Knowing he had given his position away, Mac started to step out into the open, but the girl reacted with the swiftness of a coiled rattler. Before he could call out a reassurance that he meant her no harm, she'd disappeared.

In one fluid motion, she'd snatched up her petticoats, without losing her fist full of hair, and dove behind the chest. *A quick thinker this one,* he thought as he ducked from the bullets she sent zinging over his head. She'd left nothing in his sight that could be recognized as women's clothes.

Startled by the unwarranted attack, Mac let his anger erupt. "Hold your fire," he yelled angrily. "What in tarnation do you think you're doing?"

"I'm going to blow your bloody brains out, that's what."

Mac couldn't believe the venom that poured out with the words. Fearing a stray bullet might accidentally hit Renegade, he slapped the horse on his flank and sent him out of danger. He decided to play the bumbling idiot and act dumb. The ploy had saved him before, and he hoped she would fall for his line, too. Mac raised his hands above his head and slowly came to his full height.

"I mean you no harm, boy." He'd keep silent about having seen her in the nude, no need to rile her any more. Let her think her secret was safe. His mind raced with ideas. He needed to convince her she would remain unharmed. Maybe the partial truth would serve best, he decided.

"My name is Nicholas MacNamee. I'm an army scout for Commander Williams at Fort Howard. I'm on my way to the fort to alert them about some renegade Indians. I heard the water and decided to make camp. But, if you already have this place staked out, I can just move on. Unless you've a mind to share. I don't think it's safe for you to be out here all alone."

"If you're trying to scare me, it won't work. How do I know you are who you say you are? You might be trying to fool me so you can kill me, too."

"Relax, kid. Do you see my gun drawn? I don't go around shooting children. And what do you mean 'kill you, too'? Where's your family?"

He regretted his outburst at the sight of her cutting her hair. The anxiety his presence caused her pained him. He'd thought he possessed better self-control. He realized his rapid-fire questions confused her. He'd detected the fear and uncertainty in her voice. Maybe he should try a different angle.

Before he could speak, she raised her voice. "I—I'll give you to the count of three to ride out stranger. If I don't hear your horse making tracks, I'll start shooting."

She certainly didn't like his last question about her family. Indecision cracked the girl's voice. He could tell she tried to sound masculine, and she would have succeeded if Mac hadn't witnessed the transformation.

"I can escort you back to the fort or to the next village if that's where you're headed. What's your name, boy?"

"I don't need an escort. I know how to track, and I know how to use my gun. I'll protect myself. Now, why don't you just mount up and ride away. *One...*"

Damn! Using the word escort had been a mistake. Only women needed escorts. He couldn't let on that he knew she was a woman. Edging closer to the shore, Mac pushed his way through the trees, making sure she saw his hands were free of any weapon.

"If you're good with a gun, all the better. I could use some help tracking these Indians. After I water my horse, we can decide—" Before he could finish his sentence, a branch shattered above his head and finding its mark, knocked him to his knees. He'd found himself instinctively ducking at the bark of her gun, but he wasn't quite quick enough to avoid the blow.

Damnation! What a spitfire! Rubbing the top of his head, he struggled to his feet. Was she really that good a shot, or was it just luck that sent that limb crashing down on him?

"*Two...*"

"Okay, Okay, I hear you. Just be on the lookout for Indians and remember you won't know they're around until you feel your scalp being lifted. Would you at least let me water my horse and refill my canteen? It's been a long, hot day, and I could use a cool drink. After all, it is only the water I came looking for."

"I think you've used up your time. Do you want to walk away or do you want to die where you stand." With barely a pause, she shouted, "*Three...*"

Angry now, at the girl's stubborn refusal of help, he fumed over his failure to gain her confidence. His agitation caused him to snap out his farewell with more gruffness than he intended. "Don't say I didn't warn you, boy. See you around."

Ducking to avoid her parting shot, Mac made a commotion of leaving. He raised his hands and retreated until he felt Renegade nudge his back. Mounting the big gray, he yelled a last, "Take care," and noisily rode away.

Once he was out of earshot, he retraced his steps. Ground tying Renegade a distance away, he silently circled back to his vantage point. He knew the roar of the falls would cover any noise from the slight rustling of leaves as he crept through the woods. He had to take the chance. He had to see what she would do next.

What in the hell was she doing? Mac decided to stay hidden and watch. Peeking through the branches, he watched in stunned silence as she continued to turn herself into a caricature of a callow youth. He lost all sense of time and purpose. He forgot about the darn Indians. He forgot about riding to Fort Howard. He damn near forgot who he was. If he hadn't watched the transformation, she would have fooled him for sure.

Only a few times did she betray her sex. She had gone to the buckboard and pulled out a shovel, and after looking at her hands, which even from a distance looked pretty raw, she put on a pair of gloves from the chest and began to dig a hole.

The perfect oval of her face twisted in grief, as she tenderly wrapped her shorn hair in a clean piece of cloth and buried it with all of her old dirty clothes. Next, she pulled a saddle from the back of the buckboard. He wanted to help as he watched her struggle and wince when she saddled her filly. Completing the task seemed to cross over her threshold of pain. He saw her swipe tears angrily from her cheeks with the back of her fist. Her hands seemed to be giving her most of the trouble. As he forced himself to remain silent, his stomach twisted in anxiety. Each time she winced, his discomfort grew.

Shouldering the saddlebags, she crossed to the cedar chest. She lifted out the white dress and stroked it lovingly before she carefully folded and packed it.

His only impression of the dress was that it reminded him of his stepmother's wedding dress. The recollection of standing next to his father as he exchanged vows with the only mother Mac had known shocked him. He shook his head to clear his thoughts; he had to concentrate on the present. The thought came to him unbidden. *Was it her wedding dress?*

He watched her roll a pair of fringed buckskin pants and shirt, very similar to what he wore, into the other side of the saddlebags. Who did they belong to? Who did the masculine clothes she wore belong to? Rolling a blanket for a bedroll, she strapped it behind the saddle, then tucked the gloves in her pant's pocket. Leaning into the chest she pulled out a sheath for the knife. After she checked her gun and reloaded, she holstered it. Then, she strapped it over her slim hips and hooked the Bowie knife case to the holster belt. Sheathing the knife, she rummaged in the bottom of the chest again. There didn't seem to be much left.

She took out a small pouch and appeared to put it in her shirt pocket. He couldn't tell what it contained. Next came a leather-bound book. *Looks like Ma's Bible,* he thought. Again, the memory surprised him. He watched as she reverently folded the remains of the sprigged material that she had cut apart to bind her breasts. Then, as if undecided, she replaced the cloth in the chest. The saddlebags bulged with her belongings. Most likely she couldn't stuff another thing in them. Next, she dragged the chest over to some rocks and hid it with branches and leaves.

After gathering more debris to camouflage the place where she buried her belongings, she stood up and, hands on hips, seemed to contemplate what to do about the buckboard. He realized she must have decided it was too large to hide when he saw her shrug her shoulders in resignation. Turning her back, she mounted up and rode away without a backward glance. Checking the sun, he noted she cantered off in a northwest direction.

Mac shook his head as if coming out of a trance. He cautiously raised his large body up from the leafy bed of the forest floor. He breathed deeply the musty smell of rotting vegetation from the bank of the pond, mingled with the faint fragrance of wild flowers. He knew he would forever associate this scent with his vision of the angel in the falls.

Retrieving Renegade, he started downstream to find a place to ford. He would get to the bottom of this if it were the last thing he did. Holding his horse to a walk along the shore, he came to a natural crossing about a quarter of a mile from the pool, so natural that he could see at once this was where she had passed to the other side in the buckboard.

The tracks only looked about an hour old. That meant he probably reached the pool shortly after the girl had arrived. Walking Renegade slowly across the creek, he dismounted and followed her trail back upstream to where he had witnessed her transformation.

Mac squatted on his heels to study the impression of her horse's hoof prints. He wanted to memorize the shape. Then he surveyed the clearing with a practiced eye. The only evidence she'd left of her passing was the abandoned buckboard. He looked around, and it surprised him to notice that if he hadn't been a witness, he would never have known anyone had set foot here for the last several days. Unless someone knew what to look for, they would never know where she buried the evidence of her alteration. The woman knew something about covering her trail. What was she hiding, or who was she hiding from?

He retrieved the shovel from the back of the buckboard and dug up the things she had buried. He unwrapped her hair and unconsciously held it up to breathe in the scent of her. He caressed the softness and had to swallow the lump that formed in his throat. He couldn't understand what had compelled her to cut such beautiful hair. No longer concerned about remaining silent, he groaned out loud as he recalled her self-mutilation. With a sigh, he reverently folded it back into the material and, without a second thought, walked over and put it in his saddlebag.

The condition of the dress gave him pause. It smelled of smoke. Blood and dirt obliterated the color of the gown. He paused, thinking back. No. It wasn't her blood. She appeared unharmed except for the lacerations on her hands.

The petticoat and pantaloons lay in a pathetic heap of torn rags. Two strips of petticoat lay curled and stiffened with dried blood. She must have used these to bind her hands. He pondered on what could cause the open wounds on her palms. He turned to uncover the chest. Finding it empty, he left it where she had hidden it, reburied the dirty clothes, and placed the remaining piece of clean material in his saddlebag with the bundle of her hair. Why he felt these were too precious to leave behind to rot, he couldn't have explained. He checked the buckboard next. It was in good repair except for the cut harness she'd used for a belt. This equipment had come from a fairly prosperous farm. The only thing left in the buckboard had been the shovel. Looking at the instrument again, he noticed a dark stain on the handle. Recognizing the telltale signs of dried blood, he realized she must have used it a lot to cause blisters so bad that it made her hands raw and bleeding.

He stood for a moment deep in thought. Then it occurred to him. Was it possible? He looked at the sun. There were approximately three more hours of daylight left. He could come back and track her later. First he had to see if his hunch proved right. What if Indians had attacked her home? How could he have missed a massacre?

He mounted Renegade in a single jump and raced down to where her buckboard had crossed the stream. Her tracks led to a farm where he saw the devastation and the grave. It was huge! How many people were buried there? He began looking for signs of Indians, and being agitated, he almost missed the tracks that showed where she had driven in at breakneck speed. That made him realize she had come after the carnage. He mounted up and followed the easy trail over the bush until he found the second farm. There again he found the same pattern. She came after it happened. Here, the bodies still lay frozen in death.

He would have to alert the marshal, but the heat of the day made waiting for help impossible. Mac carried the bodies down into the cellar of the burned-out cabin. It was cooler down there, and he'd be able to cover the entrance with the blackened timbers and weigh it down with rocks until he could send someone out to bury them. Puzzled, he tried to reason which farm she called home, but it was impossible to tell. He couldn't convince himself that she was responsible for the deaths. His hunch had been right—he had seen signs of Indians at both farms. Because the bodies were buried at one place and not the other, it led him to speculate that she had buried her family, but not the neighbors. Her comment about him shooting her, too, made sense now.

But, why did she disguise herself if she had nothing to hide? Is it possible she ordered the attack? Mac didn't want to believe the girl was responsible, but her actions and the evidence all worked against her. Even with everything he had seen so far, he wanted to find the woman to see if she was okay. He felt protective of her and couldn't understand why. She clearly didn't want his company, and he still had questions about her involvement, but he couldn't shake the deep need that he had to see her again. Well, he could always pick up her trail later, he knew she would be easy to find. He would never mistake her for a boy! Never!

Three

Sammy felt so sore she could hardly stay on Sassy's back. Her eyes burned from long periods of crying, smoke, and fatigue. She knew if she didn't rest soon, she'd fall and break her neck.

The sudden appearance of the scout at the falls still caused her heart to pound. She couldn't decide if his size had intimidated her or the fact that he seemed to materialize out of thin air. Thankfully, he hadn't been at the pool long enough to see her bathing. At least her disguise worked. He'd thought she was a boy. She had to chuckle to herself at his expression when her shot broke the branch and clunked him on the noggin. If she hadn't been so frightened, she'd have laughed out loud. She had to be careful, or her plan would fail before it even got started.

Thoughts of the scout brought a flush to her cheeks. He truly was the most handsome man she had ever seen. When the limb knocked off his hat, she'd gotten a good look at his face. The dark tan, probably from long hours in the sun, accentuated his high cheek bones and square jaw. She couldn't remember ever seeing a man with that much dark hair. A thick, heavy wave fell over his forehead, softening his scowl. A rawhide strip held the rest tied together at the back of his neck to form a queue. The buckskin clothes added to the overall impression and gave him the appearance of an Indian.

His size had awed her. Then, his swarthy good looks and gentle smile had seemed to beg her to recognize him as a friend. Sammy had to admit, after her initial fear for her life, the man had almost beguiled her into taking him into her confidence. But she couldn't and wouldn't trust anyone until she knew who had killed her family.

At first, she'd really thought he could be the one who'd wrecked havoc on her family's farm, but he'd never drawn a weapon and he'd enunciated his words like an educated man. It reminded her of Tim, her middle brother. He'd spoken just like that when he read to the family every night. She'd loved the way Tim stroked his mustache in concentration and every once in a while, pushed up his reading glasses with his index finger.

"I can't let myself think about family, Sassy. Those treasured memories hurt too much. But what about Nicholas MacNamee?"

If she'd entertained any idea about using the clearing as a camp, his appearance had quickly changed her mind. She knew she had to hurry. She had to put as much distance as possible between her and the farm as quickly as she could. The falls were much too close, and the stranger's appearance made her realize that the noise of the water hitting the pool put her at a definite disadvantage. She would have a hard time hearing anyone approaching unless they were as clumsy as the scout. He must have stumbled on a root. Thank God he made such a loud noise. If he hadn't tripped, she'd have never heard his advance.

Her stomach grumbled impatiently. She'd left the waterfall so hastily she'd forgotten her intention to find something to eat. Now, she felt weak with hunger as well as exhausted. She'd have to rely on everything J.R. ever taught her about surviving in the wilderness.

Maybe she should have allowed the scout to join her. As long as he didn't know she was a woman, it might have been safe. At least he might have shared his food.

Her plan to disguise herself crystallized by chance when she opened the cedar chest. It contained Ma's lovely wedding dress, prayer book, and some of the clothes she'd started to make the boys for Christmas. Samantha guessed the dress length had been meant for her. Ma would never wear a dress made from that delicate material. The pretty sprigged pattern contained all of Samantha's favorite colors. Green leaves accented tiny peachy pink flowers on a white background. The gay cloth suggested church socials and barn dances.

Well, she wore it close to her heart now and would always remember Ma's caring to choose something she would love on sight.

"Sassy, I've got to pull myself together and stop this reminiscing." Sammy shook her head to get her mind on more practical matters. She'd found a knife hidden in the bottom with the small leather pouch containing a few gold coins. The blanket looked new. Ma probably had it set aside for her trousseau. Well, she'd put it to good use now. At least she had some protection and a wee bit of money.

Dressed as a boy, she knew she could avoid some of the lewd glances she'd experienced when her brothers took her to town. A girl by herself would never get very far, and her brother's clothes were just what she needed.

Finding herself alone in the world, she knew she didn't dare trust anyone. Only one person could help her—Pa's brother, Uncle Padraig. Not one to push a plow, Uncle Paddy had left Missouri twelve years ago. For the last several years, he'd written that he'd made his fortune in fur trapping and trading.

She remembered listening in envy to his tales of wolves, Indians, and high snow country. He led such an adventurous life! If she could find him, she knew he would help her track the killers.

His last letter to the family had appeared as if an omen, folded in Ma's prayer book. Later, she'd reread it for clues to help her locate his whereabouts.

Plodding along on Sassy, she couldn't help but think something seemed strange about the raid this morning. She couldn't quite put her finger on what bothered her. Fragments of memory tortured her. She needed time to sort out all the details. Right now, her first priority was food and shelter. That thought made her aware of her surroundings, and she noticed the light had faded to dusk. She'd have to stop for the night, or she'd never survive this first day alone.

It didn't take Samantha long to realize that with each dragging step, Sassy had reached the limit of her endurance, too. "I'd better concentrate on finding a campsite, girl."

As near as she could tell from the setting sun, she'd ridden about three hours since the time she left the pool. That was probably far enough away for her to risk stopping for the night. Besides, she had no choice. She and her mount were too tired to go any farther.

It wasn't long before she spotted a huge overhanging rock. Under the rock, a hollowed-out area looked like it would accommodate her. She decided it would provide some shelter and the solid rock would protect her back. Far enough off the trail, it would be a good place to stop.

Hardly having the energy to move, she slid from Sassy's back. She gripped the saddle horn for a few minutes to allow her legs to adjust to the weight of her tired body. After she removed the saddle, she hobbled Sassy's front legs to keep her close. “Sorry, sweetheart. I know you wouldn’t wander away, but I’m not taking any chance tonight.”

Using the saddle blanket, she tried to dry the mare’s back. “You’ve had this saddle on too long haven’t you girl?” After she made the horse comfortable, she left her to graze. “This tall grass will provide plenty of food within sight of my camp. I’ll find you some water later.”

Briskly tying together a make-shift broom of sorts using old cedar branches, she swept out the area under the overhang. She didn’t want to share her bed with anything that lived under a rock. “Bless you, Pa,” she choked as she put the knife to use again, cutting fresh branches of cedar. “I don’t think I could have made it without your knife.”

With the sharp smell of crisp cedar teasing her nose, she used the limbs to line the ground under the rock. She completed her bed by laying her blanket and saddle over the branches. Her saddle would pillow her head, and the cedar limbs would soften the rock as well as dispel the odor of rotting vegetation.

As she surveyed her campsite, she detected a faint gurgle of running water. The welcome sound beckoned Sammy as she entered the woods. She cocked her head every so often to listen. She needed to find water for Sassy, and her own parched mouth had her licking her lips in anticipation.

As she started down a steep incline, she stepped on a loose rock. Before she knew what happened, it slid from under her foot and tossed her on her backside. She made a frantic grab for something to stop her fall, but she came up empty-handed. Sammy rolled several feet down the hill, banging her head, knees, and elbows in the process. A surprised, “Oh-h!” whooshed from her lungs. Her body rotated one last time, bringing her to a stop on a small rock ledge. She’d landed on her back, knocking the back of her head on the granite. The tumble stunned her for a moment, and she lay still to get her bearings.

Forest noises and the sound of rushing water finally penetrated her senses. Pain shot through her skull, and her whole body ached. Then she realized her hunch had been right. Slowly turning on her side, she reached down and trailed her fingers through the cool liquid of a bubbling stream. A little more momentum would have landed her in the creek.

As she gingerly massaged wet fingers over the back of her head, she felt the beginning of a lump. Agonizingly, she checked over the rest of her body and said a silent prayer of thanks that she didn't break any bones. All she'd have to deal with were a few bruises, and she could handle those. Sitting up warily, she turned to look up the hill. The sight of the steep rocky precipice made her gasp. The grade was too dangerously steep to attempt to lead Sassy to the water. How would she ever get back up that hill with water for her mare?

When she'd started down, the sun had just dipped below the horizon. Suddenly, she watched the trees turn to dark shadows as nightfall began to settle inside the ravine. She knew she'd have to think fast. As she contemplated her predicament, she almost cried. But, stubbornly she wouldn't let herself go. She'd find the answer. She just had to think a minute. Pa and her brothers hadn't taught her how to survive in the woods for nothing. Somehow, she'd manage.

Glancing at the length of her pants legs, which had unrolled on her tumble down the hill, gave her an idea. For the first time, she gloried in her tiny stature. Sammy quickly smoothed out the heavy twill. They were over ten inches too long. Using the knife, she whacked them off at her ankles.

Slipping one tube inside the other, she twisted one end and held it tightly as she leaned over the rock and drank her fill. Then she dipped the open end of the double pant leg into the stream, letting the rushing water fill it. Clutching the sack, bottom and top occupied both hands.

Sammy's first attempt to stand defeated her. She hurt all over, and before she could push her tired muscles into a standing position, she collapsed on her rump, spilling the water.

Swallowing the lump in her throat, she tried again. This time after she refilled the water pouch, she folded her legs under her body, struggled to her knees, and ever so slowly stood up. She remembered a lesson J.R. had taught her and studied the hill with her eyes. Next she mapped a zigzag course up the most gradually sloping path she could make out in the gathering darkness. With the open end of her makeshift container held upright, she started her painful trek up the hill.

Somehow, it worked. She reached her campsite and limped to Sassy with enough water for the tired horse to slake her thirst.

Exhausted herself, she crawled into her bedroll. Her burning eyes caught a glimpse of dark clouds as they moved across the star-filled sky, blotting out what little light they shed. A deep sigh emptied her tired body of air and filled her lungs with the freshness of cedar wafting on the cool breeze. She rolled over in her blanket, and losing the battle, her lids closed. The rumble of her stomach failed to rouse her. Sleep claimed her almost instantly, erasing thoughts of the food her body craved and the horror of the day.

~ * ~

Mac looked at the setting sun and decided to make camp. He'd stayed in the saddle until shadows made it too dark to follow the trail. *Besides,* he thought, *it had been a long confusing day.* He still couldn't figure out the mystery of the girl at the waterfall, and he didn't like the signs of the trail he followed. The raiding party had picked up a sizable herd of livestock. It became difficult to distinguish between the cows and the horses and how many there were of each.

He wanted to push on because he knew a herd that large had to travel slow, but he also knew he needed some sleep. In the morning he'd be fresh, and he would be able to catch up with them in no time. It didn't take him long to find a good campsite beside a brook. He unsaddled Renegade, removed the bit and bridle, then hobbled him to let him graze. Once he made sure his horse was taken care of, he walked upstream a little way to look for dinner.

Crouching at the base of a tree, he didn't have to wait more than five minutes for an inquisitive squirrel to peek out from behind a neighboring oak. He sat so still the creature didn't even notice him.

The bark of Mac's pistol launched a symphony of startled birds and chattering small animals. The noise didn't matter any more; Mac had his dinner. He made quick work of skinning and gutting the squirrel, spitting it to roast over his fire. As he made camp, he began to realize he wasn't as smart as he'd first thought. Staring into the dancing flames, he remembered some of the signs he'd ignored earlier at the two farms. He had been too preoccupied with thoughts of the girl.

Women were always trouble. That was one reason he never let himself get serious with any of them. As soon as he saw signs of a filly getting too possessive, he'd make tracks. No woman would ever tie him down to a plow handle.

Yes, thoughts of that girl's luscious body had made him addlebrained. Sitting there in the dark and forcing himself to replay everything he had seen step by step, made him realize he had broken one of his own rules—take time to get the facts before you rush off on a wild goose chase. Well, it was too late now. He'd just have to try to reconstruct the evidence in his mind and hope he'd retained more than he could remember at this point.

As he ate, he reviewed his conclusions. He didn't think it could be the same renegade band of Indians he'd been hunting. First, half of the hoof prints were shod horses and that meant white men. Second, something about the arrows just didn't look right. Why didn't he stop and pick one up? His reputation of being such a damn good tracker would suffer if anyone saw him now. Why didn't he take time to examine the clues better?

Third, raiding parties rarely took off with that much livestock. Usually they hit quick, killed the people, grabbed a few horses, and rode hell bent for leather. Sometimes a milk cow would turn up missing, but he had never known them to drive off cattle and horses together in such large numbers. They must be driving forty or more cows and a half dozen calves along with fifty or sixty horses. Who was he following? White men riding with Indians, odd looking arrows lying around, every animal driven off—including any dogs or cats—and no one left alive except for one lone girl, too frightened to trust a stranger to assist her.

Shaking his head to clear his thoughts, he headed for the creek to wash his utensils. Tomorrow would be time enough to start again. If he ran totally out of luck, he'd head back and pick up the girl's trail. One way or another, he'd find the answer. He always did.

Early the next morning, Mac woke slowly, opening his eyes to the gray overcast sky. He knew without a doubt a wet day lay in store for him. Eating quickly, he doused the fire and broke camp. He wanted to catch up with the culprits. They couldn't be that far ahead of him. They would have stopped for the night, too. By the time he had traveled five miles, the morning drizzle turned into a torrential downpour. The rain began to obliterate the remaining tracks, and several times he had to backtrack to regain the trail. When the tracks led into a streambed and didn't emerge on the other side, he felt a moment of annoyance.

He'd had a fifty-fifty chance of taking the right way. At first, he'd followed the stream toward the west, away from any of the towns he knew to be nearby. But he'd found no trace of where they had left the water. Could they be moving closer to settlements instead of away from civilization? If that were the case, they had to be someone local.

Mac sat on Renegade and pondered what to do. "Damnation and hellfire! Who the hell are you, and where are you headed?" He yelled to vent his anger at defeat. The weather left no choice. He had to give up the chase. Rain continued to pour down in torrents. The sky held no promises of relief. Without booming thunder or flashing lightening, a deluge of water continued to spill from the low gray clouds. At least there was no wind to slash the drops into torturing needles of pain.

With no trail to follow and water running down his neck under his raw-hide poncho, his buckskins became wet and uncomfortable. He had never felt so frustrated. His mind fought a constant battle. "What'll we do, Renegade? Continue tracking this band of thieves and obvious murderers? Daydream about the beautiful young lady in the fall? Or quit wasting time and find a campsite?" Nothing like this had ever distracted him from his job. He would have to reestablish his priorities.

"Damn!" It was no wonder he'd lost the trail. With visions of her bathing in the waterfall intruding every few minutes, he couldn't keep his mind on the tracks he followed. Maybe if he cleared up the mystery about her, he could forget the incident. But the questions kept up a litany that refused to be quiet. Who was she? How had she escaped the slaughter, and why did she disguise herself as a boy?

He tried to judge the time of day, but all he had to go on were the needs of his body. He'd skipped his noon meal in hopes of catching up with the slower moving herd. Now, his stomach demanded an early supper.

There wasn't enough daylight left to return to the waterfall to pick up traces of the girl. The rain had most likely taken care of that lead, too. "Come on, big boy. It's time to find a campsite and get dry."

He felt like he'd wasted a whole day. Tomorrow he would head for the nearest town. He'd come through Charrette Village before he had headed into the Lost Creek area where he found the girl. Knowing her disguise, he'd be able to spot her in a minute, if she'd found the village. He had an advantage—he knew his way around, and he wondered if she did. Picking up the bundle of her sheared hair had been fortunate. Now, he knew the true color of her locks.

The night before, he'd slept with his head cushioned on the cloth he'd wrapped her hair in, so he imagined he would know her scent. He wasn't sure what made him take that bundle out, but he felt very close to her and protective of her. He'd tenderly packed it all back in his saddlebags this morning. He felt as though he'd slept better than ever before, yet he knew he'd dreamt of her all night.

Four

Sammy woke with a start. She didn't recognize her surroundings or what roused her. She lay utterly still to get her bearings, clinching her jaw against the pain radiating from every muscle in her body. The rustling sound that had disturbed her sleep whispered again in the grass, and she opened her eyes to follow the noise. Not far from her bed, a rabbit lifted his head as he perked his ears in alert. Her stomach rattled a complaint that told her to wake up immediately. She needed to eat, plain and simple. Slowly she inched the Bowie knife from under her body. She'd had enough sense last night to unsheathe it and lay it within reach.

The rabbit continued alternately to nibble and hop closer, perking up to look around now and then. Seemingly wary of trouble but not sensing where it lay, he'd got to within ten feet of Sammy when she let the knife fly. She silently shrieked in sudden pain as the knife flew in a crazy somersault. Her muscles screamed so loud at the sudden movement, she thought she'd pass out from the pain. Her bad aim reminded her that the knife was much heavier and longer than any J.R. had taught her to throw. Sammy laid her forehead down on the saddle and sobbed out loud in frustration. Slowly, she clawed herself up on all fours and gingerly tried to stand. Never in her whole life had she ever hurt this bad. She should have used her gun. Yet, it just wouldn't have been wise to announce her presence with an echoing shot.

Her stiff muscles had to be the results of all the shoveling, along with her fall. Not that it would have mattered, this discomfort was a small price to pay for giving her family a decent burial. Not only Sammy's hands had suffered from all the digging. The pain seared her legs and rippled up her arms and shoulders across her back. Hunting and riding, even hoeing in the garden hadn't hardened her body enough for the previous day's arduous task. How would she ever ride today?

Her thoughts started to slip back to the day before and the vision of herself as she dragged her family into their graves. She hadn't been strong enough to carry them. She remembered silently begging their forgiveness as she struggled with each body. However, the way her limbs felt now, Sammy didn't think she could move if her life depended on it.

As she tentatively stood, she realized her life did depend on her moving. She knew she had to find her knife. It meant survival to her. Her legs barely supported her as she tried to walk. Searching the grass for the blade, she sobbed in relief when she saw the stunned rabbit. He'd lain there twitching in the last throes of death with the knife handle inches from the back of his head.

As she reached down to pick him up, she realized he had a broken neck. Apparently the blow hit him as he bent to nibble. Thank God, her aim was on target, and the knife heavy enough to break his bones! She breathed a quick prayer of thanksgiving for the nourishment this rabbit would provide. Then, she quickly laid a small fire. Taking the rabbit by his ears, Sammy carefully made her way back down to the stream. After last night's tumble, she wasn't going to take any chances, especially since she could hardly move, let alone walk. Mentally she shook herself. She had to deal with today. As she laid the dead rabbit on the slab of rock she had landed on the night before, she began to curse. She realized that taking care of her bodily functions would not be easy disguised as a boy. Sammy moved away from the stream and into the underbrush.

"Oh, hell! What am I going to do now? I didn't realize how easy all this was in my dress and pantaloons." As she tackled the belt to her pants, she vented more frustration. "Now, I'll have to practically undress every time nature calls. This is going to be tricky." Sammy contemplated the predicament she'd got herself into as she trudged back to the stream to wash.

"Pa told me often enough that I didn't think in an orderly fashion, and now look where it got me." Maybe disguising herself as a boy wasn't such a good idea, but what else could she have done?

Cleaning the rabbit took her mind off her problems for a few minutes. She completed the unpleasant chore as quickly as possible. Sammy washed the carcass in the rushing water one more time to remove the bits of hair that clung to the meat, then utilized the same path that she'd used to successfully carry the water.

In hindsight, she should have accepted the scout's offer to travel together. If she'd only been a little farther along in her disguise, she might not have panicked at the thought of discovery. *Well,* she thought as she stumbled through the woods, *I'll have plenty of time to plan what comes next while I wait for this rabbit to cook. Besides, the man was too handsome to trust. Didn't Ma always warn me to beware of a pretty man with pretty words?*

"Yes, I'm better off alone," she mumbled. She'd figure out a way to find the men who had killed her family and friends all by herself. She didn't need anyone's help, especially handsome, smooth-talking men!

Stealing some of the fringe from Ryan's buckskin pants, she trussed the rabbit on a willow stick and set it over the coals. As the meat roasted, Sammy couldn't force her mind to concentrate on any one subject for long, and her scattered thoughts drifted as she squinted into the gathering darkness.

Wasn't it morning? What happened to the light? A look upward confirmed black, boiling clouds racing across the gray, laden sky. As she came alert to the changing weather, the first rain drops started sizzling in her fire.

J.R.'s training kicked in automatically, and Sammy moved as quickly as her sore muscles would allow. This immediate problem gave her something she could act on without a second thought. Thankful for the huge, low hanging cedar tree, which had provided the boughs for her bed, she quickly cut some longer branches. As she gathered several long dead limbs that lay about under the tree, her thoughts jumped ahead to how she would build her lean-to.

Working briskly, she pushed the dead limbs into the loamy soil at a forty-five degree angle, then leaned the top of the branches against her rock overhang. She covered the angled limbs with fresh cut cedar. This would enclose her in a deep V, with the sheltering rock on one side and the cedar branches blocking out the rain on the other.

The appetizing smell of her breakfast cooking made her mouth water and her stomach growl in anticipation. She could hardly wait. By the time she'd finished her shelter, the rabbit looked ready to eat and the rain began in earnest. Settling down to contemplate this new predicament, she peeked out to check on Sassy. At least she wouldn't have to carry water for her. She already drank contentedly from the puddles that started to form.

That vision jerked her to attention as Sammy realized this was no gentle shower. It only took a second for her to remember another of J.R.'s lessons. Laying the hot meat on the piece of pant leg she'd used last night, she quickly dashed out of her lean-to. Using another dead cedar limb, she scraped a trench around and away from her shelter to allow the water to run off down the hill behind her camp.

"Now," she grumbled, "I should be able to stay dry." Looking skyward she groaned, "Is there anything else I have to do before I can eat?"

With no obvious answers raining down, she grabbed at her food. Tearing off a piece of hot meat, Sammy had to force herself not to gobble. She relished each bite as she tried to chew slowly and savor each swallow. It needed salt and herbs to enhance the flavor, but she wasn't complaining. This tasted like ambrosia to her starving body. Licking her fingers and sucking on a burnt thumb, she made herself plan while she ate. She wanted her attention fully focused, and she intended to keep it that way.

Mentally, she took inventory. Her first priority was to acquire a hat and some boots. She'd lost her sunbonnet somewhere along her wild ride. Her high-topped button shoes would be a dead give away to her disguise. She could go barefoot for a while, but surely not for long. The ground would tear up her feet, and snakes were always a danger.

As she counted her bullets and checked the load in her gun something clicked. All of a sudden, she sat up, alert. Small bits were surfacing as her mind relaxed. She began to remember the scene at the farm. She should have realized sooner that something didn't look right. Even though arrows were peppered around both farms, no one had died from an arrow wound.

"My God! Everyone died from bullet wounds and not ordinary bullet wounds. They were all shot at close range, either through the chest like Ma or a bullet through the head like the others." The multiple wounds on each body from the methodical slaughter told her whoever raided the farm wanted to make sure there were no survivors.

Indians didn't kill that way. White men did. Thank goodness she got away as fast as she did. How many other farms suffered the same fate? Sammy began to shake with fright all over again. She perceived that she could be in danger now. What if the killers knew her family? They would realize she had been missing from the farm. They could still be looking for her.

Surely the scout couldn't really be one of them. After all, he never pulled his gun, even after she shot at him. She still couldn't believe he had faced her fire as calmly as he did. He certainly didn't seem to think she posed a threat to his safety. Throughout the whole encounter, which only lasted a few minutes, he never once threatened her life. If he had been one of the raiders, she acknowledged to herself, he would not have backed down so easily. Nor would he have left without trying to kill her.

Even in fear for her own life, she had to admit she regretted hurting him by causing the branch to hit him in the head. The sight of his handsome face still made her heart skip a beat, and his glossy, black hair made her fingers itch to smooth it back into order.

"Stop it, Sammy!" she ordered herself. She knew this was not the time to moon over a handsome stranger she would never see again. Besides, she had more pressing problems right now. Anyway, she didn't know for sure if he belonged to the gang of killers or not. She just had a gut instinct that he didn't. For some reason that she couldn't fathom, she wouldn't want to see him die. If it turned out she'd made a mistake and he was part of the massacre, she would have to avoid looking into his eyes when she shot him. She had a feeling it would pain her more to kill him than she wanted to admit. But kill him she would if he had anything to do with her mother's death.

For now she would put off looking for Uncle Padraig. She decided to continue with her disguise and pretend to be an orphan. If she could find a job in town, maybe she would be able to overhear something that would give her a clue to who murdered her family and friends. She could always find her uncle later. Now was the time to plan carefully. She didn't want to go to Holstein. The town closest to her farm was too small. There were too many people who might recognize her. Sammy firmly believed people only see what they think they see, and if she looked enough like a boy, no one would guess she could be anything other than what she looked like. Her disguise would work if she went to Charrette Village. It was the next closest town. She'd never been there, and she felt confident no one would recognize her.

Charrette Village lay close enough to draw the raiders if they lived near by, she reasoned. Maybe they even lived on one of the outlying farms. Right now, she couldn't picture anyone she knew cruel enough to do the things she'd seen.

In her mad dash to escape, she'd headed northwest into the forest. To reach the old, French village, she would have to double back. The one-time fort sat on the Missouri River southeast of Holstein. She counted her meager store of coins and knew it wouldn't last long unless she watched her spending very carefully. To make sure she didn't lose it, she unbuttoned her shirt and the long johns, then slipped it between her breasts under the binding.

As she repacked her saddlebags, she laid a hand on the heavier buckskin shirt and pants she knew Ma had made for Ryan, her youngest brother. She could almost picture him swaggering into town for a night with the ladies in his fringed shirt, a broad smile plastered on his face.

She thought about the buckskin shirt with its long fringe on the sleeves and yoke. She knew it would reach almost to her knees. She could use it for a coat as the weather turned cooler. Too bad it was August. The pelt from the rabbit wasn't thick enough to save. Hopefully by winter, she wouldn't have the need for a fur-lined coat.

The gloves would hide her hands and protect them from more blisters when and if she found work. Her gun with extra cartridges in the belt and Pa's trusty Bowie knife afforded her protection as well as a means to feed herself. She had Dennis's saddle and, most important, her horse Sassy.

Ma's wedding dress wouldn't do her any good, but she'd be darn if she'd get rid of that. Ma's Bible, Uncle Padraig's letter, and her own shoes rounded out her possessions. It wasn't very much, and she predicted if she didn't get boots and a hat immediately, the whole plan would be doomed.

Sammy sat to the back of the shelter, snuggled in her blanket against the damp chilliness of the rainy day. Tears ran down her face. She couldn't shake the memories of her family. Every possession she now owned had belonged to someone she'd loved.

Her hands wrapped around her body so her fingers could knead the sore muscles on her upper arms and shoulders. After working on her upper body, she reached down with both hands to enfold them around her ankle. Starting there, she began to massage her leg all the way up to her thigh. Taking turns, she did each leg thoroughly. Then she would begin on her arms again.

Alternately massaging her arms and legs, she sat thinking. She had to put her grief aside. If she didn't, she'd never succeed. Clearing her head, she paid special attention to her legs. Then her mind veered. For the first time in her life, she pictured a man giving her a massage. She wondered if the scout's hands would be gentle.

There she went again, thinking about that darn scout. She couldn't waste time on him. He was gone, and she still had a long way to go. Sammy looked around, undecided on which direction she would need to take.

With the heavy grayness of the day, she couldn't even tell east from west. She hated to waste a day holed up, but she couldn't make up her mind if she should break camp or not. Thinking things through made her indecisive. Maybe she'd be better off just doing something. Even if it were wrong, it would be better than sitting here brooding. So what if she got wet? It was still summer, and she wouldn't melt; that's for sure.

~ * ~

Fog was settling in, indicating the night was cooling off and would probably grow chilly by morning. The warm ground generated the gray vapors that swirled around Renegade's hoofs as the pair made their way into a small glade. Mac spotted a small pond and, not finding any shelter, realized he had a wet night in store for him. He decided a warm bath would be just what he needed to chase the damp chill away. Renegade would also benefit from having the mud caked on his legs and belly washed off before it dried into hard clay. Mac dismounted and unsaddled the big gray.

It took him quite a while to forage for enough dead limbs and dry twigs to build a small fire. Stripping some bark from a cedar tree, he produced the tinder he needed to spark a flame. Satisfied that the rain would not douse his fledging blaze, he undressed and folded his clothes neatly on top of his boots. Then, he covered it all with his poncho and placed his hat on the top of the whole pile.

Renegade offered no resistance to his bath, standing quietly while Mac cleaned his glistening coat. After he tethered the gray to a big oak next to his campfire, he swam out to the middle of the pond and let the warm water soothe his tired body. He floated, completely cocooned in the shrouding fog. Cool rain hit his face as he drifted in the warm pond. It lulled him into a dreamlike state, and Mac let himself relax for the first time in days.

Only the splash of rain hitting the surface of the water and the heavier patter of raindrops slapping the trees disturbed the silence. Mac hoped it would let up so he could sleep dry tonight. He scrubbed at his well-muscled arms and chest then decided he could probably just soak clean.

Kicking out, he let his body float again. He closed his eyes and let his head fall back trying to relax. His long, lean body felt caressed by the warm water, yet stimulated by the cold sting of the rain. He savored the sensuous feeling it gave him. His long, black hair floated out around his head, and he again began to daydream about his mystery woman.

~ * ~

That does it, Sammy thought. *I'll pack up and get going!* First, she removed her button-top shoes, no sense ruining them in the mud. She added them to her saddlebags and rolling up her blanket, prepared to leave. Not wanting to waste what was left of her rabbit, she wrapped it in the piece of damp pant leg she had used to carry water for Sassy. It made a nice pouch, and she might not be as lucky later today.

In no time, she had the fire out and Sassy saddled. She rode in the shelter of the trees to try to stay out of the hardest rain, but it wasn't enough protection. After a couple of hours, her clothes were soaked through. With no hat, the rain plastered her hair to her head and water ran into her eyes, down her face and neck.

Already, she regretted leaving her camp. She couldn't tell the time of day because the sky hadn't changed from early that morning. It hung as low and gray as it had at dawn. Ahead, she saw fog swirling low to the ground and realized the air had cooled, so it must be getting on to evening time.

"What do you think, Sassy girl? There must be a pond or small lake ahead causing this kind of fog. Maybe there will be a place we can camp for the night." Suiting action to words, she headed down the hill. Heavy fog shrouded the valley as the rain continued its relentless onslaught against man and nature.

As she plodded through the endless patter, the sound of a horse snorting jerked Sammy to attention. The noise was unmistakable. A quick check on Sassy's bridle brought her to a stop. Listening intently, Sammy detected the sounds of an occasional splash. She guessed right; a pond must lie hidden in the mist. Someone had already made camp there. What if it was the raiders? She had to know. Maybe her luck had changed.

Her heart raced as she dismounted. The blood thundered through her body, stimulating her frayed nerves to heightened awareness. Fear mingled with excitement as she flipped Sassy's reins over a sapling. She whispered her apologies as she withdrew the buckskin shirt to throw over the filly's head. She wasn't taking any chances. If the other horses whinnied, she didn't want her mare to answer.

Drawing the pistol from her holster, she crept through the soft, wet grass. The scent of wood smoke wafted in the air, guiding her through the fog. When she had crept close enough to make out the flickering flames of the campfire, she saw the lone horse. A one-man camp and no one occupied it. Sammy cautiously tiptoed forward to reach the side of the huge, gray stallion. He'd been tethered to a tree at the edge of the clearing.

A small fire glowed brightly in the fog. Its sparkling light cast flickering shadows in the swirling haze. She saw the pile of clothing silhouetted by the flames. The smoke tantalized her with its woodsy fragrance, luring her to its meager warmth.

Bare feet crushed the earthen debris, causing her to wrinkle her nose at the musty smell of wet decay.

Reaching the animal on his upwind side, she nestled her face into the soft warmth of his neck. The welcome scent of horseflesh dispelled the odor of rotting vegetation. She crooned softly to the beauty, calming his initial agitation caused by her unexpected appearance. Except for shuffling his hooves, he hadn't made a sound. She smiled as he pressed his head into her hand.

"Yes," she whispered, "I know just where you like to be rubbed. Be a good boy now and be quiet. I do what I do because it's necessary, not because of malice."

Her prayers had been answered. Everything the man owned lay protected under the cover of a large poncho and topped by a black Stetson, tempting her with its promise of a sure fire disguise. She'd found what she needed. She had to work quickly if she planned to be successful in pilfering the stranger's hat and boots. For a moment, she fought an inner battle over the necessity of stealing from the unsuspecting camper. However, her dire need overcame her initial hesitation.

Giving the horse a lingering hug, she dashed over to the fire. Popping the hat on her head, she dug beneath the poncho. Her hand froze as it rested on the butt of his handgun. She had never seen a gun so large. The barrel was longer than her Colt, and it seemed to weigh twice as much. Seconds later, she'd opened the cylinder and dumped the large bullets onto the ground. Digging lower, she located his boots buried under all the clothing. Just as her hand reached for them, she heard intensified splashing penetrating the dense fog that lay like a heavy blanket over the water. She knew the noise signaled the completion of the man's bath and announced his momentary emergence from the pond.

She froze in fear as the mist parted, revealing his form. He emerged from the water like a specter. From his chest upward, it appeared as if his head was in a cloud. From his torso to his thighs, the fog wafted away to expose his body to her view. Shocked with her first sight of a man fully aroused, she couldn't take her eyes from him.

A capricious breeze shifted the fog again. Frozen to the spot, she watched him. Still unaware of her presence, using both of his open hands, he pressed the water from his hair, causing his biceps to ripple as the excess water trickled off his body. Dark hair lay shoulder length, dripping partially over the top of his well-muscled shoulders. With his arms raised above his head, the glow of the fire outlined his anatomy for her stunned perusal. Even living with her three brothers, she had never seen the bare flesh of a man's body. When she'd hunted with J.R., he'd always respected her privacy, and she'd done the same for him, one guarding the campsite while the other bathed.

Her avid inspection of the man ended as he opened his eyes and spotted her. Her mouth formed a perfect O in shocked surprise as she recognized the scout who'd interrupted her earlier. Kneeling amidst his scattered clothing, she didn't have a prayer of escaping. Instinctively, she grabbed his damp horse blanket and threw it over the fire, blotting all illumination and adding smoke to the fog.

"Please, God, I hope he didn't get a good look at me! Help me find my way back to Sassy."

She could hear him charging out of the water like an enraged bull. "Hey you, stop! What the hell are you doing in my camp?"

Closing her eyes to the image seared in her mind, she bolted. It was now or never. Swallowing her fear and closing her mind to the guilt at leaving him vulnerable to the harshness of the forest, she prayed he had a spare pair of moccasins and made her mad dash towards Sassy.

With one hand clamped on top of her head to hold down the oversized hat and the other clutching the boots, she sprinted past the gray stallion, sending him a soft, regretful farewell. “Sorry, sweetie.”

“Stop, you son of a polecat! I’ll skin you alive when I catch you! Come back here and face me like a man.”

The harsh words and savage threats didn’t frighten her near as much as the thought of dodging flying bullets if he decided to pursue her. “I’m so glad I emptied his gun. I hope he stops to put on his pants before he chases me,” she panted as she ran crashing through the woods.

“By the time he reloads and dresses, I’ll be long gone.” Reaching Sassy, she grabbed the reins and vaulted into the saddle. With both hands full, she bent forward and snagged the buckskin shirt in her teeth to pull it from Sassy’s head. Without wasting another minute, she beat a hasty retreat.

Five

Mac charged ashore with water streaming down his body. As he glanced down at his wilting arousal, he snorted in disgust and vowed to stop thinking about the woman at the falls. He'd been pitched into total darkness before he'd managed a good look at the hombre crouched by his clothes.

Trying to run through the knee-deep pond, he lost his balance when his feet came in contact with the slippery, clay mud surrounding the pool. Landing on all fours, he scrambled out of the water. Shaking mud from his hands, he groped around until he felt his saddle blanket.

"That's what smothered the fire," he grunted. Jerking it off, he fanned the coals to revive the flame and reached for his handgun. Coming up with the butt, he sited on the sound of the intruder running through the woods and squeezed off three quick shots.

Click... Click ... Click...

"Empty! It can't be empty," he muttered. Opening the cylinder, he saw the proof.

He heard the crash of someone running through the underbrush. Whoever had invaded his camp a few minutes ago thundered away and there wasn't a thing he could do about it. Frustrated, he ran his fingers through his hair and, flinging off the excess water, moved closer to the fire to dry his body and dress.

"Hellfire and damnation! Where's my hat?" He knew he'd left it on top of his poncho. It couldn't have blown away. The rain continued to fall with no wind to slant the drops. Toweling off with his shirt, he quickly dressed and reaching the bottom of his stack of clothes, realized his boots were gone, too. He spun around quickly, double-checking Renegade. Good, he hadn't been stolen. But not a sound emitted from him. He contentedly nibbled the long grass at the base of the tree as if nothing unusual had happened.

Automatically, Mac checked the ground for signs of who had been in his camp and found none. That was no specter he'd seen. Damn the rain! Damn the girl for intruding in his thoughts! If he hadn't been fantasizing about her again, he would have known when the trespasser entered his camp. At the very least, he'd have heard something. A quick inventory reassured him that nothing else had been taken.

None of this seemed real. He knew no one could steal Renegade. There wasn't a man alive who could get within ten feet of that horse without a ruckus. But wait, someone had! Renegade stood tethered only five or six feet from the campfire. "Renegade, who did this? How'd he get by you? You could have at least warned me." Strapping on his gun, he reached for the saddle blanket.

"What the hell. No sense going after someone in the dark." Throwing the blanket back in the general direction of his saddle, he mouthed more expletives.

"Shit! What happened to my charmed luck?" He walked over to his mount and ran his hands over the animal. No marks or injuries. "Of course not. You'd have let me know then, wouldn't you, boy? I'm just glad you're okay." Removing his holster again, he squatted in front of the fire.

Could he be the butt of some large practical joke? Ever since he had seen that girl at the waterfall, he'd uncovered one mystery after another. Rising to his full height, he kicked at the ground in anger. What the hell was he going to do out here without boots and a hat?

Now, he had no choice. He had to ride to the nearest town. He'd have to buy a new hat and some footgear. "Might as well head for town now rather than later," he mumbled. He could ask some questions and see what he could find out about any cattle rustling going on or how many local farms had been raided. And yes, look for that girl/boy and get to the bottom of that story.

In the meantime, he'd also be looking at all the cowboy's feet. He'd know his boots anywhere. They were a beautiful leather pair his father had tooled for him down in Mexico. He prided himself on keeping them polished to a high shine and as clean as a whistle. There was nothing distinctive about his hat. It was black suede with a snakeskin hatband. Lots of cowboys had hats just like it.

As Mac contemplated his next move, the rain abated for the night. At least now he'd be able to sleep in relative comfort. Tossing the remainder of his coffee into the fire, he walked over to check Renegade one more time. He shook his head in puzzlement and prepared for bed. The poncho made a waterproof groundcover, and he laid his blanket on top of that.

Before he lay down, he unwrapped the girl's hair again. It wasn't as dark as he had remembered it when he'd seen her get out of the pool. As he stroked the shiny, dark, red hair, he realized that being wet had made it appear darker. "Well, Renegade, at least I did something right. I kept the little lady's locks. That should make it easier to identify her." As he handled the bundle, he realized it had become a constant reminder of the woman and a major distraction that he didn't need. Snorting at himself in disgust, he deliberately decided not to use that parcel of beautiful chestnut hair for his pillow. Stuffing the offending package into his saddlebag, he lay down and tried to sleep.

Hours later, tossing and turning, he gradually woke. His sleep had been fitful and full of dreams of his angel. He lifted heavy eyelids and squinted at the morning sun peeking over the horizon. A beautiful dawn of a rose pink greeted him as he pried open his reluctant lids. The last shadows of the night were fading to leave a sky as blue as the sea with the horizon painted from a pallet of brilliant rose. High, fast-moving, white puffs of cotton chased away yesterday's gloom.

Pulling himself to a sitting position, he looked over his campsite, not sure what he expected to find. He never did like having to get up early, but years of scouting had taught him to wake before sunrise. Why had he slept so late today? Scrubbing both hands over his face to stimulate his wakefulness, he effortlessly rolled himself to a standing position.

Renegade peacefully nibbled on the dew covered grass at the base of the large oak tree that sheltered the camp. His belongings were as he'd left them. Nothing looked different from the previous night. When he crouched to rekindle the banked campfire, Mac stepped on a small ember and suffered a rude reminder of the loss of his boots. "Damn!" he muttered as he sat to brush off the offending twig. Now he had a hole in his sock and a blister on his foot. "What next?" he yelled to no one in particular.

The puzzle of how anyone could have crept into his camp and gotten away with his belongings had disturbed him all night. "Maybe that's why I didn't sleep well," he grumbled.

As he broke camp, Mac blistered the air with curses every time he stepped on an odd stone or prickly branch. Each needle of pain reminded him of his stolen boots. Satisfied he had doused his fire enough, he thankfully mounted Renegade and checked the sun for his bearings before he headed east towards what he hoped would be the nearest town.

~ * ~

Sammy slumped in her saddle, exhausted. After running from the scout, she'd continued to ride through the night and all the next day. She'd stopped frequently for short rests, mostly to let Sassy get a drink and graze. Almost every time she'd tried to catch something to eat, she failed. In fact, all she'd had in the last three days was the rabbit she'd killed the day before and just one small fish she'd caught earlier this morning. She had taken the risk of a small fire to cook her fish and examine her booty.

"Mercy sakes alive!" she exclaimed when she saw the boots in daylight. "How will I ever keep these on my feet? They're huge."

She gathered a couple of large handfuls of soft spongy moss to stuff into the toe of the boots, but that did no good. The tops came almost up to her knees, and they stuck out so far from the end of her legs she had to laugh.

"I look like a circus clown."

She could hardly walk and maintain her balance. Reaching into her saddlebags, she retrieved her own shoes. Looking at them in comparison to the boots, she had an idea. She slipped her shoe into the boot and found she could force it all the way down. Then she put her foot into the top of the boot, and it slid right into her shoe. She didn't even have to button her shoes. They fit perfectly.

She started to feel guilty about the boots again. Once she saw them in daylight, she knew they were an expensive and prized possession. They were beautifully tooled and very well-kept. She knew they would be easily identifiable. Reluctantly she coated them with a thick smear of river mud, hoping that as it dried, it would disguise the lovely design and color. The hat floated down on her forehead, but she wanted it large to hide her features.

The one thing she had to get rid of was the snakeskin hatband. She hated snakes! She could kill one easy enough and wasn't exactly afraid of them, but hated the sight and the thought of their silent deadliness. As she cut the hatband off and threw it away, she realized the hat too needed a coat of mud. Slapping the now disreputable felt on her head, Sammy grinned, satisfied with her efforts. "Now, I'll bet the owner wouldn't even recognize his property," she muttered.

Sammy reached the village after dark. The town seemed deserted. The only building showing lights was the saloon. Surveying the town, she recognized the livery stable at the end of the street and headed in that direction. She knew her talent with horses would allow her to sneak in and sleep in the hayloft without raising a lot of commotion.

Sammy guided her mount around to back of the building. "Look, Sassy, the door's open. Let's go to bed, girl." A shaft of the moonlight guided her steps to the yawning barn door. She dismounted and nearly fell as her legs tried to support her exhausted weight. Quietly, she led Sassy into the dark stable and crooning softly, used her sweet voice to calm the horses that had started to become restive. She found an empty stall and settled Sassy. After unsaddling the mare, she gave her an extra ration of oats from the wooden bin and fresh water she hauled in from the trough outside. Then struggling with the heavy saddle, she climbed into the loft. Her saddle made a soft thud as she dropped it in the hay. She listened quietly but heard nothing that meant she'd been discovered. Barely getting her blanket spread out, she sank to her knees and fell forward on her stomach in a dead sleep.

Early the next morning, loud curses and grumbling woke her. “Damn cowboys! Always stealing in here in the middle of the night using my stalls, feeding their mangy horses, then riding out again the next night, never paying a dime, and me losing money. Well, this fellow won’t find his horse when he comes back. No sir. He’ll have to pay up before he gets away this time.”

Sammy peeked over the edge of the loft and saw a big man at Sassy’s stall. He appeared to be talking to himself. A felt hat shielded his face, but she saw how large his hands were as he scratched his bushy, gray beard. Sammy disregarded her own safety, when he opened the gate to lead Sassy out of the stall.

“Please, mister. That’s my horse, and I was going to pay for her keep. I was just so tired last night, I fell asleep before I thought about looking for anyone.”

Startled, the man looked up and found her peeking over the edge of the loft.

“Get down outa’ there, boy. You think I’m running a hotel? This is a stable for God’s sake. How’d you get in here without causing a ruckus and waking me?” he demanded in a gruff voice. Shaking his fist at her, he continued, “Come on down and explain before I call the sheriff.”

Sammy scrambled down as quickly as she could, then stopped at each stall before she approached the man impatiently waiting for her. One by one she soothed the horses that had started to stamp their feet and snort with all the shouting. In seconds, she had the barn peaceful and walked up to Sassy. She laid a quiet, protective hand on her mare’s neck, then looked down at her feet. The sight of her large boots caused her a moment of panic. Sammy scuffed the toes of her boots trying to hide them in the loose hay, then lowered her voice and spoke to the astonished liveryman.

"I'm sorry, sir. I swear I wasn't going to sneak away without paying. I got to town late last night, and everything was closed except the saloon. I'm too young to go there, so I came here to sleep. I'm looking for a job in town, but have a little money to pay for boarding Sassy." Sammy mentally patted herself on the back. *No lies!* Everything she'd told him came out the truth. She'd left out a lot of details, but every word uttered was true.

The man had quickly closed his gaping mouth and instantly lost all his gruffness.

"Where are your parents, boy? Did you run away from home?"

"No, sir." Contemplating her next words, Sammy bit her tongue to force out the lie. "My folks were lost in a river accident. The cable on the ferry carrying us across the river snapped and the boat overturned. Everyone got swept away and drowned except my horse and me. I'm alone, sir, and I need a job." Regret at the falsehood caused her to hang her head in shame. At that moment the loud rumble of her stomach shattered the quiet. "I haven't eaten in days and need to replenish my supplies. I don't have anything except the clothes on my back and my horse."

With a puzzled glance around the now peaceful stable, the liveryman asked suspiciously, "How did you quiet these horses so fast?"

"I'm good with horses, sir!" Sammy replied. "I love them, and they know it. I can soothe a troubled horse in no time. I know a lot about them. My older brother raised horses, and he taught me." *Again*, Sammy sighed in relief, *the truth.*

"Is that how you got in so quiet last night?"

"Yes, sir," Sammy answered. "They weren't afraid of me."

"Look at me, boy," he demanded as he reached out to tilt her chin. "I'm not going to bite. You don't have to stare at the ground. What's your name?"

Instinctively she jumped back to avoid his touch. Then hesitantly, Sammy raised her eyes. Either her disguise would work or it wouldn't. Now was as good a time as any to test it.

"My name is Sam Turn…uh, Sam Turns, sir." She'd almost slipped, stumbling over the words. Somehow, she never anticipated having to fabricate a name so quickly. Her real name had almost popped out, so the abbreviation would have to do.

"Stop calling me sir. No one ever called me a sir before. My name is Jack Billings, and if you're as good with horses as you say you are, I'll give you a job. I need someone to sleep here anyway to check these freeloading cowboys that come in for a night at Laura's place and leave before dawn." Scratching at his beard again, he looked her up and down.

"Think you're up to the work? You're awful small. You can sleep in the loft and board your horse. I'll give you five cents a week plus meals." Closing the gate to Sassy's stall, he continued to talk more to himself than to Sammy.

"Once my wife sees how skinny you are, she'll probably be bringing extra food over to fatten you up. You can save your pay to get extra clothes, especially some boots and a hat. Everything looks too big for you, boy. Your feet aren't that big are they? Where'd you get those clothes anyway?"

Jack's rapid fire questions startled Sammy. He seemed to rattle on forever when he warmed to a subject and veer off in whatever direction his brain dictated. But she knew she needed to satisfy his curiosity enough to stop his questions, so she continued weaving a false background.

"The townspeople gave me some extras when they pulled me out of the river," Sammy fabricated with reluctance. "I lost everything."

Jack seemed to accept her explanation. His priority seemed to be finding reliable help for the stable. "Well, what do you say? Do you want to work for me?"

"Yes, sir!" Sammy exclaimed excitedly. The livery stable was a perfect place to watch the comings and goings of everyone in town.

"Then we have a deal!" He extended his big bear-like hand, and she gingerly placed her tiny palm in his. His shake pumped her arm all the way to her shoulder. "And call me Jack for God's sake. If anyone hears you call me sir, I'll never live it down. Let's go over to the house for breakfast, then I'll show you the ropes."

Stopping half way to the house, he pointed to the yard pump.

"By the way, you better stop at the pump before you come in. My wife is a stickler for cleanliness and won't appreciate the way you smell. She always says just because I work with horses all day doesn't mean I have to come to her table smelling like one. If you work for me, you'll have to wash more than once a week."

As Jack left Sammy in the backyard, she stared at his retreating back, mortified. She'd always been a fanatic about cleanliness. She pulled the collar of her shirt away from her body and bent her head. After she took a deep whiff, she felt ashamed. Mercy! She smelled so bad, she could hardly stand herself. But how could she bathe without undressing?

As she worked the pump handle, she thought about admitting she was a girl. Then, she stuck her whole head under the gushing water and scrubbed at her face and neck. After she rinsed the dust out of her hair and rubbed her hands together, she looked at her reflection in the bucket. With her hair plastered to her head and slicked back, her appearance gave her a more boyish look. She decided to continue with her plan and stick to her story. Maybe this quasi bath would actually help with her disguise.

Shyly, she stepped up to the back door and knocked, hoping no one would be able to hear the rumbling in her stomach or the pounding of her heart. She didn't know which was louder.

Jack's wife answered and, seeing the boy had made an attempt to clean up, tried not to wrinkle her nose. Jack had told her the lad's story, and she felt sorry for him immediately.

"Come on in. Breakfast is on the table." The boy ducked his head and, without a word, slid into the chair she indicated. She watched him wolf down a generous portion of bacon and eggs. Then, when she offered him seconds, he didn't hesitate to grab two more biscuits. By the time they finished the hearty meal, Sam had won her heart, and Sally had another crusade. She had a million questions for the boy, mainly when he'd had his last meal. But first, she needed to fatten him up and teach him some hygiene. As Sam and Jack prepared to return to the stable, she shook her finger at Jack.

"Don't you work the lad too hard today. You can see how peaked he is. He's probably still weak from his ordeal. I'll bring a nice lunch over about noon, and I expect you to stop your work to eat."

Laughing, Jack clapped Sammy on the back hard enough to send her flying. "Sorry," he chuckled as he caught her arm. "I keep forgetting you're so small. Anyway, I was thinking about all the good food I'll be getting now that Sally has you to fatten up. She'll be more generous with me, too. Yes, I think I'm going to like having you around."

As they entered the cool shade of the barn, Sammy inhaled the familiar tang of horseflesh and hay. She adjusted her eyes to the dimness and sought out her beloved Sassy. With her nose deep in a bucket of oats, the filly looked like she'd found heaven.

Jack's blacksmith shop occupied the front of the stable. He had artfully made doors that slid open on both the front side, facing the street, and in back, leading to the corral. Today they yawned wide to let in light and provide an escape for the heat of the forge. On the back wall of the shop, hung all the tools of his trade. Long-handled tongs and hammers shared space with iron shoes of various sizes and parts of wagon wheels. Hubs, spokes, and rims were all neatly separated, ready for use.

Handing Sammy a pitchfork, Jack indicated which stall he wanted her to start on without a break in his monologue. "I'll tell you, boy, I have a weakness for food. I never seem to get enough, and although Sally feeds me well, she's always trying to keep me from getting too fat. You can see I'm a big man. A man my size needs lots of food."

Picking up his bellows, he began to stoke his fire. The huge oven glowed and sparked to life. "You probably couldn't guess my weight, but Doc said for a man over six-foot tall it's not bad."

While he heated the iron to ready it for shaping his next horseshoe, he seemed to watch Sammy clean the stalls. "You're no slacker. You seem to know the meaning of a good day's work. Yes," he chortled. "I'm mighty glad you decided to sleep in the loft last night."

Sammy had the fleeting thought that Jack yacked nonstop. He kept up a running monologue almost all morning except for the times he was hammering away at the iron. She smiled to herself, for all she knew maybe he never stopped talking, and she just didn't hear him for all the noise he made.

The morning passed swiftly with Sammy proving she knew her way around horses. Using her gloves to protect her sore hands, she had the barn stalls cleaned out, fresh straw down, and fresh food and water carried in for the horses all before noon. She hoped Jack recognized her as a hard and industrious worker.

Sally walked in with her lunch basket loaded down at the stroke of twelve. Her spry bounce belied the woman's age. She looked tiny next to Jack's large frame. Her graying hair with its neatly coiled twin braids on each side of her head framed a round face, rosy from the sun. She handed Jack a wet towel to wipe away the sweat from working over the forge. Once he'd rubbed his face and massive arms and shoulders, he took off his felt hat and ran the towel over his salt and pepper hair. Sally waited patiently, and when he completed the ritual, she tipped her head up to receive his kiss.

Only then did she turn her attention to Sammy. Handing her a similar towel, she spread a cloth over a bale of hay and laid out the noon meal. Looking around the barn, she insisted Sam had done a full day's work already. "You been pushing the boy too hard, Jack? Looks like he finished everything in half a day. I'll be taking him home after lunch, if you don't mind."

"Since I'm well pleased with the work the lad finished, I'll let you have your way, Sally my love." Putting his arm around his wife's shoulders, he gave her a hug and whispered loud enough for Sammy to hear. "Besides, I know what you're up to. I'll wager you have water heating for Sam."

Shaking her finger at Jack, she shrugged out of his embrace and started home. "Sam, you just come over to the house as soon as you're finished eating." Sammy wasn't sure what she wanted. Did Miss Sally want her to do the wash?

After lunch, Jack handed Sam the empty basket. "You're working for me, but that includes any chores that Miss Sally might want you to do. So, you run along now. Take this empty basket back to the house. You did a fine job out here this morning, so you can spend the rest of the afternoon doing whatever Miss Sally wants."

Sammy shook her head in puzzlement when Jack went back to work, chuckling to himself. She started toward the house a bit hesitantly. Would her hands hold up to doing the laundry?

Six

As Sammy entered the big kitchen, she saw the copper hipbath filled and waiting. Steam rose in soft curls from the surface, and she tried not to look at it with longing.

"I'll take that basket, child. Now, you get out of those smelly clothes so I can wash them up. Then get into that tub and get yourself clean. And don't forget to wash behind those ears, boy."

Sammy panicked. "Miss Sally, I haven't stripped down even in front of my Ma since I was ten. I'm not getting in that tub with you in this room."

Sally turned a bright red. "Son, I never meant to cause you shame or embarrassment. I just thought you'd welcome a nice bath. I even went to Frank's Emporium and brought you a new shirt and pants so you'd have a change of clothes. There're some long johns, too. I think these will fit you better. You really look terrible in those baggy clothes."

"Thank you, Miss Sally, but I can take care of myself, and I don't mind the clothes being too big. I'll grow into them." Seeing Sally's smile fade, she wanted to put the goodhearted woman's mind at ease. "But, I do appreciate having something to put on while mine are being washed. I'll pay you back after I earn my pay from Jack."

"Well, if you insist, but I'm telling you, Sam, Jack and I can afford the little bit I got you, so don't feel obliged to pay us back so fast. Now, give me those filthy boots and I'll clean them up while you bathe."

"I'll make you a deal, Miss Sally," Sammy countered. "I'll take care of my boots, since they'll just get dirty again anyway. I'll take them off before I come into your clean kitchen if you'll lend me a little extra money to buy a pair of moccasins. I can leave them here by your kitchen door, and whenever I come over, I'll put on the moccasins and leave my boots on the step outside."

No way could Sammy allow Sally to clean them, advertising their expensive leather and causing questions of why anyone would give a poor kid their best boots.

"You've got a deal, boy. I always hated the job of cleaning Jack's boots, so now he takes care of them himself." She sighed in relief. This would be the perfect solution to the problem. She'd hated to ask the boy to take off his muddy boots before coming in her spotless kitchen.

"Here, put your foot on this piece of brown paper and I'll mark around it for size. My word, child, you have a tiny foot. It don't look like you can grow much taller and have these wee feet hold you up." Sally shook her head at the small outline, then seemed to dismiss the thought from her mind.

"I can run down to Frank's store again while you're in the tub. That will give you some privacy."

"Thank you, Miss Sally." Sammy gulped, trying to hide her feet. She'd let the remark about her size pass without comment. Oh, brother! Would she ever be able to continue this charade? As she eyed the tub again, she could hardly wait for Sally to leave. Hot water! She hadn't washed in hot water since before the fire. The second the door closed, Sammy peeled out of her clothes. The binding around her breast only caused a slight delay. She couldn't wait!

Soaping up, she worried about what she would use to flatten her chest. The cloth reeked from her sweat. She couldn't put it back against her clean skin. She'd have to think about that, but first things first. She savored the warm water, then became nervous when she thought she heard someone approaching the house. Sammy washed as quickly as possible.

Just as she started to climb into the smaller clothes, she noticed she'd started her monthly.

"Oh, God," she whispered. "Now, what should I do?"

Without her supply of rags Mama kept for these occasions, she would be sunk. Glancing quickly around the kitchen, she found a box in the corner with a neatly stacked pile of clean white rags. She guessed this was Miss Sally's supply for these times. Sammy wondered if Miss Sally would miss any if she took a handful.

Rummaging through the box, she found a piece of sheeting on the bottom that was just the length she needed to rebind her breast. *What luck,* she thought, *someone's looking out for me.* Quickly taking care of both her problems, she'd just buttoned her shirt when she heard Miss Sally return.

"I'll clean up your kitchen, Miss Sally, if you just give me a few more minutes," she hollered. *Please,* she prayed, *don't walk in on me now.*

"Take your time, Sam. I got some ears of corn at the store, and I'll sit out here in the sun and shuck them while you finish. Come out and try on your moccasins when you get done."

Bless her heart, Sammy thought. Sally was so thoughtful and considerate. After she did her laundry in the leftover bath water, Sammy bundled the telltale piece of sprigged material inside the rest of her clothes. The loft was a perfect place to dry her things in privacy. Jack would have no need to venture up the ladder now that she was working for him.

Completing her toilet, Sammy let the tail of the shirt hang out since the pants Miss Sally bought for her fit a little too snug. She didn't want her shape to give her away. She loosely belted the leather around her waist. Surveying the results, she decided it would do.

"Miss Sally, would you like me to empty my bath water on the kitchen garden?"

"Goodness, you're a sweet, thoughtful child. That would be wonderful, Sam. Except for that rain a couple of days back, it's been a dry summer."

By the time Sam had the kitchen neat and clean again, Sally announced she had to start dinner. "After I hang my clothes to dry, would you like me to come back and help you, Miss Sally? I know I put you behind in your work since I occupied your kitchen so long. I could peel the potatoes for you if you like."

"Thank you, Sam. I would like your company. Sit yourself here at the table when you get back, and I'll start the chicken a fryin'."

The next half hour passed in companionable silence. Sammy could barely keep her head up by the time she finished the potatoes.

"Why don't you lay by the hearth and rest a spell, lad? You look a mite pale." Not needing a second invitation, Sammy promptly fell asleep on the floor next to the fireplace.

~ * ~

The whole time Mac rode that day, he continually kept an eye out for tracks of the girl, the thief, and the herd. He never saw signs of any of them. It took him a full day of riding to find the village. As he rode into town, the setting sun lengthened his shadow to a long thin line that preceded him down the street. Small puffs of dust motes rose up around Renegade's hoofs like a brown cloud. His first stop was at the general store where he took a lot of ribbing from the owner when he walked in barefoot and hatless. "What'd 'ya do, boy? Gamble your boots away on a sure-fire hand?" The proprietor pointedly looked at Mac's bare feet.

Before Mac could reply, an old geezer sitting on an overturned barrel chimed in his two cents worth. "Nah, Mr. Frank. A young buck like him probably got rolled by his last lite-o-love. You better check to see if he has any money to pay for what he wants. Hee, Hee, Hee!" The old man giggled like a foolish woman.

Glowering at the two old men, Mac's patience exploded. "Neither of your assumptions are correct, and I do have the money to pay for my purchases."

"My, my," the old geezer chuckled, "the half-breed is educated."

"Look, old man, I have no quarrel with you, yet. But I happen to be in no mood for your teasing. My heritage is none of your business. All I want to do is buy a new hat and some moccasins. I'll be back for boots when my feet heal enough to try them on."

His feet were tender, cut, and swollen. There was no way he could tolerate the snugness of boots yet. He supposed with his face and neck a shade darker then normal, that he did look more like an Indian. But he wasn't in any frame of mind to argue with these men.

After he left the general store, Mac walked to the barber. He needed a bath and a haircut in that order. After he got a room at the hotel, he would stop at the saloon to see what information he could gather.

Later, thoroughly refreshed and feeling human again, he entered the barroom. The only occupants were the bartender, a not-so-young woman disinterestedly plunking at the piano keys, and one table of cowhands playing cards at the back of the room.

Mac walked over to the bar and asked, “How about a mug of beer?” While the bartender poured, he tried to think of a way to pose his questions. “I’ve been tracking some renegade Indians and came across a couple of farms that have been raided. Have you heard of any cattle rustling going on?”

“I’m just the bartender here, mister,” he snapped. “If you need information, go see the sheriff. I don’t know nothin. I don’t see nothin.” Mac had a hard time reading the man’s character.

“Well, have you seen a young boy, maybe thirteen or fourteen years old? Traveling by himself, baggy clothes.”

“I told you, man, I ain’t seen nothin.”

Mac finally decided the hombre probably didn’t know anything and tried to cover his ignorance with hostility. He might have better luck back at the hotel, should have thought about that angle sooner. If she were here, she’d go to the hotel for a room, not the saloon. He downed his drink and purposely headed back the way he had come.

The hotel lobby appeared deserted except for a large gray and white cat sleeping in a shaft of evening sunlight streaming in the open window. The feline opened one eye to check out the intruder and twitched his tail, then settled down to finish his nap.

No sounds disturbed the room’s shabby elegance. At one time, the furnishings would have been new and quite stylish. Now, they had the look of years of wear and, although free from the ever-present dust, looked faded and worn. Table runners highlighted the smoothly polished surfaces of mahogany furniture, and dainty antimacassars covered the arms and backs of every upholstered piece. They reminded Mac of home.

White lace curtains billowed in the evening breeze, shifting the pattern of sun across the floor, teasing the cat with its warmth. An Oriental rug lay precisely in the middle of the lobby, and a matching runner spilled down the steps. The pattern, while once bright in hue, had faded over the years to a soft blend of pastels.

Mac walked to the counter, ignored the dainty bell and knocked on the wooden top to call attention to his presence. Up from behind the desk flew a gray-haired, gray-bearded little man screeching like the gray and white cat he resembled. “Good Lord, man! You trying to give a body a heart failure, sneaking up like some dad burn Indian!” His sudden appearance from under the desk startled Mac, causing him to jump back, landing on the cat’s tail. With that the cat screeched and clawed Mac’s leg. Pandemonium broke loose. Mac yelled as he pried the cat off his leg. He turned, clutching the spitting cat in his outstretched arms, as a little old lady, looking like the man’s twin, came running out from the kitchen brandishing a cast iron frying pan. The tow-headed young boy, who had assigned him his room earlier, followed her on the run. The boy, glaring daggers, scooped his cat from Mac’s clutches and nuzzled his neck in sympathy.

By the time everyone had calmed down and Mac had apologized for frightening all of them, they were sitting around a table at the back of the room.

Mr. Ruggers looked like a character from one of Mr. Grimm’s fairytales. With almost identical features, he and his wife shared the same short stature and curly white hair. Her rosy cheeks glowed with health, and her brown eyes sparkled with humor. His cheeks were partly hidden by his gray beard, but his eyes held the same glint. She wore a gray dress covered with a clean white apron, and his gray trousers were topped with a white shirt and black string tie. Black suspenders supported his pants, and tiny black boots protruded from the ends. Neither one could be over five-foot tall.

Daniel's manner suggested a well-behaved young man. His neat, blond hair hung just below his ears, and with the center part, he looked very grownup. His white shirt showed the meticulous care Mrs. Ruggers used with the flat iron, and his long pants fit his growing body perfectly. Suspenders crossed over his developing back, accentuating his large shoulders. His legs were long and lanky, and his feet looked almost as big as Mac's. He showed evidence of maturing into a good-looking man.

Mr. Ruggers explained they had been in the village almost since its inception and knew everyone in town. His face lost its impish grin as he related the painful events leading to their grandson Daniel moving in with them. "One of the saddest days of my life. You don't know sorrow until you bury one of your own children." He shook his head. Mrs. Ruggers brought the edge of her apron to catch the tears seeping from her eyes.

Mr. Ruggers patted his wife's hand. Then, changing the subject back to Mac, he proved to be an unmerciful tease. "I can't believe how just having your boots stolen could cause such a chain of events," Mr. Ruggers laughed.

"If I hadn't had to buy these moccasins to wear until my feet healed up, you would have heard me walk in and none of this would have happened." Mac had explained while Mrs. Ruggers' skillet still threatened.

"Well, young man, you look like you could use a change in your luck! How about staying and having dinner with my wife, my grandson, and I? Business is slow, today being a weekday, and we'd like the company. You can catch us up on all the news from the fort," Mr. Ruggers invited. "I'm a pretty good judge of character. You look like a good sort to me. And, you can take a ribbing."

Mac laughed at the description. Delighted to accept their generous offer, he had no desire to return to an empty hotel room. Besides, maybe he could get some information about the farms in the area.

"Thanks, Mr. Ruggers. I'd love a good home-cooked meal, and I'd be happy to eat with you, but I can pay for my dinner."

"Nonsense," Mrs. Ruggers replied. "If we didn't want your company, we wouldn't have invited you. You keep your money. You'll need it to buy new boots when your feet heal up. And you never know when Mr. Ruggers might decide to inflate your hotel bill!"

With that saucy retort amid peals of laughter, she headed back to the kitchen, leaving the men to talk. Recognizing she could be as big a tease as her husband, Mac knew his hotel bill would be fair. He also understood that these good people really wanted him as a dinner guest.

Mac became serious as he watched Mrs. Rugger's retreating back. "Mr. Ruggers, do you know about any cattle rustling going on around here?" He went on to explain about the two farms he had found, leaving out what little he knew about the girl.

Mr. Ruggers sat scratching his beard, then shook his head and replied. "Why no! I never heard of anything like that around these parts before. None of the farms around here raise cattle, just crops."

"Grandpa!" Daniel exclaimed. His young face flamed and his freckles stood out as the shy young man interrupted the men. "Isn't there a farm down around Pinckney that raises cattle? Seems like I remember a fellow who came up here trying to sell Grandma a couple of beef cows for the hotel kitchen."

"You're right, Daniel my boy! It wasn't that long ago either. He came this spring. I forgot all about him." Smiling with love at his grandson, Mr. Ruggers turned to Mac. “Can you tell how many head you were tracking?”

“No, I’m afraid with the mixture of cattle and horses, all I could tell is it was a sizeable herd.”

“Well,” Mr. Ruggers promised, “I can check around easy enough for you. That Ryan is a fun-loving young man. He spent plenty of weekends up here and many a Saturday night right in this room raising a ruckus. He’s a well-liked young man, but he sure is a hell-raiser. He likes his whiskey and his women, but he’s not a troublemaker. In fact, I enjoy having him here. The place always seems livelier when he’s around.”

“Do you expect him back any time soon?” Mac asked. “I’d be interested to know if he’s heard of any cattle rustling or not.”

“Couldn’t tell you,” Mr. Ruggers replied. “He doesn’t come regular, but he’s from down around Pinckney, if you want to travel that far to talk to him. He probably gets in there a lot more often than he comes here, since that’s so much closer to his place.”

Mac had gone to college with a man from Pinckney. In fact, Tim Turner had been his roommate and good friend for over two years. If he had to go to Pinckney, he’d have to look for him. The town couldn’t be that big. Maybe he’d know this Ryan fellow.

Dinner developed into a lively evening. Mrs. Ruggers turned out to be an excellent cook, and the rabbit stew she served tasted better than any he’d had since he left home. As she cleared the table, Mac stood and gave her a spontaneous hug. “Thanks for the great meal, Mrs. Ruggers. I can’t remember when I’ve tasted better.”

“Watch yourself, young man,” she giggled. “I’ve got a jealous husband.” Her rosy face absolutely beamed at the compliment. Everyone chuckled at her flirting reply and the swing of her hips as she left the room.

"Thanks for your hospitality, Mr. Ruggers. I think I'll head back to my room for an early night. I don't get to enjoy a real bed that often, and I want to rest my feet. Maybe I'll be able to try on some boots tomorrow," he chuckled.

"Oh, just one more question before I go. I'm looking for the son of a friend of mine while I'm in these parts. It seems he ran away from home, and I promised to keep an eye out for him. He's about thirteen or fourteen years old, reddish brown hair, and about five foot two. You haven't seen an unfamiliar boy around have you?"

"No," Mr. Ruggers answered. "What about you, Daniel? You'd probably know if anyone mentioned a new boy in town."

"No, Gramps, I haven't seen anyone like that," the boy replied.

"Well, thanks anyway." Mac prepared to leave as Mrs. Ruggers rejoined the family. "I'll probably be here until tomorrow. You can find me at the general store or down at the livery stable in case you remember seeing a boy that fits that description."

They all walked Mac back to the steps in the lobby, and old man Ruggers had to tease Mac some more about his boots. "You watch that skinflint Mrs. Frank at the General Store. If Mr. Frank isn't around, she'll have you paying double for those boots. And watch out for that daughter of theirs. If she sets her eye on you, you're done for. Knowing her, she'll set her hook for a good looker like you. She don't like the pickings in this town, not good enough for her, and I hear tell she's getting desperate since she's turned twenty-five and still on the shelf."

"One look at Mac," Mrs. Ruggers chimed in, "and Ashley won't turn her nose up. I'd be surprised if she doesn't propose to you on sight. You can bet if I were thirty years younger, I'd try to beat her to it."

"Now, Mamma," Mr. Ruggers teased, "You're not going to throw me over for this young whippersnapper are you?" He draped his arm across her shoulder and gave her a squeeze. Mac chuckled softly to himself. He really enjoyed being with these people.

Mrs. Ruggers and Daniel turned back towards the kitchen. "That's a fine grandson you have, Mr. Ruggers," Mac commented. He liked the young boy.

Mr. Ruggers nodded his agreement, then waited until they were out of the room. Surreptitiously, he whispered. "Psst, Mac, would you like a little female companionship tonight?"

"Thanks, Mr. Ruggers, but I saw what was available down at the saloon, and I'm not that lonely."

"Oh, I didn't mean Lilly or Rose," he whispered. "I was thinking you might like to visit Miss Laura's. Her place is the two-story, white house at the end of the block closest to the livery stables. That's where all the gentlemen from around these parts go. Only the rougher cowboys use the girls over at the saloon."

"Thanks, Mr. Ruggers. I might just forgo a little sleep for that kind of companionship." Mac turned and headed for the door.

"I just didn't want the Mrs. to hear me supporting Miss Laura's. She'd take that rolling pin of hers to me for sure." Mr. Ruggers scurried away chuckling.

Well, Mac thought as he headed down the street, *Miss Ashley could set all the baited hooks she wanted.* He did not intend to get caught by any woman. He hadn't met one yet he wanted to give his name to, and he felt he never would. There wasn't a woman alive who loved the outdoors as much as he did. They were all afraid of anything that crawled, and he couldn't stand a squeamish woman. Settling his new hat more firmly on his head, he lengthened his stride.

However, Mr. Ruggers had voiced a good idea, and if this Miss Laura had a nice clean place, he was ready. Maybe if he spent the night in the arms of a warm, willing woman he would forget his fantasy about the girl/boy that kept distracting him.

As Mac walked down the street, he checked his pocket watch. He'd never gone to bed this early in his life. He probably would have gotten to his room and not been able to sleep anyway. His step became livelier as he neared Laura's, and he began to really look forward to a roll in the hay.

One look at the woman who answered his knock at the white frame house, and Mac wondered if Mr. Ruggers had tried to play a joke on him. She appeared to be in her forties. Tall and thin, she stood in the open doorway with a scowl on her face. Mac heard music and laughter coming from the parlor, but the woman stood like a sentinel. It made him question the happy sounds accompanied by tinkling piano music.

He'd decided to back away from the inhospitable crone when a beautiful, dark-haired woman floated into the hall, dressed more elegantly than any of the society women he had squired to the opera back east. The cobalt blue of her gown emphasized the startling whiteness of her skin. The scooped neckline allowed her generous endowments to spill over in invitation. Imported lace draped the bodice and cascaded over her graceful arms from the end of her tight fitting, three-quarter-length sleeves.

"Rebecca, what are you doing making that gentleman stand out on the porch like a lost puppy?" She scolded the matron, then continued in a soft lilting voice, directing her welcome to Mac. "Howdy, mister, welcome to my home. My name is Laura, and whom might you be, you handsome devil?"

He stepped across the threshold. "Nicholas McNamee, madam." Mac stood hat in hand, waiting for the watchdog

Rebecca to close the door. "Mr. Ruggers down at the hotel said I might find someone here to pass the time with tonight."

Laura burst out laughing at Mac's round about way of asking for a girl. "Come on in, Honey. There are four of us here, and just to keep the girls from fighting over you, why don't you come with me. I'm sure we can find something to do to pass the time." Laura linked arms with Mac and led him up the steps, laughing and talking the whole time. Her perfume tickled his senses as her soft arm encircled his. He began to look forward to the balance of the evening. Mac wasn't sorry Mr. Ruggers had told him about Laura's place.

Red satin drapery shimmered in the candlelight, creating a sensual background for the bevy of beauties clustered around the piano. Three women vied with the colors of a rainbow in their attire. They looked as sweet and demure as Boston socialites. Mac caught a glimpse of three or four men lounging around the parlor. He wondered why they weren't all upstairs.

"I see you've some interest in our musical." The gleam of Laura's brown hair in the candlelight and her ample bosom spilling from her dress caused Mac's body to harden in anticipation. Mac felt he could drown in her kind of figure. He couldn't wait to see how talented she was and anticipated the coming evening with joy.

"I was just curious, maybe a little surprised, that with all the beauty in this house, why those men choose to sit and listen to music."

Laura gave a hearty laugh. "Why, honey, it's the price they have to pay to enjoy my girls. I try to instill a little culture here. Each night we feature a different composer. All of the girls are accomplished pianists. They each have their favorites of course, but they can play almost anything." Opening the door to her room, she ushered him in and continued her conversation. "I'd have invited you in to listen to the rest of the program, but it's about over, and those who don't have an appointment will be leaving."

Standing in the center of her room, arms stretched out in open invitation, she asked. "You aren't disappointed are you?"

Mac chuckled. "No, madam. Everything I've seen so far has certainly surpassed my expectations."

From what little he glimpsed of Laura's parlor, it looked like a prosperous house. The glamour of the red satin curtains and the plushy oriental carpet that lined the highly polished stairs told Mac that Laura's house could compete with the best Boston had to offer. Everything he saw sparkled in the candlelight.

"Well then, let's see if the rest meets with your approval, too." Mac stared open mouthed as Laura's gown settled in a puddle of blue silk around her ankles. He'd never seen a dress come off so fast, and what she wore underneath left little to the imagination.

Yes, it had been too long between women. He hadn't felt this randy since he was sixteen. He remembered when he'd started mooning over his schoolteacher after her breasts had accidentally brushed his arm when she handed out some papers. Mac tossed his hat on a chair and moved toward the lovely, practically bare Laura with open arms.

~ * ~

Sammy woke curled in a ball on the floor when Jack came in for dinner. Sally hummed contentedly, and Sammy let her body unbend.

"Sh-h," Sally hushed. "The poor boy is worn out. I think he worked too hard this morning. With food in his belly and a warm bath he finally relaxed enough to rest. It's probably the first good sleep he's had since the accident."

Sammy stretched and sat up slowly. She didn't want to eavesdrop on the couple. Seeing them look her way, she bounced to her feet, warm and comfortable for the first time in days. The aroma of chicken frying caused her stomach to rumble so loud Jack and Sally both burst out laughing.

"Looks like I'll be feeding two hungry men from now on instead of one."

"Just make sure I get my fair share, woman." Jack laughed as he gave Sally a swat on her behind.

"Ah…If you'll excuse me, I'll just go out back and wash up before dinner."

"Take your time, Sam," Sally answered. "It'll be a few minutes yet."

After she used the necessary out back and washed up, Sammy returned to the warm friendly atmosphere of Jack and Sally's kitchen.

When Sammy prepared to return to the stables for the night, Jack stopped her. "Sam, I stabled a big gray this afternoon. His owner gave strict instructions that we were to stay away from his stall. He said he's the only one that can feed and curry the animal. Seems that horse is a might temperamental and can get violent if anyone but Mr. MacNamee approaches him."

Oh, no! she thought, her mind in a whirlwind. *It can't be the same man.* Jack continued to talk, unaware of her distraction.

"I've got him in the last stall towards the back, away from all the other horses. When you check the stable for the night, stay away from him. I don't want you hurt or my stall kicked down."

"Sure, Jack. Don't worry about me." Sammy acknowledged the instructions and headed for the stables. Entering the barn she moved toward the last stall immediately. Her suspicions were confirmed when she saw the gray stallion.

"So, you don't let anyone near you, huh, big guy?" The steed perked up his ears and grew restive as she approached. He tossed his head as she sang to him with a carrot in her outstretched hand. Creeping closer, her soft, clear voice soothed the big horse, and he allowed her to feed him the tidbit. Then, as if accepting her as a friend, he submitted to her strokes.

"What a sweetie," she crooned. "Your mouth is as soft as velvet." Starting from under his jaw, she worked her hand up the bottom of his face and neck, around to the top of his ears.

"I love the way you lean into my hand for more scratchin'." Confident now that the animal wouldn't raise a fuss, she wrapped her arms around his massive neck. Burying her face up close to his ear, she whispered her goodnight. "See you in the morning. You be a good boy now and don't raise a ruckus with the others. I want to get a good night's sleep."

With a final pat on his neck, she made her rounds. She had to stop and give special attention to Sassy, whom she had ignored all day. "Sorry, sweetheart. I've been so busy today I haven't had time to come see you." While she brushed the mare, she told her all about having a lazy afternoon with a wonderful bath and a good nap. With a sigh, she realized she felt uneasy, but ready to face whatever happened next—except maybe a face-to-face meeting with Mr. MacNamee.

Sammy wearily climbed the ladder to the loft. She felt exhausted even with the brief nap in front of the Billing kitchen fire. The presence of the scout would cause complications. She knew she had to keep out of sight. It wouldn't do for him to recognize his wardrobe. Even as disrespectful as she had made his boots, she worried that he might know them.

She needed to get to sleep. She had to be alert tomorrow. There was no way she could allow the man to notice her or pay her any heed if he caught a glimpse of her. Still, she had to admit, a man who could control such a powerful horse peeked her curiosity.

Sleep eluded her as she remembered what he looked like rising out of the mist and water. The recollection of the sight of his powerful chest emerging inch by inch from the depths of the pond, followed by the rest of his magnificent body, still made her face burn. The only thing that had released her feet from their refusal to budge was the sudden memory of the last place she'd seen him.

When she had recognized him as the scout she'd chased away from her campsite with gunfire the day before, her panic had caused her to bolt. That's when she'd realized what she planned went against everything she'd been taught. She had almost stopped right in the process of stealing his boots and hat.

Now, he was back in her territory again. Sammy had to avoid him. How could she defend her need to steal his things? And if he saw her, she would have a lot of explaining to do. She didn't think he would ever excuse what she'd done. She also thought he might have a good chance of recognizing her from the meeting at the falls. She wasn't sure if he knew the same "boy" stole his boots and hat, but hoped she'd doused his campfire before he got a good look at her. If she were lucky, she'd only stood out in silhouette while the fire highlighted his features for her. Squirming to get comfortable in the hay, she decided worry would accomplish nothing. She tried to put her fears aside. She'd deal with tomorrow when tomorrow came.

Seven

At least old man Ruggers hadn't steered Mac wrong. Miss Laura had entertained him delightfully. And although he couldn't seem to bring himself to actually bed her, she hadn't seemed to mind. Even though he loved big-breasted women, at first he thought he'd suffocate. It had taken all of his willpower to get through the first hour. He couldn't seem to keep his thoughts from returning to a younger, trimmer figure of a girl. Finally, Miss Laura took things into her own hands.

"Sorry, Miss Laura, I'm afraid I must be more tired than I thought. I feel a little embarrassed."

Laura just laughed and crooned, "Honey, you are so good to look at that I'm getting my pleasure just talking to you." Snuggling closer she felt his big body finally relax. "Promise me you'll come back when you aren't 'under the weather'. Now, let's just talk and get to know each other."

Mac spent the next hour gleaning as much information as he could, while being thoroughly entertained by Laura's wit.

~ * ~

The night passed quietly, allowing Sammy undisturbed sleep. Rising the next morning, she almost forgot the threat of discovery. She had a job doing what she loved most, working with horses. She exulted in her luck. Stumbling on Jack and

Sally had to be a blessing from above. Already engrossed in giving the horses their morning feed, she heard a man enter the stable.

“Morning, Jack!” he called. “How did Renegade behave last night?”

“You’ll have to ask my boy,” Jack grumbled as he nodded towards Sammy. “But since my stall’s not wrecked, and he seems as peaceful as a lamb this morning, I assume he had a quiet night.”

Renegade stood meekly, his nose buried in a bucket of oats. The scout barely acknowledged Sammy as he quickly walked up to the stall. The horse nickered in delight and pranced excitedly. “How did you manage to feed him? Usually he doesn’t let anyone near him but me.”

“My Sam has a way with horses. He keeps them all nickering for attention,” Jack boasted.

Shaking his head in apparent wonder, the man glanced at Sammy, but she ducked her head behind the boards and continued raking out the straw. “Okay, big boy! I’m in a hurry, too. Let’s get you saddled, and we’ll be on our way. Can you give me directions to Pinckney?” Mac bellowed as he slipped the saddle over the big gray’s back.

Fear of recognition made Sammy miss the rest of the conversation as she surreptitiously watched the man. He matched Jack in height, but his trim body made him look taller. She still thought he had the look of an Indian with his midnight black hair tied back in a queue at his neck. A black mustache perched jauntily above his full, sensuous lips; his dark skin accentuated his high cheekbones. The intelligent blue eyes didn’t fit in with what she knew about Indians, but it didn’t matter. The display of muscles on his arms completed the picture, making him the most handsome man she had ever seen.

He seemed to carry an air of confidence on his powerful shoulders. She could see his leg muscles as they strained the fabric of his buckskin trousers. The sight reminded her of his naked body rising from the pool, and she had to close her eyes on the image. She'd never seen a man so well built. *He must spend a lot of time in the saddle,* she thought. Her fingers tingled at the sight of his square jaw. The thought of caressing his face with her hands shocked her. The idea refused to be shaken, and she felt her heart beat quicken just looking at him. He frightened her because of the odd, unfamiliar feelings his presence caused to flutter inside her, and she breathed a sigh of relief when he finally rode away.

She had been staring at him so hard she missed most of the conversation and, not wanting to ask Jack about him, thought it best to let the matter drop. She had noticed he had a new hat and, from the way he walked, probably new boots that weren't as comfortable as his old ones. Glancing down at his old boots, she grinned when she realized he'd never know them from the coat of mud and accumulated straw and horse manure that covered the fine leather. He hadn't even looked twice at her. She began to feel confident about her disguise.

~ * ~

Renegade tried to show his displeasure from being in a cramped stall all night, and his rambunctious gallop only fitted Mac's mood. Before he had collected the stallion, Mac had stopped at the General Store to pick up new boots. He was glad he had been forewarned about the eminent Miss Ashley. Her beautiful blond hair, artfully arranged with long curls cascading down her back and over her shoulders, almost glowed. With eyes as blue as a summer sky, her complexion presented a clear and rosy picture. Her pixie face dimpled when she smiled, and though it seemed an artificial smile, it was still charming. She was tall and trim, her eyes almost even with his.

This woman's body looked made to wrap around a man. Her bosom beckoned invitingly from the low cut of her blue gown. As she sauntered forward to wait on Mac, he remembered what the Ruggers had said about the beautiful Miss Frank. Too bad she was unmarried. He might have enjoyed a little flirtation. As it was, he couldn't afford to get entangled with the woman now.

Mr. Frank was delivering a load of feed down at the livery stable, and in his absence, Mrs. Frank tried to charge him ten dollars for a five-dollar pair of boots.

Miss Ashley languidly waved a feather duster over a shelf of canned goods. She turned and gave him an exaggerated wink and a huge smile. "Why, Mama, I was right here yesterday when Daddy quoted Mr. McNamee the price on those boots," she lied. "You must have them confused with the other pair." She accompanied the fabrication with fluttering eyelashes and a coy smile.

"I'm sorry I didn't see you yesterday, Miss Ashley. I know I would never have forgotten meeting such a lovely woman. You must have been in the back while I was talking to your daddy." Not wanting to be beholding to her, Mac quickly refuted her claim, trying not to cause her any embarrassment.

"Why, thank you, Mr. McNamee," she simpered. "You are welcome to come in back and have a cup of coffee with us until Daddy returns. I know he will remember the price he quoted you, but Mama is stubborn, and she won't give in unless Daddy insists."

Mrs. Frank's lips puckered like she'd just sucked on a lemon. From the expression on her face, she clearly hadn't liked his demeanor. She scurried from behind the counter and stood between Mac and Ashley. Apparently he just wasn't up to her standards of what she wanted for her daughter. "Now, Ashley, you know if your father said those boots were five dollars, I'd go along with that. I'm sorry I confused the price,

Mr. McNamee. There will be no need for you to wait around for Mr. Frank. I'm sure you are a busy man."

Mac saw Ashley peek around her mother's massive bulk and smile demurely. He resisted the urge to wink at her only because he didn't want to give her the wrong idea. Her mother's actions were so transparent. *No wonder the poor girl hasn't found a husband yet,* he thought. Her stern countenance seemed to warn off any potential suitor, and he wondered if the woman ever smiled. She looked as sour as good wine turned to vinegar.

Mac had breathed a quiet sigh of relief after he had paid for the boots and headed for the stable.

~ * ~

For the next few weeks, Sammy relaxed and fell into a peaceful routine. She came to love Jack and Sally more everyday. They were like grandparents who looked after her with tender concern. She made friends with Daniel, the grandson of the old couple who ran the hotel, and in the month she had been in town, no one had guessed she was a girl.

The livery stable turned out to be the best possible place to work. She could hear all the town gossip. No one paid attention to the stable boy when they discussed deals, horse trading, the town whores, or the town do-gooders. In the short time she'd been here, she had learned about almost everyone in town.

Doc drank too much, and Ashley, the daughter of Mr. and Mrs. Frank, who ran the general store, had her eye on Sheriff Sudholt for a husband. Sammy couldn't deny his youthful good looks at just under six-foot tall with blond hair and blue eyes. He appeared to be a good man, and he always had a kind word for Sammy and Daniel when he saw them. When Sammy had taught Daniel how to handle a gun, she'd seen him watch them with interest, but he'd never interfered. Yes, she'd found out about almost everyone except the killers. If she didn't learn anything soon, she'd have to leave. As nice as these people were, she couldn't forget her promise.

Daniel had just celebrated his fifteenth birthday and had never held a gun before he met Sam. He'd been raised in Washington, where his father served as secretary to a senator. In the capitol, boys his age seldom saw a gun. He found it a little embarrassing that thirteen-year-old Sam could shoot so well and that gave him the determination to learn.

He'd found it a coincidence that both their parents had died in river accidents, leaving them orphaned. Because of Sam's story, Daniel never connected Sam with the boy Mac had asked about. Besides, Sam wasn't a runaway. He just didn't have grandparents he could live with and that made him an orphan. Daniel felt sorry for Sam and again thanked his lucky stars he had a family.

None of the other boys in town accepted Daniel the way Sam did. Everyone else his age had his own horse. They all knew how to handle a gun, and all of them made fun of Daniel, the tenderfoot. He always felt shy around the others, but never with Sam.

Sam became his best friend. It felt almost as good as having a brother. Daniel knew he would do anything to protect the younger boy from the intolerance he suffered. What he didn't like to admit to himself was the fact that Sam would probably fit in with the locals better than he did.

Sammy felt bad about lying to Daniel, but her story had become common knowledge around town within a week of her being hired by Jack. Since everyone accepted her at face value, she let it continue. She treated Daniel like one of her brothers. She had always known how to twist them around her fingers. This young man was no different. Sammy understood how he thought and was careful to boost his male ego while instructing him.

She also hid her swift draw and keen eye from Daniel, not wanting him to suspect how proficient she'd become at a supposed age of thirteen. Along with her size, that life span had been determined by accident when she had forgotten and let her voice betray her. Jack had laughed at her blush and clapped her on the back. "That happens to all young boys. Don't worry, Sam, your voice won't crack after another birthday or two."

So, she had let Jack assume she was younger, relieved that he didn't know the real reason for her blush. Thankfully, she hadn't given herself away. And now, everyone accepted her for the adolescent she pretended to be.

Sammy never wore her gun and holster on her hip. From the first day she had ridden into town, she had kept them in her saddlebag or just carried them draped over her shoulder. She didn't want any questions about why such a young boy toted a gun. So this pleasant afternoon as she headed over to the hotel to get Daniel for more target practice, she had the holster draped over her shoulder as usual.

Her thoughts were miles away. Sammy's disguise had worked perfectly, but she hadn't drawn any nearer to finding her family's killers. How could she find the men responsible by just listening to people talk? She needed to ask questions, and if she did, might give herself away. What a dilemma!

Sammy passed the general store as she speculated on her alternatives. Her booted feet beat a tattoo on the boardwalk, and the sound echoed loudly on the quiet street. Ashley Frank came hurrying out the door of the general store, and the two collided, sending Ashley stumbling off the step into the dust of the street, right on her back side.

"Why you clumsy oaf! Look what you did to my new dress. I'll make you pay for this." Ashley rose in a cloud of dust and dirt, slapping at her skirts. She began to draw a crowd with her screeching. Outraged indignation shook her voice. She wobbled to regain her footing as she attempted to straighten her hat. Then she picked up her parasol and whacked Sammy over the head. “You clod! You’ve ruined my dress.”

Sammy, taken by surprise by the unwarranted attack, turned her back to the blows. “Whoa! What’s going on, Ashley? Why are you beating this child?” Sheriff Sudholt grabbed the parasol and tried to calm Ashley.

Finding herself gripped by Jason Sudholt, Ashley swiftly flung herself into his arms crying, “Oh, Jason. You must arrest this young man for assaulting me. He just calmly walked up to me and pushed me off the boardwalk into the dirt. Look at my new dress. It’s beyond repair,” she wailed. “I was only trying to protect myself. He has a gun, and I thought he’d try to kill me.” She turned big tear filled eyes up to the sheriff.

Sammy snorted in disgust. The woman would try anything to turn this whole mess to her advantage. Ashley’s hysterics were becoming louder by the minute as she pressed her body closer to Jason’s broad chest. Sammy watched her wiggle against the sheriff. *Probably to let him feel her breasts,* she thought with distaste, eyeing Ashley’s over endowment with a bit of envy.

A crowd had formed. Mrs. Frank and several customers had run out of the store, and pedestrians stopped to watch. Ashley had attracted such an audience that Sammy decided she would just slip away and no one would miss her.

“That boy is a menace. You should disarm him immediately.” Ashley kept her eyes downcast as she continued maligning Sammy. Her pleas stopped Sammy from leaving. She couldn’t afford to have her guns taken from her.

“Oh, Jason. He frightened me so!” This pathetic whine caused most of those present to begin snickering. Even Sammy had to hide a grin behind a downcast head. Everyone tittered except Ashley’s mother.

"Sheriff," she bellowed, "I demand you arrest this young man immediately! He is a nuisance walking around town with a loaded gun. He might have killed my Ashley."

With that, Sammy had had enough. "She's lying," she virtually exploded. Then she remembered her disguise. She needed to calm down and think straight. She couldn't blow her cover yet. "I'm sorry, Sheriff," she stuttered a bit more calmly as she stared at the ground and scuffed her toe. *Think of Pa. Think of Ma*, she kept repeating in her mind.

"I was walking along looking for Daniel and Miss Ashley came flying out the door. We just bumped into each other by accident. I didn't mean to knock her down. She knocked me over, too, but I'm not accusing her of doing it on purpose. It was just an accident." Sammy repeated hastily.

Jason acknowledged this innocent explanation immediately as he pried Ashley from his chest. "I believe you're right, Sam. It was just an accident."

"Sirruh. I demand…" Mrs. Frank blustered with Ashley crying at the same time.

"Oh, Jason, you can't believe this lying boy over me-e-e-e." The women were causing such a scene the sheriff didn't seem to know how to handle them.

Sammy watched in fascination as he took Ashley's arm and patted her hand. "Ashley, I'm sure you would like to go inside and freshen up before anyone else sees you all mussed up. Let your mother help you, my dear. I know how you hate to appear in public in disarray."

Sammy almost snickered. She knew this casual reminder would send Ashley flying to the nearest mirror. Then Jason turned his attention to her.

"Come on, Sam, I'm taking you in until I get the truth," he bellowed in a gruffer tone than he meant. As he reached for the boy, he felt a shock run up his arm.

What a farce! he thought as he jerked his hand away from the kid's arm. He knew the truth, but he couldn't embarrass Ashley in front of all the townspeople. He had just wanted to get the boy away until he could pacify her. Ashley would forget all about the incident once the boy was out of sight.

Jason knew that after her initial anger at being tossed on her duff, she only caused the scene to get his attention. Ashley was beautiful, but he just didn't feel any spark for her. Maybe if she were a gentler soul. He just couldn't see himself constantly praising her looks to satisfy her vanity. Anyway, on his salary, he sure as heck couldn't afford to deck her out in the fancy clothes her parents bought. Somehow Ashley Frank had set her cap for him, and Jason couldn't imagine what made her think he reciprocated her feelings.

The young boy's screech of outrage brought Jason's thoughts back to the matter at hand. "You can't arrest me! I didn't do what she said I did!"

"I know, boy! Keep your voice down and just follow me." The boy's voice grated on Jason causing him to question why he'd felt such a shock grabbing his soft arm. He began rubbing his hand up and down his thigh as he walked, trying to erase the feeling. It was spooky.

He looked down at Sam and noticed for the first time what incredibility long eyelashes he had. Jeez! No boy should have lashes that long. *They were prettier than any of the girls at Laura's. Whoa!* What made him think of that? He had to get rid of this kid fast. He didn't trust himself to touch him again to see if that tingling feeling was a fluke or not.

"Look," he growled as they entered the jail, "Miss Ashley is a high-strung woman, so your best bet is to just steer clear of the store for a week or so. I'll tell her you apologized, and she'll calm down. You run along and find Daniel. And remember, I don't want to see you on Main Street for a while."

God help him, surely this protectiveness he felt for Sam didn't mean anything. He knew he wasn't that enamoured of Ashley, and the girls at Miss Laura's only eased his needs. But young boys? He shook his head. *Never, Never, Never*!

Sammy bit back a retort and turning, ran from the room. She hated that Jason would tell people she apologized. She hadn't done anything wrong! She circled around back and jogged up to the hotel through the alleyway. "Daniel, did you see that?" Fury shook her body.

"You did great, Sam," he complimented. "That Miss Ashley needed to be knocked down a peg or two."

"I didn't do it on purpose, Daniel," Sam snapped back.

"I know, Sam, lots of people who saw what happened went to talk to Sheriff Sudholt. Everybody knows Miss Ashley lied to cover her own clumsiness. There's nothing she can do to you now." Daniel in all his exuberance continued laughing. "After Sheriff Sudholt carted you off, everybody starting talking at once about what happened. Mr. Frank pulled Ashley and her mother into the store then put up a closed sign. Everyone's laughing and taking bets on whether he'll beat her or not."

"I doubt he'll do that. He's too nice. Besides, Mrs. Frank won't let him. Ashley's her pride and joy."

"Well, let's forget Miss Snooty Tooty," Daniel replied. "I practiced with tin cans all morning while I waited for you. This time, I bet I can knock more down than you. Come on, I'll race you to the creek." With that parting shot, he took off running.

Jason Sudholt scratched at his head in confusion as he watched the two young boys running off to play. Straightening his hat, he fumed at his feelings. "Something about that kid bothers me, and I don't know why," he muttered. Shaking his head, he headed over to Laura's place. Talking to her always helped him sort out his feelings.

The house always appeared quiet and deserted during the day, but come evening one could invariably hear laughter and music spilling out of the brightly lit windows until the wee hours of the morning. Laura herself was a peach, and Jason thought she was beautiful. Her brown eyes always danced with pleasure because, if anything, she seemed to savor every minute of life.

Jason knew she truly felt she provided a needed service, and she obviously delighted in the wonderful act of sex between a man and a woman. She'd told him she'd never been in love with any one man. She loved them all. Her heart had to be as large as her huge breasts. He knew she constantly tried to do what she could for the community, without the townswomen knowing she was their benefactor.

Not many people knew Laura helped pay the teacher's salary just to get a school started. She'd also bought and paid for more than half of the medicines Doc Williams dispensed to the sick. She loved helping people and thought it ironic that all the women who complained about sex didn't thank her for taking care of their husbands. If they were too prissy to do the things she loved to do, it wasn't her fault. Jason had listened to her theory so many times he almost believed it himself.

The only people barred from her place were a rough cowhand named Tyler and his cronies. They had come in once, left her girls battered and bruised, and wrecked her place. She'd finally pulled out her shotgun and forced them out the door. Jason smiled to himself as he recalled the fury in her brown eyes as she told him what had happened. He wished he could have seen their faces when she threatened to shoot them if they ever came back. They had only laughed at her and promised to return. After that, she'd hired a night watchman and told him to shoot first and ask questions later. Jason had promised her he'd keep an eye on them if he saw them in town.

Jason's knock brought Laura's cook and housekeeper, Rebecca, to the door. As he noted her stick-thin body and sour face, he wondered why no one had ever seen her crack a smile. The closest she would come was a softening in the hard glint of her gray eyes. Miss Laura claimed to be the only one allowed to see that semblance of a change in her demeanor. He wondered what caused the woman to be so unhappy.

Rebecca grunted a hello and with a nod of her head directed Jason to the front parlor. As he strode in, still upset from his encounter with Sam, Laura rose to greet him.

"Why, Jason, I am so happy to have some company on this boring afternoon," she cooed pleasantly. "Please come in." He noted her quizzical look as she took in his dour face and after a lingering glance laughingly teased him.

"Well, I can see by the bulge in your pants why you came. Do you want to go right on up?"

Jason jerked, shocked out of his thoughts. *My God!* he thought as Laura pointed out the obvious. *How could that kid make me feel so lustful? I've never thought about a man in that way, let alone a child. Am I becoming corrupted or something for that kid to arouse me?* Thoughts flashed like quicksliver through his mind. He was only able to produce a weak smile in response to Laura's observation.

Yes, it had been several weeks since he had been to Laura's. Maybe it wasn't the kid at all. Maybe he just needed a woman.

"You know what thoughts of you always do to me, Laura," he fabricated. "I do want to go right on up."

"I've always got time for you, love. You know you are one of my favorites. You look a little agitated, so sit down, and I'll have Rebecca bring us something to drink and her special cakes you like so well. As soon as you have a bite to eat, we'll go upstairs."

Laura fluttered around like a butterfly getting Jason settled. Her yellow dress bellowed out as she busily arranged a cushion behind his back and took his hat. As if she'd brought a breath of sunshine into the room, Jason relaxed.

"I…I do have something I wanted to talk to you about," he stuttered. How would he ever be able to explain his feelings to Laura?

"Rebecca, bring the refreshments in here, please." She indicated a small table she'd carried and placed in front of the settee. Then, she sat beside Jason. Hugging his arm to her ample breasts, she encouraged him to tell all.

He hesitated a moment, gulped, then plunged right in with his question. "Did you ever notice anything strange about that new kid Jack hired down at the livery stable?"

"He's a little young for me to notice, honey," she answered with a grin. "The only thing I've seen is that he's awfully shy and he's damn good with horses." Handing Jason a piece of cake, she continued, "He can hitch up my buggy and have my horse docilely waiting for me before I can finish my gossip with Jack. I don't know how he does it. Jack said the same. He told me he's never seen anyone handle a horse better than that kid. Is that what you meant, Jason?"

"Well," he answered, "you usually have a good perception of people, and I just wanted your opinion. He had a little run in with Ashley this morning, and I believed the boy's story, but something about him strikes me odd. I just can't put my finger on it." Jason ran his finger around the inside of his shirt collar. He felt like he could choke on the half lie.

"Jason," Laura replied rather sternly. "You know Ashley. I'd believe that kid or anyone else in town before I'd believe her. That girl is looking for trouble, or a man, and she'd do anything to get one. You ought to know that yourself."

"Oh, Laura, she's not after me. I'm not wealthy enough for her," Jason laughed.

"Don't you bet on it, honey. You're damn good looking, and money or not, that girl is man crazy. In fact," Laura grew pensive. "I bet she'd love working for me. All the men in town fawning over her and living the life of leisure with money to splurge on all the fancy clothes she wanted."

"Forget it," Jason urged. "Her parents would see her dead first. And then they'd come after you." Rising, Jason felt he had to escape or end up telling her how he really felt. He really needed to bed her and quick. He had to erase the wicked thoughts he had about that boy. "Well, if you can't think of anything about that kid, let's go on up. Just remember to let me know if you hear anything strange."

Laura sat a moment longer, silently pondering her assessment of Ashley. No, she couldn't have her working here. She'd do nothing but cause trouble between the girls, and trouble was one thing Laura avoided at all cost. She didn't know what Jason was thinking, but that kid Sam seemed to be just a shy, quiet boy, nothing at all for him to be worried about.

Well, she'd keep her ears open anyway. She'd do anything for Jason. She took his arm and led him upstairs. He really was one of her favorites. Shy in bed as well as out, she loved to get a reaction out of him. He made her feel so powerful. He had never come to her in the middle of the day before, and she wondered what sparked his unusual behavior.

Eight

Fall ushered itself in with crisp cool mornings, warm afternoons, and cooler evenings. The leaves changed from green to yellow, and Sammy started getting restless. She had been here two months. October was fading into November, and so far she had not learned anything to help her track down her family's killers.

Word had eventually made its way back to town about the slaughter, but as far as anyone knew everyone, including the daughter Samantha, had been killed. The general consensus seemed to be that Indians had done it. Besides the Turner place and the O'Brien's, two other outlying farms had been hit. Four places had been wiped out altogether. There was no evidence of survivors.

Sammy gathered from the talk that all four farms were in a direct line and bordered each other. She knew the other families, but not as well as the O'Brien's. The others were poorer than her family and the O'Brien's, so she couldn't imagine why they were massacred, except possibly for the livestock.

Sammy raked out a stall, lost in her memories. She couldn't think of a way to let Jack and Sally know she wanted to mosey on to the next town. Suddenly, Jack interrupted her thoughts.

"Sam! Didn't you hear me, boy? I asked you if you thought you could watch the place for a week or so for me and Sally?"

"What's going on, Jack?"

"Were you daydreaming, Sam?" He bellowed. "I told you Sally's sister took sick, and Sally wants me to take her to their place so she can care for her. They live in Truesdale. It's only about a day's ride west. I told Sally I thought you knew enough to manage the stable by yourself for a week. Think you can do it, boy? It's only busy on Saturday and Sunday." Jack scratched his beard and looked worried.

"I know it's a lot of responsibility, but you'll just have the weekend when the cowboys come in that it might get hectic. I've watched you handle most of them without a problem. You don't have to worry about any blacksmithing. Anything that crops up can wait 'til I get back." Jack raised his bushy eyebrows, then continued without giving Sam a chance to answer.

"As far as the horses, you know more about them than I do, so I'm not worried about that. What do you say, Sam? Sally hasn't seen her sister in over a year. We've never had a chance to get away before, never had a hired hand we could trust. Will you do it?"

Jack always rattled on at length, but this time he seemed so nervous he couldn't stop talking. Sammy could tell it would mean a lot to them if they could get away for a while without worrying about the livery stable. "Sure I can do it, Jack. You know I'd do anything for you and Sally. I can never repay you for everything you've done the way it is. I'll be glad to help out."

I'll just have to put off leaving for a week or so, Sammy thought with resignation. *No way I could disappoint Jack and Sally.* "You go on and take Sally to her sister's. I'll be fine, and so will the livery stable." Sammy's disappointment in delaying her departure was tempered by the knowledge that she owed Jack and Sally at least this much.

The week passed quickly enough without any problems. Sam even handled the rough cowboys who stabled their mounts for the weekend without a hitch. Most didn't give the kid a second glance. She guessed they figured Jack was over at the house. As long as their mounts were well cared for—and they were—no one questioned her.

As Sam cleaned out the last stall early Sunday morning, she heard a rowdy group approach the back door. They were laughing and joking with each other and giving a guy named Tyler a hard time about not getting in at Miss Laura's. She started to come out to help them saddle up when she heard a rude comment that made her back up into the stall and hide while she listened.

"Hey, Luke, Tyler don't care none about being barred from Laura's. Them women are too tame for him anyway. He only likes them bitches when they're fighting back tooth and nail. Right, Tyler? By the way, how did Lilly treat you last night? Ha, Ha, Ha. Hey, I think the last time I ever saw you have fun was with that redheaded spitfire a couple of months back. You should have kept that one."

"Shut up, Mark, you loud mouth." This rough, mean voice didn't sound as jovial as the rest of the group. Sammy figured it had to be the man named Tyler, the butt of all the jokes. She couldn't see the men, and she didn't dare show herself now. Nancy O'Brien was the only redheaded spitfire she knew. Then again, just maybe they were talking about someone else. She'd better lay low.

"What do you know anyway?" The loudmouthed Tyler grumbled. "That redhead was okay, but a mite long in the tooth, and she'd had so many kids I lost myself in her. If you want to know the truth, it was that bitch at the second farm that tickled my blood. She was a beauty, even though she was older. She had what it took to keep a man happy. I'll bet the daughter would have been even better. Probably still a virgin, and it's been awhile since I've had me one of those. I wonder where she was and if she'll come back."

"Hell, Tyler, how do we know?" This sounded like the one called Mark. "You wouldn't let none of us have a turn with her, then you shot her! We thought she didn't please you!"

"You wouldn't have known how to enjoy her anyway, Mark. Besides, she said something that made me see red. I've regretted that shot ever since. That's one feisty woman I'd have dragged with me and kept."

The laughing and joking continued while Sammy stood frozen in place, struck dumb. Horrified and angry, her whole body began to shake. They were talking about her mother. These had to be the despicable monsters that raped and killed her. Frantically she looked around to see how she could get to the loft for her gun. Her shaking hand caused her to lose her grip on the pitchfork, and before she could catch it, the wooden stall resounded with the clatter.

One of the men walking his horse out stopped to investigate the racket. "Hey, boy! Come out here. Help us saddle up. We're in a hurry."

She knew she couldn't beat four men. She had no choice but to continue her charade. Her body shook with impotent fury. Sammy wanted to get a good look at them, especially the one named Tyler. Tears of frustration threatened to betray her. If only she had her gun. She immerged from the stall, rage burning a hole in her gut.

"Hey, boy, what are you doing hiding and listening in on us?" The voice belonged to the one they had called Tyler. A big brute of a man, he stood at least six-feet tall. His black hair hung long and greasy; his chin covered with a full beard.

Sammy looked at his eyes and shuddered. They were dark and brooding, deep set with heavy brows. He looked strong, even though his big belly hung over his belt. A gun rode low on his hip, anchored to his thick thigh with a rawhide thong. His wicked silver spurs were the largest Sammy had ever seen. Her glance darted to his hands. She'd never seen a human paw so large. Dark hair bristled on the knuckles of his fat fingers. They were so ugly she almost got sick thinking of him touching her delicate mother.

Sammy took a huge breath of air to force the hot liquid back down her throat, hoping to quell the fear that leaped inside of her. All the feelings of that awful day roared to the surface. How helpless her mother must have been in the face of this evil man. She knew in an instant if they discovered her secret, he would rape and kill her without a second thought. These men could ride out with her and no one would ever know what happened.

Jack and Sally were gone. There was no protection, except what she could give herself. Pa's voice whispered in her ear. *Think before you act, lass.* Self-preservation won over revenge. There would be another time. *Next time*, she thought viscously, *I'll be ready for you.* This time, lying caused her no guilt.

"I was just cleaning the stalls, mister. I wasn't paying you all no attention."

"Well, you better pay attention to your job. You work here don't you? Put that pitchfork down and get our horses saddled up pronto. We want to get out of this two-bit town." He dismissed the child with a flick of his hand and swaggered outside.

As Tyler passed the tack room, he did a double take. There hung that saddle from the farm they had burned. He'd meant to grab it from the corral fence before they rode away. When he'd seem two of the Indians he'd hired ride off carrying bundles of clothes, he'd forgotten the saddle. The low-down thieves were looting the farm before he could. He had been distracted enough to forget the saddle.

At the second farm, just as he'd tried to wrestle that pretty cedar chest up on his horse, they'd spied the dust of a rider coming and had to hightail it out of there. He remembered how angry he'd been because both of his attempts to gain a little extra "pay" failed. Tyler swung back to Sam so quick it startled her. "Whose saddle is that?" he growled.

"It's mine," Sammy replied before she thought.

"Where'd you get that, boy. That's my saddle!"

"No it's not," she spat back angrily.

Before she could think, he had her by the front of her shirt and slapped her face. "I said that's my saddle. Where'd you get it?"

The blows were sharp and hard. Sammy now knew what it meant when someone said they were hit so hard they saw stars. She couldn't think. The only thing that penetrated her fear-clouded brain was that she couldn't give herself away. They would kill her for sure. Somehow, someway, she had to survive this assault. Somehow, she had to kill this man before he killed her.

The man called Luke grabbed Tyler's hand and tried to stop him. "Hey, Tyler, that's just a kid. What are you trying to do, kill him?"

Sammy sank to the ground, her head spun and her face hurt something awful. The strain of keeping all of her violent emotions under control caused her to shake uncontrollably.

Tyler's temper exploded. "He's got my saddle, and I want to know where he got it. Butt out, Luke!"

"There's your saddle, Tyler. What are you talking about? Your saddle. You only got one," Luke snapped.

"Shut up, Luke," Tyler barked. "See that mark on the saddle? That's my name. That saddle was stole from me!"

"I didn't know you could read, Tyler, but if you fancy that saddle, I won't stop you."

Tyler smirked. "At least you know not to cross me, Luke." Before Sam could think of an answer, Tyler pulled his whip off his hip and started to beat her across the back. "Where'd you get that saddle, boy?" With each blow, his yelling increased.

Sammy cowered on the ground. The searing pain in her back only magnified the hate she felt for this man. She tried to keep her eye on his next swing to protect her head. Spittle spewed from his mouth, spraying flecks in a wide arc. The madness emanating in his eyes spelled disaster for her.

Sammy felt her stomach turn at the sight. Fear invaded, insidiously creeping throughout her body, leaving her shaken and weak. Then she heard a high-pierced scream. "No, no, no-o-o-o!" Was that her voice? Her last thoughts branded themselves across her clouded eyes. She had to survive this. She had to live to kill this man.

On his way to get Sam for some morning target practice, Daniel skidded to a stop when he heard the sound of flesh smacking against flesh then a plea of denial. He peeked around the corner of the barn and saw Sam fall to the ground. He didn't stop to think, but whirled around and ran for Sheriff Jason.

Jason stood talking to Mr. Frank outside the General Store when Daniel, totally out of breath, skidded to a stop.

"Sheriff, there are four men beating up Sam in the livery!"

It didn't take Jason but a moment to respond. "Daniel, get Doc at Miss Laura's." They both took off running.

What Jason saw at the stable made his blood run cold. The boy lay on the ground, seemingly unconscious, and that thug Tyler had his whip raised to strike him again. Jason drew his gun and quietly spoke. “Drop the whip, Tyler, or you’re a dead man.”

Tyler spun around, ready to do battle. When he faced Jason’s drawn pistol, he quickly backed down a notch. “Sheriff, I’m glad you’re here. I want you to arrest this boy for stealing my saddle.”

“Which saddle is that, Tyler? Looks to me like your horse already has a saddle,” Jason answered with a deadly calm. He certainly wasn’t feeling calm. His heart thundered in his chest, threatening to suffocate him. He wanted to run to the child to see if he was okay, but for now, he didn’t dare take his eyes off the brute and his men.

Drawn by Sam’s last conscious scream and Daniel’s alarm, a crowd began to gather. Arriving red-faced and breathless, Doc and Miss Laura ran to Sam when Tyler turned to show Jason “his” saddle. The other three men allowed them access to the boy.

“See. I made my mark on it so I’d know it was mine. This kid says it’s his but won’t tell me where he got it.”

Jason walked over to the saddle. Reading Dennis O’Brien’s name, he knew the saddle wasn’t Tyler’s. “That’s funny, Tyler,” Jason ground out through tightly clenched teeth. “The name scratched on the saddle says ‘Sam Turns’. That’s the boy’s name. Did you make the mark that spells the kid’s name by mistake?” He hoped Tyler, like most, couldn’t read or write.

Tyler looked for support from his cohorts and saw they had already led their horses out of the stable. “Maybe it’s my mistake, Sheriff. I didn’t get close enough to read it right. It looks like my saddle.”

“That’s a mighty big mistake, Tyler, especially considering what you did to that innocent boy. Maybe you’d like to stick around and apologize to him. Maybe you’d let him give *you* a taste of that whip. On second thought, seeing as how he is in no condition to snap a whip, maybe I ought to do it for him!" Jason's hands itched to beat on Tyler.

"Look, Sheriff, I said I made a mistake. Let's just let it go at that. I didn't hurt the brat none. I didn't even break skin. He's just a weak-kneed sissy to pass out so quick."

Jason glared at the man with contempt. Tyler grabbed his bridle and swung up in the saddle. As he rode out, he hollered, "I'll be back. Next time, it won't be your gun against my whip."

Puzzled over the squabble about a cheap saddle, Jason walked over to where Doc and Miss Laura were tending the boy. Fear pushed his heart into his throat. He dreaded seeing the damage caused by Tyler's whip. Jason didn't understand the feelings the kid stirred up in him. He didn't like it one bit! He also wondered where a kid named Sam Turns got Dennis O'Brien's saddle. He'd buried those folks a few months back after their farm got raided by Indians.

As he drew near, Miss Laura called to him to fetch Miss Sally then asked, "Where in the hell is Jack? Doesn't he usually stick pretty close on a Sunday morning when these ruffians are leaving town?"

"Laura," Jason sighed. "Jack and Sally aren't here. Sally's sister took sick, and Jack took her to Trusdale to tend her. They should be back today or tomorrow."

"Well, we can't leave this child in the stable. Carry him to my place where Doc and I can get him cleaned up and see how bad he's hurt," she ordered.

Jason hesitated to touch Sam. He hated the thought of what physical contact might do to him. "You and Doc better see to him here or have Doc carry him. I have to make sure Tyler has left town."

Laura stopped him before he even half turned away. "Jason Sudholt, you get right over here and carry this boy. Doc can't lift his weight, and this barn is no place to nurse him! Now hurry up! Let's get him in a warm bed before he wakes up enough to feel the pain of you moving him. And, be careful," she admonished as Jason reluctantly reached to swing the boy up in his arms.

The shock that hit him as he slid his hands around Sam's slim waist and under his thighs almost made him drop the boy. The jolt sent a tingling current throughout his body. He tried to carry him low so no one could see the bulge in his pants, but that compounded the problem as the friction of walking with the boy's bottom bumping into his arousal made him even more uncomfortable. He finally lengthened his stride and almost raced to Laura's place. This soft delicate body was torture to hold in his arms. Where were the hard muscles of a young man? He shouldn't feel so pliant and cuddly.

Rebecca watched the ruckus from the front porch. As she observed Jason practically running with his burden, she knew something serious had happened. She opened the door the moment he reached the steps. Keeping her council, she led the way into the foyer. Whatever happened, Miss Laura would need her help.

Panting to catch her breath, Laura directed Jason to a first-floor bedroom. The sheriff kicked open the door and practically threw the boy on the bed. He turned to escape when Laura grabbed his arm and swung him around to face her. She looked spitting mad and didn't try to soften her abuse.

"Jason Sudholt, if you caused that boy any additional pain with your callous handling, I will *never* forgive you! I have never seen you so brutal with anyone, least of all a child. What in the hell is the matter with you? You usually have more compassion that!"

Rebecca shrank back against the wall, glad she wasn't the one on the receiving end of Miss Laura's temper. She stared wide-eyed as Jason's blue eyes turned icy cold. She had never seen such a murderous look from him. Apparently Miss Laura hadn't either. She recoiled in shock and dropped his arm as if it were a hot coal.

"If Tyler was lying about that saddle being his, so is that kid. The name scratched on it isn't his either. He has a lot of explaining to do when he wakes up. I told you there was something strange about him. I'll question him later. Right now, I have to go close up Jack's stables."

Jason's words were bitten off like he could hardly stand to speak. He twisted away to leave, but not before Rebecca saw Laura's practiced glance note the pronounced bulge he sported. Rebecca followed her quick look and muffled a snort of disgust.

She saw Laura turn with a puzzled look, to stare at the boy sprawled on his side. He had just started coming around and began to moan, "No, no, no, no-o-o," when Doc bustled into the room out of breath.

"Why in the hell did Jason take off running?" he asked no one in particular. He and Laura stepped up to the bed together as Sammy opened her eyes. She hurt all over, but quickly came to life as Laura started to unbutton her shirt.

"No! No! Don't touch me!" she screamed as she scrambled up to cower in the corner of the bed with her arms crossed protectively across her chest.

"Now, boy," Doc soothed. "We're just tying to help you. Miss Laura and I need to see how bad you're hurt. If you're cut from the whip, you might need sewing up. We won't hurt you any more. I can give you some laudanum to ease the pain if it's real bad."

"I can take care of myself," Sammy snapped back. "I don't want your help. Go away and leave me alone," she moaned. Large tears started to roll down her cheeks. She had never been abused in her life and the stiff muscles she had after burying her family were nothing compared to how her back felt now. The burning pain in her flesh seemed minor compared to the ache in her heart. Ma's killers had disappeared, and she lay in a strange bedroom.

As brave and as strong as she tried to be, she couldn't stop the flow of the silent tears that continued to streak her face. Her cheeks were still smarting from the slaps she had endured, and with a ginger touch of her fingertips, she realized her right eye had started to swell. Surely her injuries made her look less like a woman than ever, and yet she lost some of her confidence as Laura continued to stare at her with puzzled eyes.

Sammy tried to sneak a quick glance at her attire to see if anything gave her away. Between the tears and her eye, which had started to swell shut, it was difficult to see. She began to shiver uncontrollably, thinking that somehow she had given herself away.

"Doc," Miss Laura's voice sounded too nonchalant to Sammy, and she forced her attention back to the beautiful woman talking. "I don't think Sam is hurt that bad. He's just scared and probably shy from all this attention. Why don't you have Rebecca fix you a drink, and I'll just see if Sam will let me get him comfortable. Then he can rest here for a while until he feels better. If it looks like he needs stitches, we'll call you in later."

The offer of a drink after all the excitement seemed to be all Doc needed to distract him from his duties. His already florid face lit up, and he tugged his vest into place, ran his fingers through his white hair to sweep it out of his eyes, and mentally seemed to prepare himself to visit with the ladies of the house. A huge grin split his weathered face. "Well, call me if you need anything. I'll just stop in the parlor for a wee dram."

Sammy silently watched not sure what to expect next. Her posture became even more defensive as Laura calmly and quietly walked over to close the door before she spoke. Sammy stared open mouthed as the woman leaned her back against the door with her arms crossed. “Well now, young lady! What’s your game?”

Her words confirmed Sammy’s worst fears. Her charade was over.

Nine

Muttering his frustration, Mac turned Renegade and reluctantly headed back to Fort Howard. He'd been chasing shadows for two months now and still couldn't find any evidence of rustling. "All right, big boy, let's see how long you can last at this pace." He laughed in pure pleasure as the big gray picked up speed.

He hadn't ridden two hours when he crossed the trail of the Indians he had originally been trailing. The hoof prints of one of the Indian's horses was unmistakable, its left rear hoof shaped like a heart. The horse had been injured at one time and had a scar on its hoof. These had to be the same Indians he had warned Fort Howard about several months back.

He followed the rebels to their camp, and after spying on them for two days, he was no closer to finding out their plans or which one was the leader. They all seemed to be squabbling over which brave they should follow. One group of four seemed to agree with a big fellow who sported three eagle feathers in his braid. The other four sided with a shorter, stockier Indian. The only ornament he wore was a headband with a sunburst design beaded on the front that sat low on his forehead.

The big brave seemed quieter and more reserved in his arguments. The short, older Indian was loud, angry, and volatile in his behavior. Mac was hoping the young, quiet giant would win, but it seemed they just decided to split evenly and each group went their own way.

Since Mac thought the younger Indian presented no threat, he wanted to follow the five braves led by the older man. As the group split apart, he changed his mind. He reasoned older Indians were less warlike, therefore, less likely to cause problems. It seemed to always be the young bucks that spurred rebellion. Before their departing dust settled, Mac changed directions. He knew if he were being forced off his land, he'd fight. It made sense to follow the young brave. Several hours later they joined up with a larger band that seemed to be peacefully moving to their winter grounds.

He watched until an Indian woman ran out to meet the incoming riders. She carried a baby in each arm, and Mac's heart ached when he saw the young brave jump from his horse and run to meet the woman. He engulfed her and the babies in one huge hug. The joyful reunion was enough for Mac to realize he had again made the wrong choice. He'd followed the wrong Indian.

Well, he thought, *his duties came before any wild goose chase.* Reluctantly he continued toward the fort. When he'd left Charrette Village, he'd thought he'd get to the bottom of this mystery. Ever since that summer day at the waterfall, his life had gone from charmed to cursed. He still dreamt of the beauty in the falls. Even after the trials of the last two months, the vision of her continued to disturb him.

Mac reported late to the commander. There was no way to satisfactorily explain a two-month delay. In spite of his previously flawless record, he received a complete dressing down from the commander. As a further consequence, he was given the dubious honor of escorting the widows of three slain officers back to St. Louis.

After leaving St. Louis and his resentful charges behind, Mac again detoured towards Pinckney to see if he could find Tim Turner. It would be good to renew their friendship and he could ask about the man who raised cattle. The Ruggers had mentioned a man named Ryan who had a farm near Pinckney. He shouldn't be hard to find, but what he learned when he reached the town gave him pause.

With casual questions about how he could locate Tim, he found out the Turners along with three other families had been slaughtered by Indians a couple of months back. The news knocked Mac for a loop. Tim Turner, his college roommate! Why didn't he connect the massacres with Tim before? He practically knew the whole family without even having met them. Tim talked about his people all the time. J.R. hunted horses, and Ryan raised cattle. Samantha, the mischief-maker, was always under foot trying to do everything her brothers did. Ryan, the man that lived near Pinckney and raised cattle, Tim's brother! It all came together.

"You feeling okay, Mister," the bartender asked. "You look like someone just walked over your grave."

"Tim Turner was a friend of mine," even to his ears, his voice sounded hollow.

"Oh, sorry." The bartender poured him another beer and walked away, leaving Mac alone with his misery.

Once he got a grip on his emotions, he asked about the others in the Turner family. The bartender's description of Miss Samantha matched his vision perfectly. Of course he didn't let on to anyone that he had seen her alive after the slaughter.

No one knew who had buried the O'Briens and the Turners. The other two farm families had been left until some neighbors discovered them. Since neither of the graves at the two farms had been disturbed, it was assumed that everyone from both families was dead.

Mac kept his own council. He knew the girl had buried her family. He assumed the sheriff in Charrette Village had taken some men out to the O'Brien farm after he'd reported the raids. The four farms formed a line along the river. Each bordered the other. Something bothered Mac about that, and he wanted to get to the bottom of this whole mystery.

Reporting back late again to his commander a week late because of his detour, and after being sent on another wild goose chase, Mac decided to take what leave time he had coming. He hadn't had any spare time off since he had volunteered for scout duty. He figured now was as good a time as any to regain his peace of mind. He'd never get back his intuition of which path to follow or what danger lay ahead if he didn't clear his mind of his mystery woman, Samantha Turner.

In his mind he called her Sammy as Tim always referred to her. The name even fit her girl/boy identity. He had given up fighting the urge and every night slept with his head pillowed by her fragrant tresses.

Mac entered the fort to the hoots of some of the enlisted men in the main compound. "Hey, Mac, been chasing any wild Indians lately?"

"Naw, he's been too busy herding women and chasing rainbows."

Mac ignored the taunts. He'd gotten used to the men goading him. It seemed to be their only form of entertainment. Usually he tolerated it well enough, but today his temper ran short.

"You'll be wishing I was riding point next time you go out. You men better learn to read tracks because if I get my wish, I won't be around to protect your sorry hides anymore."

Stomping the dust from his boots, he entered Commander Williams's office. The commander welcomed him warmly, then listened to his plea. "You aren't tied by a contract, Mac, so I can't force you to stay. You seem to have some serious business on your mind. You've been very distracted lately. Go on and finish your affairs, and whenever you're ready to come back, your job will be waiting." Rising from his chair, he turned from his desk and walked to the window.

He remained quiet for several minutes, then turning to face Mac, continued, "However, I would appreciate it if you hear anything that might affect the security of this fort, that you send me word as soon as possible."

"Yes, sir," Mac replied. "I would do that under any circumstances. I'll consider myself on a double mission—one, to finish my personal business, and the second, to keep an eye out for that renegade band of Indians that seem to be the cause of so much trouble." With a smart salute, he left the room. Thankful he had an understanding commander, he stood on the porch and heaved a sigh of relief. Slapping his hat on his head, he adjusted the chinstrap and bounded down the steps. He was free to pursue his own path now.

Mac planned to head back to Pinckney. Since it was Sammy's hometown, he wanted to see if he could pick up her trail or at least some news of her. He could also check out the city clerk to see if anyone had purchased the four farms and maybe find a clue to the murderers.

With all the distractions his obsession with the woman had caused, he wasn't sure he'd learn anything, let alone sniff out any clues. His keen mind was thoroughly distracted at the most unlikely times by the image of that beautiful, white satin body emerging from the falls. He felt he was slowly going out of his mind and had to make a bid to regain his senses.

Out of sorts, angry that anyone, let alone a woman, could distract him enough to temporarily give up scouting, he shifted in the saddle. His confidence in his own abilities was shaken for the first time in his life, and he felt miserable because his feet hurt. The pain had been a constant reminder ever since he had to buy these cheap boots in Charrette Village. Grumbling and cursing, he made his way through the thick underbrush toward Pinckney.

As Mac rode into town, he encountered a lot of commotion outside the sheriff's office. Curious about all the excitement, he walked Renegade to the edge of the crowd.

"Paul Wilson, as sheriff of Pinckney, you should be doing something instead of sitting on you ass!" an angry man complained. That sentiment seemed to be shared by everyone in the crowd.

"Everyone calm down." The star on his vest identified the sheriff. He was a big man in his late forties. Barrel-chested with a full beard and dark eyes that looked hard and angry, he looked more outlaw than lawman.

"There'll be no running off half-cocked in my town," he boomed. "Now quiet down, the lot of you! Let's just listen to Mr. Morgan and see what he has to say."

Mac sat up straight in his saddle—*Thaddeus Morgan, his economics professor from Harvard.* The man was brilliant. What was he doing here?

After a few more disgruntled mumblings by the crowd, everyone simmered down enough for Mr. Morgan to speak. "You all know me. I'm your neighbor as well as your friend. You know since I've taken over ownership of the bank, that

I've gone out of my way to help most of you." The crowd quieted to listen.

"I've as much at stake here as any of you. I'm the largest landowner and therefore have the most to lose."

Heads nodded in agreement. Mac could tell they all seemed to respect Morgan. That didn't surprise him. He remembered he came from a wealthy family and money usually bought respect. Mac judged him to be in his early forties. Still a good-looking man, he'd always been popular. There'd been a lot of rumors about him squiring the prettiest society women. Looking at the crowd's reaction, he still seemed to be a favorite with the ladies.

"Even though I don't have a family to support as most of you do, I still have ranch hands I am responsible for." Mac watched him flirt quite openly with the females. Each one simpered and smiled as if the attention was meant for them personally.

Well, Mac thought, *they were no different from the Boston ladies who thought the sun rose and set for Thaddeus.*

"Let's face this problem as calmly as we can." Morgan waited for complete silence. "Now you all know we have one of the most honest sheriffs in the area," he began. "Sheriff Wilson would be the first to form a posse if he knew what or who you should be looking for. We have to accept the fact there are no real clues to identify these Indians who have been burning out our farms."

Morgan hooked his thumbs into his waistband. Mac chuckled to himself. For all his intelligence, he was still vain. Mac continued watching as Thaddeus spread his coat, seeming to let the men get a good look at the gold watch fob dangling from his belt and the women an eyeful of his trim figure.

"We've investigated the four farms lost this summer, and now a fifth one has been struck. I will admit it is getting worrisome not knowing who will be next. All of you living in the outlying areas have a right to protection, but let's be practical. We don't know which farms to guard, and there are not enough men to guard all of you."

Mac sat up at attention. *A fifth farm hit!*

Quiet mumbling broke out at these words, and Thaddeus commanded silence with just a lift of one soft hand. "I've written to the fort to ask the army to send out a patrol to scout our area and to help put down any uprisings if that's what we are facing. Without proof of which Indians raided our neighbors, the army will not send out a company to attack just any tribe. General Williams wrote me that he did not have enough troops to dispatch at this time anyway. We will just have to tighten security around our farms and hope we have seen the last of these marauders."

More wails rose from the women folk and angry mutterings from the men.

"Now, I know a lot of you have loans at my bank for your land. If anyone wants to sell out and return to St. Louis, come and see me. I'm sure I'll be able to work out some financial agreement with you. I'm not rich enough to buy all of your farms," he laughed. "But check with me if you are serious about moving, and I'll see what I can do. I think the best thing for all of us to do is settle down. Nothing was ever gained by going off to attack without a plan. Sheriff Wilson and I will see if we can learn any more about these predators from whatever clues they left behind. When we have some specific evidence, we'll organize a posse."

He hesitated a moment, looked at the sheriff, and turned back to the throng. "You'd best be getting back to your farms and seeing to your defenses. Come see me if you decide to leave." Dismissing them with a wave of his hand, he bid them good day.

Mac sat forward on Renegade with his left arm resting on the saddle horn and listened to the disgruntled rumblings of the crowd as they dispersed. Some were arguing among themselves. Their biggest worry was how they were going to protect their families from a bunch of murdering Indians when they were so isolated. Usually it was only a man and wife with several children occupying each farm. A family like that had no chance.

"Even the Turners with four men and the O'Briens with their brood didn't have enough firepower to drive them off. What chance will us smaller families have?" one man shouted.

"Old Pete Turner trained his brood well. J.R., Tim, and Ryan were crack shots. Even his girl Samantha knew which end of a pistol to hold."

"We have to leave," a woman insisted. "What about the children?" Several women were begging to sell out, and their men were trying to plan warning systems and defenses. The hubbub reclaimed Mac's attention. He'd better listen. He might pick up something important. Pushing his grief for Tim aside, he watched as Thaddeus Morgan clapped Sheriff Wilson on the back and headed off towards the bank. Curious now about the location of the last farm hit, Mac scratched at his three-day-old beard.

The plot thickens he thought as he walked Renegade down the street to the surveyor's office. He informed the surveyor he was interested in buying some land to start a horse farm. "Is there any good grazing land for sale?"

The surveyor didn't know about any land for sale but showed Mac the map and pointed out the farm that had just been hit. “I wouldn’t be buying land around here until the Indian problem was solved. But if you’re determined, go over to the bank and talk to Mr. Morgan. He held notes on most of those farms and he would know if any are for sale or not.” He dismissed Mac with the wave of his hand, muttering that he had an appointment. Ushering Mac out of the office, he locked up and hurried down the street. Mac thought his actions curious, but couldn’t put his finger on what bothered him.

He stood on the boardwalk a moment and rubbed his chin as he pictured the map. The last farm was the closest to town and bridged the gap between the other four farms and the town limits. All five farms formed a perfectly straight line. How had that last place been wiped out so close to civilization? Didn’t anyone hear the shooting? Striking off towards the saloon, Mac figured his best source of information would come after he bought a few rounds.

Several men were lined up at the bar, and Mac didn’t have any trouble getting the information he needed. “Henry Jones’s property lays just outside town limits. Most of it fronts on the main road comin’ into town,” supplied the first man.

“But don’t forget that old cuss liked his privacy. Why do you think he built his house and barn towards the back and most northern portion of his acreage?” another quipped.

“He wanted his house as far from town as he could get and still be on his own land.”

“Nobody could hear shots from that far. We didn’t suspect anything until we saw smoke rising over the hill early the next morning. Ole Henry never started workin’ ‘til noon.”

“Sheriff Wilson found the slaughter when he rode out to investigate. He said it looked like the whole family had been killed while still in bed, then the place torched and the livestock driven off. From what was left of the place when he got there, it looked to him like the fire had been burning several hours."

As Mac thought about this information, he guessed with the farm so close to town the people were probably killed in their sleep and never had a chance to fight back. That would have kept gunshots to a minimum and the town people unaware.

There was more here than met the eye. Mac decided to stay awhile, so he got himself a room at the hotel. He intended to investigate further, first thing in the morning.

The next day dawned crisp and cool. It was the sort of day that encouraged one to be bright and happy. Fall had arrived. Enjoying the scent of freshly mowed hay on the breeze, Mac headed for the bank with a light step. He felt good after a full night's sleep. Gut instinct told him he would find out something important today!

The first thing he wanted to do was to renew his acquaintance with Thaddeus Morgan. He'd often wondered why a man with his background and connections taught college economics instead of applying his expertise in the business world to make his fortune.

Mac entered the bank and waited until his eyes adjusted to the darkened room. The sun glowed so bright outside it made this one-window room seem dark and gloomy. He stepped up to the clerk and asked to see Mr. Morgan. "If you are thinking about selling, you'll have to get in line and wait your turn. All those folks are wanting to talk to Mr. Morgan about selling their farms." The clerk gestured to a crowd waiting outside Morgan's private office.

Something nagged at Mac's active imagination. Perhaps ole Thaddeus needed help in convincing these good people not to run scared. Mac raised his voice enough to let it carry over to the crowd of people. "Actually," he began, "I've come to see

Mr. Morgan about buying some property in the area. I've never seen better river bottom for crops and grazing." Leaning closer to the clerk in the guise of speaking confidentially, Mac continued in the same strong voice. "Anybody selling this prime river bottom would have to be crazy or scared of his own shadow. I've heard talk about Indian raids, but frankly from what I've seen, I have a notion its cattle rustlers hiding their tracks." He watched as the arguing started among the waiting couples. In less than five minutes, husbands were dragging crying wives away and no one was left in line outside the banker's door.

Mac hid a grin and sat down to wait. Thaddeus opened his door and ushered out a young couple with three children. Morgan smiled and shook the man's hand. "Well, Mr. Fitzpatrick, I think you'll have just enough to get your family safely back to St. Louis now that your loan is paid off. You'll have to agree their safety is more important than profit. Good Luck to you now."

Mac watched Morgan's smile fade as he looked up to see an empty room. The scout rose from his seat and extended his hand to introduce himself. "Mr. Morgan? Hello, my name is Nicholas McNamee. Perhaps you remember me. I had you for an advanced course in economics." Not allowing Morgan to interrupt, he continued, "Do you have a minute? I'd like to speak to you about a loan to buy some property in the area."

"Of course I remember you, Mr. McNamee. I always recollect my most promising students." With another puzzled glance around the empty bank, Morgan acknowledged the introduction and led Mac into his office. Closing the door, he remarked, "What brings you to the area, Nicholas? I thought you were headed back to Texas. Isn't that where your father bought a ranch?"

"When I left school, I did a little traveling, and now I've decided to settle here. I sure was surprised to see you. I thought you were firmly ensconced at the college."

"Yes. Well, my father passed away, and I left Boston to take over his bank."

"I'm sorry for your loss. I seem to remember you corresponded with him quite often. You must have been close."

"Yes, we were." Sadness dulled his brown eyes. "Thank you for your condolence." Straightening his shoulders, he cleared his throat. "I'm sure you are as busy as I am. Did I understand you to say you were looking for a loan to purchase some property in the area?"

"Yes," Mac replied. I want to start a horse-breeding farm."

"I'm afraid I don't know of any property for sale, Nicholas. With all the commotion around here since the Indian raids, the bank has overextended itself in aiding the loyal customers who have supported us for the last ten years."

Suddenly inspired by a new idea, Mac instantly changed his plan. He began by launching into a hastily concocted story. "Well, Mr. Morgan, do you remember my friend, Tim Turner? He and I used to room together at school. Being two lonely country boys at a big-town college kind of drew us together." Mac wished he had made the connection sooner. "I believe he majored in education."

"Of course I knew him, Nicholas. I reacquainted myself with him when I settled here. He farmed with his family, but he still had dreams of teaching school."

"Well, Tim told me if I ever decided to settle down, there was prime grazing land around his place that I could probably get at a fair price. I'm headed out there as soon as I leave the bank. I can't wait to see him again and meet the rest of his family." Hoping for some inside information, Mac was glad he hadn't let on that he already knew of the massacre.

Frowning as if solemn and reluctant to pass on bad news, Thaddeus told Mac about the Turners being killed and their farm burned to the ground. He went on to explain about the other farms and how Mac really would be throwing his money away if he bought property in this area at this time. He was taking a huge loss at the bank just bailing out his good customers.

Mac listened in pretended shock, then asked, "Do you think I could buy the Turner's property? Tim always bragged about how fertile the land was, and I'd like to think maybe I could carry on his dream."

Morgan hedged, then told him the property was owned outright. "The Turners didn't have a mortgage. With all three men helping, it was one of the few moneymaking ventures around. Most of the other farms had huge mortgages, and they were forfeited to the bank. In fact," Morgan supplied, "I've got advertisements in most of the papers out west looking for Padraig Turner. It seems Pete had a brother a few years younger than himself who didn't want to settle here in Missouri. He decided to head for the mountains out west, and we know he wrote the family about once a year. Until a letter comes from him, we have no clue how to find him. As the only known relative, he has legal rights to the property."

Mac was quiet a moment, then asked, "Do you mean all of Tim's family was killed? His parents, both of his brothers and his sister?"

"Well," Morgan replied, "someone found the Turners and their neighbors, the O'Briens, and buried them. Speculation is it was one of the other neighbors that got burned out the following day. An alarm was never raised. We figure he must have gone over for some reason, found the bodies, buried them, and returned home to warn his own family before he came to town. Only he never made it. From the looks of things it appeared as though the second two farms were hit a day after the first two. It was several weeks before anyone rode over and found those poor souls. No one had the guts to dig up the graves at the first two farms so we assume everyone was killed. If there had been any survivors, they would have shown up in town first, raising the alarm."

Gazing off into space, Morgan continued, "No. With all the visiting back and forth between those farms, especially the Turners and the O'Briens, if anyone was missing from one place, they probably died at the other. In fact, we're pretty sure a neighbor must have come riding up to scare the Indians away from the Turners. It wasn't looted as bad as the O'Brien farm, and it's possible there were people hiding inside who were caught in the fire and died in the house." Morgan seemed to be thinking out loud as he related the story, like he was trying to puzzle out an accounting of everyone.

"Well, if I can't buy the Turner's place," Mac mused, "what about one of the other farms that you foreclosed on?"

"As of now," Morgan replied, "the bank owns that land, and we can't do anything with it until we are sure there are no relatives around to claim the property and make good on the loans. However, as soon as I know of anything around here that has a clear title for sale, I'll let you know."

"Just one more question, if you don't mind, Mr. Morgan." Mac hesitated a moment to gather his thoughts. "Have you heard of anyone in the area increasing their herds?"

"No. As a matter of fact, I'm the only one who has purchased livestock. Most of what I've acquired has come from the families that are selling out. I've taken on the extra expense personally to help them out. The bank is almost over extended with the buy outs and just approving loans."

"Of course, Mr. Morgan, I understand. It was great to see you again. With your knowledge, I'm sure you'll be able to weather this trouble. Thank you for your time." Mac walked to the door and with his hand on the knob hesitated then turned back. "By the way, Mr. Morgan, you won't forget to let me know if there is a piece of property for sale, will you?"

Morgan's mouth opened and shut in irritation. "Just leave me your address, Nicholas. You'll be the first to know what's available."

"Thanks," Mac replied, "I'll be staying at the hotel for the time being, while I look around the area some more. After that, I'll be leaving to hunt mustangs, so maybe I'll just look for Mr. Turner myself if I get far enough west. I'd still like to own that property."

"Why such an interest in the Turner place, Nicholas?"

"Well, I guess you could just call it sentimental reasons, Mr. Morgan."

With that parting salvo, Mac shut the door and hustled down the street. The cultured professor, here in this little backwater town, who'd believe it? Except for knowing his background, Mac would have suspected he might be involved.

Mac knew that with Morgan's economics background he could turn a dollar into a million in no time. However, he wasn't sure of Morgan's talents in finding missing people. Maybe he'd be able to help track down Padraig Turner. If Mac wrote to his father, he might be able to find out if he or any of his friends had heard of Mr. Turner. If the man hunted and trapped for a living, he had to sell his furs somewhere. Somebody had to know him. Then, Mac could at least inform him his niece survived. What had happened to her after the waterfall, he didn't know. He just had a feeling that a woman with her spunk might be after revenge. Everything he remembered about her, including her disguise, now made sense.

Right now, he had to investigate the sheriff and the clerk at the survey office. Neither of them looked honorable. Morgan said the sheriff was honest, but Mac wondered if he knew people as well as he knew economics. His experience with extremely intelligent people often showed him they lacked common sense.

Once he satisfied his curiosity about the sheriff and land agent, he'd follow his next lead. He'd go talk to Mr. and Mrs. Ruggers again to see if Ryan Turner ever mentioned his uncle. With luck, he would find him before Morgan did. That way, maybe he could convince him to keep the land for his niece instead of selling it. Morgan meant well, but he didn't know Sammy was still alive. Mac realized her safety depended on his keeping that fact to himself.

Ten

Samantha's tears dried on her face as she stared at Laura in shock. Huddled in the corner of the bed, against the wall, with her arms clutched across her chest and her knees bent up in a defensive position, she gasped, "How did you know?"

"I never saw a boy defend his modesty by clasping his arms across his chest, honey," Laura drawled as she pushed herself away from the doorframe and started to cross the room. "Now, why don't you tell me your story while I check your back and see how badly that brute beat you." Laura's voice gentled when she saw the child shook with fright. "I hate that man as much as you must," she continued. "I sure won't tell anyone your secrets if you ask me to keep quiet. Besides, I don't think masquerading as a boy would have lasted much longer. I've got a feeling at least one person is doing some serious puzzling over you."

"Who could know?" Sammy asked. "I've been so careful."

"Well, I don't know if he knows for sure, honey. He's just mixed up about his feelings right about now." Laura tried not to laugh. She knew Jason and knew what he must have been thinking. Now, she realized why he couldn't stand to touch this child. *Won't he absolutely die,* she thought, *when he realizes he's not in love with a boy? Cool-hearted Jason, a sweetie, but so detached. It always takes me forever to get a rise out of him. What a hoot!*

"Come on, little one, let's see the damage." Laura gently coaxed Sammy out of her shirt. Once she slipped the long johns down off Sammy's arms, she saw the material binding her breasts.

"How old are you, girl?" she gasped in shock.

"I just turned eighteen," Sammy replied.

Laura's eyes widened then turned to the task of assessing Sammy's back. "Well," she said, "this binding around your breasts helped protect most of your back. You aren't cut anywhere. You just have some nasty welts around your shoulders, but that eye doesn't look too good. Let me get Rebecca to bring in a bath. I think if you soak a bit it will ease the pain."

Laura started to leave when Sammy called out, "Wait! She can't know I'm not a boy. I'm so close!" With that, Sammy broke down completely. Laura hurried back to her and, taking her to her ample bosom, rocked and comforted her.

"Hush, child, hush. Tell me what the problem is."

Totally spent, Sammy spilled out everything that had happened, even to what she had overheard at the livery stable. She explained about Dennis's saddle, her mother's cedar chest, and the impulse that caused her to disguise herself. She only left out her encounter with the scout at the waterfall. She didn't know why, but that seemed private.

When she finished, Sammy sagged on the bed, exhausted. It took all her effort to sit quietly while Laura digested everything. "I always knew there was something rotten about that no good bum, Tyler," she exclaimed. "Don't you worry, honey, I'll figure something out. Your secret is safe with me. Now, you climb out of those britches and let me get you bathed."

Laura left Sammy only long enough to return dragging a copper tub. "You climb in bed and cover up to your chin, girl. I'm having Rebecca bring in some hot water. I told her you fell asleep, and I wanted to wash your back while you were out so you wouldn't feel the pain. Hurry now, I hear her coming."

Sammy scrambled under the covers and turned her back to the door pretending to be asleep. She heard Rebecca empty two buckets of hot water into the tub.

"Just two more will do, Rebecca, then you can leave me."

Sammy risked a peek over her shoulder as Laura turned and caught Rebecca's angry expression. Laura laughed out loud. "Don't worry. He's too young for me to corrupt. I'm just nursing him until Jack and Sally return," she joked. Rebecca stamped out in sullen silence, and after closing the door, Laura started laughing.

At Sammy's puzzled expression, she asked, "You do know who and what I am, don't you Samantha?"

Sammy only nodded silently.

"Does being in my house under my care bother you?"

Sammy remained silent, then shook her bowed head. "No."

"Well, just so you won't worry, I don't plan on turning you into one of my girls, and I won't let anyone near you."

Sammy was so used to thinking the best of people she couldn't believe Laura would lie. Besides, Laura had offered the first comfort and relief Sammy had since that fateful summer day. Just being held and listened to felt so good and letting the tears flow unrestricted had lifted a ton of weight off her shoulders. She instinctively trusted Laura completely and immediately knew she would be safe here.

Laura helped Sammy bathe and wash her hair. Once they scrubbed the dirt off Sammy's face, her eye didn't look quite so bad. She would be bruised and sore, but there would be no scars. By the time they finished her bath, Sammy felt she'd known Laura all her life. Laura was so warm and caring it reminded her of all the love she had lost, and tears slowly trickled down her cheeks.

"Darlin', you're breaking my heart to see such sadness in one so young. I'll do anything I can to help you." Laura couldn't stand the thought of this sweet child caught in a sticky web of circumstances. She decided to help her untangle that web.

"You dry off, honey. I'll be right back with some clean clothes." Laura left Samantha in privacy to finish her tears and hurried up to her room to see what clothes would be best for the beautiful young girl. *And no doubt about it,* Laura thought, *she is beautiful even with her hair chopped off.* "We'll have to see what we can do so she doesn't have to disguise herself as a boy anymore," she muttered to herself as she rummaged through her wardrobe.

~ * ~

Jason hurried back to Laura's place after leaving a sign on the livery stable door saying the stable was temporarily closed. He simmered with suppressed anger and self-contempt. He knew better than to run away from problems. He had seen the green sparks fly in Sam's eyes when he was mad the day he and Ashley ran into each other. It reminded him of a mountain lion ready to spring. *Well, if you turned your back on a mountain lion, it would stalk and kill you.* Jason wasn't going to turn his back on this problem any more. He was going to face the lion in its den and find out what it was that caused such a reaction in him. He had a lot of questions for the kid, and he was going to get to the bottom of this.

Jason didn't bother to knock. He strode right into Laura's place and slammed the door. Doc was in the parlor, drinking with one of the girls, so the kid had to be patched up already.

He stomped into the bedroom where he had dumped the boy and, stunned, came to an abrupt halt.

A young woman stood with her torso twisted, trying to see her naked back in the dresser mirror. The pose arched her back and caused her breasts to thrust out at a saucy angle. Shock registered on her face as their eyes locked through the mirror's reflection. It seemed like it took her forever to react. Then, she grabbed a towel and covered her body.

"Holy mother of God!" Jason mumbled. Before him stood the most beautiful creature he'd ever seen. Her hazel eyes were huge, iridescent pools of fear. Then, staring, mesmerized, he recognized her. Suddenly, he realized he'd caused her fear. "Sam, you're a *girl*!"

She cowered against the dresser, shaking like a leaf in a gale. He watched her blanch at his statement and for a moment thought she would faint.

"I'll just wait out here until you're dressed," he said softly. Then using his most incensed tone to cover the elation coursing through his veins, he half shouted, "You've got some questions to answer!"

"Jason!" Laura screeched, running into the room. "What are you doing in here? Get out! Can't you see you're intruding on a lady's privacy?"

Laura's outraged tone mirrored Sammy's feelings. The whole time she stared at the sheriff, she felt her heart pound so hard it felt as if it was going to explode right out of her chest. Her whole body burned as the thought of a man seeing her naked finally registered. She was mortified. Then red hot fury engulfed her. Recognition penetrated her horrified brain, and her body flamed even more to see Jason standing in the room, staring at her. With his eyes laughing and his mouth curved in a slow grin, he looked as if, manners or not, he was reluctant to leave. How could she ever find out anything now? It seemed like before long everyone would know she wasn't a boy, and just when she was so close to catching those murderers.

"I'm sorry, honey," Laura soothed as she pushed the sheriff out and shut the door. "If I thought Jason or anyone else would be barging in here, I'd have told you to lock the door. I just didn't think he'd be back."

"Oh, Laura, now what can I do?" Sammy wailed. "We can't let everyone find out I'm really a girl. I'll never be able to find my family's killers." Sammy paced between the bed and the dresser, so agitated that Laura had to physically take her by the arms and gently settle her on the bed.

"Let's get you dressed, then we'll decide how to handle this," she soothed. Total silence reigned as Laura competently assisted Sammy into the borrowed clothes.

"Well, maybe Jason can help." Laura's words fell into the strained silence. "He's a good man," she continued, "and he's smart. We probably need more than our two heads to figure this out. I'll get him in here and see what we can come up with."

"No!" Samantha exclaimed. "How can I ever face him again. He saw me naked!"

Laura laughed. "Honey, you said the word 'naked' like you were pronouncing the horrors of hell. He's got enough sense to not make you feel embarrassed. Now, he knows for sure you're not a boy, and believe me, he had his suspicions before. We need him to help us out of this mess," she emphasized. "I promise everything will work out." Laura finished buttoning the day dress, and they both laughed as they tried to get the huge bodice to look halfway decent on her tiny frame.

"Laura, this will never work." Sammy's voice registered her resignation.

"You're right. But, I've got an idea." Laura opened a dresser drawer and withdrew a knitted shawl.

"Let's wrap this around your shoulders." Laura matched words to action as she crossed the ends over Sammy's exposed breasts, covering her from neck to waist. Pleased with the solution, she belted the shawl and dress together. "It will have to do for now. You stay here," Laura urged her to sit down, then walked to the door, where she paused. "I don't want anyone else seeing you until we figure out what to do. I'll get Jason. And stop fluttering around, it will be fine." Laura sighed as she shut the door firmly behind her.

Jason stood at the parlor window with a drink in his hand. He vacantly stared out at the empty street with a lopsided grin twisting his face. His thoughts seemed miles away, and Laura's touch at his elbow startled him into sloshing his whiskey.

"Sorry, Jason, I didn't mean to alarm you, but we've got to talk. Samantha and I need your help." Laura quietly explained everything to Jason as he stared at her, missing almost everything she said.

Samantha, he thought, *what a beautiful name*! It fit her perfectly. Samantha—green eyes, chestnut hair, gorgeous body, no wonder she made my pulse leap! I'm not going crazy. She's a woman, a beautiful woman. Jason's head floated on cloud nine. His thoughts rapidly ran through a litany of 'thank-you's'.

"So, will you help her, Jason?" Laura asked, jolting him back to the present.

"I'm sorry, what did you say? Help her what?" he replied.

"Jason Sudholt, I've just explained Samantha's problem, and I promise to bash your head in if you in any way embarrass her by alluding to the fact that you saw her naked! She's a young, innocent girl, and she's not accustomed to having strange men barge in on her bath. Do I have to start over?" Laura asked with exasperation.

"Please, Laura," Jason pleaded. "I'll pay attention this time. I was just so taken aback by the realization that Sam, uh, Samantha is a woman that I didn't hear a word you said."

With an understanding grin, Laura patiently took several more minutes to tell him everything the girl had related. Then she repeated her plea for his help.

Sammy had just about worn a hole in the braided carpet with her pacing as she waited for Laura to come back. Every nerve in her body crawled. She wondered what took Laura so long, and she didn't know how she would ever look Sheriff Sudholt in the eye again. On top of everything else, this fluttering in her stomach wouldn't stop, and she feared she would be sick. She continued to feel her face heat up every time she thought of the seconds Jason had stood in the room looking at her. His eyes had lost all the cold brittleness she had grown accustomed to seeing. They glowed with a warmth that almost reached out and stroked her.

"Oh, Dear Lord, how am I going to handle this?"

Her wait ended with a soft knock. Samantha stood frozen in mid stride as Laura entered with Sheriff Sudholt. She'd find out in the next few minutes if her prayers were answered.

Jason turned his back to Sammy as he shut the door, giving her a chance to compose herself and get used to him being in the same room with her. He turned back slowly and deliberately kept his eyes from making contact with her. He realized with a start he wasn't doing this to save her from being embarrassed, but to save himself from the embarrassment of revealing his feelings. If she looked into his eyes now, she'd know he desired her and that would scare her for sure.

The realization hit him that he wanted her as he had never wanted any other woman. To win this beauty, he knew he'd have to go slowly. Their hearts would be bound together. Once she felt comfortable with him, she would then come willingly.

Jason couldn't stop himself from looking directly at her. Courage sparked green fire in her eyes as she struggled to maintain her dignity. *This was the woman of his dreams.* Jason took a deep breath, swallowed his delight, and very professionally began to ask questions.

Sammy seemed to visibly relax when she saw him avoid direct eye contact. It cost him a great deal of effort to make sure she realized he wanted to make this as easy for her as possible. Hesitantly, she told her story from the beginning up to what she'd overheard in the livery stable.

"Those men knew I was supposed to be at the farm, and they didn't find me. I have to stay in hiding until I have proof that they killed my family. And one other thing—" Sammy hesitated then, for the first time, looked straight into Jason's sky blue eyes before she continued, "I know not one of those men is smart enough to be the leader. The man that beat me must have recognized Dennis's saddle and that's why he was so brutal. I'm sure it never entered his mind that I'm Samantha Turner. However, he sure remembered the last place he saw that saddle."

Jason sobered rapidly as he listened to Sammy's story. He continued to sneak looks at her while her eyes were glazed in remembering her loss. He ached to wrap his arms around her and protect her from any more pain. The sight of her swollen eye made him wince, and he wanted to inflict mortal agony on Tyler. He thought if he had the man in his sights right now, he'd kill him without a second thought. He also realized, as Sammy did, that Tyler probably only did the dirty work on someone else's orders. There had to be someone directing him.

After Sammy finished her tale, the three of them sat in silence for a long time. They all started speaking at the same time, and Laura laughed. "All right," she said, "we've all thought about this, but now we need a plan. Jason, you go first!"

Jason sat with his elbows on his knees. He rubbed his chin and continued staring at his boots. "Well," he replied slowly, "I think Samantha should stop dressing as a boy, but how do we sneak her into town and into the community without a lot of questions?"

"I can't be a girl," Samantha shot back. "If Tyler spots me, he'll know who I am. He'll kill me before I even know he's seen me."

"Wait a minute," Laura interrupted. "I've got an idea about all this. Samantha, how well do you know Jack and Sally? And even more important, are you willing to let them in on your secret?"

"Sure, except for the fact that the more people I take into my confidence, the more chances there are of everyone finding out about me. I love Jack and Sally. They're good people and I think I can trust them, but they won't be back until tomorrow or the next day."

"That's all right. That will give us some time," explained Laura. "Here's what I have in mind. Judith dyes her hair black because she has some gray hairs and she doesn't want the men thinking she's too old." At Jason's shocked look, Laura laughed and continued, "I think we can keep Sam Turns under wraps until he heals up. By that time, Jason can talk to Jack and Sally, and if they agree, you can be her sister's daughter come to live with them because your ma is ill. We'll curl your hair and dye it black. No one will ever guess. We'll say Sam Turns got scared because of the beating and ran away." Jason realized Laura was on to something as he listened to her plan.

"Rebecca will have to know, but she won't breathe a word to anyone. She hates most of the people in town for turning on her just because she needed a job and I gave her one. She's an excellent seamstress, and she can whip out a couple of dresses in no time. You can't be seen in town with any hand-me-downs from my girls. Someone might recognize them. The underwear is no problem." Laura paused as she seemed to think of more details.

At Sammy's startled gasp and immediate blush, Jason looked at Laura. Catching her eye, they instantly realized her mentioning undergarments was the cause of Samantha's alarm. Laura quickly changed the subject.

"The only thing is you'll have to come up with a name."

Sammy didn't react for a minute, then surprised Jason and Laura with her answer. "I can't do it."

"Why?" They yelled in unison.

"I can't give up Sassy. She's all I have left. Sassy is Sam Turn's horse. He wouldn't leave town without her."

"Who knows about Sassy being Sam's horse?" Jason asked. "I never knew you had a horse or a saddle until today."

"Well," Sammy replied. "Jack and Sally of course, and Daniel knows, too. I'm not sure if anyone else is aware or not. Anyway, after all the ruckus today, half the townspeople probably know about the saddle."

"Look," Jason answered, "You said you rode in after dark, and no one saw you go into the livery stable. What if we just say Jack gave Sam the horse to use while he worked for him, and he's just thankful he didn't steal the horse and the old saddle when he ran away? We can tell Daniel Sam was probably bragging about the horse being his," he continued.

"Daniel knows me better than anyone," argued Sammy, "and he knows I'd never run away without telling him. We're best friends, and I wouldn't want to hurt him or lie to him for anything. He lost his family, too. We understand each other." She sounded obstinate as she fought for her right to do this her way.

At first Jason felt a stab of resentment. Then, he and Laura looked at each other, and they both turned to look at Sammy. She seemed dejected and so sad it tore his heart.

"Well," Laura said, "what's one more person in on the secret? Daniel did save your life by going for help as fast as he did, and he will make an excellent ally. He always knows what's going on. He may hear something important. No one pays attention to a kid."

"Now, you know the reason I disguised myself," Sammy countered. "It worked perfectly. I hate to give up now that I'm so close."

No one spoke for a long minute, then Sammy relented. "I guess that settles it. If Jack and Sally will take me in, I reckon we can try it."

"All right!" Laura exclaimed. "I've got to get to work. I'll get Doc so drunk he'll be swearing to everyone he meets tomorrow that you are so beaten up you can't be moved. I'll need to get Rebecca started on your clothes right away, and all you have to do is come up with a name."

Laura hurried out, leaving Jason and Sammy in an uncomfortable silence.

Jason couldn't tear himself away even though Sammy seemed embarrassed to be alone with a man in a bedroom. Neither looked at the other, and yet heightened senses sent sparks vibrating through the room. Sammy's cheeks began to flame again. Jason felt his heart pounding so loud it seemed to echo in his head.

Sammy's heart slammed in her chest. She thought she would pass out like a baby if it didn't slow down a bit. She had admired Jason since she first came to town. He was an honest sheriff and well-respected. For the first time she looked at him as a man. *Why,* she wondered, *hadn't she ever seen how good looking he was?* Not as tall as Nicholas MacNamee, he didn't intimidate her with his size. He wore his blond hair shorter than Nicolas did, and it hung straight and fine, not a smidgen of curl. Parted down the middle and combed back on each side, it gave his long face the perfect frame. His eyes weren't as blue as the scout's either. *Why am I comparing Jason to that tall, dark stranger?*

Shaking off her thoughts, she stood up from her chair and turned her back, letting the silence drag. Crossing her arms protectively around her body, she tried to understand why she never paid attention to Jason before those bullies beat her. Was she only this aware of him because she realized he had seen her totally naked? No, she saw a warmth in his eyes that she had never noticed. Previously, whenever she'd caught his glance, his eyes had been icy cold and glaring. She'd thought he hated her, so she'd avoided him as much as possible. Now, when he looked at her, her pulse leaped and she wasn't sure if she wanted him to leave or to wrap his arms around her and hold her safe. She felt secure with him there and knew if he was with her, she would be protected from harm. Gradually, she felt the tension ease and the anxieties melt away. Her arms dropped to her sides, and she quietly walked back to her chair and sat down in resignation.

Jason cleared his throat. "Umm, do you want me to help you pick a name?"

"No," Sammy replied. "Do you think anyone would guess if I kept Samantha for my first name and my father's name, Peter, for a last name? I could be Samantha Peters. You could call me Mandy. I think, that way, if anyone slips, it won't matter. Especially Daniel, he may have a hard time with this. So will Jack and Sally. Oh, what will they all think of me?" Suddenly the enormity of their plan began to worry Samantha. "This will never work!"

"Don't worry," Jason soothed. "They'll want to do all they can to help you. I think your name will be perfect unless anyone knows Sally's sister's name. You might have to take her last name if that's the case. As soon as Jack and Sally return, we'll find out." Jason continued in a softer voice, almost to himself as he reflected. "It's not hard to see why those whom you have gotten close to in the last couple of months have come to love you."

Sammy jerked around at that remark, not sure she had heard him correctly and caught his full gaze. She saw the flush begin at his neck and crawl up his face, and felt the matching heat flow through her veins.

Jason cursed, half to himself. "Dammit anyway. Sorry if I embarrassed you again." He quickly looked away and made his excuses. "I'll let you rest now. Laura will have you busy for the next twenty-four hours. I'll send Daniel in to see you, and you can use him as our go-between if you need to see me for anything."

Sammy kept her eyes on the floor and mumbled, "Thank you," not really taking a breath until she heard the door softly close.

"Need him for anything!" she mumbled. She didn't want him to leave! She started shaking in delayed reaction, whether from the beating or her disturbing emotions she wasn't sure. She did know she didn't feel as safe now that Jason left. Her active imagination began to haunt her with all kinds of horrible possibilities. She had to shake herself out of this or she'd be beat before she started.

Eleven

Sammy watched as Laura bustled around, bringing Jason's prediction to reality. She immediately began to organize everything. Explaining she wanted to talk to Jack and Sally before anyone in town knew they were back, she sent Daniel to watch for the Billings. She recruited Rebecca to begin sewing a dress that would fit Sammy, then tackled the job of helping Doc forget the rest of the evening.

Daniel had taken the news that his thirteen-year-old friend was really an eighteen-year-old girl pretty well.

"You're still my best friend, Daniel. It doesn't matter that I'm a girl. The circumstances of our parents' deaths are different, but we still have a common bond," Sammy assured him with a quick hug. "And don't forget, you saved my life. I won't ever forget that."

"Ah, Sam... I mean Samantha, I'd do that for anyone, but when I saw those men beating you, I really came close to using my gun. Then I remembered your lessons. I knew I had to get Sheriff Jason. They outnumbered us."

"I'm glad you used common sense, Daniel. I would hate to be responsible for you getting hurt. Believe me, those men would not have hesitated to gun you down if you drew on them."

Daniel grinned shyly and backed out the door. “I’ll let you know as soon as I spot Jack and Sally coming into town.”

“Thanks, Daniel, you’re a true friend.” Samantha turned to include Rebecca in her warm smile.

“You, too, Becca. I can never repay you for all the hard work you’re doing to make a dress so fast.”

“I don’t mind, Miss Samantha. At least you aren’t too snooty to help me sew up your outfits.” Rebecca looked over her shoulder as if to check on eavesdroppers, then continued, “Unlike the girls here at Miss Laura’s, at least you’re willing to help yourself. By the look of those stitches, you even seem capable.”

Samantha laughed. “Oh, I know enough, Becca, but you will have to do the fitting and cutting of the patterns. I can’t do that. I can only piece together the parts if you tell me what gets joined to what.”

To keep Rebecca from asking any questions she wasn’t ready to answer, Samantha gently quizzed the woman as they sat and sewed.

“How’d you come to work for Miss Laura, Becca? You seem to be a very talented seamstress.”

“When my no-good husband was killed in a shootout during a failed bank robbery, I couldn’t find work anywhere. No one wanted to hire a bank robber’s wife.”

Samantha covered her shock with a soft murmur. “I’m sorry, Rebecca.”

“Me, too. But, Miss Laura needed a housekeeper, and my talents with a needle saved her the expense of sending away for the girl’s dresses, so she hired me. As soon as the good people of this here Charrette Village found out where I worked, they immediately shunned me.”

"But, Becca, surely they knew you weren't one of the girls for hire? Didn't they realize you needed to support yourself as best you could?"

Rebecca smiled at Samantha.

"Honey, most of those folks just hoped I would up and disappear. They couldn't stand the reminder that I used to be their friend and my husband turned out to be a bank robber. They just wanted to forget I ever crossed their threshold." Shaking her head in sadness, she continued, "What they don't remember is that my Tom was a good man until crop after crop failed and sent him over the edge. He was desperate. He never let me know how bad our finances got. I didn't piece it together until after the funeral when they came and foreclosed on our farm. They took everything—every stick of furniture, all the household goods and every animal on the place, all auctioned off to pay the debt."

With a huge sigh, she finished. "If Miss Laura hadn't given me a job, I'd have starved to death and not a person would have cared."

"Rebecca," Samantha nudged her quietly. "Miss Laura's a good person. She cared. You have nothing to be ashamed of. You couldn't have known what your husband had in mind that day. And even if you'd suspected, I bet you couldn't have stopped him. You have a job that supports you and no one has the right to look down their nose at you." Samantha got up from her chair and hugged Rebecca.

"That's all over now, Becca. Put a smile on that pretty face, and let's see if we can fool the whole town."

"You're a sweet girl, Miss Samantha. You're the first one to ever call this sourpuss 'pretty'. You don't think I'm bad just because I work here, and you appreciate my help. I'm grateful for that."

"Well, you are pretty when you smile. You should do it more often. Ma always said a cheerful smile could make the saddest soul lift its spirits."

As they finished the first dress, Rebecca commented, "You know, maybe your ma had a point. Your smile has lifted my spirits, and I feel a might better since we started talking. Now, stand up. Let me see how this looks."

Rebecca slipped the finished dress over Samantha's head. Rebecca tilted her head one way than the other. Sammy held her breath and waited for the verdict. It seemed to take forever before Rebecca finally voiced her opinion.

"You know, this soft fern color brings out the green specks in your eyes. I think it suits you. You look beautiful."

Accepting the compliment with a shy smile and a quiet nod, Sammy brought another smile to Rebecca's face as she exclaimed, "Becca, who would ever believe such scandalous underwear beneath this very demure dress. I feel absolutely wicked."

"It would take more than all that silk underwear to make you wicked, Miss Samantha. Besides, I had to get that underwear. Mrs. Frank would never believe any of Miss Laura's girls would wear cotton drawers. Anyway, no one will ever see it, so don't worry about it. That silk will help you realize you are a woman and not some tomboy running around town." Rebecca rose from her chair and walked over to the door. Cracking it open, she peeked out and returned to her chair.

"Look, Miss Samantha. Even I get to indulge a little." Lifting her drab gray skirt, Rebecca revealed the black silk petticoat. "Wouldn't any of the women in town just die for this luxury?"

Samantha gasped, then burst out laughing. Rebecca joined in after hesitating a moment. Sammy thought she seemed to enjoy the sound of their merriment as much as the joke on all the proper women of the town.

"Oh, Becca, I think I'm going to miss having the freedom of my disguise," Sammy moaned.

"Freedom," Rebecca barked, "you can't tell me you found it easy to get in and out of those long johns and britches just to go to the necessary!"

They both laughed over the picture that brought to mind. Samantha doubled over in giggles, and Rebecca clamped a hand over her mouth to stifle the noise. Both of them tried to sober up as Laura hurried into the room.

"What's going on in here?" She looked from one to the other, surprise written all over her smiling face.

"Rebecca, I don't think I have ever seen you smile, let alone laugh aloud. What could possibly be so hilarious?"

"We were just discussing Miss Samantha's disguise," Rebecca answered as she tried to smother her glee.

"Sorry, Miss Laura. We didn't mean to make so much noise," Samantha mumbled contritely. "It's all my fault. I was trying to cheer Becca up."

"Becca?"

"Oh, I mean Rebecca. It's just a habit. My family always gave each other nicknames." Samantha turned to Rebecca. "I'll address you by your full name from now on if you prefer."

"Oh, no, you won't." Rebecca jumped to her feet. "This is the first time anyone thought enough of me to give me a nickname. You just keep calling me Becca if you want. I kinda like it."

"So do I," agreed Laura. "But I'll stick to Rebecca since that's how I think of you." Laura turned to look directly at Samantha. "I didn't mean to interrupt you, but Jack and Sally are back. Daniel met them on their way in. He brought them in the back way, and since it's dark now, we're sure no one saw them enter town. They're in the kitchen."

Samantha gasped. It seemed the moment of truth was here. She wasn't sure if she was ready for it.

"Don't worry." Laura walked over and hugged her. "As soon as they know the circumstances, we'll know if our plan will work or not."

Sammy paced back and forth in the small room. She felt so nervous she thought she would be sick.

"Once the Billings find out how I lied to them for three months, they'll refuse to help." Voicing her deepest worry made her anxious. She began wringing her fingers and pacing again.

"Calm down, girl," Rebecca admonished. "These people are your friends. They'll understand."

"Come on, Samantha." Miss Laura took her by the hand. "That green dress looks lovely, and Jack and Sally will be enchanted with you." Leading the way, Laura opened the door and gently tugged her through the hall past the opulent parlor and stairs into the practical, but well equipped, kitchen.

Sally sat stiffly at the kitchen table with a cup of coffee untouched before her. Jack stood behind her chair. His huge hands lay protectively on her shoulders. Daniel nervously shifted from one foot to the other, then edged his way to the door. With a nod in the general direction of Miss Laura and Samantha, he made his escape.

Samantha stood in awe. She'd never witnessed the Billings looking so intimidating. Jack looked like he could start smashing things, and Sally had her nose so high in the air it was a wonder she could breathe. Her eyes glared at Miss Laura with enough heat to blister the Madam.

Miss Laura pulled Sammy forward and gently ushered her to sit at the table. Sally seemed affronted by being forced to sit at the same table with her and turned her head to avoid eye contact. Miss Laura gave Samantha a reassuring smile, then turned to the Billings.

"Jack, Miss Sally, I'd like to introduce you to your niece, Miss Samantha Peters."

Samantha's gasp was as loud as the Billing's. She didn't know what she expected, but it wasn't the kind of introduction Laura had just used.

Jack was the first to recover. "What are you talking about, woman? We have no niece. And if we did, she wouldn't be working for the likes of you." Sally reached for her hankie and bowed her head into the white cloth.

Samantha couldn't stand the pain she saw in Jack's eyes. "Miss Laura, please let me explain."

Before she had a chance to speak, Jack interrupted. "I don't know why you had us brought here, but I'm taking my wife out of this sinful place right now." Pointing to Samantha, he continued, "That hussy is not our niece. You can keep your dirty baggage right here. We want nothing to do with it."

"Now, just you wait one minute, Jack Billings," Laura's voice thundered through the kitchen, shaking Samantha down to her boots. "Sit down and listen to me." Her voice held so much authority that Jack sat. Samantha noticed that even in his agitation, he never let go of Sally. His arm lay protectively across her shoulders as he scooted his chair closer to her.

"I'm sorry I startled you with that introduction." Miss Laura's voice was gentle and sweet. "Your hired hand, Sam, met with an accident this morning." Ignoring a collective gasp from the Billings, Laura continued, "After he was beaten, I brought him to my house for Doc to patch up. As soon as I got Sam here, I found out Sam was Samantha."

Sammy felt her cheeks heat up as all eyes turned toward her. She could hardly maintain eye contact with the Billings. She was ashamed of lying to them, but knew she'd had no choice. Her life had been in danger. Jack and Sally continued to stare at her. They still didn't recognize her. Their baffled expression left no doubt. They didn't know her.

"What are you talking about, woman?" Jack bellowed. He surged to his feet. "We never saw this girl before. Our Sam is a young boy."

"No." Laura looked directly at Jack. "Your Sam is a young girl."

With that, Sammy couldn't take any more. She jumped up and threw herself into Sally's lap. Sobbing she tried to explain why she had to disguise herself. Hiccuping through her story, she only made things more confusing. Finally Miss Laura sat down and explained everything. With her calm rendition, all disbelief melted away.

Once they were told the whole story, the Billings immediately joined forces with Sammy and vowed to do all they could to help. Tears of relief swelled Sammy's heart and seeped from her eyes.

"I'll be proud to call you niece, Samantha," Sally said. "I'm mortified that you have had to rough it in the stable all this time. Truthfully child, I really didn't recognize you with that black hair. If I didn't know you after you've sat at my table for all this time, I don't think you have to worry about anyone else in town seeing through your disguise."

"Jack, you've been so quiet. Please say you're not angry with me!" Samantha had noticed that Jack stood silently, listening and even now hadn't said a word. He appeared deep in thought, and Sammy needed to know how he felt as she prodded him to attention.

"No, Miss Samantha," he answered. "I'm not at all angry. I'm just trying to puzzle out how you could've fooled me all this time! We worked together every day. It's so obvious you're a woman, I can't believe I didn't see it. Besides that, I feel bad about all the hard work I had you doing."

"Please don't feel bad, Jack. It's only obvious now because you see me in a dress. The hard work didn't bother me. I really enjoy working with horses. Anyway, I hesitate to embarrass you by telling you all the times you almost caught me with my britches down out back."

Sammy shocked herself into a pink blush with that remark, and the laughter in the room broke the tension. From that point on, plans flew fast and furious. An hour later, Sammy snuck out back with Jack and Sally, and fifteen minutes later the three of them rode down Main Street at a good clip. They slowed down in front of the saloon to greet one or two of the men and introduced Samantha to Mr. Ruggers as he came out to investigate the racket. Jason was included in the introductions as he made his rounds past the hotel.

After ten minutes of conversation, while Jason filled Jack and Sally in on the happenings at the stable in their absence, they said their good nights.

"Jason," Jack called out, "I'd appreciate it if you would go to Miss Laura's for me and see if Sam is well enough to be moved." Taking Miss Sally's hand, he patted it and continued, "Miss Sally insists on taking over his care since the poor boy is in our employ, and now that Miss Peters is going to be living with us, she'll have the extra help." At Jason's agreeing nod, he picked up the reins and chucked the horses. Turning in his seat, he called back, "Jason, come by the house in the morning. I'd like a more detailed accounting of what happened while I was gone." Jack kept his eyes on the road, but directed his questions to Samantha. "Do you think that was convincing?"

"You did great, Jack. I can never thank you and Sally enough for agreeing to this deception."

"Think nothing of it, girl," Sally piped in as she reached for Samantha's hand. "We're glad to help you."

By morning, Jason brought news that word had spread about the Billings' visitor. "Everyone in town knows you returned with a house guest." He turned to include Samantha in his wide smile. Looking at her, he spoke as if she weren't present. "Miss Peter's beauty has been widely touted, and everyone is eager to see this paragon in the flesh."

She felt her skin heat to a boiling point. Jason must have noticed because she saw him begin sliding the rim of his hat through shaking fingers. Sammy risked a glance at his face and realized he'd turned his attention back to the Billings.

"Gotta finish my rounds. I'll be back after lunch if I have any other news for you." He nodded a quick goodbye to Sammy and hurried out the door.

~ * ~

The first visitor the next afternoon was Ashley Frank. Sally answered the knock at the front door and had to hide a grin when she saw her afternoon caller. Ashley had never graced the Billings door before, and Sally knew just why she was here now. She silently thanked the Lord that Samantha's eye was healed enough to use the makeup Miss Laura had given her. A little touch of powder had hidden the last of the bruises. The two of them had just practiced applying the powder, laughing over the idea of Sammy being a painted woman. *Just in time*, Sally thought.

"Why how nice to see you, Miss Ashley. Please come in," Sally cooed as she pasted a fake smile on her face.

"Thank you, Miss Sally. I've brought you some fresh-baked cookies. I know you've been gone for a week or so and probably haven't had time to catch up on your baking." Handing Sally the paper-wrapped package, Ashley never once looked at her while she spoke. Her blue eyes darted around as though she were searching for something or someone. Sally knew just who that someone was.

"Why, thank you, Miss Ashley. You are so thoughtful. Will you let me take your wrap? Can you sit down and stay for a cup of tea?" Sally invited. Sammy needed to be warned. Miss Frank was pure venom, and usually, no one ever saw her on a cold November afternoon like this.

"I'm honored you left your warm hearth on such a blustery day." Sally watched Ashley dramatically swirl off her black cape. She took the girl's pelerine and hung it on a hook by the door. Masking her surprise, she took in the young woman's elegant gown. *Wouldn't you know?* Sally thought. *She's not going to miss the chance to wear her newest outfit.* Ashley seemed eager to show off the gown as she lifted the skirt and held it out away from her legs. She made a graceful turn and walked toward the parlor. Blond head held high, her sausage curls bounced on delicate shoulders covered in midnight blue wool.

Indeed, Sally thought, *the color set off Ashley's good looks to perfection.* She watched as the girl turned to see if she'd noticed and quickly hid a smile. *She is so transparent,* Sally thought masking a smile.

"Please sit here, Miss Ashley." Sally indicated a small stiff-backed chair that she hated. "It's the most comfortable chair I have. I'll just bring these cookies into the kitchen and fetch some tea." She stopped in the doorway and in studied innocence asked, "Oh, would you like me to see if my niece has finished her letter writing? I'm sure she'd love to meet you. There aren't many young ladies in town and perhaps the two of you will become friends."

"I would love to meet your niece, Miss Sally. Actually, that's just the reason I stopped by. It's so lonely not having someone my age to visit with."

Sally stepped into the kitchen and warned Sammy. “Ashley Frank is here to meet you, and her claws are out, so be careful.”

“I’ll be fine,” Sammy answered. “As long as she doesn’t recognize me, I can play along with whatever she dishes out. Let’s get this over with before I chew off all my fingernails. Until I meet everyone in town as Mandy Peters, I’ll always be wondering if someone coming around a corner will recognize me.”

Sally ushered Samantha into the parlor and watched Ashley’s hard, assessing look turn into an ingratiating grin as she introduced the two girls. Ashley seemed to dismiss Samantha immediately as absolutely no competition. She acted as if she was prepared to offer her a benign friendship.

“I am so happy to meet you, Miss Peters. I didn’t realize you were so young. I had hoped you were closer to my age so we could become bosom friends, but I still think we might take tea together sometimes. The winter can drag on so. It will be nice to have company, occasionally.”

At first Sammy seemed surprised by this backhanded remark, but she must have remembered her promise to play whatever hand Ashley dealt. She pretended not to notice Ashley’s condescending attitude. “Thank you, Miss Frank. I’m sure I’ll be able to count my afternoons with you as my most memorable here in Charrette Village.”

Sally retreated to fetch the refreshments before she broke out laughing and spoiled everything. She had no worry about Sammy holding her own.

As she reentered the parlor and set down the tea tray, she caught the gist of the conversation and had to beat a hasty retreat back to the kitchen. She ran through the kitchen and out the back door before she released her breath and exploded in laughter. Goodness! Where had Samantha come up with the story of having to sell her hair? The cold wind sobered her quickly and, gathering her composure, she returned to excuse herself from the tea party.

"I understand you came more to meet my niece than to visit with me, which is perfectly acceptable, Miss Ashley," Sally interjected as she noticed Ashley begin to deny the real reason for her visit. "I'll just let you girls get better acquainted while I start dinner."

Samantha jumped up instantly. "Let me help you, Aunt Sally. I'm sure Miss Frank will understand if I have to cut our visit short."

"No, no." Sally replied. "I don't need help, and anyway you just relax. This is your first day here and you need to rest from the trip. You get acquainted with Miss Ashley. I'm sure you'll be good friends."

Sally watched Samantha's eyes round in innocence. Then she turned the look on Ashley and gushed. "Oh, there's nothing I'd like better than to be best friends with Miss Frank!"

Ashley preened herself in the homage she felt was rightfully directed toward her by the younger girl. Yet, she wasn't sure from the story she had just heard if this girl was the right class of person to be associated with. After all, this was the first person she ever knew who had to sell her hair for money. Heavens! If she was that poor, Ashley didn't want to be associated with her. In fact she had been hard put to keep her face from registering the shock she felt when she received that answer to her rather blunt question as to why Miss Peters had cut her hair in such an unbecoming length.

"I suppose you could be pretty if it wasn't for your hair. It's such an ugly color, and you cut it so short."

Ashley noticed the poor child tilt her chin down and clasp her hands tightly in her lap. "Not everyone can be as beautiful as you are, Miss Ashley."

"Oh, I'm so sorry. Sometimes I forget myself and speak my thoughts out loud. But I must say, your hair just doesn't seem to fit your face or your fair coloring. That black shade is truly unbecoming, and it makes you look sickly pale."

Now that Ashley had satisfied her curiosity and was confident this girl would be no competition, she was prepared to be generous. Besides, the girl had acknowledged her own exceptional good looks. "Thank you for a delightful afternoon, Miss Peters," she sniffed as she rose from her chair. "You must come and visit me at the store. Perhaps I could give you some pointers on more stylish clothes. I have excellent taste, and I'm sure I could help you choose prettier dresses than the one you have on now. I love looking at all the catalogues. We could have a lovely afternoon browsing through Godey's Lady's Book."

Samantha looked aghast. She must think her dress is beautiful and very up-to-date. *Poor dear,* Ashley thought. Then, she let her observation speak for itself. "My dear Miss Peters, have you ever considered dyeing you hair a lighter color?"

Samantha sputtered but didn't answer.

"Oh, dear! I've done it again. I am so sorry. I should have realized you would not think in such modern terms. But believe me, it's quite the thing back east. No one thinks anything of it."

With no answer from the bemused young girl, Ashley gathered her gloves and nodded a dismissal. "Please come soon," Ashley invited as she prepared to depart.

"Thank you, Miss Frank. I'm sure you can teach me a lot about hairstyles and the latest fashions. However, I'm afraid I can't afford any new clothes right now. My mother is so sick. All our money is going for doctor bills. In fact that is why Aunt Sally has taken me in for a while. My poor daddy can't afford to feed me and pay for mama's medicine, too. As for dyeing my hair, why, I would never do such a thing."

"Well, it doesn't cost anything to look at the catalogues, Miss Peters, and we can still enjoy an afternoon daydreaming about what we'd like to buy if we could. Give my regards to Miss Sally. I've got to run."

Ashley waved a cheery goodbye as she smugly left the Billings' feeling totally superior to Miss Peters. She was so naive to fashion and color. Ashley knew she could steer the young girl into some really ugly clothes and hairstyles. Idly, she pondered where the girl had bought the lovely frock she was wearing.

Ashley wondered if it had been jealousy that glinted in those insipid eyes when Miss Peters saw how beautiful she looked. Her soft, blue, wool gown had been designed to attract attention to her tall shapely body, and Ashley never failed to enjoy the looks she received. Whether it was admiring glances from the men or envious looks from the women, as long as she remained the center of attention, she didn't care what emotion sparked that regard.

She loved to sway into a room causing her taffeta petticoats to rustle and smiled to herself at how pleasant that swishing sounded even now, as she swept down the boardwalk. She mentally prepared to put this girl in her place and make it clear there were certain men in town who were off limits. Mainly, Jason Sudholt! Even if he wasn't wealthy, he was certainly the best looking man in town. Ashley's smugness changed to consternation as she met Jason on his way toward the Billings.

"Walk me back to the store, Jason. It's so cold and windy, you can be my anchor so I don't blow away." Latching onto his arm, she pleaded coyly as she batted her eyes.

"I'd like to," Jason replied, "but I'm on my way to welcome Miss Peters to town."

"Oh, you'll have to come back another day. Miss Peters is so exhausted from her trip. I just left her so she could lie down and rest. You don't want to disturb her, now do you?" Ashley's blood boiled. Why would Jason stop to visit with that young chit? She'd heard talk in the store about the attractive Miss Peter. Maybe he'd heard the same rumors and wanted to look for himself. Well, she'd have to see about that.

"In that case," Jason answered, "I'll just stop at the stable. I wanted to talk to Jack anyway. Miss Laura just told me that young Sam Turns must have been afraid of that cowboy Tyler coming back and beating him again. It seems he ran away in the middle of the night while everyone was sleeping."

"Well, good riddance," Ashley retorted. "That kid was a brat anyway, and he probably did steal that saddle. Miss Laura better check her silverware."

"Jack lent that saddle to Sam so he could ride that extra horse of his. He bought the horse and saddle off a prospector passing through who needed a grubstake and a mule. That saddle wasn't Tyler's. It did belong to Sam because Jack gave him free use of it and the horse. That child has had a hard life, but he is honest and is a good kid."

"Maybe so," Ashley conceded, "but he was extremely rude. Remember how he knocked me down. I could have been hurt!"

"Now, Ashley, that's over and done with. Besides, all that got hurt was your pride because you landed in the street." Patting her on the hand, he reassured her there was no need to be embarrassed. "Think about it, Ashley. Neither of you were hurt. It was just an unfortunate accident." Jason gave her a rakish grin that had her simpering as he continued, "Now, admit it, if it had happened to someone else, you'd have thought it was quite funny."

Funny indeed! she thought. That was one of the reasons she'd gotten so upset that day. She could see the smirks and grins people tried to hide from her. It was one of the reasons she'd allowed herself to vent her spleen on the young boy. She had been embarrassed to death, and he caused it. She couldn't bear to be the laughing stock of the town. It was bad enough they gossiped about her single status, but to add the indignation of clumsiness on top of that was just too much.

Yet, Ashley couldn't help laughing. "You're right, Jason. I did overreact. It was just that my new dress got all dirty." She tried to pout, but she knew her eyes gave her away. She felt so pleased that Jason actually spoke to her for a change instead of ignoring her like he usually did that her laugh bubbled out with genuine pleasure.

Jason burst out laughing. "You are a minx! You better hurry home before you catch cold. I've got to talk to Jack." He gently detached himself from Ashley's grip.

Since she couldn't lure him away, she continued on to the store with a sigh. After walking a short distance, she turned to watch Jason to make sure he headed for the livery stable and not the house. Satisfied that he believed her about Miss Peters napping, she headed home.

Stepping into the warm livery, Jason greeted Jack and related his encounter with Ashley.

"You know, Jack, I don't think Ashley realizes it's her attitude and not her marital status or her grace that causes so much derision from the town folks." Jason removed his hat and scratched his head in contemplation. Then giving up on analyzing the proud Miss Ashley, he continued.

"I knew if I told Ashley about the saddle and the horse it would be the best way to have it all over town before sundown. Let's hope that gossip reinforces our story." After a good laugh, he slipped out the back door of the stables and headed towards the Billings' kitchen.

Sally answered his knock, and he entered the warm, cheery room. Finding both women busy preparing dinner didn't surprise him. He had known Samantha wouldn't be napping this time of day. He figured either she told Ashley she was tired just to get rid of her or Ashley's blue eyes were turning green. She'd have to come up with a better story if she were going to be successful in trying to keep him away from Samantha. He was hooked, good, and he knew it.

"Sit down, Jason. Samantha, fetch Jason a cup of coffee."

Jason watched Samantha reach for the coffeepot. Her breast strained against the fabric of her dress, causing his heart to trip. He ached to touch her, to wrap his arms around her. He never wanted to be apart from this beautiful girl, and he had to think fast because he wanted to convince her that she needed him as much as he needed her. He had dreamt about her all night. Convinced she was the woman he had waited for all of his life, he didn't know how he was going to be patient long enough to make her his own.

Both Samantha and Sally seemed glad to see him. Sally enjoyed a good laugh again, relating the yarns that Samantha had spun for Ashley. Samantha didn't wait for Sally to finish her story about Ashley's visit. "Please, Sally, excuse me," Samantha interrupted. "I've been looking forward to seeing Jason."

Jason almost knocked his chair over backwards as he rose and reached for her hands. "I've been waiting for you. You must tell me how you plan on catching Tyler and his gang. I need to know how soon I'll be free to be myself. I also want the satisfaction of knowing that justice was served and those killers were punished. When are you going to arrest them?"

Both Jason and Sally looked at Samantha as if she had lost her mind. Jason recovered first. "Samantha, maybe I didn't make it clear to you yesterday, but there is no way I can arrest

Tyler yet. First of all, I can't leave the town unprotected while I try to trail them. Second, we have no proof that they burned out your family and friends. I just can't walk up to them and say, 'I'm arresting you for the murder of the Turners and the O'Briens.' Do you think those men would just turn over their guns without a fight? I can't do this alone, and until I get word from the marshal, I won't know if he can spare any extra deputies."

Startled by her reaction, Jason watched Samantha's face cloud up as if she had been betrayed. He hastened to continue his reasoning, "Samantha, I'm not afraid of going after Tyler if that's what you are thinking. We need a posse and we need proof to back us up with the judge. If we don't have an iron-clad case, they'll get off and we'll never find out who the ringleader is."

"Jason," she cried, "I heard them brag about what they did! Isn't that proof enough?" Snatching her hands from his grip, she began to pace. "I can't wait much longer. I set out to find the men who killed my family and I did! Now, I want to see them die for it. I am not going to sit here under Jack and Sally's protection and do nothing while they're still free. I will go crazy living a lie. It was one thing while I was Sam Turns—I was still searching. To live a false life as Mandy Peters and do nothing about those murderers is asking too much. I was willing to disguise myself for my own protection, but I never planned on it being for long. I *won't* do this much longer. I *can't*!"

Samantha's voice had risen steadily, and she was shaking with anger by the time she noticed their pained expressions. She stopped yelling and hung her head. Her posture sagged in defeat.

Samantha's forceful argument for his immediate action shocked Jason. He'd thought she would be satisfied to remain in disguise. He knew her life was in danger if Tyler ever found out her identity, and he meant to protect her even if she didn't want it.

"Samantha, I never said I wouldn't try to bring in Tyler. I just said I can't do it alone, and I need reinforcements. I will continue to investigate his activities. I'll try to find out if he is employed by any of the local ranchers. And I will keep looking for evidence to use against him until we can bring him to justice. In the meantime, you have to keep up this charade of pretending to be Sally's niece. It can't be helped. It's the only way to protect your identity. One thing is certain: if Tyler ever finds out who you really are, you're dead. He can't have any witnesses, and if he finds out that you escaped the slaughter at your ranch, he'll figure out there's a chance you might have witnessed what happened. When he comes to that conclusion..."

Leaving the obvious unspoken, Jason wearily scrubbed at his chin. With a heavy sigh, he gentled his tone. He hadn't meant to react so vehemently, but he had to force her to understand the danger. "You have to agree with me on this masquerade, at least for a little while."

Samantha's eyes widened and her lips parted at Jason's harshness, but then she frowned and seemed to think about what he'd said. She paced between the table and the window, practically stomping, and he knew she was miffed at the idea of just sitting back and doing nothing. A crease deepened between her eyes then melted away. He braced himself for her decision.

"I'll give you one month, Jason Sudholt. After that, I will go to the closest fort myself and enlist the help of the commanding officer. I won't let that man get away with killing my family. I'll see him dead if it's the last thing I do!" With that parting shot, she stormed out of the room, leaving Jason and Sally awed by her vengefulness.

Jason felt dejected. Sally tried to assuage his despair by explaining Samantha's actions. "Really, Jason, if you had to bury your family and friends after the atrocities those men did to them, I think you'd be bitter, too. She just needs time. She never received the comfort of friends when her family died, and she's never been able to grieve properly. Once she becomes a part of this community and accepts our love and friendship, she'll be able to put all of this behind her."

"I don't know, Sally. I'm worried about her. She shouldn't feel so personally responsible for catching those murderers. Besides, she's no match for Tyler and his thugs. I have to persuade her to let me protect her."

"And how are you going to accomplish that feat, Jason Sudholt?" Sally taunted.

"I'm going to marry her," he exploded. He turned on his heel and, snatching his hat from the peg, slammed out of the kitchen. He'd never felt so angry. Why did Samantha have to be so stubborn? She'd upset him so much, he'd spoken his thoughts out loud. He'd just have to trust Sally's good sense not to spread this piece of gossip all over town. The letter he'd sent to the commander at Fort Howard had gone out this morning, but now he couldn't wait for a reply. He stormed back to his office to compose another missive explaining the urgency. Maybe he could hire Daniel to deliver this one.

Twelve

Sammy paced her room in frustration. She felt so useless. There weren't even any chores she could do to keep herself occupied. Her room shined with perfection. Not a speck of dust marred the furniture. Sally had given her what she called the guestroom. Much prettier than the other bedroom, this one hinted at elegance. White lace curtains hung under heavier drapes of forest green. Tonight, because of the blustery wind, her drapes were closed against the cold. They were heavy enough that they didn't even sway as gusts of frigid air rattled the windows.

The counterpane consisted of two parts. Delicate hand-crocheted, ecru cotton covered an under slip of forest green satin, allowing the rich color to show through in a flowery pattern. Matching doilies graced the dresser and vanity.

Sally had said her mother had crocheted the bedspread and scarves to match. They were something she'd always wanted to hand down to a daughter, but they'd never been blessed with children. Samantha felt a moment of regret that Sally and Jack had never gotten to know the pleasure of having children. She remembered her ma saying they were the joy of her life. She hoped someday, when this painful time in her life was past, that she would have children of her own to give her comfort. She pictured sturdy black-haired little boys circling her legs. Would they have blue eyes? Shaking away the mental picture, she paced over the pink and green oriental carpet. The beautiful design drew her attention and she marveled at the length of the fringe that paraded around the entire edge.

Maybe she should do her pacing on the bare floor. The rug was too pretty to wear a path in the pattern. Sammy tried to calm herself. Her lower lip ached from where she'd chewed it raw. New tears threatened as she remembered ma's scolding whenever she caught Sammy biting her lip.

She'd expected Jason to tell her how he planned on capturing Tyler and his cohorts. She didn't understand how he could just let the situation ride without taking any positive action. It was bad enough that her identity had been discovered. Now her hands were tied. She couldn't do anything as Mandy Peters, and she really did intend to keep her word. If Jason didn't have any answers in a month, she would ride over to Fort Howard and enlist the help of the commander herself.

In the meantime, she would write to her uncle in care of General Delivery. His last letter had come from a town in the mountains. She'd have to reread it. Vaguely, she remembered he'd said something about leaving trapping to prospect. Pa always said he'd never settle on what he wanted to do.

"I wonder if he stayed in the same area," she mused aloud. "I know he'll come after I explain what happened." If all else failed, she would don her disguise again and go after Tyler herself.

She'd been practicing with her pistol whenever she taught Daniel and hoped she could shoot as well as that bully Tyler. It wouldn't be a problem to leave town some night and just head out in another direction. She'd done it before, she could do it again. Her only regrets were leaving all the good people who had been doing their best to help her. The thought of worrying them nagged at her conscience. This beautiful room Sally gave her didn't help to ease her mind.

Walking over to the fireplace, she stretched out her hands toward the warmth. Maybe she could come up with a plan to let them think she was going to join her uncle and give up looking for Tyler. "They might think that's my best bet and let me go without too many questions," she muttered. She'd have to think about that. It might work as an alternative plan. "If Jason doesn't find any answers soon, I just might do that." Satisfied that she now had a purpose, she moved across the room and sat at her vanity to compose a letter to her uncle.

~ * ~

Sally was so upset about Samantha losing her temper she couldn't wait for Jack to come in from the stables. She had to talk to him, now. As she reached for her shawl, she mumbled, "I hope he's alone." She didn't want anyone else hearing what she had to tell him.

At first, she hadn't been sure if Jason was serious or not, but seeing the look in his eyes as he left dispelled any doubts. For someone so much in love, he sure left angry. Yet, she could understand his frustration over Samantha's being so adamant about revenge. Sally knew Jason only wanted to protect her. She hoped he'd keep his feelings about the girl to himself for a while. She knew Samantha well enough to know she would refuse him outright if he said anything about marriage now. The wind had kicked up, and it pulled and pushed at Sally's skirts as she hurried across the yard to the back door of the stable. She got an eye full of dust as she scurried into the warm barn. The back door slammed behind her, and Jack looked up as she stopped to scrub at her eyes.

"What are you doing, coming out in this weather? Can't you see we have a storm brewing? Now, look what you did! Here, let me help you." Jack tenderly cradled Sally's head in his large hand as he took a clean corner of her shawl and wiped her eyes.

"Is it the dirt in your eyes making them water or are you crying?" His tenderness and concern warmed her heart. She knew he considered her the love of his life and would curl up and die if she were hurt in any way.

Sally quickly laid Jack's fears to rest. "I'm fine," she said. "I just have something very important to talk to you about and I can't wait until you come in tonight. Besides, I don't want to discuss this in front of Samantha—it's about her." Looking over Jack's shoulder to make sure he was alone in the stable, she related all that had happened that afternoon.

"Jack, I'm worried. What if Samantha doesn't have the patience to let Jason do his job as he thinks best? What if she does try to go after those men by herself?"

"Calm down, Sally, love. What can a young woman like Samantha do against Tyler and his wild bunch? She has enough sense to know there is nothing she can do by herself. Let's give it some time. She'll simmer down when she realizes Jason is doing his best. She's not unreasonable. Right now, she's just emotionally spent. Give her a day or two to come to grips with what's happened in such a short time."

"That's what I'm afraid of, Jack. She's had three months to adjust to the loss of her family. She should be a little more practical by now. Then there's Jason! Do you think he really means to marry her just to keep her from going off after those men?"

"Well, from what I saw of the way Jason was drooling over that girl when she wasn't looking, I'd say he meant to marry her no matter what!"

"Do you really think he loves her? Heavens, he's only just found out she's a woman!"

"If you remember right, my dear, it didn't take us long to know we were meant to be together." Jack winked and stroked her cheek. "It still wouldn't take me long."

"Oh, Jack, that was different. Our feelings were mutual. I don't think Samantha sees Jason as anything but a lawman. I think she sees him as just someone to catch Tyler for her."

"Don't be so sure of that, Sally my love." Jack became serious again. "Right now, our Samantha isn't thinking straight. Once she sees Jason working towards the same goal she set for herself, she will start to see him as a good catch. I think Samantha already has some feelings for Jason—she just doesn't recognize them yet. I watched her close last night. You know how shocked I was! I studied her real hard while she told us her story, and I couldn't keep my eyes off her all night. It was as if I had to convince myself that she and Sam were the same person. She had me that fooled. Anyway, I saw her look at Jason when we met him on the street. I saw her flush at the introduction. Women don't blush like that unless there's a cause. I think the reason is she's attracted to Jason, whether she knows it yet or not."

"Maybe you're right, Jack. If she does marry Jason, it would solve all her problems. She could let her hair grow out and be herself as Mrs. Jason Sudholt." Sally allowed her eyes to glaze over as she thought about playing matchmaker. Jack's hearty laugh boomed out his amusement, bringing a sheepish smile to her lips.

"Come on, Love, let's close up shop and go in. If anyone needs me, they know where to find me. I've gotten a yen to cuddle in front of the fire tonight."

They wrapped their arms around each other's waists as they turned down the lanterns and closed the big door against the cold wind. *Like youngsters again*, Sally thought as they ran across the yard to their warm and cozy kitchen.

~ * ~

Samantha finished her letter and tried to think of a way to post it without anyone being the wiser. Thoughts of Jason caused her to blush again. Every time she had seen him in the last couple of days, all she could think about was that first glimpse he had of her as a woman. She felt so humiliated to know he'd seen her standing at the mirror buck naked. She couldn't stop the heat that gave away her thoughts and caused her to blush even more whenever their eyes met. She had to admit Jason had not done or said anything to remind her of the incident. He'd been a perfect gentleman. She would have to acknowledge the embarrassment and try to forget it ever happened.

Her thoughts veered off as she remembered another man, this one tall and dark. His good looks were embedded in her mind. She wondered where he'd gone. As a scout, he probably knew a lot about tracking. Could she enlist his aid in going after Tyler? "I wonder if the commander at the fort knows him?" she muttered. *Here is another possibility,* she thought. Would she have the nerve to ask about him? Thinking about all the obstacles in her way vexed her all over again.

Samantha rose from the vanity and walked to the window. Pulling the drapes aside, she peered out into the darkened street. Voicing her frustration, she gripped the curtain in her clenched fist and threatened, "Jason, don't be too slow in following through with Tyler's apprehension. I don't think you'll like what I have in mind."

~ * ~

Pinckney had turned out to be a dead end. Neither the sheriff nor the surveyor led Mac to any plot. Morgan had kept him informed on his efforts to locating Padraig Turner, which so far had produced no results. Without a lead, he couldn't waste more time here. Mac paid his bill at the hotel and walked towards the livery stable to get Renegade.

Suddenly, the peaceful town exploded with the sound of hoofbeats as four men on horseback galloped down the street. They immediately caught his attention because of their reckless horsemanship and roughshod appearance. He watched them rein in and walk their mounts towards the bank.

At first Mac thought they planned to rob the place. They dismounted, looked up and down the street, then hurried inside. He quickly made his way back to where he could stop them when they tried to escape. Professor Morgan deserved at least that much help from him.

After several minutes with no evidence of violence, his curiosity got the best of him. He crossed the street and made his way around to the back of the bank. There he found the window he remembered seeing in Morgan's office. Looking both ways and not seeing anyone in the alleyway, he tiptoed closer.

A curtain in the partially opened window prevented Mac from seeing inside, but he hoped their conversation would drift through the opening. The thought entered his mind that perhaps another farm had been hit. But why didn't they go to the sheriff?

"What do you mean you never found out where that kid got that saddle? Are you sure it was the same saddle that was at the O'Brien farm?"

"Yes, boss. I know it was the same saddle, but that sheriff said the name scratched on it was Sam Turns. That was the name of the boy that was working in the livery stable."

"What? Sam Turns! You dunderhead! Think! Sam Turns… Samantha Turner. I thought you said you beat up a boy. Could it have been Samantha dressed as a boy? How else would he or she have that saddle? That couldn't have been his name on the saddle. Whoever it is must have been at the O'Brien farm.

That's probably why you didn't find her. She must have been hiding! You've got to go back to Charrette Village and find out. If that is Samantha, you know what you have to do! If she was hiding at the O'Brien's, she might have seen what happened."

"If she was there, she'd have come running into town with her story. I don't think she saw anything."

"What do you know, Mark? You don't know anything about women. You just stick to horses."

"Boss, we can't go back right away. That sheriff will still be looking for us. I'm surprised we got away without spending time in jail the way it was."

"Shut up, Luke! We'll go back. I owe that little girl a kiss or two, and I aim to see she gets all the squeezing she wants."

"Tyler, keep your britches buttoned. Luke's right, we don't want anyone to connect you with her murder. You go out to the ranch and stay under cover for at least a month. You can go back to Charrette Village after all the hullabaloo has died down. I want you to make sure 'Sam Turns' is really Samantha before you do anything else to him...er...her. I don't want you seen in town before or after you take care of this little problem."

"Right, boss. Let's go!"

"Tyler, one more thing—this was too important to wait until I returned to the ranch, but I don't want you seen coming in here anymore. If you come into town, we don't know each other. Is that clear?"

"Sure, boss. I understand. You're getting too highfalutin to know the likes of me. That's okay. As long as the pay envelope stays as fat as it's been, I don't know you from Adam."

Mac heard general laughter from the four men as they trooped out of Morgan's office. He leaned weakly against the wall as he digested what he'd overheard. It was hard to believe that Professor Morgan could be mixed up in something so evil.

His family represented the elite of society back east. Mac stumbled into more information than he'd bargained for, but he wasn't complaining. He would need more proof, but now all doubts were laid to rest. He only had to substantiate what he heard and he'd have a watertight case against Mr. Morgan and his cowhands.

Mac tried to remember the boy at the stable who he had thought was Jack's son. What had he said? "You'll have to ask my boy." At the time he'd thought "my boy" had meant "my son". All he could picture was a small kid in an oversized hat staring down at the ground as he raked out the stalls. He hadn't seen his hair color, but the clothes were not the same. They didn't appear to be as big and baggy as what he had seen the girl dress in at the waterfall. Morgan was right, though. It had to be her. If the sheriff said the name on the saddle was Sam Turns, he must have been covering for her. It was too much of a coincidence that there would be a boy named Sam Turns and a girl named Samantha Turner living so close together.

At first, Mac thought about riding to Charrette Village immediately. He wanted to determine if the boy at the stable really was Samantha and, if so, to warn her. He planned to go there anyway to talk to the Ruggers again, but now he felt that he had a little time on his side. Morgan had told the men to lie low for a month, and he felt so close to getting the evidence he needed, he had at least three more weeks to look into the motive. He decided he had time. If he'd figured right, he would arrive in Charrette Village at least a week before Morgan's men. That would give him the opportunity to warn the girl.

He shuddered to think what she would suffer in the hands of that mean one. He had only heard three names, Tyler, Luke and Mark. He didn't know who spoke, but from the gist of the conversation, Tyler seemed to take orders from Morgan and the others followed Tyler. Mac heard hoofbeats retreating from town and knew his shock had kept him anchored out back too long.

He pushed himself away from the wall and slowly walked back to the boardwalk. Not wanting to walk past the bank, he crossed the street and headed over to the saloon for a drink. He would be the most popular man in town if he kept buying drinks at the rate he was going. It had proven to be the easiest way to get information without appearing to be nosy and worth every penny.

~ * ~

Morgan paced from his office door to the window. Why did he have such dunderheads working for him? Tyler used what hung between his legs to think, and the others were too intimidated by the brute to make any sensible suggestions.

He had to get rid of that Turner girl. She represented the only link that could keep him from gaining title to all the land along the railroad right of way. He needed the money that land would bring when he sold it to the railroad. So far he'd been able to cover the fact that his father had embezzled money from the bank, but if he didn't get these farms sold, everything his father did would come to light. He'd die before he let his mother suffer that indignity.

When he'd been called to his father's sick bed from college, he'd been appalled by the news his mother gave him. It hadn't taken him more than three days to travel to their family home in New York, but he'd arrived too late. His father never had regained consciousness, and his mother had been hysterical. He could hardly make sense of her ramblings. Finally he'd managed to calm her enough so she could explain what had happened.

He would never forget the shock of learning that his father jumped from the roof of their mansion after telling her that he'd lost all the family money to gambling. His mother had maintained the house while his father managed several banks, traveling from one to the other as often as necessary. She'd been unaware of his addiction or financial problems. Thaddeus helped her cover the fact of his father's suicide by concocting the story of heart failure after an accidental fall. He'd needed to buy time to find a way to restore the family fortune. His mother had great confidence in his ability to do that legally.

After he investigated the extent of his father's betrayal, he realized he could never successfully pay back all the money stolen and still keep his mother in the style she'd grown accustomed to. At first he used part of his personal savings to restore the pilfering from one of the banks. When he had the books of that one in order, he'd sold the bank and used the proceeds to mend the next bank. It wasn't until he reached the Midwest that he saw his plan, while saving the family name, did nothing to supply his mother with an income.

Morgan walked over to his desk and opened his humidor. Then he sat at his desk and lit a cigar. Leaning back in his chair, he savored the rich aroma of the tobacco and smiled as he remembered his last trip home.

He'd gone to New York to check on his mother. While there, he met with some businessmen he knew in hopes of getting a tip or two on the stock market. News was buzzing all over town about the new railroad. He immediately realized the potential of a railhead in the midwest. He thought about the possibilities in connection with cattle. If the railroad got as far as Missouri, he could make a fortune shipping cattle back east. The animals would not have to be driven over trails with the potential danger of Indian raids, swollen rivers to cross, and loss of life. Both animals and men suffered on those drives.

Thaddeus became excited about the idea and talked to as many of his friends as would listen. Everyone discouraged him from the venture. They advised that it would be years, if not decades, before a railroad would reach the Midwest and that was dependent on the blasted thing being accepted in the east. All the information from his investigation of the new venture proved his friends right. Trains were noisy and dirty to ride. It took years for rails to be laid, and the engines needed a lot of wood to keep a head of steam.

Nothing deterred Thaddeus. He had a vision, and he knew he could succeed. When he returned to Pinckney, he began by embezzling a little more money. He needed to buy a ranch. He wanted an established place that raised cattle, and he knew exactly which one he could get.

With a little manipulation of the books, the landowner fell deeper and deeper in debt. It took just over a year, but he finally got his farm. He named it, "The Free Spirit", and designed a butterfly for his brand. Once he found out how easy it was to sucker the first landowner into losing his ranch, he decided his father was a wise man after all.

He'd only resorted to Tyler Morris's brand of eviction when his methods failed. Now, all this work to get rid of the rightful landowners along the railway route he envisioned was finally paying dividends. He now had the potential of owning all the land needed to build his railroad. Just one person stood in his way—little Miss Samantha Turner. By the first of the year, with that problem out of the way, he could start to build his empire.

Morgan leaned forward and ground out his cigar in a crystal butterfly ashtray. He waved the smoke from in front of his face in aggravation. Tyler better not mess up this time. If the man couldn't do his job, he'd have to see about arranging a little accident. He had become too dangerous anyway. Too many people complained about his cruelties. Everyone knew Tyler worked for him. To keep his respectability, he couldn't afford to have a man like that on his payroll. Morgan got up from his chair and walked over to slam shut his window. He'd finished his smoke for the day and the room was getting cold. His frustration showed in the force of his action. The glass rattled and he cursed as he wondered how things had become so complicated.

~ * ~

Samantha knew Jason had proven himself a tireless laborer in his efforts to find and capture the men. He'd told her he had received word back from Commander Williams at Fort Howard explaining he did not have spare troops to send because of an outbreak of fake Indian raids:

"I am trying to contact one of my scouts on leave. If you have to do any tracking, he is just the man you need. I've sent word to the man's father, my best friend,to request him to have his son get in touch with me as soon as possible. I believe the scout, Nicholas MacNamee, is still in the area attending to some personal business."

When Jason read the part about Nicholas MacNamee, Samantha kept her surprise to herself. In the nick of time, she gulped down the nasty curse she'd almost muttered. Nicholas MacNamee! His image seared her inner vision. He'd told her the truth. He really did work for the army. As a scout, he probably would have known how to help her track down the killers. Why, oh why, didn't she trust him? If she had let him share the water at the pool and joined forces with him like he asked, she'd have ended up at the fort—safe. She'd have been able to talk to the commander and tell him about the atrocities done to her family. Mr. MacNamee would have been assigned to track down the culprits. This would all be over and she could be herself. Samantha chewed at her lip in frustration.

Jason finished reading her the letter. "I'm sorry, Samantha. Don't look so worried. I promise I'll continue looking for those hombres even without help from the fort." She couldn't ask for more.

Samantha saw Jason every day. He always gave her a detailed account about what he did and a full report of what little information he'd gathered about Tyler and his men. No one seemed to know whom they worked for or where they came from. Samantha could not fault any of Jason's tactics or his efforts. He really seemed to be trying, and she knew he had pursued every avenue she'd thought of herself.

She became more comfortable around him and began to look forward to his evening visits. She always received his report first, then they would settle in the parlor in front of the fire with Jack and Sally to just talk. She liked Jason and knew he liked her. A couple of times she had caught a look in his eye that caused her to blush. *Why did this man seem to crawl into her very soul?* she wondered.

It didn't take long for Samantha to realize he was courting her, and she started looking at him in a different light. Sally forever dropped hints about how nice it would be if Samantha would settle down in town and live here always.

She reflected on her feelings about Dennis O'Brien and realized he had never made her heart skip a beat or made her blush the way Jason did. Had she really been in love with Dennis? In retrospect, she supposed not. Was she starting to fall in love with Jason? She didn't know. She enjoyed his company, and she enjoyed the little thrill she received when she caught that special look.

Nevertheless, she continued to compare him with her vivid memory of a tall, dark stranger.

Thirteen

After two weeks of seeing Samantha everyday, Jason decided his patience had ended. He made up his mind to speak to her that night. He wanted to marry her, and he didn't want to wait. They could continue their search for Tyler after they were married. He wanted her with him all the time so he could protect her. If she were married to him, she would no longer be a threat to anyone. Perhaps then, they could all relax.

The way it was now, his heartbeat threatened to rob his breath every time a stranger rode into town. He felt too jumpy to do himself or anyone else any good. After dinner that night, he walked over to the livery stable. He hoped to catch Jack alone, and for once, he timed it just right. The liveryman had just finished making his evening rounds and appeared ready to head back to the house.

"Hey, Jason, come on over to the house with me. I'm finished for the night, and the girls will have some hot coffee brewing to go with that yummy cake Samantha baked today."

"Wait a minute, Jack. Can I ask you a favor?" With a go-ahead nod from Jack, he continued, "Do you think you could take Sally over to the hotel for coffee? I'd like to speak to Samantha in private."

"Jason, you know darn well Sally won't leave you and Samantha alone at the house. She's worse than a mother hen over that girl. I know there's no way she'll leave. She'd be worried to death about Samantha's reputation."

"Sorry, Jack, I didn't think of that. It's just that I've made up my mind to ask her to marry me, and I am determined to do it tonight."

Slapping Jason on the back, Jack boomed out his hearty laugh. "I knew it was coming, but you move fast, man. You've only been courting her for two weeks now."

"It only took me two minutes to know what I wanted, Jack. These two weeks have been killing me. I've tried to go slowly. I just don't want to wait any longer."

"Don't look so down, Jason! I think those feelings of yours just might be reciprocated."

"Do you think so?" Jason could hardly believe his good fortune but he knew from experience that others noticed his feelings before he did. Didn't Laura always know just by watching others how people felt about things? Maybe he did have a chance.

"I'll tell you what, Jason. I'll get Sally to stay in the kitchen with me on some pretext and that will give you some privacy with Samantha. It's the best I can do. Sally won't leave the house."

"Thanks, Jack. I appreciate that. It really means a lot to me. If it weren't so cold, I'd ask Samantha to go for a walk. It's just too bitter now that the sun is down and the wind's picked up."

"Come on, Jason. Let's get this over with now. You're as nervous as a cat in a room full of rockers." As the two men hurried through the blustery winter evening, Jason couldn't tell which of them was more excited.

Jack pulled Jason through the kitchen door and they brought laughter and love into the room. The two women didn't seem to know what to make of all the joviality, which made Jason realize they probably sounded like a couple of schoolboys. He turned his back to hang his hat on a peg and to hide the flush he felt creep up his neck at the sight of Samantha. Sally recovered first.

"Hurry up and close that door, Jack. You've just about let all our warm air out. It's cold enough in here without you trying to heat all the outdoors."

"Hush, woman," Jack teased. "Give me a minute, and I'll warm you up real good."

"Jack! Behave yourself!" Sally slapped his hand away from her backside as she skirted her husband's attempt to cuddle.

Samantha watched their antics with a shy grin on her face. She'd gotten used to Jack and Sally lovingly teasing each other, and she knew, as much as Sally protested Jack's attention, she loved it. Samantha looked over at Jason as he hung his coat on the hook by the door. They smiled shyly at each other, tolerant of the affection they saw in Jack and Sally.

"Fix me a hot toddy, Sally my love," Jack implored. "I have something important I need to talk to you about. I'm sure Jason and Samantha won't mind giving us a little privacy by going into the parlor."

"Jack?"

"It's all right, love. I'm sure they understand. We'll be right here in the kitchen, so it's not as if we're leaving them alone or anything. We'll join them in a few minutes. You don't mind, do you Jason, Samantha?"

"Of course not, Jack. Jason and I will wait in the parlor for you. Would you like a cup of coffee, Jason?" Samantha was sure her presence in the Billings household had limited Jack and Sally's intimacy, and she was anxious not to intrude on them any more than absolutely necessary. It didn't take her more that a couple of minutes to fix a tray with two coffee cups and some cake. She led Jason into the parlor, closing the door to give the Billings all the privacy they needed.

"I'm sorry, Jason. I'm sure Jack and Sally won't be long, but if you want to leave and return later, I'll understand."

"Don't worry, Samantha. I prefer a little privacy with you anyway." Jason watched Samantha's shocked look bring a flush up her neck and flood her whole face with a warm glow. "I think Jack manufactured an excuse to keep Sally in the kitchen just for me, and I'm not sure how long he'll succeed. I won't waste time on preliminaries. I'm too nervous anyway."

Jason saw Samantha eye him closely. All of a sudden, she seemed apprehensive as she sat down clasping her hands tightly into a ball on her lap. With Samantha's stricken face looking at him so imploringly, Jason couldn't procrastinate any longer. "Samantha, I think you know how I feel about you. You've come to mean the world to me in the last few weeks, and I don't think I can live without you in my life. No matter what the outcome of this mess with Tyler, I want to marry you. I want to take care of you for the rest of your life. I love you!"

At Jason's first declaration, Samantha felt her face flame again. She felt so hot; she thought if she touched her cheek, she would burn her hand. Oh, why did she have this horrible inclination to blush every time Jason spoke to her? It seemed to give away her feelings. Her heart pounded painfully, and she wasn't sure if she could speak past the lump in her throat. *Did he say marriage? It couldn't be.* As she sat there trying to comprehend, he kept talking as if he had her consent.

"I'll continue to hunt for Tyler. I want to do that for you. Commander Williams hasn't heard from his scout McNamee yet, but he assures me that once he arrives and gets on their trail, we should have some answers. Christmas is almost here. If it's agreeable with you, I'd like to have our wedding on Christmas Day."

Christmas! Forcing herself to think, she mentally calculated the time. "Jason, that's only ten days away!" Surprise caused her to protest at his impatience.

"That's plenty of time, isn't it, Samantha?"

"I haven't said 'yes' yet, Jason!" Samantha still felt like she floated in a state of shock. Her thoughts and feelings were tumbling so fast she couldn't keep them straight. All she could grasp were fragments. It was too soon! She wasn't sure if she loved Jason let alone if she loved him enough to spend the rest of her life with him! She didn't want to live with black hair forever, either. Where did that thought come from? Oh yes, if she married Jason and lived here, she would have to continue this charade. She didn't have a dowry! She would be bringing almost nothing into this marriage.

Samantha's chaotic thoughts were running away from her. She sat limp, in a daze, only focusing her eyes when Jason approached. He placed a strong hand on each of her arms. She looked down at his large fingers. They engulfed her tiny frame. His thumb almost met his forefinger as they encircled her upper arm. His grip, though firm, wasn't uncomfortable. He gently lifted her out of her chair.

As he bent his head forward, she realized he meant to kiss her. She'd never been kissed by anyone except her family and wasn't sure what to expect. She stood expectantly, curious of what it would feel like, and watched him lower his head. As his lips softly brushed hers, she relaxed. It felt nice. She wasn't frightened. Trusting Jason, she let him embrace her and press a firmer kiss to her pliant lips. Just as he seemed ready to deepen the kiss, the sound of Jack and Sally's voices came through the door.

Jason moved away from Samantha and faced the fireplace, bracing his head on the mantle. Samantha tried to calm her beating heart so that Jack and Sally wouldn't see how red she had turned. Again!

Having explained to Sally why he wanted to give Jason and Samantha a few minutes alone, Jack couldn't wait any longer to know if Jason had popped the question. He watched Jason lift his head from the mantle as they entered the room. With a huge sigh he continued to stare at the fire. Samantha sat stiffly in the rocker, head bowed, hands clasped and chewing her lower lip. Jack looked expectantly at each of them, waiting for someone to break the silence. When no one spoke, he feared the worst—that Samantha had refused Jason's offer.

Trying to cover the awkward stillness in the room, he launched into a story he had heard that day. Sally laid a quiet hand on Jack's arm catching his attention and shook her head.

Again the silence started to build tension. Jason turned from the mantle and faced the room. Inhaling deeply enough to visibly expand his chest, he declared, "I've asked Samantha to marry me. Sally, do you think you can help her arrange a wedding by Christmas?"

With that, everyone started speaking at once. Jack and Sally burst into enthusiastic congratulations, and Samantha protested that she hadn't decided yet.

"I think it's wonderful that you and Jason fell in love so quickly." Jack pumped Jason's hand and grinned at Samantha.

Sally pointed out that they might need a little more than ten days to get ready, but she was sure they could manage a wedding before the end of the year. Sammy became silent. She withdrew into herself as she half listened to all the hubbub. Was this the right thing to do? Were Jack and Sally right? Did she really love Jason, but was too naive to know it? Everyone seemed ecstatic except her. Her emotions were in such turmoil she began to shake. A fine bead of perspiration broke out across the bridge of her nose. She ran a finger around her neck, pulling the lace collar of her dress away. Embarrassment threatened, as she forced the bile in her throat back down into her queasy stomach.

Sally saw Samantha tremble, rushed over, and put her arm around Samantha's shoulders. "Come on, Samantha, let's sit down with a nice cup of coffee and we'll iron out all the details. I know this must seem impossible, but you'll see, we can do it. Here, sit by the fire. You're shivering, girl. Jason, get my shawl from the hook by the door. Samantha's cold."

When Jason left the room, Samantha looked up at Sally imploring her to listen. "Please, Sally, listen to me. This is happening too fast. I don't know if I want to marry Jason or not."

"It's okay, Honey," Sally answered as she fussed over Samantha. "This is the right thing to do. Jason can take care of you and protect you. You'll be able to live here in town, and we can always be friends. I was afraid after Jason caught those crooks you would leave. I'm far too attached to you to have you move on, never to see you again. This way we can stay family. I'll get to enjoy your children! It will be as if Jack and I were their real grandparents. You know you have a soft spot for Jason, what are you afraid of?"

Sally changed the subject so quickly, Samantha guessed she saw her shocked reaction at the mention of babies. Her whole body stiffened as she straightened her spine. She visualized her mother laying in the dirt, blood running down her legs. No, she couldn't think of that now.

"I don't know, Sally." Samantha sat still in a daze as Jason wrapped the shawl around her. Keeping his hands on her shoulders, he began to gently rub her upper arms to warm and comfort her. Samantha turned her head to look up into his eyes. Her heart skipped a beat as she saw the smoldering look of love on his face. He did love her. What was she worried about? It might be the best thing she ever did. She wasn't sure if she loved Jason, but she knew he kindled a spark of something in her.

"If you're sure about this, Jason," she stuttered. "I will marry you!"

With wild hoops of joy from Jack and Sally, Jason picked her up and twirled her around the room. From that point on, the evening progressed from celebration to planning.

Jason insisted on paying for everything himself, but Jack and Sally firmly declared they would give the couple a party after the ceremony.

Samantha mentioned rescuing her mother's wedding dress, and she and Sally thought they could alter it to fit without any problems. "We can ask Rebecca to help," Samantha suggested. "She is a whiz with a needle, and I know she keeps up on all the latest styles because of Laura's girls."

Samantha noticed Sally wrinkle her nose and turn away. "What is it, Sally? Rebecca is my friend."

Taking a deep breath, Sally turned with a smile. "If you want Rebecca to help, I'll accept that. I just never had much to do with her after she started working at Laura's place."

"Please don't hold that against her. She had to support herself. Miss Laura's the only one who could afford to hire her. She's really a very sweet woman."

Sally embraced Samantha. "If she's your friend, she's welcome here."

"Thank you, Sally."

"I'll stop by Laura's when I leave here," Jason volunteered. "I want to check with her anyway to see if she has heard anything new about Tyler. She promised to ask a few discreet questions. If anyone can help us with information, it's Laura."

Jason prepared to leave at about eight o'clock. He had to make his rounds before he stopped at Laura's. Jack and Sally quietly left the couple alone so they could say goodnight. When Jason enfolded Samantha in his arms and lowered his head to kiss her goodbye, she still seemed a little hesitant. Especially when he tentatively tried to push open her lips with his tongue, she withdrew in skittish haste. Jason attributed her reluctance to shyness and the fact that she was so innocent. He gently kissed her forehead and bade her goodnight. The cold night air didn't even chill his warm body.

Leaving his coat unbuttoned, he bounced down the steps and settled his hat on his head, feeling like he was walking on air. All his dreams were coming to pass. For this woman, he would have all the patience in the world. He planned on loving every inch of her gorgeous body, but he would give her time to be comfortable with his lovemaking. Before the next couple of weeks were over, she would become familiar with his touch. Then she wouldn't pull away from him anymore.

Once they were married, he would convince her to relinquish her revenge. He wanted all of her thoughts to be centered on him. He pictured the two of them entwined in a hot embrace. His walk to Laura's became uncomfortable. Maybe he could ease his desire with Laura or one of the girls. No. None of them measured up to Samantha's perfection. But he knew he could be out of there in ten minutes flat tonight.

~ * ~

After Jason visited with Laura, it wasn't long before the whole town knew of the upcoming marriage. Ashley stomped her foot furiously. She blamed herself for not cultivating Samantha and keeping an eye on her. She could attribute it to the cold weather that had kept her close to her own hearth, but she realized she had underestimated the ambition in that young chit. She credited Samantha with being devious enough to fool everyone with her innocent face and kicked herself for dismissing her as no competition. Now, she would be the laughing stock of Charrette Village.

How could this young girl catch the best-looking man in town in less than a month? Ashley had known Jason for years, and he had never been more than gentlemanly and polite with her. She wondered if she could undermine the relationship before the wedding took place. She'd have to think about this. Perhaps it was time for a second visit to Miss Sally's. Yes, she would go tomorrow and invite Samantha to come Christmas shopping with her. It was the perfect way to show off her new emerald green dress and drop a few little doubts into Miss Samantha's head.

~ * ~

Rebecca was thrilled to be asked to help make Samantha's wedding gown. Ever since she had made that first dress for her, the girl had let everyone in town know that she helped her sew a few new dresses. People were beginning to nod and offer her a good afternoon whenever she visited the general store. Rebecca knew her improving reputation was due to Samantha, and she loved the girl for defending her. Miss Laura had been the only person in town to offer Rebecca employment and not just empty platitudes. Rebecca appreciated Laura's assistance, but inwardly felt ashamed of her job.

Her shame was one of the reasons she always wore her hair in such an unbecoming style and dressed as soberly as she could. She never smiled except when Samantha made her laugh because before she married, one of her many suitors told her that her smile transformed her face into a thing of beauty. Maybe he was just telling her lies to flatter her into an indiscretion, but even so, secretly she always believed the compliment. Even her no-good husband told her she was beautiful when she smiled. As a consequence, she made herself into a hag to keep gossips from talking about what her job really entailed at Miss Laura's whorehouse.

She knew those feelings along with folk's prejudices had caused the rift between herself and the women in town. Samantha with her quiet support had helped people recognize Rebecca's need. With that, they came to understand that Laura was the only one who could afford to hire her and perhaps just working for Laura didn't mean that Rebecca condoned what went on in that house.

Since it was unseemly for Samantha to be seen going into Laura's, Rebecca came to her two days later. "I'm so happy for you, Samantha. I can't wait to start on your wedding dress."

"Oh, Becca, thank you. This is happening so fast! I'm a little apprehensive."

"Child, all brides feel that way. Don't you worry, as soon as the wedding is over, you'll know you did the right thing. Now, let's get started. What do you have in mind?" Rebecca rubbed her hands together in joyful anticipation.

"Becca, the only thing I have of my mother's is her wedding dress. Could you look at it? I would love to wear her dress. It would help me feel as if she were with me and perhaps approved." Samantha hung her head. "Every time I think of her it always brings back that last painful time I saw her lifeless eyes staring nowhere. I wish I could remember her as the happy, beautiful woman who raised me with so much love."

Rebecca took hold of Samantha's chin and lifted her face. As she looked into those beautiful hazel eyes, brimming with unshed tears, her heart softened. She engulfed Samantha in a hard, bony hug and tried in her awkward way to cheer her. "You fetch that dress right down here. If you want to wear your mother's wedding dress, that's just what you'll wear. I'm sure it will be beautiful on you. Hurry now," she urged, "let's see how much work we have cut out for us."

When Samantha entered with her mother's dress lovingly draped across her arms, Rebecca gasped. "Why, Samantha, I think what you have there is a real treasure. That is real Irish lace. This dress is beautiful! Look at the beaded bodice, those sleeves, the train." Rebecca stopped in utter stupefaction. "This is delightful. Quick, try it on. Let's see how it fits."

Rebecca's enthusiasm was contagious. Samantha called Sally in, and together the three women began to fit the dress. Samantha's mother had been a tall, stately woman. The dress had to be shortened by about five inches and taken in all over to fit Samantha's petite frame.

"Look, Samantha, I can shorten the dress in the front and leave a short train in the back. I wouldn't change a thing in the style. It's a beautiful dress. Just nipping in the waist and bodice is all the work it needs. We can use the lace I cut from the hem in front to make you a beautiful little hat to wear with the dress. I'll get some tulle from Mr. Frank's and fashion a short veil to come down over your face."

As Rebecca pinned and measured, and Sally fluttered around in admiration, Samantha began to get excited. She still didn't know if she had made the right decision, but the upcoming nuptials might not be anything to fear. After all, she knew Jason loved her. She was also flattered that Jason, the most eligible bachelor in town, wanted to marry her. She smiled to herself as she remembered how sweet his kiss felt and how easily she'd acquiesced to his attentions. Maybe they *would* be happy together.

Rebecca finished the fitting and, as Samantha changed back into her day dress, Rebecca dropped a bolt from out of the blue. "Samantha," she hesitated, "Miss Laura heard a piece of gossip I think you should be aware of. It seems Miss Ashley is quite put out about your upcoming wedding and is determined to foil your relationship with Jason."

"I don't understand," Samantha gasped. "Why would she do that?"

"What you don't understand," Sally explained, "is that Ashley wanted to marry Jason herself. She's jealous and will probably start a few rumors designed to cause you and Jason to argue and break off the engagement."

"Oh, Sally, I didn't set out to make Jason fall in love with me." Samantha wrung her hands in agitation and began to pace.

"Calm down, honey," Rebecca soothed. "What Ashley doesn't understand is you can't make someone fall in love with you. It just happens. Jason would have never married Ashley. He barely likes her, let alone loves her. She thinks everyone shares her own selfish motives and probably believes you set out to steal Jason away from her so you could feel superior."

"My gosh! I think I was the last person to know that Jason loved me. Jack and Sally saw it, so did Laura. They seemed to be sitting back and waiting for Jason to tell me. I never had a thought to 'steal him away' from Ashley. What's she saying, Rebecca?"

"Well, first she said there must be a reason for such a hastily arranged wedding; said she'd be counting the months next summer when a baby happens along."

Samantha couldn't help the gasp that escaped, and poor Sally collapsed into a chair clutching her chest.

"Last night was the first time Samantha and Jason were ever left alone in my parlor," she exclaimed. "There's no way."

"Please, Sally." Samantha took Sally's cold hand. "No one will question you. Or me, for that matter. Everyone knows you well enough to realize you wouldn't leave Jason and I without a chaperon."

"Everyone in town knows Ashley, and no one will believe her stories. So, don't you worry, Samantha." Rebecca patted her hand. She didn't want to upset the girl. "She won't be able to stop your wedding. Well, I have to get back to Miss Laura's. I'll just take this dress with me so I can work on it. We'll have you all fixed up in no time. I'll see you tomorrow."

Rebecca picked up the dress and, after giving Sammy a reassuring hug, started for the door. "Miss Sally, don't you take on so. Everything will be fine." With that, Rebecca let herself out the front door. Samantha caught Sally's eye, and nervously they both burst out laughing at the absurdity of Ashley's accusations.

~ * ~

Mac had spent the last three weeks digging around for the information he needed. He just about had all the evidence he could get without tipping his hand. Morgan seemed to be getting suspicious of him so he decided to lay low. Right now, Mac didn't know who to trust in town. He wasn't sure how many were on Morgan's payroll. He had his doubts about the sheriff, but no evidence. The surveyor seemed suspicious but, there again, no evidence supported his mistrust.

So far, Mac had kept his own counsel and was glad he had. He'd learned that Morgan employed Tyler, Mark, Luke, and Joshua as ranch hands. Tyler was the foreman and seemed to be Morgan's strong arm. Mac had also learned that Morgan's herds had been growing abnormally fast. His ranch, The Free Spirit, supported a mixed herd of Shorthorn cattle. Information had come in about the horses that were broken and sold to the army. It seemed that number had also recently increased.

Mac did a little imaginary drawing of the brands of the Turner and O'Brien families. They'd both used their initials to make the simplest of brands. J.R. had used his two initials sharing the same spine, creating a brand with a vertical line down, an upward curve on the back side for the J, and a rounded curve with a leg on the front for the R.

Peter Turner had used the same idea with the T superimposed over the P and Tim had just used the T. The O'Brien's had used the OB together in the same manner creating the rounded half of the O on the backside and the two rounded humps of the B for the front. *The Free Spirit* ranch used a butterfly as its brand, and all four of the previous brands could be converted into the butterfly design with a minimum of change. It was so simple, it was scary. Mac looked into the brands of the other farmers and found that Morgan's complex design would cover every one of the other brands.

Mac decided the time had come to head over to Charrette Village. He would arrive at least a week before Tyler planned to eliminate Sam Turns. Christmas would also have arrived by the time he reached the village. Not one to be sentimental, Mac thought of the Ruggers and decided if he had to spend Christmas with anyone, he might as well spend it with people he enjoyed. By then, his quest would be fulfilled. He would have found and saved Sammy Turner alias Sam Turns, and he could return to duty at the fort with all the evidence he had on Morgan and his gang for the federal marshall. Then maybe he could sleep in peace again.

Mac knew that Commander Williams did not have the time to pursue civilian criminals, but he thought he could count on the commandant's help if he couldn't enlist the assistance of a marshal out of St Louis.

In his mind, Mac had successfully completed another assignment. Granted this assignment was self-imposed, but again his wits were back on track. What he would do once he exposed Sam Turns as Samantha Turner, he wasn't sure. He felt he owed his friend Tim the favor of taking care of his beloved sister. It was the least he could do for the man that had been his closest friend. At least, he knew he could tell the girl that she didn't have to disguise herself any longer and that her land would be returned to her to sell or do with as she pleased. He wasn't sure if he would return her hair to her or not. He decided sleeping on that sweetly scented bundle was good for his peace of mind, and he just might keep it.

Fourteen

Christmas fell on a Sunday, and since Samantha's dress only needed to be altered and not made from scratch, everything was ready for the wedding on time. Jason and Samantha decided to be married after Christmas services in the late afternoon. Jack and Sally were giving them a party at the hotel after the ceremony. Jack had told everyone that he planned to give Samantha his extra horse as a wedding gift, so Sassy officially became Samantha's again.

Ashley's snide remarks about Jason being stolen from her had gone astray. As with some of her other 'tall stories', they discredited her more than Jason or Samantha.

Samantha felt sorry for Ashley. She'd heard people asking each other why Ashley didn't just go to St. Louis where no one knew her and try her luck there. It seemed everyone wanted her out of town. Her selfishness was so transparent it became a standing joke.

Jack heard through the grapevine that Mr. Frank finally had a good, hard talk with his daughter and her mother about their airs, explaining how it hurt their business. Mr. Frank had told him that once he laid down the law to Ashley, she'd finally realized she better button her mouth. Spoiled as she was, Mr. Frank had decided she'd gone too far and he'd told her so.

Samantha insisted the Franks be included in her wedding invitations. She didn't want to live in town with anyone having hard feelings. She thought, after Ashley calmed down, that while they would never be close friends, they could get along passably well.

~ * ~

Mac arrived in town on Christmas Eve. After settling Renegade at the livery stables, he headed over to the hotel. The "boy" Sam wasn't at the stable. He wondered where he would look for him now.

Whoops of joy from Daniel and a joyous welcome from Mr. and Mrs. Ruggers greeted Mac as he entered the hotel. Doling out a good ration of teasing, they wouldn't let him forget how he'd lost his boots and hat. As soon as he could tactfully distract them, his first inquiry was about Sam Turns. He felt instantly depressed to learn that the boy had run away after the beating Tyler had given him. Mac's only consolation was that Tyler wouldn't find the girl here when he arrived next week.

The Ruggers also informed him about the biggest upcoming event in town. Nothing this exciting had happened in the last couple of years. It seemed the sheriff, who was a very popular man, planned to marry the Billings' niece. The celebration would be held right here in the hotel, and the whole town was invited. The Billings' niece, they explained, was a sweet girl, and everyone liked her.

"Ha," laughed Mrs. Ruggers, "everyone except Miss Ashley Frank. She sure got her nose tweaked when Jason fell in love with Mandy instead of her."

Mac's ears perked up at the pet name. "Mandy? Is that a nickname?" With a nod from Mrs. Ruggers, he sat up straighter in his chair. He remembered Tim's penchant for shortening family names.

"Tell me about this bride. What's her full name? How long has she been around? What does she look like?"

"You're too late, Mac," Mr. Ruggers chuckled. "Her full name is Samantha Peters, and she's already taken."

To the general laughter at his own joke, Mr. Ruggers continued, "She's a sweet young thing. Her hair is coal black, and it makes her skin look as white as milk. She's a beauty all right. Small boned and delicate, she looks as if she'd blow away at the first stiff wind."

Daniel, knowing better, added to the story generally accepted in town. "Mrs. Billings' sister fell ill in November, and Jack and Sally went to take care of her for a week. When they returned, they brought Mandy with them because her mother was so sick her father couldn't look after both of them."

"Is this girl sickly?" Mac asked, at once all concerned. If this was his Samantha, maybe Tyler's beating injured her permanently. His heart raced unusually fast, and he dreaded what he might hear.

"Oh, no," replied Daniel. "She's as healthy as a horse."

Mac slowly expelled the breath he had been unconsciously holding. "Then why didn't she stay to help her dad with the care of her mother?"

Everyone looked at Mac. "No one thought of that. Why indeed, did Miss Peters leave her father as the sole caretaker of a sick mother?" Mr. Ruggers asked.

Daniel, the only one to know the truth, tried to cover his revealing statement. "Apparently, Mr. Peters, that's Mandy's father, had so many expenses with his wife he couldn't afford to support Mandy any longer. Jack and Sally pretty much volunteered to adopt her and to help Mr. Peters financially with some of his wife's medications. Miss Peters didn't want to leave her mother, but her father insisted. She had no choice. She wasn't too happy when she first arrived here, but everyone made her welcome. Then Jason fell in love with her. Everyone said it was love at first sight, and I hear tell he had to do a lot of talking to persuade Mandy to marry him." Daniel took a gulp of air.

Mac sat in silence for a few minutes. Maybe it was a coincidence. His Samantha didn't have black hair, that was for sure. He'd just have to get a good look at this girl before he made up his mind. "Well, when is this happy occasion to take place?" Mac asked.

"Why, it's tomorrow," Mrs. Ruggers exclaimed. "Jason wanted a Christmas wedding, and since the preacher will be here for Christmas services, it works out just right."

Tomorrow! God! Mac thought. *How can I get a look at this girl before the ceremony?* Brides were usually kept under close wraps right before a wedding. He couldn't be this close and lose. Wait! What was he losing? This might not be the girl anyway. Even if it were, she was never his to lose. How could her marriage make any difference to him? He didn't even know her.

For all he knew, the girl in the waterfall was only an illusion. Just because he built up some romantic dream about her in his mind didn't mean she would have lived up to that dream. He just needed answers to the questions that tormented him. His mystery woman, Samantha Turner, had dominated his conscious and unconscious mind since that day in August. It seemed like a lifetime ago now. He had to put this to rest.

Four months was too long to be obsessed by one woman. He had to stop thinking about her as *his mystery woman.* She wasn't his, and if this were the same girl, she never would be.

Daniel was speaking to him, and Mac had to shake himself out of his daydreams. "I'm sorry, Daniel. What were you saying?"

"I said, since you are staying at the hotel, I'm sure Jason and Mandy won't mind if you come to their party. I know you'll like them. They are my favorite people."

"Well, I don't know, Daniel. It wouldn't be right, me a stranger going to their wedding."

"I'm going over to see Mandy later. I told her I'd run any last-minute errands for her. I'll just ask her if it's okay."

"Don't bother, Daniel. I'll probably be leaving town after church services tomorrow anyway."

"Why so soon?" Mr. and Mrs. Ruggers asked in unison.

"Well, to tell you the truth, I'm still looking for my friend's son. I think he might have been that Sam Turns that was here this fall. I got word that those men that beat him up are looking for him to finish the job. I need to find the boy to warn him. If Tyler and his gang find him first, he's a goner."

Mac noticed Daniel's pallor, his flimsy excuses, and hasty departure. Something strange appeared to be going on, and he decided to follow the boy. He bid the Ruggers goodnight and quickly left the hotel.

Mac heard rather than saw Daniel as he ran down the boardwalk towards the jailhouse. Knowing the dirt would muffle his footsteps, he quickly stepped into the street and trailed the boy. He reached the jail minutes after Daniel, but it wasn't easy to eavesdrop.

The door was shut tight against the cold December wind, and there were no windows on the side or back that he could use to peek into the office. He only caught snatches of words and sentences. "Tyler coming...wants to kill Sam Turns...set a trap...catch him." Jason demanding "How?...find out? Who? Let's go...need to talk"

They both burst out of the door as Mac jumped back into the shadows on the side of the building. "Hurry, Daniel," Jason urged. "This is the break we have been waiting for. McNamee must have received the telegram Commander William's sent."

Mac scratched his head, confused. He ran around the back of the building and sprinted all the way back to the hotel. Finding a drainpipe on the corner, he climbed to the second floor and luckily found the window in the hall partly open. Quickly, he climbed over the sill.

He had barely made it to his room when he heard Jason and Daniel thundering up the steps. Mac unbuckled his gun belt and slipped out of his boots. A thundering knock rattled the door. He rumpled the bed covers and tousled his hair before he opened the door. Daniel stood clutching his side as he gasped for breath. The sheriff skidded to a halt, careening into Daniel.

"Why didn't you wait for me?" he bellowed.

Mac hid a grin. The sheriff was obviously put out that the young boy had outrun him. "Daniel, Sheriff, come on in, what's the problem?"

"Mac, you know Sheriff Sudholt. He wants to know if he can speak to you a minute about Tyler and his gang."

"Of course, Daniel. Sheriff, good to see you again. Did you find the bodies at the O'Brien farm like I told you?" Mac extended his hand in greeting as he welcomed the two into his room.

"Oh, yes. It was just like you said. We found them in the cellar, and we buried them. I'm glad you let me know about it as soon as you did. If they'd have been down there any longer, I'm sure some animals would have found them." The man seemed to shudder at the remembered scene.

Mac tried to size up the sheriff as he related the story. He judged him to be a gentle man, perhaps not cut out for the tough job he held. He wondered if he held the position because of the goodwill of the townsfolk or if he did indeed have the ability to deal with the likes of Tyler. Hiding his doubts and masking his curiosity, he motioned for them to be seated. "Now, what can I do for you?"

"McNamee, I am hoping you are here in answer to the telegram Commander William's sent to you," Jason began.

"I'm afraid I don't know what telegram you are talking about, Sheriff."

Jason took an instant liking to this man who Danie said had seemed to have information about the illusive Tyler. He looked at the tall, good-looking stranger and realized he had the advantage of knowing this man came highly recommended by Commander Williams.

On the heels of that thought, Sammy came unbidden into his mind, and he was glad he had her promise of marriage. Still unsure of how strong her feelings for him really were, he didn't know how she would react to this tall, dark stranger who could give her way more information about Tyler than he ever hoped to know.

Well, they'd be married by this time tomorrow. Once she was his, it wouldn't matter how much information this man had. Sammy's loyalty would be his. She wouldn't violate her marriage vows. Having appeased himself on that score, Jason began.

"Let me explain. We had some trouble back in November. A mean son of a—sorry, Daniel, anyway this brute came to town and beat one of our local boys pretty bad. We have been trying to locate him ever since. I've appealed to Commander William's for help, but he didn't have any extra troops to send us. He did offer to enlist the aid of one of his top scouts, a Nicholas McNamee. I remembered your name from last September, and when Daniel said you were back, I assumed you were in town to lend assistance or bring us some information."

"I never received Commander William's telegram," Mac replied. "I've been away on personal business, and I didn't leave word where he could reach me. He probably contacted my father, who is a good friend of his. However, my father isn't aware of my whereabouts either."

"Then you haven't been sent to help us!" Jason's knew his voice betrayed his dejection. He hadn't been able to mask his disappointment.

"I haven't been specifically sent to help you, but perhaps I can be of some service. I need to ask you a few questions and I would appreciate some honest answers. I have information about Tyler Snodgrass that will most likely help you."

"Fire away, you already know more than we do. We were never able to even learn Tyler's last name." Jason became excited about the prospect of new information. What a wedding gift for Samantha! She would be so grateful that Jason was getting somewhere.

"First thing I need to know is about this beating that Sam Turns took. How badly was he hurt?"

"Actually not bad, Doc and Miss Laura patched him up. He only had a few bruises. The whip didn't break any skin, so there were no stitches required. He had a bit of a black eye, but by the second night when he ran away, he seemed to be okay." Jason answered easily and almost by rote. He was so used to thinking of Sam and Sammy as two different people that his response was instant.

He noticed Mac freeze. "What's the problem, MacNamee?"

"That thug slugged a kid? Gave him a black eye? I'll kill him!" The venomous tone of Mac's voice sent shivers down Jason's back. He looked at Daniel and saw him staring wide-eyed at the man. There was a hard side to this scout. Jason mentally thanked God he was on the right side of the law.

"We tried to locate Tyler," Jason continued, "who he worked for, where he lived, but no one seemed to know. I sent word to the fort for help and to the federal marshall in St. Louis. So far, I haven't heard anything. I was really pinning my hopes on you."

"Sheriff Sudholt, I need to ask you a rather strange question." Mac hesitated a moment. "Is there any way Sam Turns could have been a girl in disguise?"

Daniel's cough momentarily distracted Mac. The boy sounded as if he were choking to death. Jason used the distraction to recover, as he poured a glass of water, from the pitcher on the dresser and gave it to Daniel.

"Sorry, Mac, Jason. I must be catching a cold." Daniel recovered enough to hide his emotions, and Jason breathed a sigh of relief.

"There's no way Sam Turns was a girl," Jason answered with confidence. *Lord, what a close call. How much does this man know?* Jason was unsure of him now. Could he really trust him? Why did everything have to be so complicated?

"No way," piped up Daniel. "He taught me how to handle a gun and how to shoot. No girl could know as much about guns as he did."

"Maybe you're right, Daniel. It's just that with all these people named Sam or Samantha, it's really confusing. We must be talking about different people." Looking at Jason, he smiled. "I'd still like to meet your betrothed."

"I'd be pleased to introduce you." Jason's response came quite naturally. He felt proud of his woman and wouldn't be worried about introducing her to anyone.

"Great! By the way, call me Mac. Everyone does." Jason took the man's hand and smiled, his instinct reassuring him Mac was a man to be trusted.

“Well, here’s what I know about your Tyler Snodgrass.” Mac proceeded to relate all the information he had discovered about Tyler, where he worked and lived, who he worked for, and what Mac had overheard. Tyler was headed this way, to Charrette Village, to kill the boy Sam Turns because Morgan thought it might be Samantha Turner in disguise. He wanted her dead, and Mac outlined what he thought his motives were.

It took them another hour before they satisfied each other with their respective information. Jason beamed in happiness. The information Mac had provided would win Samantha’s gratitude. As a gesture of goodwill, he invited the scout to his wedding. “It will be your chance to meet my lady.” Confident that Samantha’s disguise as Mandy Peters was solid, he didn’t hesitate to include Mac in the celebration. After all, he reasoned, this scout had never seen Samantha Turner or Sam Turns, so he would have no reason to think she was anything other than Sally’s niece.

By the time Daniel and Jason left Mac’s room, the men were comfortable with their first-name basis. Mac slipped on his boots and grabbed his coat to head over to Laura’s place. He had a few questions for Miss Laura. After all, if she were the one to help Doc nurse the child, she would know if he were a boy or a girl. Somehow, Mac figured Sam Turns had everyone in town fooled. He just wasn’t so sure about the gun part. Would a young girl know that much about guns, much less how to shoot one with any accuracy? Tim used to brag about how well the whole family could handle a gun, but Mad’d always taken Samantha’s skill with a grain of salt. Hell, the real Samantha Turner could be in the further Western Territories looking for her uncle. He was probably chasing a wild goose.

The same ugly stick of a woman answered Laura’s door. She stepped back to allow him entry and without a word closed the front door. Indicating he should go into the parlor, she disappeared toward the back of the house. What a strange creature. You would think Laura would have a beauty to answer the door. Well, the woman certainly didn't deter business. It seemed that all of the girls were occupied and the parlor was empty except for Doc. Mac found him sprawled in a wingback chair with a bottle on the side table and a glass in his hand. "Where is everyone?" Mac asked.

Doc looked up and squinted to focus. He didn't seem to recognize Mac, but he must have realized he meant no harm.

"They're all upstairs. Busy tonight, my boy. You're too late if you want a woman. Now, if it's only a drink you're needing, you're in luck. I still have half a bottle. Grab a glass and pull up a chair."

"Thanks, I think I will." Mac exchanged small talk with Doc until he felt the doctor was mellow enough to answer some questions. "Do you remember treating that young boy Sam Turns a month or so ago?"

"Sure do! Those thugs beat that poor boy to a pulp. He didn't need stitches. No cuts or anything that bad, but his body was one huge black and blue bruise. The poor kid couldn't move for two days, then he upped and ran away. Told Miss Laura he wasn't sticking around for another beating. Said he was heading west. I felt sorry for the kid." Doc refilled his glass and held out the bottle to Mac.

"The only thing he had going for him was he knew horses. Never saw anyone have a way with horses like that kid did. He was even better than Jack. It was a sight to see."

Mac's skin bristled at the mention of the beating the kid took, but before he could pose any other questions, Doc dropped his head and began snoring away. Mac sat a minute in thought. If Doc patched him up, he would have known if Sam Turns were a girl. He never faltered in his gender at all. Could it be that this kid really wasn't the girl he was looking for? Just when he thought he was at the end of the trail, here he was, foiled again. Well, he'd talk to Miss Laura next and go from there.

After about fifteen minutes, the stick lady came into the parlor.

"I'm sorry, sir, Miss Laura sent word down that she will be engaged for the rest of the night. All the other ladies have an overnight guest, so I'm to put Doc to bed in the downstairs bedroom and close up for the night." Rebecca seemed anxious to get rid of him. She probably wanted to retire for the night herself.

Mac sighed. Oh well, tomorrow was another day. He'd stay for the wedding and get a good look at this Mandy Peters, and after the ceremony, he'd come back and talk to Laura. Maybe he'd have a better feel for the situation by that time. Sitting in a daze, he watched Rebecca try to handle the doctor. Suddenly aware, he realized she would never be able to manage Doc by herself.

Mac surged to his feet and effortlessly hoisted the doctor over his shoulder. "Here, let me help you. He's dead weight, and you'll never be able to get him into bed by yourself." Turning to give the startled woman a smile, he asked, "Where would you like me to put him, Miss Rebecca?"

"Why, thank you. Mr. MacNamee, isn't it?" After he acknowledged his name, she continued, "There's a bedroom downstairs he can use, right this way. It's just across the hall."

The man's offer to help astonished Rebecca. No one ever gave her a second thought. He'd picked up Doc as if he weighed nothing and inclined his head for Rebecca to lead the way. She scurried ahead and opened the door for him.

"Don't bother with the lamp. I can see by the light from the doorway. You just turn down the covers. It'll be cold tonight, and he'll need them." This man's concern for a stranger further impressed Rebecca. *What a gentleman!* she thought.

"I appreciate your help, sir. Usually I can get to Doc before he passes out cold. I'm glad he won't have to sleep in an uncomfortable chair tonight." He nodded an acceptance to her thanks, then bent to remove the Doc's suit coat.

"Let me take his coat," she whispered. "I noticed a button came off. I can fix it tonight so he'll look nice for the wedding tomorrow." Taking the coat from Mac, she gently covered the doctor. Then, she tiptoed out of the room and showed him to the door.

She'd anticipated Samantha's wedding with so much joy that she couldn't wait for the morrow. Never had she felt so excited or happy for another person. *Just once*, she thought, *I'll share my happiness with someone who looks lonely tonight.* Beaming with all the jubilance she felt, she smiled at Mac. "Merry Christmas, sir. God's speed."

Her soft, gentle voice surprised Mac, but not as much as the change in her features when her smile lit her face. Maybe she wasn't as hard as she looked. It seems as if he was being fooled by looks all the time lately. Just think, he used to have the intuition of a bird dog. He bid Rebecca goodnight and Merry Christmas and headed back to his hotel room. Tomorrow he'd have a few more answers. Whether they would be the ones he anticipated or not, he didn't know.

Fifteen

Christmas Day dawned crisp and bright, one of those bright, sunny days that fooled you into thinking it was warmer than it was. The sun rose in a spectacle of beautiful rainbow colors. The bright blue sky lacked even a single cloud to mar its brilliance.

The Billings household teemed in a beehive of excitement. Earlier, Sally had prepared her traditional Christmas breakfast, even though Samantha had protested. "Sally, there'll be enough food for the rest of the day to warrant skipping breakfast."

"I won't hear of skipping a meal, Samantha. It's only seven o'clock. You have a long way to go before we eat lunch." Reluctantly, Sammy sat down to a table groaning with all of Sally's specialties.

"Sally, you've outdone yourself," Sammy exclaimed. "The Christmas stolen is beautiful." Sally's specialty graced the center of the table, and platters of ham, eggs, biscuits, and hotcakes surrounded the masterpiece. Crockery of fresh butter and newly boiled maple syrup combined to send a tantalizing aroma throughout the kitchen. "Who's going to eat all this food?" Sammy groaned in mock horror.

"Don't you worry your pretty little head over these victuals, Samantha. I plan on eating whatever you girls leave on the table." With that, Jack pulled up his chair and rubbed his hands together in anticipation. "Let's say grace so we can get started."

Everyone laughed, and Sammy tried to do justice to all the effort Sally had made. While they ate, they discussed last-minute plans. "Your wedding is set for four o'clock, Samantha, so I think we should start getting ready by at least one o'clock. We'll get you a nice bath and wash your hair. Too bad we'll have to take the time to color it again."

"I know, Sally. I hate that awful stuff. It rubs off on the pillowcases, and if I'm not careful, it gets on my dress collar. I'm always afraid people will see it and think I'm dirty." Taking a sip from her coffee cup, Samantha looked at Sally in horror. "Laura warned me that if I get overheated in the summer time, it may cause black sweat to run down my temples. Ugh, can you imagine!? I hope by this summer we will have Tyler hung, and I can be myself."

Just talking about her disguise reminded her about the delay in any progress and she grew irritated. "I can't stand all the lies and subterfuge. When will I ever get to be Samantha Turner again?"

"Well, Honey, after today you won't ever be Samantha Turner again. You'll be Samantha Sudholt." Sally's laughter brought a smile to Samantha's face. Then she turned serious.

"I haven't had an answer from my letter to the new governor, asking him to send a federal marshall. I wonder how long it will take to hear from him."

"You know how unreliable the mail is. It could take weeks. Don't you fret." Sally patted Samantha's hand and put another hotcake on her plate. "Eat up child. You'll need your strength later."

"Sally, stop it! How can you tease about something so serious?"

"Sorry, Honey. I'm just trying to get your mind on today's events, not what might happen tomorrow."

"I know, and you're a sweetheart, but don't forget how important this is to me." Samantha absentmindedly cut into the tender hotcake. "Remember, I told you I did receive a reply from Commander William's. The letter explained how he notified one of his scouts about my request. He said he asked him to help us track and locate this outlaw. I'm not sure how much one man could do, but I'm grateful for any help."

Sally tried to quell her disappointment that Samantha's main thoughts were still about Tyler and not on her own wedding. She began to have second thoughts. *Did they rush Samantha into this wedding business?* She certainly didn't act like an eager bride. It didn't seem to matter to her if this wedding took place. The only thing that dominated her emotions right now seemed to be the apprehension of Tyler and his gang.

As she rose to clear the table, Sally prayed her thoughts would prove to be wrong. Samantha's nerves had to be the cause of her apathy. "Let's exchange our presents now," Sally decided. "The rest of the day will be too busy, and I want Samantha to wear what we got her."

Hoping that opening their gifts would get Samantha's mind off the killers, Sally ushered everyone into the parlor. The room looked festive with the cedar tree by the window and all the red satin bows hanging from the ends of the branches. Three big boxes rested under the tree covered in brightly colored paper cut outs. Handing Samantha her package first, Sally held her breath. She couldn't wait to see her face when she opened it.

Samantha eagerly opened the package and moving the tissue aside, uncovered the delicate undergarments. Sally watched the inevitable red flush creep up her cheeks as her fingers gently moved over the beautiful handwork. "I've never seen anything so lovely." Her quiet whisper told Sally how much she liked the present.

Sally'd paid Rebecca to make Sammy a beautiful white chemise and matching petticoat to wear under her wedding dress. The chemise was decorated with white ribbons and tiny white satin rosebuds. The petticoat had four rows of ruffles edged in matching ribbons and flowers. The garments were elegant and yet serviceable enough to wear under everyday clothing. Besides that, she'd added a split riding skirt. The girl chafed at the bit to ride that horse of hers, and she couldn't do so until after the wedding. At least now, she'd be properly dressed when she could ride.

"Oh, Sally! Jack! Thank you, thank you, thank you! Now I'll be able to ride Sassy. I was so worried about how I would do that."

Once hugs were exchanged, Sally and Jack opened the presents Samantha had made for them. Jack's box held a new vest. The black-and-white-checked material would set off his black Sunday go-to-meeting suit. He admired her stitches and donned the garment immediately. Then Sally opened her box.

"Oh, Sammy! How lovely. This must have taken you hours to finish."

She held the white bib apron to her chest. The edges, from the skirt all the way around to the top of the bib and both shoulder straps, were outlined with tiny red apples among bright green leaves. "I wish I could wear this to church," Sally declared. "At least you two can show off your presents today."

"I don't think I'll be showing anyone my petticoats at church, Sally," Samantha quipped. They all laughed. Then, Samantha went upstairs to put her gifts away.

"I hope we did the right thing to encourage this wedding, Jack."

"Ah, love, don't you worry your head over that. Jason loves the girl, and everything will work out all right." Jack gave Sally a tight hug and a long kiss. "Let's get ready for church."

Sally had told Jason it was supposedly bad luck for the groom to see the bride before the nuptials, and she didn't want to give Samantha any reason to delay the wedding. So by prearrangement, Jason had agreed to avoid talking to Samantha before the ceremony.

When the Billings family arrived at church, Sally saw Jason standing with the Ruggers and a tall dark stranger. She noticed Jason had honored her wishes and waited until they ushered Samantha into church before he slipped into the back and stood close to the door.

Samantha had hurried into the church, but her eagerness seemed to be only to escape the bitter cold. Sally wondered how she really felt. She seemed so distracted lately; it amazed Sally that she even completed her own toilette this morning.

As the morning had journeyed towards the ten o'clock Christmas service, the cold air that penetrated anyone brave enough to venture outside seemed to intensify. Samantha couldn't believe how cold she felt. Granted the wind blew sharp today, and although the sunshine blinded her, she'd felt little warmth radiate from the brilliant sky. Thoughts of a long soak in a hot tub dominated her mind. She'd heat the water extra long and not add much cold water so she could stay in longer. How she longed for her own home where she could bathe as often as she pleased for as long as she pleased. That was one thing she really looked forward to more than anything.

Jason had shown her the rooms above the jail, and she and Sally lamented that they would never be able to cheer them up properly. The walls were papered with a dark, paisley pattern that jarred the senses. The two rooms only boasted one window in the front and one window at the back. The building faced north so little light penetrated the dismal chamber.

Shabby and scarred from water stains and scratches, the furniture appeared dark and meager. Deep burn marks scarred one of the side tables in the sitting room, most likely from a careless smoker. The two chairs that sat under what served as a dining table were missing slats in the back. One looked worse than the other.

The front room contained the sitting room and dining area combined. It accommodated a settee, a single-caned chair with the burned table next to it, and a small dining table with the two offending chairs. The back room served as the bedroom. There was a washstand with a chipped bowl and pitcher for bathing, a large wardrobe, and a rather small bed.

Samantha and Sally found a bedpan under the bed for nighttime use. She would have to go down the steps and out back to use the outhouse. Each room had a small fireplace, and Samantha wondered if enough heat escaped to warm those barren rooms. There were no rugs, pictures on the walls, or any other decorations to make the place look more like a home. Samantha wasn't sure she would like living there.

However, she wasn't one to complain so she'd never say a word to Jason. Shivering in the cold church, she hoped Jason had a fire roaring today. She couldn't imagine what the next twenty-four hours had in store for her, and she quaked again in anticipation.

~ * ~

Mac entered the church with Mr. and Mrs. Ruggers and Daniel. He nodded to Sheriff Sudholt and took a seat in the last pew. At Daniel's inquiring look, Mac indicated they were to go ahead up front. He always liked to stay near a door, and he wanted to avoid being noticed anyway. The room emanated the scent of pine. Every window sported a crown of greenery, decorated with a red bow. A huge cedar tree stood in the corner behind the pulpit. Popcorn and cranberries were strung together to make a red and white garland that encircled it. A few red and green paper rings hung from the branches. Someone had attempted to imitate icicles with white paper streamers attached to the tips of each bough, and the top supported a beautiful angel.

Seeing the heavenly spirit, Mac remembered his mortal angel in the falls. He looked around trying to locate Mandy Peters. He spotted Jack Billings from the livery stable and the gray-haired woman next to him. That had to be his wife.

Craning his neck to see around the people in front of him, he finally spotted the short girl next to Jack's wife. Well, no one lied about her hair. It was coal black. Her bonnet hid most of it, but from here she didn't look anything like the girl he thought she might be. Damn! Now what!? Well, he'd stay for the wedding and tomorrow he would head farther west. At least he didn't have to worry about Tyler killing the boy Sam Turns. He had disappeared.

Mac didn't catch too much of the church service. His thoughts were jumping ahead to how he would locate the girl. Sam Turns had to be the girl from the waterfall. Daniel had said Sam's hair was a reddish brown. Morgan was probably right about that much—Samantha Turner and Sam Turns were one and the same. The uneasiness Mac felt when he found out Jason planned to marry this girl, Mandy, started to dissipate.

Mac felt lighthearted again and with that burden lifted, realized how uptight he had been about this wedding. Why should it bother him if Jason married Samantha Turner? It shouldn't. After all, he didn't know the girl. There was no reason he should feel so territorial about her. And, if she was Tim's sister, the burden of taking care of her would be Jason's, not his. At least now, he could enjoy the wedding festivities.

Catching sight of the housekeeper from Miss Laura's, he smiled at her with all his joy. What a contradiction. The woman was all starch, piss, and vinegar, but when she smiled—wow! The man she favored with that face would be luckier than most. If he remembered right, Miss Laura called her Rebecca.

There was Doc, seated next to the housekeeper. She seemed to be taking care that he followed the service. She caught Mac's smile and returned the salute. Mac's smile turned to a grin as he watched Doc do a double take. Rebecca's face lit up the room with joy. *Well, now,* he thought, *maybe those two would be good for each other. Doc could stop drinking, and Rebecca could start smiling.*

All of a sudden he felt the Christmas spirit and joined in the ending Christmas carols with his strong baritone voice, drawing admiring glances from those seated around him.

Jason couldn't help looking at Samantha. She was so beautiful in her green dress! He had bought a lovely shawl in soft, white wool to keep her warm. When he'd sent it over this morning, he'd included a note that said he hoped she liked it enough to wear it with her wedding dress. It pleased him enormously that she wore it to church this morning.

His quarters above the jail left a lot to be desired. She would need the shawl inside most of the time. He'd hardly taken notice of the drafts until he looked at the rooms with Samantha in mind. They were fine for a bachelor, but he wasn't sure if they were worthy of her.

Perhaps he could use some of his savings and build them a small home on the outskirts of town. That way he would be close enough to still be effective, and Samantha would be isolated from the coarseness of the jail.

His thoughts were on their future and not on the service as he daydreamed about their life together. Before he knew it, the service ended and the hustle and bustle of people taking their departure roused him.

Mac and Jason were the first outside after the services and Jason excused himself hurriedly. "Sorry I can't stay to introduce you to Mandy, Mac. I promised Sally I wouldn't talk to her or look at her until the ceremony—these women and their fool superstitions. Don't tell Sally, but I couldn't keep my eyes off Mandy's back through the whole service. I don't know how I'm going to keep away from her until this afternoon."

Satisfied that the black-headed wench in church wasn't *his Samantha*, Mac laughed and clapped Jason on the back. "Come on, I'll walk you over to the saloon for a healthy shot. That will calm you down."

Samantha watched Jason's retreating back as he and another man walked companionably down the street. They were half way to the saloon by the time Samantha and her party finally made it to the front door of the church. From the back, she couldn't tell who accompanied Jason, and she couldn't recall anyone in town that tall.

His clothes sparked a memory. Buckskin. He towered over Jason by a good six inches. Could it possibly be the scout, Nicholas MacNamee? They were just too far away for her to get a good look. But no, it couldn't be. She's the one who'd sent the letter asking for assistance. If it were the scout, he'd have come looking for her. She wasn't hard to find. Dismissing the idea, she turned to accept another proffered handshake.

So many well wishers delayed them that it seemed to take them forever to make their escape. "Hurry, Samantha, it's after noon already, and we still have all that water to heat. As cold as it is, it will take us forever." Sally took hold of Samantha's arm and pulled her away from the last of the gossips. Waving a cheery goodbye, she hurried her home.

~ * ~

Jason only had one drink with Mac, then headed back to his rooms above the jail. He wanted to make sure everything was perfect for Samantha. He carried up extra logs and laid a fire in the bedroom as well as the parlor. He wanted the place to be warm and cozy. Mrs. Ruggers had promised to prepare a late evening meal for the two of them to share after the party. He had an idea that Samantha would be too nervous to eat much during the celebration. He placed a bottle of wine on the windowsill to chill and set the table for two. Everything looked perfect.

Sally had sent over some curtains that he'd hung and that alone had softened the rooms. He knew he would want more for Samantha before too long, but for now this would have to do.

He could hardly believe his good fortune. He felt light enough to fly. He'd never been so happy. Just the anticipation of holding Samantha in his arms caused his heart to race. The smoothness of her skin awed him. He longed to touch the hidden places on her body. The nuptials were just a formality—what he ached for would come later.

Jason looked at the bed one more time. The cover lay stiff as a board over the hard mattress. He walked over to plump up the pillow. Why did everything look so shabby to him? Never before had he noticed the lack of curtains or whether the spread had a wrinkle. Today he wished for a castle.

His one and only suit was newly pressed and his white shirt starched to perfection. He had a bolo tie with a turquoise clasp that matched the color of his eyes.

Jason opened his dresser drawer and took out a small box containing a gold ring. The band seemed plain and narrow. He hoped Samantha would appreciate the sacrifices he'd made to purchase it. Mr. Frank had rushed the order for him so he'd have it in time. He'd regretted having to withdraw money from the bank to buy it. He hated to dip into his savings. It meant they might have to call this dingy room home a lot longer then he had planned.

Glancing at his pocket watch, Jason noted the time and hurried to get dressed. Shrugging into his suit jacket, he put the ring box into his breast pocket. He took a last glance around the room and finding everything to his satisfaction, bound down the stairs. He would be bringing his bride here tonight, and his heart thundered at the prospect of returning a married man. Samantha stirred his blood as no other woman ever had.

Jason entered the jail and hung his gun and holster on the peg next to the door. He wouldn't need it at church. Locking the jail, he left and headed over to the hotel. He wanted to check with Mrs. Ruggers one last time to make sure that everything was ready.

~ * ~

Christmas holidays weren't any different for Tyler than any other days. He and the boys were up early as usual and, after a hearty breakfast at the bunkhouse, decided they did not want to wait any longer to find Samantha Turner. "We've got the next couple of days off because of Christmas, we might as well not waste any more time." Slapping Mark hard enough on the back to knock him forward in his chair, Tyler laughed. "Let's go. If we ride hard, we can get to Charrette Village in less than two days."

"We might be lucky enough to find the kid alone at the stable and, being Christmas with no one around to hear us, we can grab her and get out of town," Luke volunteered as the men gathered their gear.

"Sam Turns and the girl, Samantha, have to be one and the same. It explains why the kid passed out so fast after a couple of cracks from my whip," Tyler reasoned.

"We'll go to the stable first. If she isn't there, Joshua, I want you to go to the saloon and ask some questions. You're the least known of the four of us, and being youngest, you still look as innocent as a newborn lamb." Booming a hearty laugh at his own joke, Tyler led the men into the cold, crisp day. "Mount up. Let's go, we'll have something to celebrate when we get back."

Although the sun shown brightly, a steady wind blowing from the north made the air bitter enough to penetrate hands and feet. Tyler grew surlier by the mile. He'd always hated winter. Cold and grumpy, they reached Charrette Village about four o'clock in the afternoon on Christmas Day. The town seemed quiet. Not many people were on the street, and after a quick search of the livery stable, they realized this wasn't going to be as easy as they'd thought.

"It's too dang cold to stand around twiddling our thumbs. Let's go over to the saloon to warm up a little." Tyler led the procession down the street at a slow walk. He sent Joshua in first, then the rest of them sauntered in and migrated to a corner table.

The room reeked of stale smoke and sour beer. Mark grumbled about the odor, and Tyler took offense. "Just sit down and shut up, Mark. You ought to be used to places like this by now."

Joshua stood at the bar and after ordering a drink, casually began to talk to the bartender. "Last time I was in town was about three or four weeks ago. You all had some trouble back then with someone beating up the young boy at the livery stable. How is the kid? I hope he wasn't hurt too bad."

The bartender didn't look inclined to be drawn into a conversation. He seemed a taciturn man with a sour disposition. "Can't say. I never saw the kid!"

"Well," Joshua asked, "didn't you ever hear any talk about his condition?"

"Might've, might not!"

Joshua ordered a second drink and laid a gold piece on the bar indicating the bartender could keep it for an answer or two.

Before he answered, the bartender eyed the money and seemed to be sizing up the young cowboy while he continued to dry glasses. Finally he replied. "All I know is the kid got scared and up and ran away after Doc patched him up. Said he wasn't staying to be beat again for something he didn't know nothin' about." The bartender picked up the gold piece, flipped it in the air, caught it, and tucked it into his vest pocket. With that, he nodded to the cowboy, turned and walked to the other end of the bar, indicating that was all the information he planned on giving out.

Joshua finished his drink, gave Tyler and the boys an exaggerated nod, then walked out of the saloon. He ambled along slowly waiting for the others to catch up to him and told them the news.

"Looks like we wasted our time. We should have come back right away. The kid took off as soon as Doc patched him up, and no one has seen him since."

"Damn!" Tyler exploded. "Now what do we do? The boss won't want us to come back without her. We've got to find out if anyone knows more than that. The town seems deserted today. I wonder where everyone is."

"Don't forget," said Luke, "it's Christmas. Everyone is probably home with their families. Why don't we go over to the hotel and get something hot to eat? Then we can decide what to do. We can always spend the night with the girls at the saloon and head out in the morning."

"Good old Luke, always thinking of his two most important body parts." Mark teased and laughed as the four walked down to the hotel.

"It sounds like a good idea to me," Tyler grumbled. "It's too cold and too late in the day to head back, anyway."

"Besides," Mark continued, "maybe one of the girls knows more than that sourpuss behind the bar. They usually know everything that's going on in town."

Tyler clapped Mark on the back as he laughed. "You know, Mark, sometimes you ain't as dumb as you look."

As the four entered the hotel dining room, they realized something special was happening. Tables were set throughout the dining room, barely leaving space to maneuver. Across the lobby, the parlor, cleared of all furniture, looked like a dance hall. A fiddle and banjo waited idly on a chair in a corner. The room looked bare without rugs, but quite festive. Paper streamers hung from the ceiling and someone had strung a paper bell from the chandelier. Brightly colored paper flowers clustered wherever the streamers met, creating brilliant splashes of color in the drab room.

In the dining room a young girl of about twelve stacked heaping plates of food on a trestle table. The aroma of fried chicken penetrated the air along with the appetizing smells of turkey and beef. The added bouquet of fresh baked pie was enough to start their stomachs rumbling.

"Hey, Missy." Tyler's voice boomed loud enough to echo in the vacant parlor. The girl jumped and almost dropped a pie. "Do you think we could get something to eat before the party starts?" The child scampered over and skidded to a halt in front of them.

"Did you come for the wedding party?"

"Don't know what you're talking about, kid. Just serve us up some vittles, and we'll be outa here."

"I'm sorry. Th… the dining room is closed today. The sheriff is getting ma... married, and everybody will be coming over here a...after the ceremony for the cel...celebration." The girl gripped her apron in both fists as she tried to speak without stuttering. "Th...the service started at fo...four o'clock, and they should be getting out about fi...five."

"You mean we can't get anything to eat?" Tyler's roaring voice scared the poor girl so bad she started shaking.

"May... maybe I can fix you each a plate, and you ca... can take it over to the saloon to e... eat," she suggested. "I do... don't know what else to do. Th... the wedding party will be here in less than a ha... half hour." She visibly trembled in her boots, and Tyler let his temper flare.

Mark watched as his face turned red and it looked like he would explode. He feared for the girl's life if Tyler didn't control himself. Mark turned him away from the child.

"Easy, Tyler. This kid can't help what's going on today." With Tyler's back to the girl, Mark continued to reason with him. "Let's just get us a plate and go back to the saloon. There's nothing going on here, and at least over there, we can listen to the piano and look at the women." He breathed a sigh of relief when his argument worked. You never knew with Tyler.

"We'll do more that just look at those fillies," Tyler agreed. Mark relaxed as Tyler addressed the girl. Smiling at the other two men, he gave a thumbs-up signal.

"Okay, little miss. Fix us four plates of food. Make sure you put enough on since we won't be here to get seconds. And wrap them good. I don't like my food cold."

"Ye...yes, sir." The girl practically ran back to the kitchen. It didn't take her long to return with a big tray. "You can ta...take the tray. I'll get it back tomorrow. I wr...wrapped everything tight, and I put in some extra."

Tyler grudgingly paid the girl and told Mark to get the tray. “Come on. Let’s get out of here before this shindig gets going. I want my food and a woman, and I want ‘em both hot.” Laughing at his own crude joke, Tyler led the group out of the hotel.

Sixteen

Mac had decided to visit Laura while the wedding took place. He wasn't interested in seeing the ceremony, nor going to church a second time in one day. He also thought it would be the perfect time to talk to the madam since he'd seen almost everyone in town headed for the church.

Smiling, Laura herself answered the door and, with Mac's questioning look, readily volunteered the information that her housekeeper was at the wedding. "I'd be there myself if it wouldn't cause a scandal in town. Jason is one of my favorite people, and I really like Miss Mandy."

"What do you know about her?" Mac turned his back as he took the drink Laura offered and started towards the couch. He hoped his question sounded as casual as he tried to appear.

"Not much," Laura answered. "She came home with Jack and Sally when Sally's sister took sick, and she's been here ever since. My housekeeper, Rebecca, has helped her sew a few dresses. It seems her family is pretty strapped for money, and she didn't have much when she came. Jack and Sally have helped her a lot." Laura seemed to study Mac's face as if she were trying to decipher why he was so curious about Samantha.

He abruptly changed the subject. "I understand you helped nurse Jack's stable hand when some rough hombres beat him up." Mac wasn't sure how to continue, but decided just to be upfront with Laura. "I've been looking for him to warn him that Tyler is out to get him. I wanted to warn him to stay out of his way."

"Well, you're too late to do any warning" Laura answered cautiously. "He ran away as soon as he could move. Maybe if Jack and Sally had been here when it happened, they could have persuaded him to stay. However, he took off the night they returned to Charrette Village without even knowing they were back."

"You helped nurse him didn't you, Laura?" Mac asked.

Again she seemed to eye him carefully before answering. "Yes, why do you ask?"

"Was Sam Turns a boy or a girl in disguise?"

"Whatever gave you that idea?" Laura looked away and fussed with her coffee.

"I'm trying to find a Samantha Turner. Her farm was burned to the ground, and her family killed. I think she disguised herself as a boy to escape the attention of the men who killed her family." Mac set his glass on the side table and rose from the couch. He stood before Laura and looked her straight in the eye. "If I'm right, she made a smart move. The same men who beat Sam Turns are looking for Samantha to kill her. I have to find her before they do."

Laura continued to stare at Mac as if he'd lost his mind. He decided to tell her all he knew. "They have the idea that Sam Turns is the girl they're looking for, and they plan to track her down."

"How do you know all this?" Laura had raised her voice, and all gentleness disappeared from her demeanor. She gave Mac a glimpse of what it would be like to cross this elegant lady. "It sounds to me like you're barking up the wrong tree, mister. Why are you so interested in finding this girl anyway?

Are you a relative or something?" She growled. He wondered why she took his questions so personal.

"No, I'm not a relative. I'm a scout for the army. I was tracking some renegade Indians when I happened on the Turner farm. It was made to look like an Indian raid, but there were white men riding with the Indians."

Turning away from Laura, Mac walked over to the piano. He absent-mindedly plunked at a few keys. Deep in thought, he finally looked up and smiled. "I just got caught up in this when I followed the trail of the raiders and realized Samantha Turner was still alive and in danger. I just don't want to see these men kill anyone else, if I can help it." Mac hoped his nonchalance covered his real emotions. He had to find this girl and put his haunting vision to rest.

"Well, I don't know about your theory. I nursed Sam Turns, and I think I would know a boy from a girl." Laura laughed, but it sounded forced. She seemed to realize it didn't come out the way she planned. Straightening her spine, she turned serious and faced Mac. "I'll put out some feelers and see if I can get any information about where Sam ended up. The men that come here are loose with their talk when they're sated. Why don't you come back tomorrow afternoon? Maybe I'll have something to tell you then." Looking him up and down rather suggestively, she smiled and offered, "If you're not here for just information, my bed has a thick down cover we can snuggle under."

Mac laughed at Laura's boldness. "Maybe you're just what I need, Miss Laura. Lead the way." Mac hoped to God he could perform. All he needed was to fail with this woman twice.

Mac's impassioned reasoning caused Laura to pause. She glimpsed more to his concerns than he admitted. It also caused her heart to jump in fear to realize Samantha was still in danger. Laura needed to find out if she could trust this man. She had instinctively liked him the last time he visited her, and he seemed to be an honest person. But she didn't intend to take any chances with Samantha's secret. Everything he told her fit the girl's story, yet what did she really know of this man. He could even be the ringleader.

Laura had to talk to Samantha before she told Mac anything. It would have to wait until tomorrow. She knew she could never see Samantha tonight. She'd send word with Rebecca and maybe they could meet at Jack and Sally's. The more Mac had explained, the closer Laura had come to believing him. They could check out his name with the army, and if he was who he claimed to be, she knew the Samantha would be happy to have help in finding her family's killers.

In the mean time, he was just too good looking to pass up any opportunity to entertain him. Everyone was occupied over at the church, and she knew she wouldn't have any visitors at the house until after the party at the hotel dispersed. The rest of the girls were already upstairs taking a nap. They'd wanted to be ready for the randy bunch that would stop by later because once the bride and groom left, the revelers would begin to think about Sally and her girls.

Tucking her arm into Mac's, she gave him her most flirtatious smile and hugging his biceps to her breast, led the way upstairs.

~ * ~

The afternoon went by too fast for Samantha to dwell on the stranger with Jason, though it triggered the image of a tall dark man rising out of the water. Try as she might, she couldn't shake the memory. Her distractions barely left her time to complete her toilette.

The church appeared packed when she arrived with Jack and Sally. "Goodness, Sally. There seem to be more people here now then at this morning's service."

"It just goes to show how well-respected Jason is and how much everyone in town likes you." Sally patted her hand, then took hold of it. "My word, girl, your hands are shaking." Sally snuggled the warm white shawl around her shoulders and gave her a hug. "It's just like Jason to be so thoughtful. This shawl is perfect to wear with your wedding dress. It will warm you up in no time." She'd told Jason that Samantha didn't own a winter coat, so the shawl was a welcome gift. "Are you cold, dear?"

"Yes and no," Samantha laughed. "I'm so nervous, I'm not sure if I'm freezing or just getting cold feet."

Rubbing Samantha's hands, Sally tried to reassure the girl. "There's nothing to be afraid of. Jason will take good care of you. All brides feel this way before the wedding." Quickly changing the subject, Sally held out a small prayer book. "Here, I'd be honored if you'd use my prayer book for the ceremony. I had Rebecca save me a piece of lace from your dress, and I covered the book with it so it'd match your dress."

"You look beautiful, Samantha." Sally's voice cracked with emotion. She rapidly blinked trying to restrain the tears that threatened. "Honey, you are the closest thing I ever had to having a child, and I love you like my very own."

"Sally, that's the nicest thing anyone's ever said to me. Thank you." They embraced in a bone-crushing hug until Jack broke them apart.

"You don't get all the hugs, Sally my girl," Jack boomed. Turning Samantha into his arms, he seemed at a loss for words.

"Jack," Samantha teased, "I can't believe you don't have anything to say." Her smile faded as she saw tears glisten in his eyes.

Then he chucked her under the chin. "Samantha, you are a vision of loveliness."

Head bowed in shyness, Samantha peeked up at him. "Rebecca did a beautiful job of fitting the dress. I look like this because she's so talented. Look, she even took the border she trimmed off the length of the skirt and fashioned a lovely lace headpiece for me to wear."

"Don't give all the credit to Rebecca, my dear," Sally chirped. "The dress was old-fashioned, but its beauty is in the intricacy of the lace and the way it hugs your lovely shape. Who'd have guessed you had all that hidden under those baggy clothes of your brother's."

Samantha felt the heat of a blush again. All she could think of to say was a quiet "thank you." Rebecca had left the length in the back, and it formed a small train that Samantha had difficulty managing. She pulled the heavy material behind her as she leaned forward for Sally's kiss. She hoped she wouldn't trip.

As the music started, Sally hurried to her seat up front, and Jack stepped in to walk Samantha down the aisle. Rebecca bustled up to straighten the train and gave Samantha a swift peck on the cheek. Then she scurried to her seat. Samantha's last conscious thought filtered through her brain. *Oh, my God! Am I really doing this?*

The ceremony blurred into a hazy dream, and Samantha didn't recall any of the words. She wasn't sure she'd even said, "I do," but she supposed she must have answered appropriately. The next thing she knew, she and Jason were receiving congratulations, and the laughter and talking sounded like bedlam. Jason tucked her shawl around her tighter. Then they were outside. His arm around her shoulder felt like a tight band that she wanted to break. The sun had set already, leaving the early evening in full darkness. The buggy waiting for them glowed with a soft wash of lantern light, illuminating decorations of white ribbons and cedar branches.

Being the dead of winter, there were no flowers for Samantha to carry or to use for decorations. Sally and her friends had done such a good job with ribbons and paper bells that no one seemed to notice the lack.

As Jason handed her into the buggy, Samantha realized that Sally's thoughtfulness in providing the Bible, covered in white lace, embellished with evergreens and bows, camouflaged the absence of a bouquet. She must remember to thank her again.

The hotel didn't offer any relief to Samantha's feelings. It seemed packed with townspeople, all wanting to speak to Jason and herself at one time. The noise threatened to blow off the roof, but Samantha felt as if she were isolated. She wasn't sure if she could repeat one word of what anyone said to her. She felt totally disjointed, like she floated in a kaleidoscope of swirling dancers, faces, and noise.

Rebecca stood with a glass of punch and watched with pride as Jason and Samantha danced around the parlor. Several women had approached her and complimented her on the workmanship of Samantha's dress. One even asked if she could spare the time to make an outfit for her daughter.

"Being with child again, I just don't have the time or the energy. Marilou has grown so fast these last few months, nothing fits her anymore."

"I think I can find the time," she laughed. "She's such a wee mite, it won't take but a few hours. I can do it in the evening." With the ice broken, more women came over to speak with her. Rebecca felt an inner glow. This is what it used to be like to feel the respect and friendship of her neighbors. She owed it all to Samantha.

She watched as Ashley Frank preened and simpered as if she were the main attraction. It was just like Samantha to forgive her malicious rumors. There she sat, with her emerald green dress spread out so far that no one could sit next to her. Mrs. Frank stood to the side, nibbling on a piece of wedding cake.

Rebecca watched as Daniel came over and spoke to Mrs. Frank. He carried a chair, and at her nod, Daniel set the chair next to Ashley for her. *What a thoughtful boy,* Rebecca thought. Mrs. Frank lowered her huge bulk onto the chair and visibly sighed in relief. Rebecca had to hide a grin. It was so enjoyable to watch all the people.

Jason did his duty and asked each of the ladies to dance. Rebecca knew he hated the social necessity. She saw him approach Ashley, and the woman practically jumped out of her seat to accept his hand.

"Ripppp!" The sound reverberated around the room.

"Ahhhh!" Ashley's anxious scream seemed piercing enough to shatter glass. Her mother's face mirrored her horror. Ashley frantically tried to collect the yards of material that had only moments before been attached to her waist.

The music stopped, people froze as if they posed for an artist. The whole scene had Rebecca choking to stifle the giggles that tried to escape.

"Get up, Mother." Ashley screamed. "Your chair leg is pinning down my skirt.

Sure enough, three of the four legs were firmly planted on Ashley's extravagant velvet skirt. Anchored by the hefty weight of her mother, the material had parted from the waistline when Ashley had risen to dance with Jason. The resulting rip left Ashley standing there in her petticoat.

As much as she despised the haughty Miss Ashley, Rebecca hurried over to help. The readymade dress, though surely expensive, had been poorly made. All of the gathers had come undone, and the skirt only hung from the bodice by a few stitches on one side. Three-fourths of the skirt had separated with the tug. "Allow me to help, Miss Ashley." Rebecca stiffened at the snobbish sniff she received for an answer.

"If you would be so kind, Rebecca." Ashley's reluctance in accepting her help hurt, but in moments several other woman joined them. Once they secured the release of the dress, Rebecca became aware of the condition of Ashley's petticoat. Several patches of different kinds of material supported the ruffles. Its general condition looked worse than anything Rebecca had worn during her poorest days. Women began to point and titter. Then she heard a loud hoot from one of the men. Turning towards the sound, Rebecca saw Doc elbow another man to hush.

Bless him, she thought. Ashley didn't deserve to be humiliated anymore. She handed Ashley's mother the yards of velvet she'd picked up and watched as she escorted the poor girl from the room with the help of one of her cronies. Several women tried to shield Ashley from the prying eyes of the assemblage.

Rebecca glanced around the room, looking for Daniel. He stood with several other young boys his age. They all wore delightfully devilish grins. Daniel had his thumbs hooked into his waistband. His chest puffed out like a bandy-legged rooster, and he actually seemed to be raising and lowering himself on the balls of his feet. She had to shake her head and laugh.

Except for a few titters, the room returned to normal within minutes. Jason had looked stunned then relieved. Ashley had been the last of the ladies he needed to dance with to fulfill his obligations as host. He rescued Samantha from her enthusiastic dance partner, and together they joined the Billings.

When Jason left her for a moment, she panicked. He hadn't left her alone all night except for their social obligations, and now she felt she had been cast loose in this eddy of bodies. She saw him take Daniel aside and speak to him, then he returned to her side. He placed his arm around her waist, and she sagged against him in relief and apprehension. Such conflicting emotions. She really didn't understand her feelings at all.

"Let's start saying goodnight, Samantha. You are exhausted, and you haven't eaten a thing all evening. I asked Daniel to carry a late supper over to our rooms and to light the fires. By the time we escape this madhouse, our rooms will be warm and we can eat and relax."

Jason's smile held the warmth of a blazing fire. His thoughtfulness touched her, and she tried not to let her anxiety show as she nodded her agreement. Samantha had no choice but to follow Jason around the room saying their farewells. His arm never relaxed its grip from around her waist.

She should have realized they wouldn't escape the party peacefully. Almost everyone crowded around the buggy as they clip clopped their way down the street. The whole noisy, cheering crowd saw them up the steps to their rooms. As they entered the room, Jason closed the door against all the hullabaloo to lead Samantha over to the roaring fire.

"Sit here in front of the fire, Samantha," he indicated. "Let me bring the table over here, and we can eat our supper while it's hot and toast our toes at the same time."

Samantha relaxed and laughed at Jason's gallantry. Maybe this wouldn't be so bad after all. She did take pleasure in Jason's wit and humor. Her hand shook as she sampled Mrs. Rugger's superb cooking. Eventually she became aware that the noise in the street had quieted.

"Thank goodness it's as cold as it is tonight. It sounds as if everyone decided being inside out of the wind was more comfortable than shouting at us all night."

"They wouldn't stay out there all night would they?" Samantha asked, shocked. "Why would they do that?"

"Some people think it's fun to harass the bride and groom all night so they don't get any sleep."

Samantha blushed and looked down at her plate. Would she get any sleep this night? She wasn't sure. With or without people yelling outside their window, she didn't know if she'd be able to sleep in the same bed as this handsome man sitting across from her.

To cover her nervousness, she lifted her wineglass. Her hand shook so that the wine sloshed out of the glass and onto the white cloth. The red stain spread starkly across the table, and it reminded Samantha of spilled blood. She'd have dropped her glass in shock if Jason hadn't reached across the table and gently removed the goblet from her cold fingers.

Their eyes met and locked. He reached down and took her elbow gently in his, then pulled her to her feet. "Come, my dear. It's time we went to bed. You've only picked at your food, and you're shaking with cold. Daniel has a good fire started in the bedroom. You go on in and get ready. I'll clean up this mess and join you in a few minutes."

Jason couldn't have been kinder. Samantha didn't have the heart to refuse him. She knew what was coming. She hadn't been raised around livestock without seeing the animals mate. She just felt so scared. Sally had told her it only hurt a little, right at first. Then the joy she would feel would obliterate all the pain. She hoped she would feel joy. Right now she only felt trepidation and fear.

Closing the door to the bedroom, Samantha saw the bed turned down invitingly, and indeed, a good fire burned in the hearth. The room didn't feel as cold as she'd feared. She decided not to light the candles. The firelight illuminated the room adequately, and Samantha found her nightgown and changed her dress without a problem.

She had just finished rinsing her face when Jason came in and startled, she swung around, splashing water across his brow. He started laughing at the slap of the water on his skin, but then he sobered immediately. He reached for her towel and gently patted her face dry. He looked so intense Samantha began to shake.

"Come here, my love, you're freezing. Let me warm you." His voice sounded husky as he folded his arms around her body. Jason sighed deeply, as if in pure pleasure. He lifted her effortlessly and carried her to the bed. Samantha hid her face in his shoulder and clung tightly to him.

She was totally unprepared for the look of adoration on his face and seeing the love in his eyes forced her body to relax. Jason laid her on the bed and covered her before he turned to strip off his shirt and pants. She closed her eyes against the possibility of seeing him without clothes. She didn't want to look at him. In seconds he crawled under the blankets with her and gathered her tightly to his chest.

"Ah, sweetheart. I've always cursed this tiny bed, but now I'm grateful for it. We have to sleep in each other's arms just to fit. I'll have to remember not to get too physical or one of us will end up on the floor."

That broke the ice. Suddenly they were both laughing and teasing as they kissed and touched. Samantha's heart pounded in anticipation. Maybe she really didn't know what would happen next. Jason certainly wasn't making any attempt to mount her, and she did enjoy his kisses. When he tried deepening the kisses, she still felt uncomfortable enough to turn her head. He allowed her to withdraw and began an assault with his hands. They felt wonderful on her back, rubbing up and down, causing warmth to flow into every limb.

She had her arms around him, and as he stroked her, she automatically repeated the strokes on his back. His skin felt rough, not as smooth as hers, and she could feel the cords of muscle as he strained to hold her tighter. Jason rained kisses all over her face, and she laughed as he tried to nibble an ear.

When she turned away, he caught her nose. *Nothing to worry about here,* she thought. *This is fun.*

Suddenly the atmosphere changed and became serious. Jason scooted down in the bed to snuggle his head between her breasts. *What is he doing?* her mind screamed. That's private. He kissed her breasts through her nightgown, but before she could protest she felt his hands slide down her hips and begin to bunch up her gown. She wanted to stop him, but didn't know how. By the time she knew what he had in mind, she felt his hands on her bare skin.

She stiffened and held herself tight, waiting for his next move. Her hands clinched at the sheets to keep from slapping him away. Her pulse raced so quickly she felt faint. Fear raised its ugly head, and her breath escaped in short gasps.

His hands moved up her sides then in front to clasp her breasts. He held one in each hand as he rubbed his face between them. *What did he think he was doing?* Could she tell him to stop? Would he understand she wasn't ready for this? *Lord, I don't think I can endure much more. Please help me.* Her silent prayers went unanswered.

In seconds he whipped the gown over her head and pulled the covers around her shoulders to keep her warm. Her arms automatically crossed in front of her body for protection. She tried to turn away, but the narrow bed left no room for movement. Jason seemed unable to contain his passion any longer. He laid the naked length of his body on top of her. She felt the ridged shaft of his manhood against her thigh and shuddered in revulsion. She had to escape. Whimpering, she tried to scoot out from under his weight. No longer fun and games, Samantha's mind whirled. *How can I get away? This is wrong. I can't do this.*

Jason took her hand and led it down to his engorged member. She jerked away violently.

"Ohh... Easy, love. Go easy." He gasped, and his chest heaved against her. She wondered if she'd hurt him. "Hold me. Please, just touch me, Samantha."

Tentatively she tried to do as he asked. Her fingers encountered a stiff muscle, covered in silken tissue. It felt like such a contrast, her curiosity got the best of her. Gingerly, she closed her hand. She could feel the veins pumping blood. It felt alive, like it had a life of its own. She let go quickly, as if she'd accidentally touched something hot. *How will that huge thing get inside me?* she wondered.

Suddenly, the vision of her mother intruded. Someone had done this very thing to her mother, leaving her broken body a mute testimony to his brutality. Samantha panicked.

Jason had reached his limit. He had no practice in readying a woman for what he wanted. His only sexual experiences had been with whores who'd prepared him and never seemed to need more than his movement in their bodies to give them pleasure. Samantha seemed to be hesitant. Only moments ago, she'd laughed and seemed to be enjoying his ministrations. Now, she shied away from him. He raised to his knees and lifted her by the hips. Then he pulled her under his body and began to try to penetrate her secret place. He gasped in surprise when he found her tight and almost impenetrable. He seemed too large for her, and with her whimpering, he couldn't force his member into her body. Her dry sheath felt painful for him as it stretched him unmercifully. It just wouldn't go in. Samantha squirmed and wiggled as she tried to escape his invasion. He didn't know how to hold her still without hurting her. Only the tip of his member penetrated her entrance, but the warmth of her and all the wiggling around caused him to spill his seed. The fluid helped him to enter a little farther as his body bucked in reaction, but Samantha continued to back away from him using her heels to push at the mattress.

The whole ordeal only took a matter of seconds. Jason gathered Samantha to his chest and breathing hard, tried to apologize. "I'm so sorry, love. I became so excited I came before you were ready. I'm sorry it hurt. They say it only hurts the first time."

Samantha's body shook violently. He wondered if she felt any pleasure. The firelight shimmered in reflection on the tears that streamed from her eyes. He tried to wipe them away with his fingertips, then gave up and used the sheet.

"I wish it felt as good for you as it did for me."

"It's okay, Jason. It only hurt a little." Samantha shuddered in his arms. Jason, never having taken a virgin before, hadn't realized it would hurt so badly. He felt sure the next time would be better.

He wanted to feel the length of his member enclosed by her warm sheath. He wanted to feel the pulsing of his blood surging against the walls of her womanhood. He'd known she felt apprehensive about this first time, but he wasn't prepared for her tears. Her pain tore him apart. Next time, he'd have to be more patient. He would give her the time she needed to relax with him. The next time would be better.

Concerned that he'd hurt her, Jason decided to leave well enough alone for the night. To think that he caused her pain plunged him into despair. He rolled to his side and lifting her, helped her cover herself with her nightgown. With her back to the fire, the light shown through the gauzy material and seductively outlined her body. He felt his body harden almost immediately. Patience, he cautioned himself. She's had enough for one night. Cushioning her body, he wrapped his arm around her and, with her head pillowed on his shoulder, he fell asleep within minutes.

Samantha lay awake most of the night lamenting what she'd gotten herself into this time. She wondered if Laura's girls felt this way when a strange man violated their bodies. She'd let her compassion for Jason's obvious contrition overcome her revulsion. Forgiving him for hurting her seemed right. After all, they were married, and he had a right to do with her body as he saw fit. She knew he didn't mean to hurt her. If she were truthful with herself, she'd admit he didn't even bruise her. She just didn't want to share her body with him. It was that simple.

Seventeen

Laura walked Mac to the door several hours later. "You know, I usually don't extend this courtesy to all my guests, but, honey, you're welcome in my bed anytime. And I'm sure glad you weren't 'under the weather' tonight."

Mac felt a sheepish smile curve his lips as he accepted the compliment. Settling his hat on his head, he opened the door. Laura slipped up close behind him and sent him on his way with a lingering pat on his butt. A wide grin crossed his face, and he swiveled and caught her peeking around the opening. Mac mischievously winked when she blew him a kiss, then turned on his heels as she closed the door against the cold wind.

Mac practically raced down the street. Apparently he'd pleased the madam, and his chest swelled with relief only because it kept her from being suspicious. He was disgusted with himself and felt Laura wasn't the only one to sell her body. He'd pretended it was Sammy he held in his arms. It was the only way he could function. When would he ever get that woman out of his head?

He entered the hotel as most of the revelers were on their way out and realized he'd missed the whole wedding party. Jason and his bride were already gone. He'd traded four hours with Laura for being introduced to the new Mrs. Sudholt. Well, he'd have liked to meet the sheriff's wife, but his time with Laura would pay dividends. He'd invested his time and his honor in the hopes those dividends would pay off. He had a feeling she knew more than she pretended. Once she checked with her source, he bet he could count on some new information. Mac stayed downstairs long enough to get a bite to eat and help Mr. Ruggers move some of the tables back into place.

"I'll be saying goodnight now," he announced. "I'll probably head out again tomorrow. I just have one more lead to check before I leave. There's someone who might have some information for me about Sam Turns."

Mr. Ruggers stopped rearranging the furniture, a chair held suspended in front of his body. He couldn't restrain his disappointment. "Oh, Mac, come on now. You've barely set foot here, and you're off again? I know you mentioned yesterday that you weren't staying past tomorrow, but I thought you'd change your mind. The missus will be sore disappointed to see you disappear so soon. Why, she's been so busy with this wedding that she hasn't even had time to visit with you."

Mac had to hide a grin as old man Ruggers tried to cover his obvious emotion by using his wife for an excuse.

"What's this I hear?" Mrs. Ruggers bustled into the room, drying her hands on her apron. "You can't be off again already. You only just got here."

Mac walked over and eased her hands out of the tangle of cloth. Holding both her hands gently in one of his huge fists, he pulled up a chair with the other hand. He lowered her to the chair and knelt at her side to be at eye level with her. "I wish I had all the time in the world to spend with good people like you. But you know duty calls, as they say. Like I told you yesterday, I have to find Sam Turns. If Tyler and his bunch locate him first, they'll kill him. Once I do that, I still have a job to do, you know." He raised the corner of her apron and wiped a tear that escaped from her worn eye and trailed a shiny path down her wrinkled cheek.

How had these people become such an important part of his life so fast? He felt closer to them than he did his own mother. Well, stepmother. Although she'd treated him kindly, she'd never gone out of her way to show him love. She'd avoided all contact with him—never a warm hand to ruffle his hair, a pat on the back, or even a hug. As a child he'd missed that warm contact. All her energy went into pleasing his father. She'd only tolerated Nicholas.

Whenever he returned home, his father welcomed him like the prodigal son. He never tired of embracing him in a huge bear hug every time he saw him. When they walked around the ranch, his dad always maintained contact with an arm around his shoulders as if he couldn't bear to part with him. The last visit he'd made after college, his father had told him the story of his real mother. She'd belonged to the Shoshone tribe. She'd been left for dead when another tribe had raided their village, and he'd discovered her when he rode over to investigate the shouting and screaming.

He'd been a young man on his way west to make his fortune. Then he'd found Kimama. Her name meant butterfly. By the time he'd arrived, the raiders were gone. The only one left alive, he didn't have the heart to abandon her. He'd nursed her back to health, then they'd set out to find the remainder of her tribe.

During that time, they fell in love. Fergus MacNamee had found a priest among the Indians and persuaded him to marry them. They'd lived with her people until she gave birth to Nicholas. When she didn't recover from the birthing, Fergus allowed her to be buried in the Indian custom. Then, he took his son and returned to the white man's world.

Nicholas had to give his father credit. He'd kept him near all the time. As a measure of his love, he'd never allowed anyone to persuade him to abandon his son. He'd raised him as a white man, but also instilled some of his mother's customs. Nicholas favored his father. Not many people picked up on the Indian heritage in his blood, but Nicholas never forgot it.

At times when he dreamt of Sammy he woke in a sweat. If he ever found her, would she accept a half-breed as her protector? He hoped the raid on her farm hadn't poisoned her mind against Indians. Rising to his feet, Nicholas planted a soft kiss on Mrs. Rugger's creased cheek.

"I'll stop by to visit whenever I'm close. I promise." After shaking hands with Mr. Ruggers, he retired for the night.

~ * ~

Doc walked over to the saloon when Jason and Samantha left the hotel. He wanted another drink. The memory of Rebecca's smile haunted him. Her quiet presence eased his tortured mind, and he wondered if she would put up with him on a permanent basis. Then he chastised himself. "What woman would want a drunken old fool for a husband. Better put that thought out of your mind, old boy," he muttered as he pushed through the swinging doors. "Besides, I don't think I could live through the agony of another woman dying on me."

Doc looked at his glass of whiskey. The amber fluid had always helped him forget the horror of losing his young wife in childbirth. Tonight the invitation of hazy forgetfulness didn't beckon with its usual force. The Christmas festivities at the saloon sounded almost as loud as the wedding party. When the gathering in the barroom began to get out of hand around midnight, Doc noticed the man Tyler as he became belligerent.

"A hostile drunk," he muttered into his glass. He couldn't tolerate men that became aggressive when they drank. At least he was a quiet drunk. He just fell asleep when he had too much. This was not his idea of a good time. Maybe he'd be wise to go on home and go to bed.

Fingering the button Rebecca had sewn on his suit coat, he marveled at her thoughtfulness. He'd never even asked her to mend anything for him. When he'd tried to thank her, she'd just sassed him back. "You men never realize what people think of you when you walk around all sloppy. I just didn't want Samantha to be embarrassed by your carelessness." He'd bristled up at that.

"Miss Samantha's so sweet, she probably wouldn't have given a second thought to my coat missing button." He remembered Rebecca's "humpf" as she stalked off and had to smile.

"I wonder if Rebecca will be busy all day tomorrow," he mumbled as he turned and left the saloon. "Maybe if I go to bed sober, I'll be sharp enough to sass her. That oughta' be worth a chuckle or two. God knows I haven't had much to laugh about lately." Doc slid the barkeep a coin for his drink and tipping his hat to the man, straightened his shoulders, and walked out the door without missing a step.

~ * ~

The more Tyler drank, the angrier he felt. He began to rant and rave about having to carry his evening meal down to the saloon to eat. "The hotel is a public place. How could they refuse to let me eat there? It's that sheriff again. It's all his fault."

"Shut up, Tyler." Mark grabbed Tyler's arm. "Let's go upstairs." Mark enlisted the help of Luke, and together they half carried the grumbling Tyler up the steps.

"If it hadn't been for him, we would have killed that kid, and Morgan wouldn't have to worry about Samantha Turner showing up in Pinckney wanting her property," Tyler argued as they tried to get him to bed. "The sheriff is the reason they turned us away from the hotel, too. His private wedding party, ha! Maybe I'll have to teach this sheriff a thing or two about messing with me more than once." His last statement gave Mark pause, then Tyler passed out cold. Luke and Mark just pulled off his boots and let him lie on top of the covers. Closing the door softly, they went back down to each grab a girl and hit the sack themselves.

Tyler woke early the next morning not remembering what had happened. He shivered with cold. The bed looked like he'd tossed all night. The covers lay scattered on the floor, and the lumpy mattress sagged beneath his weight. He mouth tasted like sawdust. Gingerly he placed his feet on the cold floor and held his aching head between stiff fingers. His stomach lurched like a butter churn, and for a minute he thought he'd be sick. He remembered the reason he felt so miserable. It was all the sheriff's fault, he reasoned. He would have to do something about that, but first he needed some coffee.

Tyler stood up and stumbled to the door. Thoughtlessly, he charged into the hall and almost tripped on one of the girls as she came out of her room. Forgetting the coffee, he grabbed the girl and dragged her back into his room.

"Seems like I missed something last night, girlie." He threw her across the bed, jumped on top of her, and began to rip at her robe.

"Get off me, you lunkhead. Go soak your head in the privy," she yelled.

"Don't insult me, you piece of dung." Tyler began to slap her. Didn't she know who she was dealing with? She couldn't talk to him like that. Her screams turned from angry insults to cries of pain and torture. Tyler totally enjoyed her wails as he beat and savagely raped her.

When he finished, he rose from the bed, buttoned his trousers, and wiped her blood off his hands. Calmly, he left the room. Surprised, he found Luke and Mark in the hall along with the surly bartender.

"What's going on in there?" the barkeep demanded.

"None of your business," Tyler replied as he pushed past the man. Turning, he shouted, "You should teach your girls to be more accommodating."

Luke and Mark eyed each other, then Mark went to get Joshua while Luke followed Tyler downstairs. Luke fingered his gun nervously, trying to think of a way to get Tyler out of town as soon as possible. If he'd beat up another woman, they'd never be able to show their face again. They were already barred from Laura's place. All they needed was to be barred from this sleazy tavern, too. "Let's get out of here, Tyler. We need to report back to Morgan and let him know that Sam Turns ran away. It probably wasn't really Samantha anyway. Lily and Rose didn't know anything different from what we already heard."

"We're not going anywhere until I kill me a sheriff," Tyler blustered. "He's the reason we didn't get Sam Turns the first time, him and his interfering. It won't happen again."

"Are you crazy? You can't kill a sheriff! We'll all hang if you do that."

Tyler spun on his heels and backhanded Luke, knocking him up against the wall. "Shut your mouth. You want to tell the world my plans? Anyway, they have to catch us first, and they haven't caught me yet. Come on, let's get out of this dump." Throwing an arm around Luke's shoulder, Tyler acted like the slap that left his handprint on Luke's cheek was just a friendly poke.

"Don't you worry, Luke, stick with me, and we'll get rid of that pest and find Samantha, too."

Before Luke could protest any further, screams erupted from upstairs. Luke grabbed Tyler and started pushing him toward the door as Mark and Joshua came running down the steps. It took the three of them to drag him out the back way.

"We've got to get out of here, now. The bartender roused one of the girls to check on Lily. When Rose went in the room, she started screaming uncontrollably." Mark pushed at Tyler and Luke to get them moving.

"What happened?" Luke asked.

"I peeked in. Lily is beyond help. The sight of her body had Rose and the bartender retching in the corner. I didn't even recognize her." With a disgusted look at Tyler, he continued, "It looked like Tyler raped her, then beat her to death."

"We're not going anywhere 'til I kill me a sheriff," Tyler commanded in his make-no-mistake voice.

"We'll take care of the sheriff later," Luke argued, "come on." The four men ran down the alley to the livery stables, and because Jack stepped out front to see what the fuss was about, they were able to saddle their horses and ride away unobserved.

~ * ~

Some time before dawn, Samantha fell into a fitful sleep and woke to pounding on their door at daybreak.

"Jason, trouble over at the saloon. We need you, quick."

"Be right there, just give me five minutes to dress."

Samantha rubbed the sleep out of her eyes and tried to get the circulation back in her arm after Jason had lain on it all night.

"Stay in bed a little longer, sweetheart. I put another log on the fire, and it will warm up in here in a minute. I'll try not to be too long. I wanted our first day together to be private, but looks like somebody has other ideas." Giving her a lingering kiss, Jason buttoned his shirt as he ran out the door.

As Jason ran down the steps, he remembered that he'd forgotten to tell Samantha about Nicholas McNamee. He should have mentioned it. He'd hoped Nicholas would have come to the reception. Then he could have introduced them, and she could have heard the news from him. She would have been thrilled to hear they had some leads to follow.

Well, he'd tell her when he got back. After he saw to the trouble at the saloon, he might as well stop by Laura's and find out what he'd done wrong. He knew Samantha didn't enjoy her wedding night, and he didn't want a repeat performance.

Samantha decided to get up immediately. She had to go over to Sally's and get the rest of her things. All she had sent over the day before was a dress to change into this morning. She wanted to pick up her saddlebags. She intended to keep her brother's clothes and everything she had brought with her from the farm. She never wanted to part with her past.

Samantha heard Jason stop downstairs to pick up his gun and talk to the men who had come for him. She didn't waste a minute. Barely taking the time to run a comb through her tangled curls, she splashed some cold water on her face and dressed in a flash. When she ran down the stairs and out the door, she saw Jason walking toward the saloon. Practically running, she headed in the opposite direction to Jack and Sally's.

Sally seemed shocked to see her so early and even more uneasy when Samantha remained so taciturn. Samantha wasted no time on pleasantries. She wasn't in the mood to talk about last night. She knew Sally's manners kept her curiosity at bay. Samantha realized it had to be hard for her to not ask questions. To appease Sally, she joined her for a hasty cup of coffee, then she went to her room to gather the rest of her belongings. There wasn't much.

Yesterday she'd packed the saddlebags with the shirts and pants that had been meant for her brothers. She picked up the boots that she had stolen and gave them another polish with her sleeve before she put them in her bag. When she had turned into Samantha Peters, she'd lovingly cleaned and polished the boots. She'd hated having them dirty all the time, and to make up for the abuse she'd put them through, she'd spent a lot of time and elbow grease getting them back into good shape. The leather didn't suffer too much, especially after several coats of saddle soap. The hat also received its share of refurbishing, so Samantha had salved her conscience. Handling the boots reminded her she'd forgotten to ask Jason about the man in buckskins. Too much had occupied her mind yesterday. She'd have to remember to inquire about him today.

With a quick peck on the cheek, she told Sally she would see her later. She hurried to the stable to saddle Sassy, avoiding Jack, who was busy with a customer. She decided to ride over to Jason's rooms and drop off her baggage. She could change into the new split skirt Sally had given her then take a ride. She needed to think about this marriage business. Maybe she could sneak over and ask Laura what she'd done wrong. She felt very dissatisfied with the whole business of "making love". She knew it couldn't be like that forever or she would never be able to tolerate Jason's touches again.

Rubbing the ring on her finger, she wondered if she'd made a mistake. Why did she have to be so impetuous? J.R. was right. She never thought things through before she acted on an idea.

~ * ~

Mac had just finished breakfast. He walked out of the hotel and prepared to mount Renegade when he heard all the commotion. Glancing down the street, he took in the whole scene.

Jason's new bride pulled her horse to a stop in front of the jail and looked ready to dismount. Jason stood in front of the saloon with a group of shouting and gesturing people. He seemed to be trying to calm down their hysteria. Then Mac noticed a glint of sunlight off metal and looking up, saw a man on the roof across the street. He was pointing a Kentucky flint rifle at the group in front of the saloon. Glancing around Mac spotted two more men lurking between the buildings.

"Yoo-hoo, Mr. MacNamee."

Before he could spot their target, Ashley Frank bounced down the steps in front of Frank's Emporium, waving a hanky to get his attention.

Her shrill voice and wild gestures caused Renegade to rear. Mac had all he could do to keep the powerful stallion from stomping the woman into the ground. He reined the horse in a tight circle to settle him.

"Miss Frank, back off a little." His harsh command erupted with all his impatience. The woman acted affronted. Gathering her skirt in a huff, she straightened the feathered concoction sitting cockeyed on her blond locks. Her mouth opened to protest his lack of manners when a volley of shots fractured the quiet morning. Mac saw Jason hit the ground, just as he calmed Renegade. All Ashley's intentions of continuing her rebuke were forgotten as she ran screaming for the safety of her father's store.

People scattered in all directions trying to get away from the gunfire. Jason's bride, totally disregarding the flying bullets, remounted and raced her horse towards the fallen man. By the time Mac reacted and raced after her, she knelt on the ground next to Jason's body, sobbing his name and screaming an endless, "noooo…".

She seemed oblivious to the bullets that continued to kick up the dirt around her as Mac barreled down the street. He bent from the saddle, grabbed her around the waist, and kept riding. She fought like a maniac, almost unseating Mac and throwing them both to the ground. He had to find a way to restrain her before she got them both killed.

Regretting the action, he slapped her to stop the hysteria. The woman fainted dead away. Whether it was caused by the shock of being hit, or the horror of Jason's body covered in blood, he didn't care. She'd escaped reality in her own way. Mac gathered her limp form in his arms and continued to ride as he realized the bullets were now aimed at them.

In all the confusion, the girl's horse had taken off running after the big gray stallion. Mac didn't know why, but someone had killed the sheriff and now they were chasing the woman. Mac gained a little ground by riding into the hills. He took a chance and slowed Renegade so he could look back. The four riders still followed their trail. The girl's horse drew even with them and he murmured a quick thanks. Renegade was strong, but carrying double on a long ride would wear him out too soon.

Mac clucked for the girl's horse, and the mare obediently ambled over to the side of Mac's mount. After checking her pulse and finding it strong, Mac knew she could safely continue the ride. Her white wool shawl was her only covering against the cold, and he cursed as he realized she could freeze to death if the weather stayed this cold. Releasing his bedroll, he wrapped her in the blanket and gently placed the girl over her saddle. The dark blanket would hide the white of her shawl, and they would have a better chance of hiding.

With a quick twist of his wrist, he tied her to the saddle with his rope. He hated restraining her that way. It would be a bruising ride. Yet he knew Renegade couldn't escape their pursuers carrying the extra weight. Grabbing the mare's bridle, he continued riding, turning into the woods.

Her ribs jarring against the saddle seemed enough to wake the girl. She struggled against her bindings, and since she hadn't been secured too tightly, she began to slip off her horse's back.

Mac, alert to her movements, pulled up as soon as he realized she'd awakened. They had a little lead on the four men, but they were still being followed. As Mac began to unleash her, she turned into a spitting, fighting wildcat again.

"Let me go! Let me go! Who are you?" she screamed.

"Quiet," Mac cautioned. "Whoever killed the sheriff is after us. We have a little lead, but they are still on our trail."

"They killed Jason? Oh, no! It can't be true. Not again! Everyone I love dies." Tears streamed down her face, blinding her with their onslaught. "What's going on? Who are you? Why did you take me away from Jason? If you're kidnapping me, I don't have any money. You've got to take me back." Samantha's thoughts were tumbling again, and she heard her tongue gave voice to every disjointed supposition. How could this happen a second time? She didn't know if she could go through another trauma like last summer.

The last thing she remembered was a band of steel wrapped around her waist and whisking her away from Jason. The arm that had grabbed her so tightly had felt rock hard. The same strong arm held her again.

Did this stranger say Jason was dead? It couldn't be! Nevertheless, deep down she knew it had to be true. She had seen it herself. Jason had been shot right through the chest, and from the size of the hole in his back, she knew he'd been killed instantly. He'd probably died before he hit the ground. She remembered bullets kicking up the dirt around her as she knelt to cradle his head, then she'd been snatched away.

It was true. The shots were turned towards Samantha and her rescuer. She knew because she had felt a bullet graze her. Unconsciously, she reached under her shawl and touched her side. Pain made her cringe, and she pulled the blanket and shawl aside. Awareness widened her eyes when she saw the blood staining her dress.

The man seemed to watch her as the emotions chased across her face. He'd followed her glance. When he saw the blood, he let out a string of curses that turned her ears blue.

"Damn! We have to get you to a doctor. I didn't realize you were hit. My first thought was to get you out of the line of fire. Before I knew it, we were the targets." He helped her settle on Sassy, then glanced back the way they'd come.

"Can you ride? We have to keep going." At her nod he grabbed her reins and took off in a flash. She wanted to fight him for control of her horse, but he started speaking again, and she tried to catch his words as they galloped away.

"You were fighting me so hard I was afraid you'd unseat both of us. I had to subdue you to keep you from falling and dragging me down with you. I didn't expect you to faint." He looked at her intently and she shuddered. His eyes seemed to bore right through her.

"I only slapped you to stop your hysterics." He turned to check on the advance of their pursuers. "We have to find shelter so I can see to your wounds. If we can hide out from those four men until dark, maybe we can circle back to town and get you some help."

"I only have one wound," Samantha snapped haughtily, "and it's probably only a scratch. I don't think I'll need Doc. However, I would appreciate it if you'd let me have the reins to my horse and bring me back to town as soon as possible."

"I'd like to oblige, ma'am, but those four men seem to have different ideas. Tuck this bandanna against your side to stop the bleeding. And try to keep your arm pressed to your side to make a compress. Hurry," Mac urged as he held her one arm to steady her while she followed his instructions. Once she had the bandanna stuffed under her arm, he handed her the reins. "Let's try to lose our friends back there."

With Samantha riding Sassy properly, instead of being bounced like a sack of feed, they made better time. By noon, the sky clouded over, and the weather began to look threatening. Every time they tried to circle around back towards town, the four men trailing them seemed to read their minds and cut off their trail. Mac led Samantha deeper into the woods to try to lose their pursuers, but she could tell he was beginning to worry about her.

"You look pale and listless. I know you have to be cold." His blanket and her shawl were little protection against the rising wind. He pulled up in a small glade and frowned at her in concern. "I wish you had some warmer clothes. This weather looks as if it can turn nasty, and you're not dressed for being outdoors, let alone this wild ride we are on."

Samantha seemed to stare at Mac in a daze. She shivered uncontrollably and slumped forward in the saddle. He didn't know if she trembled from the weather or seeing someone she cared about gunned down in front of her. Suddenly, she straightened in her saddle. “I have some pants and shirts in my saddle bags. If we can stop for a few minutes, I can put those on. They should help keep me a little warmer.”

Wasting no time, Mac jumped from his horse and hurried to help her down. He lifted her saddlebags and opened one side to find some twill pants, a cotton shirt, and a pair of buckskin pants with a matching shirt. He did a double take. He looked at Samantha and back at the clothes. The black hair had fooled him, but this was the girl from the waterfall! He was sure. His pulse quickened, and he almost grinned.

Now he knew why those men were shooting at her and who they were. Well, it sure had taken him long enough to find her. At least now he would be able to protect her. Not letting on that he knew her identity, he handed her first the cotton pants then the buckskin. He instructed her to put the buckskin on over the cotton and turned his back while she struggled to pull them on under her skirt.

Then he took his blanket and her shawl from her shoulders. He made her slip the cotton shirt on over her dress and the buckskin shirt over that. The buckskin shirt was so big and long on her it acted as a coat. The leather would also effectively stop the wind from cutting through her clothes.

“There, you should feel warmer now.”

“Yes, I already feel the difference.”

“This shawl is useless for riding.” He packed it back in the saddlebag and wrapped the blanket back around her.

“Let me help you remount.” With a wink and a grin that she found irresistible, he continued, “You won’t have to worry about the pants falling off while you’re in the saddle.” Turning serious, he mounted while he spoke. “If we could find some shelter before this storm hits, I could help you arrange your clothing better."

Sammy felt the heat of another blush. Would she be doomed to suffer this affliction all her life? She thought being a married woman would have stopped her inclination to turn red every time a man joked with her. It was hard to be lighthearted when everyone she ever loved seemed to die. She wished she could go back to last August and relive her life.

As for now, they didn't have any time to waste on fashion or her sensibilities. He rebuckled her saddlebag, and they urged their mounts to a gallop. Samantha knew she looked ridiculous with the blanket over her head and shoulders, but she didn't care. The extra clothes were a godsend, and she could feel her body responding to the additional covering. She remembered she had some gloves in the other side of the saddlebag and vowed the next time they stopped she'd retrieve them. For now she wrapped the edges of the blanket around her hands as she guided Sassy through the trees and followed her rescuer.

Eighteen

Sammy's rescuer rode slightly ahead, head bent over the neck of his stallion. His buckskins stretched tautly over the muscles rippling across his back. Something tickled the back of her memory. She just couldn't grasp what. When he'd first grabbed her, she'd neglected to register any details about the man or his mount except that his smile was enchanting. He'd never answered her questions. She supposed she should be thankful he rushed her away when he did. She could be lying there dead, too, and if that had happened, there would be no one left to avenge her family.

She had to live. Somehow she would find those men and kill them herself. She had received little help from anyone else. Everyone seemed to think she needed to be protected. They all thought her too young and inexperienced to go after those killers. Well, she'd show them. As soon as they could get rid of these men tracking them, she would get away from this well-meaning stranger and head out on her own.

She just wished her side didn't hurt so badly. Maybe then she could concentrate on remembering where she'd seen this man before. "Look," Samantha cried. "An Indian Thong tree, it's pointing over there. Sometimes they point to water or shelter or to a trail."

Mac frowned in surprise. How did this girl know about Indian trail markers? Riding over to the tree, he saw the circular carving. Glancing up, he realized this was a real indicator. Some Thong Trees were bent in the wrong direction to throw off anyone trying to follow the Indian trail. Indians would bend a young sapling and tie it parallel to the ground with a thong, then let it grow. Years later, after the thong had rotted away, the trunk stretched up from the ground about three to four feet, bent in the direction it had been trained, then made another turn on it's own, reaching for the sky. Some trees, like this one, had messages carved on the trunk to indicate their purpose.

This one marked a cave. If they could find it, they could hide until their pursuers left. Mac found the entrance. A crack in the bluff about ten feet high indicated the opening. It looked small, but it might be big enough to hide them and their horses. He removed the brush hiding the access, and after checking that there were no winter inhabitants, led Samantha and the horses inside as quickly as possible.

The opening had been easy to find once he'd read the thong tree. The small fissure, just wide enough to admit a riderless horse, led to a large cavern that would hold them and their mounts comfortably. He cautioned Samantha to keep her animal quiet and crept back out to wipe away their trail and recover the cave entrance.

"We'll have to stay quiet until I'm sure they're gone." Mac handed Samantha his canteen. "See if you can tell how bad your wound is. Try to clean it up while we wait. When you get done, I have some beef jerky we can chew on. Sorry we can't have a fire." Mac stayed close to the opening. He pressed his back against the stone wall and drew his gun.

"Stay toward the back of the cave. I know it's dark, but keep the horses between us. If they find the entrance," he whispered, "I'll try to convince them you rode away."

She didn't know how he expected her to see anything in this dark hole, but at least she could wet the bandanna and wash off the blood. She wondered if she would be able to tell the extent of the damage just by feeling. Samantha unbuttoned the two shirts and her shirtwaist dress. She couldn't think of a way she could get to the wound without undressing, and she didn't intend to do that. Not only did the weather forbid it, she didn't completely trust this stranger yet. Her dress and chemise had torn where the bullet entered, so she ripped them further, allowing her to place the bandanna tight against her skin. Blood continued to run down her side, but she couldn't see if the wound needed stitches or not.

The bullet had grazed her under her arm just below her left breast. The gash felt about two inches long and a finger wide. As soon as she placed the wet bandanna over it, she winced. She bit her tongue to keep from mouthing any expletive. Reaching for her saddle horn, she hung on to keep herself upright as she pressed the cloth tight against her skin. Samantha finished as best she could and stepped around Sassy. She reached for Renegade and began to stroke him.

Mac sensed rather than saw her and kept a tight grip on Renegade's rein. "Careful," he whispered "Renegade doesn't let anyone near him except me. He may snap at you if I get distracted and have to let loose of his rein."

Samantha didn't answer. Let him think what he wanted. No horse had ever snapped at her or probably ever would. Just then, something clicked.

This was the same gray horse from the waterfall and again at the pond! The same one at the stable back in November. This had to be the man she stole the boots from, the scout from the waterfall. *Oh, Lordy*, Sammy thought, *it's a good thing he didn't look in the other side of the saddlebags. He would have found his boots and his hat.*

How would she get out of this mess? She remembered him as he rose from the mist swirling on the pond. His gleaming body had looked so strong and beautiful. Her heart pounded as it had when she saw him again at the stable. His name flashed in her memory, Nicholas MacNamee. She almost whimpered aloud. Trapped with him in a small cave, she didn't stand a chance if he ever found out she'd stolen his boots. Lordy! She really had something to be afraid of now. He wasn't one she could fool for long.

She wished she knew why he had ridden off with her. Surely if it was just to rescue her from the flying bullets, he could have doubled back and brought her to her friends. She wondered why the four men were following them, why they had tried to shoot her as well as Jason. She wished she'd gotten a better look at the culprits.

Samantha's curiosity ate at her, and just as she decided to start asking some questions, she heard voices outside the cave. Placing her hand over Sassy's muzzle, she leaned forward to listen. Mac did the same with Renegade as they moved in unison.

"Quit arguing with me, Luke," Tyler exploded. "I'm telling you that girl was ridin' Samantha Turner's horse and sittin' on Dennis O'Brien's saddle. I don't care what color her hair is, she has to be Samantha Turner. 'Sam Turns' never ran away. He just turned back into who he really was to start with, the Turner gal!"

"You're crazy, Tyler," Luke shouted. "You are so obsessed with finding the Turner girl you see her in every woman who rides a chestnut horse. You beat Lily to death and killed the sheriff. You're going to get us all killed before this is over. Look at the sky. We're on a wild goose chase and, from the looks of things, we are about to be caught in a hell of a snowstorm. I say we turn around and head back while we can."

"Luke, you are so dumb sometimes, I wonder if you would know your own mother if she said howdy to you on the street."

"Hell, Tyler, you know I never knew my mother. How could I recognize her?"

"Shut up, Luke, and listen. I know, as well as I know my own name, that the woman who rode up to the sheriff when we shot him is the same woman who used to come riding into Pinckney with her brothers every month. I know that horse, and no matter what color the gal's hair is now, I know her face, and I know her size. I recognized that saddle, too."

Reaching for Luke's bridle as he started to turn away, Tyler gave it a vicious tug. Luke's horse reacted to the pain and shied away with a whinny. Jerking on the reins again, he continued, "It's the same saddle that hung on the fence at the O'Brien's place, and it's the same one that was in the stable with the kid. I'm telling you this gal we're chasing is Samantha Turner. I swore to myself I'd be the one to deflower that little filly, and if she married the sheriff yesterday, and he beat me to her, I'm double glad I killed him."

Releasing Luke's horse, he tossed the reins to him and he studied the trail. "That don't mean I don't want to get my hands on her before I kill her. That's why I only tried to wound her this morning."

"Well, if you weren't so horny," grumbled Joshua, "you could have saved us a lot of trouble by just killing her when you had her in your sights. Now look at what you got us into. Some knight in shining armor comes along and rescues the fair maiden from right under your nose, and here we are stuck out in no man's land without shelter and a lulu of a storm brewing."

"Shut up, Joshua. You listen to too many fairy tales. Start looking for those tracks we lost. We must have missed their trail farther back. That hombre, who rode off with Mrs. Sheriff, is a might too clever. I know I hit her. They can't ride without stopping. Let's try to catch up to them before this snow covers their tracks."

~ * ~

Mac could feel Samantha's agitation. He knew, if she had a gun, she would charge out of that cave with no regard to her own safety. He had been intensely aware of her every emotion as they listened to the boasting of those louts. Only his hand on her arm had restrained her. Mac had started to give Samantha directions when he'd felt her move to quiet her horse simultaneously as he placed a hand on Renegade's nose. *Smart girl*, he'd thought.

The voices faded away, leaving Samantha and Mac in stunned silence. He'd reached out instinctively to comfort her with a soundless promise of support. It wasn't a good time to confront these men. He didn't feel the need to speak aloud. He knew they had been speaking to each other in their thoughts, and he felt awed by the power that filled him from their speechless communication.

Samantha shook in reaction. Right outside this cave were the men who had killed her family, her friends, and now her husband. She quivered in anticipation of that brute Tyler in her gun sights. She knew if she had reached into her saddle bags for her pistol she'd have made enough rustling noises to alert them and felt Nicholas sending her signals to wait. When she'd felt his hand on her arm, she'd known that he'd anticipated her action. She would have lost the element of surprise if she'd made any noise at all, and surprise was her only chance of getting all four of them. *Yes*, she had answered him in her thoughts, *I'll wait*.

They were gone. Mac remained as still and quiet as he had been when the men were right outside the cave. Samantha did not want to break the silence. They had communicated without words. She had read about that before, but never knew it could really work. She stood, shocked into wonder by what had just happened.

After several minutes of silence, they both had the same awakening. Snow!? They'd been unaware that the silent fall of white flakes had begun. Mac whispered for Samantha to stay in the cave, and he crept to the mouth of the cavern and peeked through the brush. The snow was falling so hard he could barely make out the trees on the other side of the clearing. The tracks from the four horses were already half obscured. Even though the sun should have been half way across the sky, the heavens had turned a heavy, thick gray. This looked bad.

Mac could tell they would be in for a long day and night. They couldn't go anywhere in this weather. To top that, he wasn't sure just how far the others would go before they found a campsite and settled down for the night. Mac rubbed his chin as he thought. Samantha needed her wound tended to and she needed to get warm. The cave would keep them dry and out of the wind, but without a fire he wasn't sure how long they could hold out before they began to lose too much body heat. He made a sudden decision and returned to the girl.

"I've got to track them until I know they are far enough away that we can safely start a fire and not be detected. You stay here in the cave and don't leave for anything," he instructed. "You don't have a weapon, and you're injured. I should be back in less than an hour. Stay close to your horse for warmth, and don't leave, no matter what!" he repeated.

Not waiting for a reply, Mac led Renegade out of the cave and mounted.

Earlier, when he'd heard her wince in pain, Mac had jumped as if he had been stabbed. The thought of her being injured had caused rage to build inside his chest. He'd wanted to kill the man who shot her. What caused him to react to this woman by losing his self-control? This was the woman he'd dreamt about for almost four months. Now that he'd finally found her in the flesh, he didn't know how to act. His thoughts were jumbled, but his senses seemed tuned in to his phantom lady.

He rode through the increasing snowfall, wondering how he could save this woman from the certain death that awaited her at Tyler's hand. He'd never been a violent man, and yet this woman made him yearn to protect her from anything and everything, especially the likes of Tyler. Mac didn't expect the group to go much farther before they made camp, and yet the distance they'd traveled already showed Tyler's tenacity for finding Sammy.

As Mac caught up with fresher tracks, he knew the snow was slowing them down without fail. From the direction of their meandering, he realized they were still hunting for the girl. They were actually far enough away from the cave now that he could return to her. He knew it would be safe enough to build a fire for the night. However, he wanted to get close enough to make sure they'd stopped and made camp. He also hoped to try to eavesdrop on them and discover their plans.

Disturbed snow showed evidence of their milling around undecided then continuing on in a disorderly pack. Mac could just imagine the arguing and bickering among them about stopping for the day. The white powder muffled sound so he couldn't hear them. He had to be careful. He might be getting too close.

Several shots rang out at close range, knocking Mac's hat from his head and causing Renegade to rear in panic. Only his iron control kept the horse from unseating him. He quickly took cover behind a large bolder. Squinting through the blurring snow, he tried to judge the origin of the shots.

Mac freely cursed himself for not dismounting sooner and continuing on foot. Tyler's gang must have stopped to set up camp and posted guards already. Peering ahead, Mac could barely make out the lay of the land ahead of him. He had been traveling down a slope and assumed the ground continued to drop off to a creek. Tyler had probably camped at the bottom of a hill near running water and left a man near the crest as a precaution. Mac could smell the smoke now, even though he couldn't see it.

He traded a few shots with the guard, hoping to figure out his position. He soon found out that all his shots had accomplished was to pinpoint his hiding place for the others. In a matter of minutes, shots exploded from several locations. Pinned down on two sides, he had to watch his back. There were four of them, so Mac knew it would be only a matter of time before one of them circled around behind him while the other's kept him pinned behind the rock. Mac's thoughts shifted back to the cave and Sammy. He had to get out of this mess so he could get back to her.

Left alone in the cave, Sammy would never know she could safely light a fire. She would probably think he had deserted her. Mac checked his ammunition. He was good for several rounds, and he had another box of bullets in his saddlebags. Even so, it wouldn't be long before he ran out of ammunition. Regret clouded his vision. He'd never have a chance to know her.

~ * ~

Back in the cave, Sammy grew colder by the minute. She couldn't stay inactive any longer. With her decision made, she dug into the other side of her saddlebags and retrieved her gun and holster. Strapping the gun to her side, she took out the hat and gloves. It only took her a minute to add the boots to her outfit, wrapping the extra buckskin around her feet for a tighter fit. The heck with being discovered. He'd find out the truth soon enough anyway. Rolling up his blanket, she stuffed it in the saddlebag and led Sassy out of the cave.

She mounted and set out to follow Mac's trail. She had to find out if he was part of the gang or the army scout sent to help her. Regardless of his guilt or innocence, she knew she had the skill to track the men and kill them. Her vengeance burned a hole in her gut.

Sammy realized she'd traveled far enough that no one would detect the smoke from a fire in the cave. Could it be possible that the man had just ridden off and abandoned her? The buckskin shirt kept her torso dry, but her skirts grew heavy with snow and were becoming wet. She thought about returning to the cave to dry out, but her need to find these men impelled her to continue.

She froze when she heard the first muffled shots. She tried to spur Sassy a little faster, but the snow had piled so deep she didn't gain any speed.

The intensity of the shots warned Sammy she'd gotten close enough. She dismounted and ground tied Sassy's reins. She heard a volley of shots to her right and a single return shot from her left. The scout had to be to her left. Then she heard another burst of shots farther to the left and his single return. They had him pinned behind a boulder! Well, that answered her question about whether he was on her side or not. Her heart thundered in her chest. She felt elated but decided it had to be excitement that caused her pulse to quicken. It couldn't be the sight of MacNamee, alive and well.

Well, maybe she could even the odds! She'd wanted her chance at these men, and now she had it. Sammy crept behind the trees until she approached on Nicholas' right flank. She drew her gun and checked the load. Then she crept closer until her eyes adjusted to the distortions caused by the falling snow. A slight movement helped her distinguish the man from the boulder. With his attention directed toward Nicholas, she crept to within 20 yards of him. She recognized him as one of the men from the livery stable and knew exactly what she had to do. At this range, she knew she wouldn't miss. Using the butt of his Kentucky flint rifle as a target, she steadied her gun and cocked the hammer. She took aim from the notch in the hammer to the brass sight at the end of her barrel and squeezed off a single shot. Her bullet dropped the man cold. Not giving him a second thought, she quickly circled back to Sassy.

As Sammy scrambled around to Mac's left, she became hampered by the weight of her wet skirts dragging around her legs. To be of any help, she needed to be more mobile. Apprehension tensed her muscles, and blood surged through her veins. She forgot how cold she'd felt only minutes before, as sweat trickled between her breasts from exertion.

When she found shelter behind an outcropping of rock, she removed her holster and drew her Bowie knife from its sheath. Quickly, she separated the skirt from the bodice. The two pairs of men's trousers she had on beneath her dress would have to be enough protection. After cutting off her skirt, she untied the strings holding her petticoats and kicked out of all the restraining skirts. Now, she could move. Using the holster as a belt, she buckled it back on over her pants. Cinching it as tight as possible, she prayed it would hold up her pants. She rolled on her belly and peeked around the boulder trying to see through the falling snow.

She saw Mac on her right. He must have been puzzled by the gunshot that had dropped one of the outlaws. He peered around trying to spot his support. She wondered if he thought one of Tyler's men mistook one of their own for him in the blinding snow. The confusion caused by one of their men being hit seemed to make the outlaws careless. Like a specter rising from the swirling snow, someone stood to yell. "There's more than just one man."

She said a quick prayer that the snow would not hamper her vision and squeezed off another shot.

~ * ~

Mac had hit the ground as the first bullet winged past him to drop the man who had been sneaking up on him. Trying to see anything in this soup was like peering into a crystal ball. Nothing but swirling white snow. It only allowed glimpses of shapes. Only a few minutes had passed before he heard a man shout and another shot rang out on his left. He rolled to his left to see where that shot came from and heard a short scream. He saw a second man drop.

With two men out of action, Tyler and his remaining ally scurried for cover. Mac realized someone had come to his aid. He could relax and not worry about his back.

Concentrating on his attackers, he was able to wound one of them as he ran for cover. The odds were suddenly looking better. Before he could advance, Mac heard shouting and cussing followed by muffled hoof beats as the last two men rode away from the deadly crossfire. They'd left their companions in the snow.

He worked his way forward to check the bodies, making sure they were dead and no longer a threat. He recognized one as the man called Luke. He had a bullet hole right between his eyes. The one he had shot had only been wounded. Mac saw a trail of blood leading to the trampled snow where the horses had been tied. The third man was off to his left with a bullet hole through the temple. Whoever had helped him knew how to use a gun.

Mac kicked snow over the fledgling fire, then turned back up the hill to thank his rescuer and retrieve Renegade. His only thought was to get back to the cave and Sammy as fast as he could. He saw someone struggling down the hill towards him.

The man looked as small as a kid, and he was dressed in outrageously baggy clothes.

He stood rock still in shock as he realized the "man" had to be Sammy. She stumbled down the hill breathless and fell into his arms. "Are you O.K.?" she gasped. "Are they dead? Did I get Tyler?" She struggled to release herself. "Let me go, I need to see if I killed Tyler!"

Anger boiled up and out of Mac. As he took her by the shoulders, he began to shake her. "I told you to stay in the cave. Are you crazy? You could have been killed!" He knew he was overreacting, but he couldn't control his fear. What if she'd been harmed? He couldn't bear to think about it. "You're not going anywhere. There are two men dead, and one was wounded. You don't have to go look. The fourth man rode off with the wounded one."

Sammy jerked back as if he'd slapped her. Reaction seemed to set in as soon as he'd answered, "There are two men dead". She began to shake uncontrollably. He wondered if it was the first time in her life she had aimed at a human being.

"They're dead?" Tears glistened in her eyes. "Oh, God! What did I do?" He felt sorry for her. She really didn't seem to understand what had happened. "I'm sorry. I'm sorry. The shots I fired were the deadly ones, weren't they?" She seemed to know, and he could only nod in agreement. Then, as if to explain her actions, she exploded with a temper to match his. "I saved your life! Those men were sneaking up to get behind you. You didn't stand a chance. You'd be dead now if I weren't here. Besides, they deserved to die."

Ignoring the truth, he changed the subject. "Where's your dress? You'll freeze out here!" Mac shouted as he wrapped his arms around her.

“Quit yelling at me,” Sammy replied as she twisted away from his cruel words and his hard hands. “I had to cut my skirt off so I could move faster.”

“Come on, let’s get back to the cave. We can build a fire now and get you dry.” Mac shook with rage, angrier with himself than with her. He’d wanted to be her protector, and instead she’d come to his rescue. “I guess that makes us even,” Mac mumbled as he took her elbow.

They struggled up the hill, stopping to retrieve Sammy’s skirt and petticoats, which were covered in snow already. They looked like a sodden heap of rags. “We may never find that cave again,” Mac muttered as they mounted their horses. The snow had covered all of their tracks already.

“Just follow me,” Sammy snapped as she clucked Sassy into the lead. When they reached the crest of the hill, Sammy reached up into a laden cedar tree with her Bowie knife. She finished cutting off a small dangling branch. She continued to lead the way reaching up every now and then at eye level as she removed the markers that she’d obviously made. Her anger at Mac seemed to simmer at a slow boil. She withdrew into herself, and for a minute he wondered if she wished she’d killed him, too.

When they reached the cave, she looked back and caught the look of awe and question in his eyes. “I don’t want anyone else following my trail markers.” She looked back the way they had come. The prints from Sassy and Renegade were already half full and would be obscured in a few minutes.

Sammy threw down all the cedar branches she had collected and dismounted. Leading Sassy into the cave, she marched back out to collect the branches as Mac brought Renegade into the warmth. With the pieces she had cut, she had enough cedar to start a small fire, and by the time Mac had unsaddled both horses, she had a small, cheery blaze crackling.

They worked in silence, each of them, absorbed in their own thoughts. Questions filled Mac's mind, and he knew Sammy had the same queries running through her head. He wondered if the one question, how they worked together, ever entered her mind. It seemed as if they'd already discussed and decided which chores each would assume.

Mac left the cave to gather more wood and once outside, looked around the clearing. He realized he probably would have missed the cavern. How in the hell did this slip of a girl track him, come to his rescue, kill two men, and find her way back without once losing her way? It promised to be a long afternoon and evening, and an even longer night. They had to start talking. He needed some answers.

He broke his daydreams to bring in the wood and, without a word, stomped out of the cave again. The beef jerky in his saddlebags would not be nourishing enough. He had to find some game. They needed a good hot fire, and she needed her wound tended. Then, he would see about food. *My God! I forgot all about her wound.* It couldn't be too bad if she felt strong enough leave the cave earlier. But, did it still pain her? He remembered how hard he'd shaken her, and he felt immediate remorse. The shock of recognizing her and the thought of her being in danger had driven him out of his mind.

Nineteen

Sammy stared at the fire in confusion. The dancing flames reminded her of her jumping thoughts. Now that they were out of danger, she started shaking from reaction. She shivered in cold and in pain. Although the heat drove out some of the dampness from the cave, she could still smell the mustiness that indicated mice. She shuddered.

She'd felt the warmth of blood running down her side as they had ridden back to the cave, but she didn't dare say a word about her wound. The brute would probably tell her it served her right for disobeying him. He hadn't even said thank you for saving his life.

She'd hoped one of the dead men would prove to be Tyler. She knew the others only followed his lead. If Tyler weren't in the picture, she might be able to find out the name of the ringleader a lot easier from the others. Even with the wish for his death, Sammy hated the thought that her bullets had ended two lives. Her need for revenge diminished, and she prayed for forgiveness. Then she prayed for the strength to see justice done. What those men did to her family and friends was so horrendous that the memory hardened her resolve again.

Sammy stumbled to the entrance of the cave to see what could be keeping Mac. He'd told her to tend her wound while he was out, but she wanted to make sure he wasn't going to walk in on her before she opened her dress. She caught a glimpse of him crouched behind a tree with his gun drawn. *Well*, she thought, *let him stand guard. I need to clean my wound.* With the blaze roaring, Sammy wet her bandanna with snow and let the heat warm the cloth. She still hadn't stopped bleeding, and it hurt terribly.

With the light from the fire, she could see the damage. A soft expletive voiced her concern. The red, raw, open wound made her feel queasy. The edges were ragged with the flesh torn a good quarter of an inch deep. She tried to press the sides together, but the pain halted that attempt. She cleaned the bandanna as best she could in melted snow, then redressed the wound. She laid out her skirt and petticoats to dry, then settled down with her back against her saddle. After she'd bathed the wound, it felt a little better. Perhaps the shock of seeing it caused the numbness. She wasn't sure but breathed a sigh of relief as she tried to make herself comfortable. Right now, she didn't feel too much pain. Now, all she had to worry about was infection.

The sound of the gun shot startled Sammy so much she jerked and winced as she felt her side tear open yet again. The warmth of the blood as it ran down her side caused her to spit out another curse. "If that's you, Tyler, you're a dead man." She grabbed her gun and charged out of the cave as Mac returned carrying a rabbit by the ears. "You could have warned me you were hunting," she yelled. "You scared the heck out of me."

"What was I supposed to do, get us some supper or worry about your sensibilities?"

Sammy glared at Mac and turned her back on him. "Clean your own rabbit." A glance over her shoulder showed her parting shot had been delivered to his back. "He is the most ill-mannered, obnoxious man I have ever had the misfortune of meeting," she grumbled. "Outside of Tyler!" she added with resignation.

He swiveled in shock at her remark. One look at her retreating back, and Mac did an about-face. He'd only wanted to show her he'd caught supper. He headed back to the stream to clean the rabbit. The woman probably didn't know the first thing about wild game. Conditioned to taking care of himself, he hadn't planned on asking for her help anyway.

When he returned, the cave felt quite cozy with a roaring fire and the body heat from the horses. Mac had enough light to finish his tasks and in no time had the rabbit on a spit over the fire. A thousand questions buzzed in his head, but he didn't know where to start. He owed her an apology and a thank you, but he found that hard to spit out, too. Mac watched her silently through lowered lids. Her arms were crossed in front of her chest, and he could see her right hand soothing her left side. He knew her wound had to be causing her some discomfort, but he didn't know the extent of the damage. Taking a deep breath to prepare himself, he supposed now was as good a time as any to get some questions answered.

"How's your wound? Do you think I should look at it?"

"It's fine. There's nothing for you to see."

Ha! That's what you think, but he didn't voice his sarcastic reply. No, now was not the time to think about her creamy white body.

"Do you feel up to talking some?" Mac gingerly tried again. "I'm sure your mind is snapping with as many questions as mine, and since we'll be stuck here together for probably the rest of the night, we ought to set each other's minds to rest."

"I just want to know if I killed Tyler." Sammy spoke in a quiet voice, almost dreading the answer. She'd never intentionally hurt anyone before, let alone kill a man. At the time she pulled the trigger, she didn't think of revenge, only of helping this mysterious man. Why she cared about his well-being, she couldn't say. She only knew she had been compelled to go to his aid. Now, after the fact, she needed to know if she had avenged her mother in the process.

"No. He wasn't one of the dead." Mac replied. "Will you tell me why it's so important for you to kill him? I know what you overheard when they were outside of the cave, but you should let the law go after him."

Nicholas looked at her with what appeared to be sympathy. Could she confide in yet another stranger? She wasn't sure if she could relate everything that had happened to her, again. If she unburdened her heart, it would show that she trusted him, and she didn't know how she felt yet.

"Who are you? Why did you snatch me away from Jason?" Sammy continued in a soft, quiet voice. It sounded like the voice of defeat, even to her own ears. By answering his question with one of her own she could delay talking about what had happened back in August. Her body sagged in total exhaustion and exasperation. Tyler lived, and he still wanted to kill her. She didn't know if she could trust this man yet, so she had to turn the questions back to him.

Mac's heart went out to her. She deserved some straight answers. However, he wasn't ready to reveal his original participation in her life. He decided to explain only his involvement from the time he'd spoken to Jason the night before their wedding. "My name is Nicholas MacNamee. I am a scout for the U.S. Army on personal leave. Word had reached me that Jason Sudholt needed some help tracking some wanted men. I arrived in town Christmas Eve, and I spoke to Jason just before your wedding. I was on the street when he was ambushed, and I saw that the bushwhackers were trying to kill you, too. I rode in to grab you out of the line of fire, found myself being chased by those four men, and you know the rest."

Sammy's body jerked erect as if pulled by the strings of a puppeteer. "Jason never told me you'd arrived! He must have known how much that news would have cheered me. I had written to the commander at the fort myself." As if talking to herself, she continued, "You're the man that walked with Jason Christmas morning, aren't you?" At his nod, she sighed. "It just didn't seem as if Jason moved as fast as I wanted him to. I had to take things into my own hands." Sammy lowered her head and sobbed.

Mac's heart broke for her, but he didn't dare try to comfort her at this point. She must have loved Jason very much. He felt awkward and remained silent as she cried out her anguish. He wanted her to have the privacy she needed in this moment of grief. As far as he knew, this was the first time she'd allowed herself to cry over her husband's death. She only seemed to allow herself a brief moment before she forced her emotions under control again. He wondered how long she would mourn. Would she ever love again? He hoped in time she'd regain her will to go on with her life.

Mac saw her resolve and the hard glint in her eyes as she raised her head and wiped away her tears. He distracted himself by busying his hands, checking the rabbit. Finding it done to a turn, he offered Sammy half and without another word began to eat his portion.

Sammy ate in silence and found she was hungrier than she had imagined. Nicholas remained quiet, and she let her mind drift. She wouldn't give in to grief. Her father had raised her to be strong. She wouldn't allow herself to cry anymore. She felt another layer of steel close over her heart. It would take a stick of dynamite to crack her reserve now. Each trial hardened her heart a little more. No one would get close to her again! She wouldn't allow it!

When she finished, she took her bandanna and, wetting it in the snow, carried it back to the fire to warm the cloth. After washing her face and hands, she repeated her actions then offered the clean cloth to Mac to wipe his hands. Her thoughtfulness seemed to touch him, causing him to smile his thanks. That smile! It caused her heart to leap for a moment, then it was gone. He still maintained his silence. Sammy grew uncomfortable with the strain and decided to confide in him. She settled back against her saddle and began her story.

She could see his straining forward to hear every word. He listened without interruption until she heard him gasp as she shyly revealed the part of her story she had never before told anyone. "I'm afraid I'm the one who stole your boots and hat." She tried to see his reaction without really allowing him to make eye contact with her. "I'm sorry. But I needed them to complete my disguise." She finished her story and looked at him directly for the first time. Then she stuck out one small foot and said, "I'll trade you. It's obvious that these boots are custom-made, and they are so big on me that it won't matter if I have these or the ones you are wearing now."

After a brief moment, Mac's hardy laugh ricocheted off the walls of the cave. "You've got a deal. I just have one question. How did you get past Renegade?"

"That was the easiest part," Sammy laughed. This part of her story brought her a feeling of superiority. Her heart swelled with joy in remembering. She stood up and walked over to the horses. She sensed Nicholas tense immediately. He seemed ready to jump up to keep her from being stomped by his powerful horse. She glanced over her shoulder at him as he waited in a half crouch. Renegade whinnied, and she smiled as she sang to the beautiful horse. Before Nicholas could move, she embraced the horse and rubbed her face against his. Renegade almost purred in contentment. Nicholas sank back down on his heels. He wore a look of utter astonishment.

Sammy continued to stroke Renegade until Sassy voiced her jealously and, laughing, she administered the same love to her sweet mare. From her position between the two horses, she continued the story of her training by her father and her brothers and of the different skills she learned.

“Jason didn’t know about my skill with a gun although he’d witnessed me teaching Daniel.” She explained how she had always masked her real expertise so that no one would question her. Walking back to the fire, she also offered to trade hats with Mac as she sat and removed his boots.

“I’ll take you up on the trade.” Mac laughed. “My poor feet haven’t been the same in these cheap boots. The hat doesn’t matter near as much.” Doing a double take he questioned, “What happened to the hatband?”

“I can’t stand snakes. I threw it away.” Sammy answered so matter of factly that Mac laughed again. This woman made him feel so good. He hadn’t laughed aloud with such enjoyment in a long time. Something about Sammy made him feel whole for the first time. He felt contentment and peace. He hadn’t even touched her, yet he knew this woman was one he could spend the rest of his life with in total contentment.

Wait a minute. Spend the rest of my life with! What am I thinking? He was afraid she wouldn’t have anything to do with him once she found out about his mother. Anyway, he couldn’t and didn’t want to settle down yet. He’d better get a grip on his emotions. Besides, she was so wounded both spiritually and physically that he instinctively realized she wouldn’t let anyone close to her for quite awhile. He knew she still wanted to bring Tyler to justice, and he firmed his determination to help her.

His first priority was to get her to a doctor and safety. Then he would go after Tyler and his boss, Morgan.

Mac rose. He picked up his saddle blanket, his oilcloth poncho, and her bedroll. He crossed to her side of the fire and laid out the oilcloth. “Lie here. You can use both the blankets. You need to keep your body warm so you don’t become ill. I’ll keep the fire going all night. In the morning, we’ll see if we can make our way back to town. I’d like a doctor to look at your wound, and you’ll be safer in town with some protection.”

As Sammy wrapped herself in the blankets and prepared to settle down for the night, Mac started talking. He wasn’t sure what unlocked the dam that allowed the words to spill out of his mouth like a raging river. Somehow, he had to show her she’d placed her trust in the right person. If he confided in her, he’d be returning the compliment.

He told her all about his life as a scout and how he had come across her burned-out farm and become suspicious. He had left out the part of seeing her bathe in the waterfall. He didn’t want to embarrass her. He’d save that story for some night when he had her wrapped in his arms, and he could tell her with words as well as action what he’d thought when he first saw her. That he would make love to this woman he had never doubted. That he was in love with her he couldn’t yet admit.

As Mac related the part about Morgan, she became agitated again. Her excitement seemed to bubble out like the fizz of champagne. “You’ve discovered more than I ever guessed was possible. Did Jason know all this?” she asked.

“Part of it,” Mac replied. “He said he wanted to tell you the news as a wedding gift. Didn’t he mention it?”

“No!” Sammy looked dejected again. “He just never thought I was serious about finding my family’s killers. Everyone underestimates me. Don’t you make that mistake!” With that she turned over and pretended to go to sleep. He could tell by her breathing that she kept herself alert.

Don't worry, thought Mac. *I won't make that mistake again. You are one woman who knows how to take care of herself. You are the one woman who can be my equal. I'll do everything I can to help you find your family's killers. If you can accept my heritage, I'll never let you out of my life. Together we'll make a hell of a team.* Mac stoked the fire and, pounding his saddle, lay his head down and tried to sleep.

The next morning, Sammy awoke with a start at the sound of a single shot. Clutching her side, she jumped from her bedroll and grabbed her gun as she ran to the cave entrance. She took note after several minutes of silence that Nicholas' footprints led off into the woods. Not hearing any return fire, she forced herself to relax a bit, then waited. Where had he gone? Had Tyler returned? Thoughts of the outlaw made her heart race again.

"Calm down," she muttered. "He's probably acting the great hunter again."

The morning had dawned crisp and clear. The sun struggled to break the gloom of night, and the snow had finally stopped. The depth of Nicholas' prints showed they had received a major snowstorm. All around her, the trees glistened with a coating of white icing. Cedar trees bowed under the weight, and many were bent in half. It looked like a fairyland, and the beauty of the setting did not escape her notice.

However, right now her wound screamed for attention. She felt another warm trickle of blood run down her side. Returning to town became a priority. Besides, she needed to lay Jason to rest. She just couldn't leave that part of her life with loose ends. Secondly, she knew her friends would be worried sick about her. Sammy's mouth felt pasty, and she ran her tongue around her teeth to relieve the feeling. Her stomach growled as a reminder that she hadn't eaten since mid-afternoon yesterday. She needed to relieve herself, but she didn't dare leave the safety of the cave until Nicholas returned.

"Where are you?" she wondered aloud. Shivering with cold, she checked her skirt and petticoat. The material had dried overnight so she slipped them on over the pants to add another layer of warmth. Just when she decided she couldn't wait any longer, she saw movement. He came trudging through the woods dragging a heavy burden. Reaching the clearing, he struggled through the deep snow, plowing a path for his payload. Without a word, Sammy holstered her gun and fought the deep snow to reach his side. When she got close enough, she saw the young doe he had shot. He'd field dressed it, but it wasn't skinned. As she approached, his face lit with a smile that caught her breath.

"Morning, Sunshine."

Too embarrassed to answer, Sammy wordlessly reached for the doe's back legs. Together they carried it to the cave.

"Thanks, I wasn't making good time by myself. This snow turns every chore into a challenge."

Sammy nodded in reply. His easy banter made her feel uncomfortable, and she couldn't seem to find her voice this morning.

She needed to get outside and fast. "I'll gather more firewood while you skin and quarter the deer." With that parting remark, she beat a hasty retreat.

Rounding the corner, she saw he'd tried to clear a path for her. She made note to thank him for his consideration then saw to her morning toilet. The clean snow refreshed her as she rubbed some across her face and hands. Then taking some more, she tried to rinse out her mouth and clean her teeth. The cold moisture penetrated every nerve and made her teeth hurt. Reluctantly, she gave up the effort. She tried to clean Nicholas' bandanna in the snow, but it only made the cloth soaking wet and useless to absorb more blood. To reach a clean, dry portion of her petticoat, she had to use her knife to cut off the bottom ruffle then remove part of the second flounce. Once she folded and stuffed the wad under her chemise, she used another length to wrap around her middle to hold it tight against her skin. “It’s the best I can manage”, she muttered. She dismissed the wound as a minor inconvenience and set out to gather firewood.

Returning to the cave with an arm full of tree limbs, Sammy set about helping Nicholas prepare a deer haunch for roasting. They worked together in silent companionship. She thought they seemed comfortable with each other. She wondered if it was because of that amazing connection that allowed each to know what the other needed without words.

Sammy handed Nicholas a length of rope. He looked up at her in wonder. “How did you know what I needed?” He asked, breaking the silence.

“I know what I would have done with the remaining meat to keep it from spoiling and to save for later. I just figured you were at least as smart as me,” she replied matter of factly. She was so used to baiting her brothers that she instinctively knew what his reaction would be.

“Why you little minx,” he laughed as he made a lunge for her.

Sammy dodged him and, holding out her arm to ward him away, grinned. “Don’t forget, I’m wounded. You don’t want to reopen my side by any roughhousing do you?”

Stopping short, he apologized. “You’re right, I almost forgot you’re hurt. You’ve been so brave, no complaints, no crying. I watched you work just as hard as I have all morning. Your father and your brothers trained you well. I wish I could have met them. I think I would have loved your family.”

His speech startled her into quiet withdrawal. She hated the reminder of all she'd lost. Not wanting him to see the shine of tears that threatened to spill, she turned her back to him. Defensively, she used anger to cover her feelings. "How can you talk about loving my family? You never knew them. You have to know people before you can love them."

Walking up behind her, Nicholas gently laid his hands on her shoulders and turned her to face him. He lifted her chin and used his thumbs to wipe the tears that brimmed each eye. "You're right. I didn't know them, but I'm beginning to know you, and I…" *damn! I almost said, 'and I knew your brother.'* "I like what I see," he finished. "You are the product of your family's upbringing, and you do them proud."

Before Sammy could respond or decipher the intent look in his gleaming blue eyes, Nicholas bent his head and gently touched his lips to hers. It was a butterfly kiss of barely perceptible contact, and yet it caused such a rush of blood to her heart that it threatened to pound itself right out of her body. Heat flooded her neck and rushed to the top of her head. She watched a smile transform his face and cursed her tendency to blush. How dare he laugh at her?

Sammy shrugged away from him, thoroughly flustered. The nerve of him. Kissing her! Then laughing at her embarrassment. Why would he do that? And, why had he turned so gentle at the last moment that it caused her to feel safe and protected again? It was a feeling she hadn't realized she missed until now. It made her imagine she was huddled deep in the heart of her family again. This man posed more than one danger for her. She'd better be prepared for anything.

Reluctantly, Mac released her. "Keep turning that meat while I hang the rest of this carcass outside." How could she be so innocent? She'd been married. Maybe only one night, but Mac knew if he had spent the night with her, she would have been thoroughly initiated into the art of love. Yet, she blushed like a maiden.

He stayed out long enough for her to regain her composure and, on entering the cave, became matter of fact to cover any lingering embarrassment. "I've scouted around a little, and I don't think we'll be able to make it back to town today. The snow is so deep it will be hazardous for the horses. I'm afraid you'll get too cold, and with your wound, it might be wise to hole up here another day. We have enough meat, and there is plenty of wood to keep us warm. One more day will help you recover. Then when the snow melts, we'll be able to make better time. That will get you back to shelter with the least exposure to the weather."

Seeing her about to respond and not wanting to argue with her, Mac continued, not allowing her to interrupt. "I also want Tyler to have enough time to get farther away from here. He won't return to town after killing Jason. I expect he'll go back to Morgan for reinforcements. He is too much of a coward to continue hunting you with only one wounded companion."

"If we wait another day before we return," Sammy finally interrupted, "it will be too late to bury Jason. I need to return as soon as possible to set Jack and Sally at rest. Rebecca, too, she will be beside herself with worry. Then after I see them, I want to go to Pinckney and expose Morgan myself."

"No, I won't allow it." Mac exploded. "You don't seem to realize how dangerous this man is. He's had at least five families wiped out without even batting an eye. Do you think he'll hesitate to kill you if you show up in Pinckney?" He knew as soon as he saw her eyes flashing green fire that she fully resented his authoritative manner.

"Who do you think you are to 'allow' me to do anything? You have no say over my comings or goings!" When she snapped right back at him, he had to suppress a grin. God, she had spunk, he'd give her that. But, it didn't change the fact that she couldn't go after Morgan by herself.

"If I want to go after Morgan, I will. I'm smart enough to figure out a plan to trap him or something. I've got to do this! Don't you understand? He is responsible for what happened to everyone I ever loved. He can't get away with this!"

So she had loved Jason. He marveled that she expressed her feelings without hesitation, even though her voice shimmered in anger.

"Simmer down, Sammy," Mac pleaded. "I do understand your need to get Tyler and Morgan. I didn't say we wouldn't go after him. We just need to plan this out so he doesn't escape, and you don't get hurt. Maybe I neglected to mention it, but I want to help you."

"Don't be condescending," she screamed.

"Sammy, I'm not. I'm trying to say I'll help you."

Her mood changed abruptly. "Thank you, Nicholas. I could use some help. I realize how dangerous these men are, and I wasn't planning anything rash. It's just now that I know who's behind all this and where to find him, it's hard to hold back."

Nicholas. God! No one except his father used his real name. It sounded wonderful when she breathed it out like that. Mac was having a harder and harder time keeping his hands off her. He wanted desperately to sweep her up and cover her body with his. He just knew they would make magic together. Knowing how much she had been hurt in the past, both by the deaths of her family and what was more important, her husband, he realized he had to exercise every bit of patience he had.

"Come on," he said, "let's see if that venison is done. I'm starving, and the smell of that meat cooking is driving me crazy."

"You men, all you ever think of is food." Her laugh had broken the tension, and he smiled.

"Not all," he quipped. He avoided looking up at the quick snap of her head in his direction. *Lord, I've done it again. Why can't I keep my mind outta the gutter and my mouth shut?* Mac sighed in relief when Sammy chose to ignore his comment.

"Do you have any salt?" Sammy kept herself busy turning the spit to avoid eye contact. She didn't want him to see how much his use of her nickname had affected her. No one had called her Sammy since she'd lost her family. It was a reminder of gentler times. It made her feel like Nicholas could fill that gap.

"My possibles pouch is in my saddlebag. I'll get it." Nicholas retrieved a leather bag and untied the drawstring. He removed a piece of thin leather and unfolded it to reveal a small mound of white granules.

"I don't have much, but use what you need."

"This will be more than enough. Thank you." Sammy held out her hand for the seasoning and accepted the packet from Nicholas. She started at the contact their hands made. A shiver chased goose bumps across her body. Why did this man affect her so?

To still her shaking hand, she busied herself cutting portions of meat for each of them. After she sprinkled a tiny bit of salt on the pieces, she pushed Nicholas' tin across to him. She wasn't taking any more chances of making contact. She didn't want to feel the sparks, he alone seemed to ignite, flare across her skin.

Jason. His name entered her mind like a sharp reprimand. She couldn't let this strange feeling erase Jason's image. To break the uncomfortable silence, Sammy asked Nicholas about his life. "How long have you been a scout?"

"I've worked with Commander Williams a couple of years now. I finished college, and when I came back west, I decided I didn't want to return to my father's ranch."

"You went to college?"

"Yes, what's so amazing about that?" She watched his eyes turn a steely, blue gray.

"Why, nothing. I guess I was just surprised. My brother Tim went to college. J.R. and Ryan didn't have an interest in more schooling, but Tim wanted to be a teacher. Where'd you go to school?"

"Harvard."

When she heard his answer, she almost dropped her food. "That's where Tim went." She knew her voice registered her shock and surprise when she saw Nicholas squirm. He set his dish on the ground and looked at her. His eyes softened to a warm, sky blue, and she marveled at how his emotions changed his looks. She held herself still, almost dreading what he seemed to be preparing to tell her.

Twenty

Sammy felt the air crackle with tension. Even the horses stopped shifting their weight. She took a huge breath, inhaling the familiar scent of horseflesh and leather mingled with the mustiness of the cave. Nicholas seemed to hesitate, then he broke the silence.

"Sammy." He paused, and she stiffened, holding her breath. "I knew your brother." The air whooshed out of her lungs.

"What?"

"Your brother and I were roommates."

"That's not true. He roomed with a man named 'Mac', and he was an Indian." As soon as the words left her mouth, she realized it had to be true. MacNamee, Mac. It was just like Tim to give him a nickname. He would never have called his friend "Nicholas."

Before she could say anything else, Mac watched as acceptance and recognition softened her face. He'd debated telling her about his acquaintance with Tim, then he'd decided to start building her trust in him. Once she knew he'd been a friend of her brother's, maybe she'd be more receptive to his help.

"Yes, it is true, Sammy. Your brother nicknamed me, and it's stuck all through my scouting days. Most people call me

Mac now. I hardly knew you were speaking to me when you said Nicholas. Only my father and stepmother call me Nicholas anymore."

"Tim wrote us about you. He said your mother was an Indian. Is that true?"

He couldn't tell if the thought repulsed her or not. He'd hoped to win her love, making her forget about Jason and anyone else she might have known, before he revealed his heritage. Since she already knew part of it from Tim, he'd better tell her the whole story.

"Yes, it's true. Does that bother you?" He hadn't planned on asking her that already. Somehow, it had slipped out without thought. He realized his future pivoted on her answer.

"Of course not. Why should it?"

Her answer came so quickly, he knew she spoke the truth. His heart swelled with happiness. Her words were exactly what Tim had blurted out when he'd learned of his origin. Well, there was one impediment he could quit worrying about. "A lot of people have a hatred for Indians and especially half-breeds. I'm glad you're as tolerant as Tim." When he beamed his pleasure at her answer, she ducked her head. He wondered if she would ever return his smile without embarrassment.

"I never knew my real mother. She died when I was born." Sammy winced. He shook his head to dismiss her sympathy.

"My father was born in Scotland. He came to America to make his fortune. When my mother died, he left the tribe and took me with him. I was raised and educated as a white man." He smiled at her again. "Your brother talked me into growing this mustache. He said with my blue eyes, the mustache would make me look more like a white man. Indians don't grow facial hair you know."

Sammy smiled at him in a moment of shared memory for Tim. "Yes, I can well imagine what a joke Tim thought it would be to fool everyone."

"Well, he was right. Once I grew the mustache, no one commented on my resemblance to the Native Americans." Laughing, he continued, "But I got my revenge. I challenged him to grow the muttonchops. I told him, if I had to have hair on my face, so did he. We made a pact that neither of us would shave. By the time we got used to the way we looked, neither one of us wanted to."

He and Sammy laughed outright at that admission, and he felt at once in total harmony with her. "I've never been ashamed of my Indian heritage. It's just that people can be so cruel. When I was growing up, I received countless taunts and snubs. It wasn't until I could hold my own in the schoolyard that the kids finally stopped teasing me. After that, I never made excuses for my parentage or my looks."

"No one should be made to feel ashamed of their nationality," Sammy responded. "Our family and the O'Briens were always ridiculed for being Irish Catholics. The German community around here finally accepted us when we proved we weren't lazy."

"Yes," Nicholas laughed. "Tim told me some stories about the scraps he and his brothers got into at school." Finding it easier to relate his history, he told her about the coldness he'd suffered at his stepmother's hand, his reluctance to return to his father's ranch, mostly fueled by Juliana's treatment. "My stepmother would never allow me to call her mother. It was always Juliana. At first, she insisted I call her 'Miss Juliana', but my father threw a fit. He told her I wasn't a servant. If 'mother' was unacceptable, then just plain Juliana would have to do. She didn't like it, but she accepted it."

"Nicholas, I'm so sorry. We had such a loving family, I can't imagine what it would be like to be only tolerated."

He didn't want her pity and had to marshal his thoughts before he answered. "There's no need for concern. My father more than made up for her lack. I've never been given a moment to doubt his love for me."

"I'm so glad, Nicholas."

He had to change the subject. He couldn't take much more of her goodhearted concern.

They finished their meal, and Nicholas took the utensils out to rinse in the creek. He noticed when he returned that she'd laid out the bedrolls, one on each side of the fire. Would she ever lie by his side? He wondered if he would be able to sleep tonight. Could she feel the tension as much as he did? No. She'd loved Jason. She wouldn't think of her brother's college roommate as anything other than a friend. He hoped he'd have the patience to wait for her to forget her husband.

~ * ~

The next morning, Sammy woke to the smell of venison cooking. Suddenly, she became shockingly aware of her surroundings. She cracked her eyelids open to see if Nicholas still slept. He was nowhere in sight. Gingerly sitting up, she found herself embarrassed about being stranded with him. She had never spent the night alone with a stranger before, and now she'd just woke up from her second night with this man. Why wasn't she this self-conscious yesterday, she wondered.

Then she remembered her disturbing dream. It had been Nicholas making love to her on her wedding night and not Jason. In her dream she had welcomed him with open arms. When his powerful body came down on hers, she'd wrapped her legs around him and her hips had risen to accommodate him. Her body still hummed from the quivers he'd stirred with just a touch. The visions that came with the memory made her glad he wasn't sitting across from her to see her blush. It seemed like she knew Nicholas better in the two days they'd spent together, than she'd ever known Jason. After he'd courted her for a month, Jason had still been a stranger to her. Nicholas had become a friend, practically overnight. Nicholas. She could never think of him as Mac. The nickname seemed so ordinary. It didn't suit the extraordinary man that he had turned out to be. The name Nicholas gave the impression of someone strong, masculine, and independent. Yes, it suited him well. She could never call him Mac.

She stood hesitantly, nervous and relieved that he hadn't tried to put his hands on her. Except for that one brief kiss, he hadn't touched her again or made any move by word or action that he intended to pursue her. She didn't think she could bear for a man to touch her like Jason had ever again. Her one experience had left her cold, and she feared she'd never want to get married or have children if it meant enduring another night like her wedding night. *Children*! The thought shocked her. She would have made a wonderful mother. She loved children. One of her favorite past times had been to help Nancy with her brood. Forcing herself to forget the painful memory, she wondered why her dreams hadn't frightened her. Instead, they had excited and thrilled her. She didn't need these confusing feelings.

As she walked to the narrow opening and peeked out, she realized she'd been left alone. The cave echoed the sound of her breathing, emphasizing her solitary presence. Even the horses were gone. The only noise, disturbing the silence, came from the cracking and spitting of meat cooking. Suddenly, she felt fear run down her spine leaving a trail of goose bumps. She bolted out of the cave. What if Nicholas had left her all alone again? What if he didn't intend to help as he promised? She saw the footprints left by Nicholas and the two horses. They led away from the cave.

The snow appeared to be at least two feet deep. How could he travel today? It would wear out the horses and going would be slow. She decided he must have taken both horses so he could alternate mounts, and she began to mourn the loss of Sassy. Then she cursed herself for beginning to trust a stranger. Tim might have known him, but she didn't. And, even though he'd been educated, he was still an Indian. She instantly regretted the biased thought, but her trust was shattered. She realized the absolute silence was what must have awakened her. The familiar snorts and rustling of the horses had been missing.

Devastated she walked back to the fire and steeled herself not to cry. At least he'd left her enough food for a few days. Hearing a whinny, she drew her gun and ran back to the cave entrance. Heart pounding, she hoped Tyler's ugly face would emerge from the trees. She felt like shooting someone. Her body trembled in relief to see Nicholas returning on foot, leading both horses. Her hand shook so badly it took her two attempts to return the gun to her holster. She had to get control of herself.

Nicholas raised a hand in greeting when he spotted her standing at the cave entrance. "Breakfast ready?" he shouted. "I've brought us more firewood. The way things are looking this morning we'll be here at least two or three more days. The snow is over five-feet deep in places where it's drifted, and nothing is moving. I'm glad I got that deer yesterday. It should last us until we can ride out."

Sammy stared in awe, almost not taking in his cheerful chatter. The horses were harnessed to two huge tree trunks and they were dragging the wood right up to the cave entrance. "Don't just stand there gaping, woman, help me unhitch these poor beasts and get them into the cave. I'm near frozen myself.

As soon as I eat and thaw out a little, I'll get some logs chopped and we can have a real fire. We need a blaze that will warm us tonight and keep our breath from smoking out every time we open our mouths."

Mac sounded so cheerful it was almost disgusting. Didn't he realize they didn't need two whole trees for firewood? They certainly wouldn't be here much longer. However, his playful manner got the best of her, and Sammy jumped to do his bidding. She rushed to Sassy first and crooned into her face. Her spirits had soared to see the mare again. She really didn't know what she would ever do if she lost her, too. The filly helped her think of better times. Her eyes closed and a soft smile caressed her face.

Mac watched her stroking Sassy and something tightened in his gut. He wanted her to greet him with that same sweetness. What made him feel so protective and yet, *jealous* of a *horse*? No one had ever evoked these emotions in him. She had to be the most self-reliant woman he had ever met. She'd saved his life and found her way back to the cave in a blinding snowstorm. He hated to admit it, but she had saved him twice in one afternoon! *Who am I kidding? Protect her! Hell, I need her to protect and care for me!*

About the time he decided to remind her of her duties, Renegade pawed the ground and whinnied. Sammy laughed and turned to the stallion.

"All right, I love you, too."

Mac gulped. Would she ever direct those words to him? Would she ever hug and stroke him with that same tenderness? His body hardened instantly with that thought. He had to stop thinking like that.

Mac couldn't let her see his eyes. He knew they almost shouted out his need. His tongue rebelled as he bit it to keep from asking, "When is it my turn?" To distract himself, he helped her unhitch both horses. One at a time, she led them through the narrow opening, bringing them into the warmth of the cave. Then she returned to Mac.

“Can you manage for a minute? I need to rinse off my face and hands, then I’ll cut some venison for you.” Without waiting for a reply, she slipped past him and disappeared into her mutually agreed upon private place.

By the time Sammy returned, Mac had his emotions under control. The more time he spent with her, the more difficult it became for him to hide his feelings. He hadn’t told her he had seen signs in the sky of another storm headed their way. To reinforce his predictions, he’d seen the snowbird. It had seemed to chirp a warning to prepare for more. She seemed so anxious to get back to find Tyler and bring him to justice he didn’t have the heart to tell her she’d probably be stuck out here for a lot longer than they had thought.

That was one of the reasons he had dropped two dead trees this morning, that and the fact that he needed to work off some of the intense feelings he’d begun to experience. The physical exercise of chopping down the trees and now the labor he had in front of him splitting them into logs for the fire should wear him out enough that he would be able to sleep tonight. Last night had been the worst. They had spent the day getting to know each other, talking about their families and friends, about their dreams and ambitions.

Mac couldn’t remember ever sharing his thoughts with anyone else, but it came so natural with this woman. She seemed to be his other half. Together they would make a perfect whole. He couldn’t, even after this short period of a time, imagine being without her company ever again. She seemed as necessary to him as breathing, and yet he knew he had to use caution. She was as skittish as an unbroken mare. Sometime during the last twenty-four hours, perhaps during the night as he watched her sleep, he realized he wanted her for all time and not just for the momentary pleasure he always enjoyed from bedding a woman. This was one filly he intended to make his own, even if he had to marry her to do that.

~ * ~

After riding through the snow for an hour, Joshua passed out and fell off his horse. Tyler, not wanting to be held up any longer, left him where he lay. Taking the other man's horse, he continued on his way. He didn't feel a bit of remorse at leaving the man.

"Damn fool, letting himself get shot up," he muttered. He planned on circling back to the ranch and getting reinforcements. Once this blasted snowstorm ended, he intended to pick up Miss Turner's trail and carry out his revenge. He'd make that little gal sorry she'd ever been born.

Tyler made camp late that night. He felt safe enough to build a fire. No other fool would be out in this storm, so he wouldn't be detected. Besides, he reasoned, he needed to get warm and eat something to keep up his strength. He couldn't remember ever seeing such a bad snowstorm. It had gotten harder and harder for his horse to pick his way. Even switching between the animals to conserve their strength hadn't helped. Finally the snow grew so deep he couldn't go any farther.

Once he'd set up camp and built a skimpy fire, he'd made some coffee and diluted it with whisky. The frigid wind chilled him to the bone, and he gulped the mixture down, trying to warm his insides. Tyler had used Joshua's bedroll to fashion a lean-to. With the fire in front of him and the blanket keeping the wind and snow off his back, he rolled himself in his bedroll and drank himself into a deep slumber.

Morning found him hopelessly befuddled. At first he couldn't remember why he was sleeping in the snow. His fire had gone out, and he couldn't control his shaking. The lean-to he'd strung over his body had collapsed on top of him, burying him under at least a foot of the cold white stuff.

Clawing his way out of the cocoon created by the blizzard, he tried to clear his head and think. He shivered as the wind whipped through his damp clothes, and he looked at the snow-covered blanket. He almost crawled back under that insulating envelope. *No*, he thought, *I've got to get help. Got to find that gal.* A glance around his camp chilled him even more. He didn't see his horses. He took two steps and sunk up to his thighs in the deep snow. A harsh white mantle of iciness covered everything. There were no dead limbs visible to use for firewood. He remembered he'd left his hatchet in his saddlebag. Another befuddled look confirmed that he'd neglected to unsaddle both horses last night.

He stood, dazed and disorientated. There were no tracks to show which way the horses had wandered. Digging in his pocket, he brought out a piece of beef jerky and began chewing. He scooped up hands full of snow to quench his thirst while he contemplated his next step. Then he remembered his bottle. Scrambling under the snow-covered blanket, he retrieved the whiskey. He'd need it later. As the fog began to leave Tyler's brain, he realized he faced the biggest problem he had ever had to deal with alone. He knew he wasn't the kind of man that coped well in harsh conditions. He liked his comforts. If he needed anything, he'd always been able to bully it out of someone. He'd never had to work to satisfy his needs. He just took them.

Out here in the wilderness, all alone, he realized he'd have to fend for himself. "Damn fools," he muttered. "Why'd they have to go an' get themselves shot up. If they'd stayed hidden like me, they'd be alive." He only had his own abilities to rely on, and he knew that he courted disaster. "It's all your fault, you stupid idiots," he yelled into the empty forest. "I wouldn't be all alone if you'd used your heads." He began to sweat with anxiety, and the rapid increase of his heartbeat caused him to panic.

He snatched up the two blankets. His subconscious told him he needed them. A vicious shake dislodged most of the snow. Then, he threw them over his arm and began a frantic half run, plowing through the snow. He hadn't taken more than seventy-five awkward steps before he became totally exhausted. He stood panting and scared. Nothing but a white wilderness lay before him. All landmarks were obliterated. No animal tracks were visible, and even the birds were quiet. Tyler's throat hurt from breathing through his mouth. His lungs strained from the pain of the cold air. With the depth of the snow reaching well over his knees, the inside of his boots had become packed. His socks were saturated, and his feet began to turn numb.

Looking back at his tracks, he could see that he'd wasted a tremendous amount of effort in the erratic path he'd taken. He beat his fist against a tree in frustration because he could still see the trampled snow where he'd spent the night. The broken branch that supported his blanket tilted at a crazy angle. At this rate, he would never reach civilization. He would die in the cold, alone. For the first time in his life, Tyler felt the unfamiliar sensation of fear raise goose bumps over his body.

Pulling the whiskey bottle from his pocket, he drained it. He knew that without help he could die. That despair made him angry. He screamed his curses to an invisible audience and pounded the empty jug against a tree in his uncontrollable rage. Falling into the snow to sob his frustration, he lapsed into unconsciousness, his head pillowed by the broken shards.

Like a silent ghost, Swift Arrow crept forward, leading his band to where they found the unconscious white man. Seeing him face down in the snow and apparently defenseless, one of the braves ran to the body, turned him over, and prepared to lift his scalp. Swift Arrow's hand stopped his upraised arm. The young brave looked questionably at his leader for a moment as he immediately stayed his blow.

As their chief, Swift Arrow knew if he wanted the man alive, his men would obey. His band had broken off from the weaker members of their tribe, those who wanted to live in peace with the white man. Swift Arrow knew there would be no peace with the greedy white man always wanting more of their land and driving off the game they needed to survive. Even now he'd had to lead his small band to hunt farther afield to find food for their women and children.

"Don't you want to kill this dog?" The brave asked.

"No. I stopped you for a good reason. I recognize this man." This was the man who had hired Swift Arrow and four other braves to help him kill the settlers along the river. This man had paid them in liquor and guns. Swift Arrow had not been happy with the number of guns he and his braves had received, so he'd taken his own payment.

In the confusion during one of the raids, he'd stolen five young children. He'd never seen a human being with hair the color that adorned the heads of everyone in that family. He knew the children would be valuable as slaves. Many tribes would be willing to have a child blessed with the touch of red sunset on their head. It had been so easy to outfox the greedy one, the man who lay before him. He had been so busy satisfying his baser needs with the woman, it had been a simple task to hand the children off to his braves and have them disappear into the woods to wait for him. This poor excuse of a man hadn't even missed the braves who had ridden off with the five children.

In a few short words, Swift Arrow identified him to the other braves and told them what he thought about him. He wanted nothing more than to bring him to their camp and torture him with all the subtle art his forebears had developed. However, he knew the value of this man's connections. Powerful friends had given him the guns and firewater to trade. He would know where to get more. Since he had not paid enough for their help with the slaughter of those families, maybe they could ransom the life of this worthless dog.

Not wasting any motion, the braves had Tyler bound and wrapped in his two blankets, forming a makeshift travois. Minutes later they started their trek back to camp, dragging the unconscious man behind like a dead carcass.

By noon the Indians approached their camp. Ten teepees circled the main campfire. Swift Arrow envisioned Night Flower running to meet him. Her smile would hold that heart-warming glow that Swift Arrow would give his life to keep on her lovely face. His chest puffed up in pride and happiness that he had given her the gift that brought joy back into her life.

She'd been in the depths of despair when he first rode out to accept Tyler's offer. The temptation of guns and the headiness of his first taste of the firewater had warped his judgment on that decision. Yet, the addition of the twin babies he'd brought his wife made him glad he had gone.

They had sold the older children on their way home, but Swift Arrow had kept the youngest babies. He knew that the twins with their thatches of red hair would bring his teepee a distinction no other had.

What he hadn't foreseen was that these babies would give his wife the will to live again. Owning these sun gods had brought her honor, and her joy in caring for them had helped her put their baby's death behind her. Swift Arrow recalled that day more than four moons ago and smiled for the change it had caused. Maybe today would bring the same good fortune. The winter had dragged on, long, cold, and with more snow than the few elders could remember. On this late afternoon, the camp looked deserted except for the smoke of cook fires. The women and children huddled in their teepees, staying as close to the warmth as possible.

Inside her home, Night Flower tucked another blanket around the sleeping babies and stewed over Swift Arrow's decision not to accompany the rest of the tribe to winter quarters. He'd insisted on staying close to the white men, always looking for a job helping to raid farms and receiving payment in guns and firewater. Less than a dozen families had stayed with Swift Arrow. She felt the camp was in danger, lacking the protection of larger numbers.

She had to admit that Swift Arrow had chosen this site well. It was nestled along the side of the creek with hills directly to the north to cut down on the wind. They had water and small game, but the larger animals had disappeared. With this last snowstorm, the men had been forced to range farther searching for bigger game.

The twins were sleeping curled together in the furs. They were almost a year old and beginning to walk. Night Flower smiled as she watched their innocent faces reposed in peaceful sleep. She wished her tribe could all be that innocent. She hated the violence they had to live with every day.

The peace and quiet suddenly erupted with the sounds of horses and the shouts of the men. Their excitement was evident. This was no ordinary homecoming. Night Flower hesitated only a moment before she grabbed a sleeping fur and wrapped it around her shoulders. A glance at the boys assured her the noise hadn't disturbed them. Satisfied, she stepped out of the teepee.

Her joyous laugh froze on her face when she saw the travois her man helped drag through the snow. At first she thought they were returning with an injured brave, but when she and the other women reached the blankets, they could see the white man. Night Flower's heart stopped then felt as if it would pound itself right out of her body.

The presence of a white man in their camp posed a threat to her tenacious hold on her children. Was Swift Arrow loco, bringing him to their camp? He would see her boys and demand their return! That could never happen. She barely heard her husband's explanation as her mind raced to contrive ways to keep the active boys out of sight. They would drive her crazy with demands to play outside. Their antics in the snow entertained the whole village.

In the four moons through which she had mothered and loved the two white babies, Night Flower had learned that they were more important to her than her own life. She couldn't risk the chance of losing them and would protect them at all cost.

As Swift Arrow's words penetrated, she realized the white man was a captive, and his care was being left to the women. When she detected he was the man responsible for bringing firewater and trouble to her people, she immediately offered to feed him. Approaching her sister-in-law, Moonwalk, she made the arrangements.

She darted into the teepee to check if the boys were still asleep. They were cuddled together under the buffalo robe as warm and comfortable as she had left them. She brushed the red gold hair from the smooth forehead of each child. Then she placed a kiss on her fingertips and touched their sweet cheeks. With her mind and heart at rest that they were still sound asleep, she stepped back into the bright winter sun to find out what she could about this new prisoner.

Her husband boasted about his capture and told the braves gathered around that this man would be the key to more guns and even more of the firewater they were all beginning to crave. Night Flower listened to his bravado, and her stomach churned. She knew that guns and firewater would be the death of her people. As she listened to Swift Arrow's plan, she began to form one of her own. Many of the other squaws felt as she did, and she perceived she would have all the help she needed. Together they would conspire to make sure the white man never bothered their people again. Her decision made, she returned to her teepee.

Swift Arrow entered the teepee in jubilation that soon turned to a pout. Night Flower didn't care if he knew she didn't share his enthusiasm. She served him his meal in silence. As she gathered the remnants of food, she made her request. "Will you watch the babies while I bring the prisoner his food?" Knowing Swift Arrow loved the boys and looked for excuses to play with them, she was certain he'd agree.

"Feed him well," he chuckled. "He is worth his weight in barter."

"I will feed him until he can eat no more, my husband," she replied. Hurrying through the deep snow, she circled around to meet Moonwalk. Her friend had married Tall Feathers, brother to her own husband. Tall Feathers was the shaman, so she would have access to his potions.

"I found some Indian tobacco and rootstock of the mayapple. We can brew the tobacco into a hot drink, or we can grate some rootstock into his food," Moonwalk whispered.

"Which one works the fastest?" Night Flower didn't want to take a chance of this man seeing her twins.

"Let me think. The Indian tobacco is dried for the men to smoke. If we brew it, we might have to give him several doses. The mayapple will be faster. He will suffer as his body fluids leave from every opening. Soon he will fall into the sleep of death, and by sunrise, his spirit will depart."

"I will use the mayapple."

A small pouch passed between the women. "Tall Feathers uses the root as a charm against evil spirits. He never touches it with bare hands. He said its power could be absorbed into the skin and cause red bumps. He makes me keep these pouches where the children cannot reach them. I brought a rock to scrap the root. Hold it through the pouch when you handle it."

Night Flower stirred the gratings into the corn meal mush. She used as much as she dared to insure a quick death.

"It smells strange, Moonwalk. Do you think he will eat this?"

"Maybe if we give him some firewater, he won't pay attention to the taste."

Night Flower hugged her sister-in-law. "What a great idea," she laughed. "We can be rid of him with his own poison." It served him right. He was killing her people slowly with the firewater. She would pay him back in kind.

Twenty-one

As the day wore on, Sammy grew quieter and more lethargic. Mac kept busy chopping wood, and she had nothing to do but bring in the logs as they tumbled free and stack them near the entrance of the cave. The piece of venison on the spit would be enough food for all day. Her only other chore had been to neatly fold their bedding, and she'd accomplished that hours ago. The sky outside maintained it's gray and ominous appearance. Perhaps that was why she felt so out of sorts.

By lunchtime, she had to force her feet to move and had developed a pounding headache. Later in the afternoon, she watched absently as darkness began to descend like the closing curtains of the last act, blotting out the last visage of light.

Mac had noticed Sammy's initial restlessness and how she'd gradually slowed down, but rather than teasing her, he began to worry. Perhaps she was becoming depressed. How stupid of him to forget she'd just lost her husband. She must have loved him very much. He knew from Jason's talk and manner that he'd loved Samantha. The grief from her loss must be catching up with her. *Besides,* he thought, *she probably missed Jack and Sally more than she wanted to admit.* Still, she'd worked hard all day. Carrying those logs had been heavy labor, and she was such a little thing. He'd probably worn her plum out with all the lifting. As they settled down for their evening meal, Mac noticed she'd removed the buckskin shirt.

"Sammy, it's getting colder now, you better put your extra shirt back on."

"The fire is so warm, and with carrying all that wood, I got too hot. I think I'll turn in early if you don't mind Nicholas. I really feel tired tonight."

Her voice came out a mere whisper. It seemed like the effort of talking was just too much. Mac had to strain to hear her words. He could see the fatigue around her eyes and knew she had to be exhausted.

"I don't mind a bit, Sammy. It will give me an excuse to grab some extra sleep. All that chopping wore me out, too." His attempt at teasing fell on deaf ears, and Mac worried about her silence. Not exactly sure how to draw her out, he opted to let her sleep.

Sammy slipped the buckskin shirt back on and rolled herself into her blanket. Without a word, she turned her back to the fire. Within minutes, he heard the deep, regular rhythm of her breathing. He smiled in pleasure just to watch her sleep.

Mac turned his coffee cup in his hands and stared vacantly into the fire. Yesterday they had enjoyed each other's company, and he'd felt like they were becoming really good friends. He knew he wanted her for more than a friend, and was willing to give her time to get used to him. Today she had been quiet and lackluster all day. Was she really so much in love with Jason that she could never forget him? His thoughts perplexed him.

Mac walked to the entrance of the cave and, as he had expected from the snowbird's warning, falling snow again blotted out the world. Well, he had better turn in himself. His muscles ached, and he felt emotionally exhausted from all the strain of trying to keep his distance from Sammy.

The dream intruded into his sleep. He watched a red-tailed hawk flying with his mate. In his dream, the female hawk appeared to be wounded and unable to keep up with her mate. It started to fall to the ground. Mac heard the male hawk screaming. "Wake up, wake up. Your mate is in trouble."

Mac woke to a whimpering cry. His dream flashed before him. In his mind's eye, he saw a wounded animal. He lay still as death as his ears perked to identify the animal. Slowly he inched his hand to his pistol. Once he had the grip wrapped in his palm, he opened his eyes.

The glow from the dying fire cast enough light that he could see the two horses. They didn't seem too upset. Sassy tossed around a little, but her movements were of unease rather than fear. Maybe he had just imagined the noise. It probably reflected his discomfort during the dream. As Mac relaxed and settled back down, he heard the sound again. This time he sat straight up and looked towards Sammy. She whimpered and moaned in pain.

It took him less than a second to surge to his feet. He crossed to her side of the cave and wondered if he should wake her. Then he had a horrifying thought. The cave was so warm from the big fire they had left burning all day. What if a snake came out of hibernation and decided to snuggle with her? Surely the sting of a snake bite would wake her. Her blanket had become twisted all around her body. Her legs thrashed and her head rolled side to side. His heart pounded so hard and fast, he wondered if he might die right there.

Holding his gun in one hand, he slowly tried to extract the blanket without touching her. As he strained to see in the flickering glow of the dying embers, he couldn't detect anything slithering away from her body.

Maybe she's having a bad dream, he thought. He quickly laid his gun down and tried to recover her body with the blanket. While he debated if he should wake her from her nightmare, his hand brushed her shoulder as he tucked in the blanket. His initial reaction caused him to snatch his hand back from the heat. He felt as if he'd burned himself with that slight contact. He shook himself out of his daze, surely he wouldn't feel that kind of heat from just a touch. Cautiously he laid his hand to her forehead. *My God! She is hotter than blazes.*

He rose and reached for another log in one motion. He added more fuel to the fire, stirred the embers, and in seconds had a blaze roaring again. In the light cast by the flickering flames, he could see Sammy's hair plastered to her head and beads of perspiration covering her face. Kneeling at her side, he realized she ranted deliriously. Her clothing clung to her skin. Fever raged through her body.

Gently he levered her to a sitting position. She didn't wake up, but she continued to moan and whimper. He slid the buckskin shirt off her shoulders and pulled it down her arms and off her body. Under the buckskin the rest of the clothes were so wet they outlined every luscious curve. Mac's hand reached to the medicine bundle that hung around his neck. He touched it in thanks to the red-tailed hawk that came to him in his dream. The Indian lore his father had taught him sometimes surprised his white man's brain.

Right now, Mac couldn't let himself think of her curves. He knew he had to bring the fever down and get the wet clothes off her drenched body. Wondering how she'd gotten so sick, he stripped off her brother's cotton shirt and began to unbutton the shirtwaist of her dress. Removing it was easy since she had cut the skirt from the waistline. He'd gotten down to her chemise when he saw the dirty piece of cloth she had used to wash and pack her wound. Horrified, he stared at the blood-stained clothes. He had forgotten all about her wound. She had never complained, and he'd assumed it was a mere scratch. He should have insisted on looking at it himself. Not that she would have allowed that, but he should have remembered to at least ask about it. The wound looked worse than he'd imagined.

He tried to figure out how to remove the chemise without cutting it off. She really needed every piece of clothing she had. Finally he just braced her back against his bent knee and pulled it over her head. The movement caused her to cry out in her sleep, but he'd had no choice. She had stuffed a rag into the hole the bullet had torn in the corset. It was held in place by a piece of petticoat wrapped around her middle. The material bore an ugly brown stain.

As he tried to pull it away from her skin, he could see it adhered tightly to the wound. Mac lowered Samantha gently to the ground and covered her with the blanket. He poured the last of the coffee into a cup. He'd need it later. Taking the coffeepot to the entrance of the cave, he used a hand full of snowdrift to clean out the pot. Then he filled it with fresh, newly fallen snow. Returning to the fire, he set the pot on a rock next to the blaze. The heat would melt it down to warm water. While he waited, he spread her wet clothing over a big boulder close enough to the fire to dry the material.

Mac hesitated a moment and returned to her to finish what he had started. He stripped her down completely, returning to her only after he finished draping the rest of her things to dry. Her body glowed just as beautifully as he remembered. Her proportions were perfect for her height. His eyes followed the shape of her frame, from her softly rounded breasts, so sweetly inviting, to her tiny waist that flared, to gently curved hips. He saw the soft triangle of chestnut hair that guarded the entrance to her most secret place, and he knew he had to control his thoughts. He wouldn't risk losing this woman he'd searched for and finally found by letting his instincts to touch her overcome his self control.

He covered her with both blankets and tested the water to be sure it wasn't too hot. Lifting the covers so that he only exposed the wound on her side, he poured the warm water over the rag to loosen it and free it from her skin. As he gently pulled the cloth away, the stench that arose almost gagged him. He whispered a prayer that she would remain asleep. Maybe her deep unconsciousness wasn't a good sign. At the moment, he was just glad she slept so that he could tend to her wound without causing her more pain.

Moving aside so his shadow wouldn't block the light from the fire, he saw that the wound had festered with yellow pus. He needed more water to clean the wound. He only knew of one way to halt the infection and, not stopping to think, he placed the blade of his knife in the fire. If he delayed the inevitable, she might die. Melting more snow and heating his blade seemed to take forever. As soon as he tested the water, he rinsed her side, taking up the red-hot blade, he laid the burning metal in her wound for just a second. Sammy jerked, then screamed in pain. He felt her distress clear down to his toes.

As he settled her back against the ground, she fell into a deeper sleep. Thankful that she had fainted from the pain, Mac set about bandaging the wound. Going to his saddlebags, he removed the piece of material he had saved from her cedar chest. He used it to bind the wound as tightly as he could, wrapping the cloth around her body and up over her shoulder to hold it in place.

Cauterizing the wound had burned off the infected part, and he knew it shouldn't bleed. All he could do now was to keep it as clean as possible. It took him countless trips to bring in fresh snow to melt so that he could wash the fever-induced sweat from her body and cool her skin.

After several hours of sponging, he noticed she'd begun to shiver. Her things were still wet, so he retrieved a clean shirt and trousers from his saddlebags and dressed her in his clothes. Then wrapping her in the two blankets, he lifted her into his lap and cradled her tightly as he sat leaning against his saddle, in front of the fire. He spent the night alternately sponging her forehead and holding her while she shivered from the chills of the fever.

As Mac became aware of the graying light signaling the start of another day, he wondered if Sammy would live to see it. Exhaustion from nursing her and holding her all night had finally caught up with him. Shifting his body to lie down, he rested his head on the saddle and tucked Sammy closer to his chest. Before he drifted off to sleep, he heard her sigh as she turned her body intimately against him. She snuggled deeper and slept the peaceful sleep of one safe and secure.

He heard the screech of the hawk outside the cave. It had warned him of danger and stayed around as a protector and guardian until the danger passed. *I could die happy if this woman burrowed next to me every night like this*, he thought as he drifted off to oblivion.

Several hours later when he opened his eyes, he realized he still held her. He noticed the angle of her body and how she slept with her arms wrapped around him. He grinned in spite of the pain his numb limbs suffered, knowing she'd made it through the night. He didn't move for fear of waking her and also for the pleasure he felt in just holding her in such a loving position. Just as his discomfort became unbearable, she stirred and sighed.

Sammy nestled her head against Mac's chin and woke with such a start that she yelped in pain as she moved and disturbed her side. Sparks of green fire shot from her eyes. The glare pierced him to the core. He could almost hear her questioning desperately why he held her. His grip automatically tightened so she wouldn't jerk away from him. He knew she wondered what had happened while she had slept. He watched the fear and uncertainty turn to cold fury before he spoke.

"Try not to move too quickly, Sammy. You are sure to be weak after the night you spent."

Her thoughts ran amok. *What was he talking about*, "after the night I spent." *Oh my God! What happened?* She knew Nicholas had seen her eyes jump in fear. She'd tried to hide it, but he held her in a vice like grip and she couldn't move. He continued trying to explain to her that she had been burning up with fever, how her wound had festered, and how he had cleaned it to lower the fever. She barely listened. She had to get away from him. Mercy! She had the length of her body draped across him. It was the same position Jason had used on her. Angrily, she struggled to push away from him.

"Easy, you'll hurt yourself again. Let me help you." Nicholas sat up slowly, turning her first to sit across his legs then easing her onto the ground. He picked up the blanket she'd lost and draped it around her shoulders.

Sammy looked down at her self and realized that she wore different clothes. "Where did these come from?"

"They're mine. I needed something dry to put on you."

"You undressed me? How could you? You shouldn't have touched me? My God! You saw me with nothing on?" She felt panicky, knew she ranted. Did the fragmented sentences pouring out of her mouth even make sense? She tried to stand and collapsed to her knees clutching her side in agony. Embarrassment clouded her judgment. She felt the betraying red flush creep over her whole body, warming her to her core.

"Sammy, please understand." Mac tried to take hold of her shoulders. He started to explain how he had to help her.

Sammy wrenched away and gasped in pain. "Don't touch me." Her voice sounded as cold as the driven snow, even to herself. "Where are my clothes?"

Silently Nicholas pointed to her things spread out over the rocks to dry. She rose unsteadily to her feet and almost fell again. Mac started but didn't move to help her. She was aware he would have caught her in an instant if she had faltered and thanked the Lord she didn't.

As she crossed to her clothing, she realized he had told her the truth. Her things were stiff and smelled from her dried perspiration. She almost cried to have to put them on again, but she had to get out of his clothes. They seemed to be burning her body. She sensed every movement that caused the loose hanging shirt to brush against her taunt nipples. She felt naked. She wondered if he could see right through the clothes she wore. What was she thinking? He had seen her naked! How could she look him in the eye again? It was the same as when she knew Jason had seen her.

Seeing her hanging her head in embarrassment and keeping her back to him, Mac knew her thoughts as though she had spoken out aloud.

"Don't be embarrassed! I did what I had to do to save your life. Don't you realize you could have died last night?"

Sammy swung around at his first words. How did he know what she was feeling?

"It was dark, Sammy, and I didn't look." Noting the cryptic glare she gave him, he knew the lie didn't work.

"All right, so I looked. What's the big deal? I've seen plenty of naked women before. It's not like you're the first. But you are the first woman I've had to nurse through the night, and believe me, I was more worried about you dying than what your body looked like."

Mac looked exasperated and exhausted. How could she stay mad? There wasn't anything he could have done different. What did she expect anyway? Did she want him to just let her die because he shouldn't undress her? He couldn't go for a doctor. He had done the best he could.

Sammy was immediately contrite even though she still suspected his motives. She hated that things had happened the way they had. Besides, he was right, she was sure he had seen plenty of other women naked. A man like him wouldn't look twice at a girl like her. She shocked herself with the jealousy in her thoughts. Why should she be concerned whether or not he thought she was attractive? She was a widow, and she should only be thinking of Jason.

This man was more than she knew how to handle. The last two days, she had learned a lot about him and had begun to really like him. It was almost easy to forget that she ever had a husband or that he had died. It seemed like that part of her life had never happened. She felt as if her life began when Nicholas swooped down on her and carried her away from Jason.

She realized her knuckles were aching, and she looked down to see her fist clutching the waist of his trousers, which hung from her hips. She had to get out of his clothes, but hers were so wretched she hated the thought of putting them on again. Nicholas solved her problem when he approached her with the length of rawhide she had used to belt up her brother's pants.

"I know you want to feel the comfort of your own clothes, but we need to clean them first. Put this on and wrap yourself in the blanket while I brew some coffee and get our breakfast. You need to eat and rest today." Mac spoke in a soft understanding voice. He seemed to know her feelings and appeared to want to reassure her. She had the feeling her health concerned him more than anything else.

Sammy reached for the makeshift belt with a shaking hand. She had to get control of her emotions, and she realized as she stood there that her strength had chosen that moment to desert her. Snatching the belt, she turned her back and sank to her knees. Mac gently draped the blanket across her shoulders and, without a word, picked up her sweat-stiffened clothes and left the cave.

Sammy felt so overwrought she didn't even question where he was going with her things. She gathered her strength and tied the belt around her waist. She needed to visit her private spot. As soon as she stepped out of the cave, she noticed how much deeper the snow was. Then, she took note of Mac's footprints. Reassured he was heading away from her assigned place, she proceeded to fight her way into the trees. *Mercy!* she thought, *there must be at least six inches of new snow on top of what had fallen the first day!*

It took her longer than normal to relieve herself and return to the cave, in part because of the depth of the snow, but mostly due to her weakened condition. Her body poured sweat, and she was breathing in gasps by the time she finally made it back. Her legs only had the strength to stagger to the fire before she collapsed. Once there, she pulled the blanket back around her numbed body, curled into a ball, and fell asleep.

When he returned, Mac found her shivering like an aspen in a windstorm. Working quickly, he laid her wet clothes on the rock by the fire and added more logs to bring the heat back up in the cave. *She must be freezing,* he thought. Not wanting to wake her, he lay down next to her and covered them both with the second blanket. Mac didn't think he could fall asleep holding her shivering body so close. However, as the heat of the fire, coupled with the warmth of holding her, seeped into his chilled flesh, he felt the languor steal over him as his eyelids fought a loosing battle.

Mac woke first to the growling of his stomach. He was afraid to move lest he wake Sammy from her much-needed, healing sleep. She lay quietly and no longer shivered. He eased away from her, keeping the blanket tucked around her so that she wouldn't feel the lack of warmth. First, he checked her clothes. He'd taken them to the stream, and after breaking through the ice, he'd rinsed them as best he could in the cold water. They were almost dry.

He added more logs to the fire and stepped outside to try to gauge the time of day and to wash the sleep from his eyes. They must have slept longer than he thought. With no sun to measure the sky, he judged it to be past noon, but he couldn't be sure. It didn't matter, they couldn't go anywhere anyway. He lowered what remained of the deer carcass and cut some meat to roast for dinner. Silently, he entered the cave and began preparations for their meal.

She'd slept too long. He couldn't decide if he should wake her or not. He worried about her coming down with a fever again and knew he had to get her back to the village as soon as possible. He had steeped some willow bark to make a weak tea. He knew the brew could aid in reducing any fever. His indecision resolved, he reached over to feel her forehead.

Sammy woke with a start the second he gently touched her forehead. "Sorry, I didn't mean to wake you. I wanted to be sure the fever hadn't returned. You've been sleeping so long, I was beginning to worry." Mac felt uncomfortable. He didn't like having to explain his actions to anyone, and yet he owed her an explanation. He didn't want to spook her and give her any reason to mistrust him. "I've made some willow bark tea. It should help."

"I'm fine," Sammy yawned. Then as she became more aware of herself, she rose up on her elbow and tentatively smiled. "Actually, I feel much better. How long have I been asleep?"

"I'm not really sure," Mac answered. "It's been cloudy all day so I don't know what time it was when we woke up this morning. From the looks of the light outside now, I would guess it is late afternoon. It's seems we slept all day."

"We?" Sammy looked at Mac with suspicion. "What do you mean, *we*!"

Too late, Mac realized the slip he'd made. However, she didn't have to know they had slept together, with his arms protectively locked around her. "Well," he countered, "I was up all night nursing you, so while you slept, I took a nap, too. Anyway, my stomach woke me up and reminded me that I hadn't eaten all day, so I got up and started dinner." *There*, he thought, *that wasn't even a lie.* He'd just neglected to tell her he took his nap with his body wrapped around hers. To change the subject quickly, he indicated her clothes drying on the rock. "I took your things down to the stream and rinsed them out. They still need to be washed with some soap, but at least I have the sweat washed out, and maybe they won't be so stiff."

Sammy's eyes lit with gratitude. "Or as smelly," she responded with a hint of her former humor. "Thank you. I'll feel much more comfortable in my own clothes." She rose slowly, shocked at how weak she felt. Mac jumped instantly to her side to support her. She felt his heart pounding. Did he fear that she'd fall? She had to reassure him.

"I'm stronger than I look. I'm okay. Really," she protested at his skeptical gaze. She let her eyes express her renewed warmth and friendliness. She trusted him again. Reaching for her clothes, she felt that they were nearly dry. She raised the shirt to her face and breathed in the smell of clean cotton. Her heart sang in the pleasure of having clean clothes next to her skin. She wished she could have a bath but knew that was impossible.

"We'll get you home soon, where you can bathe in a warm room in a tub of hot water. You can't take a chance of bathing here, it's too cold." Again, Mac had shocked her with his comments.

Sammy looked at him and knew her fear showed. "How did you know I longed for a bath? I never mentioned it out loud!"

Mac rubbed his hand over the side of his face and his head. "I don't know! I've never experienced anything like this before. Maybe it's because we have been in such close quarters for three days now, but sometimes I can hear you speaking in my head."

She narrowed her eyes and gave him a scathing look. "Don't look at me like that, I'm not crazy. I'm just as amazed as you are. It's like we communicate without words! Does that make sense?" Mac seemed clearly puzzled.

After her first feeling of shock, Sammy burst out laughing. "Then there really is such a thing as telepathy. My brother read about it, but we all laughed at him." Sammy sobered at the thought of Tim. She could almost see him as he slipped on his glasses and prepared to read to the family.

The sound of Sammy's pure, spontaneous laugh flew right to Mac's heart. He was lost. He watched the changing emotions chasing across her face and knew in his heart he loved her.

"We studied telepathy in college," he gulped. "I never held much store in it either. Do you think that's what it really is?" He could hardly believe it himself. What kind of bond did they have to know each other's thoughts? *Oh, God! Could she hear him speak in his mind, too?* Watching her face for any telltale sign, he gently inquired. "Sammy, can you hear me think, too?" His heart hammered against his chest, and he feared her answer.

"When Tyler was outside the cave, I somehow knew you were restraining me, warning me not to give our position away. I didn't know what to attribute that feeling to, but yes, to answer your question, I must have heard you mentally pleading with me to keep quiet. Were you?" When she answered her voice rang with innocence. The tone told him she must feel as incredulous as he did.

"Yes." Mac shocked himself with his answer. They simultaneously sank to the ground on each side of the fire and stared at each other.

God! If she can hear me think about how bad I want her, she'll run like a scared rabbit.

Oh, Lord! If he can hear how I wonder about him, and how handsome I think he is, he'll think I'm a hussy. The sizzling of the cooking meat woke them from their respective musings. Mac shook his head and pretended nonchalance in preparing the evening meal.

"Drink the tea while I bring in some snow for you to wash with, and I'll leave you to change into your own clothes." Mac's words broke the long silence, and Sammy avoided eye contact as she thanked him.

It was almost funny. Sammy felt as if each of them were trying to read the other's mind all during the meal. Perhaps their thoughts met and crashed, falling into the burning fire, never making it across to the mind of the other. She knew her mind had been blank of any message, and she felt sure from the set of Mac's face that he had not been able to tune into her either. In a way, she was kind of relieved. It would be awful if even her thoughts weren't private. This enforced sharing was almost more than she could bear. It had been different on camping trips with J.R. Of course, he was her brother, but their trips had always held a mood of jocular camaraderie. With Nicholas, she felt an intimacy she couldn't explain.

She was intensely aware of his maleness, more than she ever felt for Dennis or Jason. Dennis she dismissed as a partner in adolescent puppy love. Jason had been much more in love with her than she was with him. She admitted to herself now that she probably hadn't really loved Jason. She had been grateful to him for trying to help her, and she supposed she had believed he was her ticket to safety and freedom—safe from Tyler and free to be herself again. Both reasons together didn't add up to love.

She realized she had been bulldozed into the marriage by well-meaning friends and Jason's strong will to have her. She had been attracted to him because he was a strong, good-looking man. He was good-hearted and generous, and she had confused the physical attraction for love. She realized now that she had only truly loved her family. No one else had held her heart as much as they had. She would have died for them without a qualm. She supposed she would never find a man to love like that. Nicholas? No! She didn't, couldn't love him. He disturbed her. He frightened her. He confused her. That had to be the reason she felt strange around him. Their telepathy was no more than a phenomenon. It couldn't mean a thing. After all, it didn't work when they tried during dinner. It had probably been a fluke and would never happen again.

Twenty-two

As Sammy changed her clothes, the sight of the cloth bandaging her wound startled her back into the present. It looked like the same material she left behind at the waterfall after the fire. She ran through a series of possibilities without coming up with a plausible answer. Nicholas had a lot more questions to answer. Where did he get the material? Her mind grew weary of the endless grilling, and she gave up waiting for Nicholas' return. Feeling better after she changed and had her own clothes wrapped securely around her body, Sammy sank wearily to the ground. Minutes after wrapping the blanket around herself, she fell sound asleep.

Mac entered the cave an hour or so later to find Sammy in an exhausted slumber. He came in refreshed from a quick wash at the stream and although his skin felt cold from the icy water, the sight of Sammy's peaceful countenance quickly warmed him. He had done his own soul searching at the water's edge and concluded that as much as he wanted this woman physically, they were also linked spiritually. The more he came to know her, the more he knew they belonged together.

He had laughed to himself over the battle of their minds, trying to see if this telepathy thing worked. He supposed they had tried too hard, and in his mind's eye, he saw words flying through the air to meet and mingle, to become entwined and intercepted, so that they never reached their destination.

He smiled to himself. Both of them were strong-willed. There would be arguments and disagreements, but oh, the making up time would transcend all limits. The sun, hidden behind the gray blanket of sky, had just set. That meant at the latest it was only about five in the evening. It seemed too early to go to sleep, especially after sleeping most of the day. Right now, all he wanted to do was to curl up next to Sammy and hold her again.

Mac sat for a couple of hours staring into the fire and contemplating his future. He didn't know what he wanted anymore. He thought about returning to his father's ranch in Texas and building a home there for Sammy. He didn't want to continue scouting and leave her for months at a time, but he wasn't sure if he wanted to be tied to the ranch all the time either. What he knew and loved the most were horses. It was something else he shared with Sammy.

Somehow he had to come up with a solution so that when the time came, he could go to her with a proposition that would appeal to both of them. He had to help her bring Tyler to justice first. Thaddeus Morgan was the real culprit. Somehow he had to find the evidence to lock him up for good. He would then be free to convince Sammy that she belonged with him, wherever that was! He just didn't have an answer for that yet.

His first priority was to get Sammy back to Charrette Village. Jack and Sally would keep her safe while he tracked Tyler, then, with his testimony, he would see that Morgan paid for his sins. He hoped to have enough evidence to hang them both!

The long evening stretched into an endless kaleidoscope of jumbled thoughts, problems with no solutions, and confused emotions. Mac finally decided to call it a night, and after checking the horses and banking the fire, he rolled into his blanket and tried to sleep. He tossed for what seemed like hours before he finally gave up and took his blanket over to Sammy's side of the fire. Lying next to her, he covered them both with his blanket and, settling her spoon shape into his lap, he put his arms around her and fell instantly asleep.

Sammy woke warm and comfortable in the middle of the night. She snuggled closer to the warm body behind her until the weight of an arm around her waist intruded into her consciousness. She came instantly awake and struggled to rise. Mac surfaced from his somnolent state.

"What's wrong?" He queried as he rubbed the sleep from his eyes. "Are you hurting? Did something scare you?"

"You scared me!" Sammy shouted. "What are you doing sleeping next to me?"

"I couldn't sleep. I've gotten so used to sleeping next to you that I had to come over here before I could get comfortable!" If Mac had been more awake, he would have watched his words. As soon as he spoke, he realized he had more explaining to do.

"What do you mean? 'So used to sleeping with me.'" Sammy stood, hands on hips, demanding an explanation. "You call holding me last night while I was sick, 'sleeping with me'?"

Mac stood and faced her. He lowered his head, appalled with himself for forcing this situation. In his frustration, he raked both his hands through his hair. He had to wake himself up and try to think at the same time. He needed her to understand it wasn't sexual desire but a desperate need to be near her that drove him to her. How could he explain without causing her to feel contempt for him or to fear him?

"Sammy. I'm sorry I upset you, but try to understand. I'm not going to hurt you. I would never do that. Last night I held you all night while you went from burning fever to bone-shaking chills. I held you to add my body warmth to yours. Today, while you slept, your body shivered with chills again and I lay beside you, just like I did last night, but only to add my body warmth. I wasn't trying to take any liberties. I was just trying to help heal you." Turning on his heels, he paced in the tiny confines of the cave. *Might as well be honest,* he thought.

"Tonight, I tried for hours to sleep on my side of the fire, but I couldn't. Tonight, I needed you to help me sleep. I needed to feel your body warmth next to me to chase away my chills and to bring me comfort."

Embarrassed, Sammy fidgeted as she vacillated between compassion for his discomfort and anger at his presumption. "You confuse me, Nicholas MacNamee! I don't know what to make of you."

"You can make me a happy man by coming back to bed with me." He leered mischievously.

Sammy stared in shock at his audacity and burst out laughing as he quirked his eyebrows at her in a mock come-hither look. "You are impossible! I wish I had a frying pan to knock over your head!" Turning on her heels, she stomped out of the cave.

"Wait a minute!" Mac called. "Where are you going?" He dashed after her, only to see her plod off into her section of the woods. He ran back for his gun and quickly followed her.

"Sammy! Talk to me, sing, make noise, anything," he yelled. "I'll come for you unless you let me know you're okay. I've got my gun, and I can be there in a second if you need help! Answer me!" He paced in agitation, trying to decide if he should follow her or not. She'd headed for her private place, but he didn't like her out of his sight.

"For heaven's sake, Nicholas, calm down. I just need a little privacy for a minute. It's probably been twelve hours since I've been out here."

"Keep talking, Sammy. I mean it!" Mac's nerve ends pierced his whole body. The snow wolves were sure to be hunting, but he feared bobcats the most. To see a bobcat meant you were being stalked by an enemy. A bobcat would be a sign that Tyler had come back. She wouldn't know that the wolf is considered a good sign, a protector, and her scream might cause it to attack in self-defense.

"Shall I sing you a song?" She laughed. The next thing Mac heard was the beautiful melody of "Greensleeves". She emerged from the woods smiling as she finished the first verse, and Mac was so shaken he just grabbed her in a bear hug.

"Don't ever scare me like that again."

Sammy's smile disappeared from her face as she watched him lower his head to take her lips in a consuming kiss. Once he tasted her lips he couldn't seem to stop. He sucked on her lower lip and ran his tongue over the sensitive corners of her mouth, causing her to open her lips in mute surrender.

She started shivering. He scooped her into his arms and carried her into the cave and the warmth of the fire. Gently he lowered her to her feet and, cradling her head with his two large hands, began an assault on her eyes, her nose, her cheeks, and her ears.

Sammy's knees weakened. The emotions spiraling through her body confused her. Everything was happening so fast. She'd never felt like this before. Jason's kisses were pleasant, and she'd liked the way they made her feel, but they were nothing compared to this.

This made her body vibrate like a fiddle string and burn like a torch. Nicholas' kisses seemed to be the only thing to quench that heat. She knew she should stop him, knew his kisses were causing these feelings but she didn't want to stop. When he returned his attention to her mouth, she went slack and helpless. Her mouth opened to admit his tongue, and she melted in the passion of his embrace. They were both shaking when Mac lowered her to the discarded blankets and lay beside her.

"I knew it would be like this," he whispered. "I knew it! Now, can we please just go to sleep?" He turned her so her back was to him. Then, like that afternoon, scooped her into his lap and covered them with the blankets. He wrapped his arms around her and snuggled his chin on top of her head.

Sammy froze, stunned, first, by the force of his kisses and the feelings they evoked, and second, by the abrupt cessation of his assault and their resulting position. How could she sleep with him curled up behind her? It felt even more intimate than the night she'd spent with Jason. For one thing, she could feel his arousal against her backside. She wiggled frantically for a moment trying to move away until he whispered in her ear.

"Please stop moving, Sammy. If you don't, neither one of us will sleep the rest of the night. Of course, if you don't want to sleep, I'll be only too happy to stay awake with you."

Instantly, Sammy ceased moving. *My lord, how does he expect me to sleep like this?* Fear kept her from verbalizing her feelings. She didn't trust her voice. She wanted to be mad at him, but she couldn't maintain the anger. All she could feel was the heat of his kisses and the throbbing it caused between her legs. What was wrong with her? She couldn't allow herself to go from one man's bed to another's. Sammy argued with herself the rest of the night, succumbing to sleep only just before dawn.

Mac knew the minute she finally drifted into her dream world. It had been the longest night of his life. He had kept his fingers crossed that she would acquiesce to his wishes and let him hold her. He wanted to make love to her so bad he ached, but he would never take her unaware. Her acceptance of his love had to be as great as his need. He wanted to make her forget Jason Sudholt ever existed. She had to recognize their mutual attraction and welcome it. He knew he suffered from jealousy and berated himself for not finding her sooner. He wished he had been the one to initiate her into the intimacy of husband and wife. He would have to school himself never to let her know how much it hurt that Jason had been the first.

He consoled himself with the thought that he would be the last. From this night on, no man would touch her. She would be exclusively his. He wasn't one to share, and he wasn't one to give up what belonged to him. This woman had been created for him, and he meant to keep her. He didn't care if it took a hundred nights of torture like tonight. If that's what it took to win her, that's what he would do.

Mac realized that he could have made love to her very easily that night, but he also knew her enough to understand she might hate him for it afterwards. He didn't want her contempt. He wanted her love. When he finally felt her even breathing, he allowed himself to drift into oblivion.

~ * ~

Mac woke to the sound of birds and the brightness of the morning sun. For the first time in three days, the sun deigned to show itself. The brilliance penetrated the dark cave and lit his surroundings. He buried his face in Sammy's hair, inhaling the scent of her. Careful not to actually touch her, he soothed the tendrils away from her brow. The ache to wake her with his kisses forced him to leave her. He quietly eased his body away, and after tucking the covers around her, he stoked the fire and went to tend the horses.

The trees were dripping, shedding their coats of snow like giant, shaggy dogs shaking water from their fur. The air felt much warmer, and the snow seemed to be melting rapidly. Mac realized today would be the last day in the cave. By tomorrow they should be able to travel, but so would Tyler. They would have to be careful, but he thought he could get Sammy back to the village and safety. Mac cut another leg of venison and entered the cave as Sammy stirred.

Her first sense was of something missing. She tentatively moved her foot to feel if Mac still lay behind her and when she met empty space, allowed herself to take a breath. When she heard his step, she opened her eyes and saw him tying the meat to hang over the fire. She watched him add logs to the embers. Their eyes met and locked. Mac smiled.

"Good morning, sleepyhead, time to rise and shine. The sun is up, and it looks like a beautiful day. Everything is dripping, so if you go off into the woods, I suggest you take a parasol or you'll be soaked before you get back."

His teasing helped to ease the strain, and Sammy returned his sally, "And where do you suggest I find that convenience, kind sir? Or do you happen to have a magic wand you can wave to produce one for me."

"Your wish is my command, Angel. Just give me a minute." Mac rose and disappeared in seconds. Sammy found herself smiling as she stood up and stretched. He was still an enigma. She never knew what to expect from him, and he never reacted the way she expected him to. She instinctively knew his endearment, "angel" wasn't said in jest. It at once made her feel uncomfortable and yet very special.

When Mac returned, he held a tree branch. He trimmed all but the top twigs and taking his poncho, draped it over the top. Gallantly, he handed it to her with a flourish. Laughing, Sammy took the makeshift umbrella and ventured out into the elements. It was quite ingenious. However, she couldn't hold the umbrella and attend to her needs at the same time. She needed both hands to manage the britches. Still and all, Nicholas' invention saved her from a complete drenching, so it had been worth the effort. She emerged from the woods with a smile and, curtsying very prettily, thanked him for the loan of his 'umbrella'.

Breakfast became lighthearted, and by mid afternoon they both knew this would be their last day in the cave. Nicholas began to outline his plan of returning Sammy to the village and proceeding to Pinckney to see if Tyler returned to Morgan's ranch. His intention to leave her behind infuriated Sammy.

"This is my fight, and I intend to be there for the finish." They argued all day about the wisdom of her participation, and by bedtime neither one of them had conceded to the other.

Mac had decided they needed to get to sleep early so they could be up by dawn. Sammy returned from outside to find he had made up their bed together again.

"You don't have to sleep with me tonight, I don't have the chills anymore," she remarked. "And don't tell me you have the chills either because I won't believe you."

"Who said anything about chills?" Mac replied. "Come on, get over here and go to sleep."

"I'm not sleeping next to you tonight, Nicholas. It's not necessary."

"Oh, but it's very necessary. If you don't, I won't be able to sleep, and we'll never get to leave early enough to make it back to the village before dark."

"Well, if you can't sleep without me next to you, you'll have to take me with you to Pinckney won't you?" Sammy's saucy reply made Mac laugh.

"Oh, honey, it's just having you so close that causes the problem. If I leave you at Charrette Village, then you won't be there to tempt me and keep me awake. However, if you can't sleep without me..."

"You know very well I can sleep perfectly fine without you. You're the one that has the problem!"

"Ah! Then you'll be glad to stay in Charrette Village while I go to Pinckney. That way you won't have to sleep with me every night."

She'd walked into her own trap. Sammy stood with her fist clinched. She stamped her foot. She could almost feel her blood steaming.

"Why, that's blackmail, and you know it!" Why did he provoke such extremes of emotion in her? She couldn't win. She had to find a way to go and to stay out of his bed. There had to be a way. She just couldn't think of it right now.

Nicholas patted the blanket in front of him. It was a good thing he kept any kind of knowing smile off his face. She knew she'd have exploded if he so much as grinned.

"Come on, love. Time to say goodnight." His voice sounded gentle and coaxing.

Reluctantly, Sammy knelt on the blankets. Another endearment he probably didn't mean. Does he call all his women "Love"? She felt emotionally exhausted from arguing with him all day, and if last night was any indication, she had nothing to fear from him. So what or whom was she afraid of? She realized the only thing she dreaded was her own lack of control. She had to admit, she felt very much at home in his arms when she had allowed herself to relax. She remembered last night—once his arousal dissipated to the point that she no longer felt its ominous presence—she began to enjoy the comfort of being wrapped in the warmth of his arms.

Sammy gingerly lay on the blanket with her back to him, keeping her distance to avoid contact. Nicholas gently turned her on her back and whispered, "I just need a goodnight kiss, Sammy," as he took possession of her willing lips. Sammy drank in the ardor of his kiss like a person dying of thirst. It seemed like she'd waited all day for him to kiss her again without realizing that what she had longed for was the warmth of his lips.

He traced her lips with his tongue, and she readily opened her mouth to receive that questing member. She matched his ardor with a passion of her own, following his tongue back into his mouth and mimicking the play he taught her. Somehow her hands found themselves around his back, and she pulled him closer. She marveled at the hardness of his muscles. She remembered the strength of steel she felt when he had lifted her to his horse. That brought back memories of Jason's body lying in the street, and she sobbed in her throat.

"What is it, Love?" Mac whispered. She shook her head in silence, telling him to help her forget the horrors of her past. He kissed the tears from her eyes, licking the salty fluid, drinking her soul, merging their spirits. Her passion became so furious that Mac knew he would lose control if she continued.

"Sammy, I want you. I want you so bad it hurts. If you want this to stop, now is the time. I can't take many more of your sweet kisses. I won't be able to quit. Last night, I stopped us before it went too far. Tonight, I don't want it to end, so it's up to you."

Sammy buried her head in his shoulder. She shook with passion, and she didn't understand her feelings. A few days ago, she swore no man would ever again know her intimately, and here she was burning for Nicholas' touch. Jason had never excited her like this. Her body burned hotter than the fever, and only Nicholas' caress seemed to sooth her. Maybe he could help her forget. One thing for sure, if she let him stroke her, and it felt anything like what happened with Jason, she knew she would never let another man near her.

Sammy's hands lay against Nicholas's shoulders with the slightest pressure, to push him away. However, she made the mistake of raising her eyes, and in doing so became paralyzed by the thread of desire that wound itself through her body. Her breasts swelled, and the nubs pearled of their own volition. A shiver of anticipation curled through her middle to moisten her sheath and tighten the muscles in her abdomen.

The look she captured in his eyes was like nothing she'd ever seen. It wasn't the look of lust that had frightened her many times. She'd seen men use that look when they thought they were unobserved. It wasn't even the same as Jason's measured observance that she took for love and devotion. This felt different! This spoke of total surrender to her power. This offered the gift of Nicholas' body and soul, to do with as she willed. It told her of his utter trust that she would not abuse his love. He laid his heart in her hands with the knowledge that she would not hurt him.

Her mind registered his thoughts as surely as if he spoke aloud. She heard his words echo in her mind. He would honor her will, but he wanted to claim her as his own. He needed to brand her with the stamp of his love, to bind her to him with invisible ties of passion and commitment.

Nicholas thought he would snap if she didn't make a decision soon. The seconds that she held him at bay seem to last a lifetime. He registered the confusion in her mind, the wonder, the doubts, the fear, and finally her capitulation. He took a ragged breath of relief just as she moved her hands up to shyly pull his head down for a kiss and utter what he knew was the answer he wanted with his whole being.

Nicholas wanted to give her a love so great as to totally blot out any memory of Jason. He would use the patience of a saint and the love in his heart to give this woman the most sensual experience of her life. He fleetingly wished they were in a soft bed in a fancy hotel, but he would do his best to make her forget the chill of the cave and the unyielding rock mattress. He wanted to make her first time with him a memory that would last her a lifetime. His last rational thought was to tell himself to have a care for her tender skin. His four-day growth of beard would leave her raw if he weren't careful. Then, as their lips met, all actions and intentions were swept to a sea of spontaneous passion erupting in them simultaneously. Wave after wave engulfed them, emersing the two lovers in a world neither had ever suspected could exist outside of heaven.

Mac's feelings exploded. In a blink, he deepened his kiss then pushed himself up to kneel above her, one knee gently moving between her legs to rest inside her thighs. Smiling into her eyes, he slowly slipped his hands around the flare of her hips and squeezed. As her eyes widened and a tiny gasp escaped her lips, he slid his fingers up to spread around her taut breasts, pushing them up. Thumbs and index fingers found her pearls through her shirt and tightened. She moaned, throwing her head back, closing her eyes. Her thighs gripped his knee and her hips and pelvis rose, seeking his thrust. Nicholas dropped his head to murmur words of love in her ear and against her neck.

Sammy became so wrapped up in the sensations he caused that she barely heard him. Her body tingled, and goose bumps ran up and down her spine. The shivering it caused seemed to stimulate Mac into a frenzy. He gathered her against his chest and rolled on his back.

The intimacy of the position stirred Sammy even more. She felt his shaft hard against her mound as he raised her to sit on top of him. He lay there quietly unbuttoning her shirts, one by one, until he reached her chemise. His finger traced a soft, gentle path from her jaw down her throat to the juncture between her breasts. She could feel the roughness of his skin against the smoothness of hers. The contrast caused her heart to pound. He seemed to be worshiping her body with his eyes as his hands moved to her shoulders and slipped her straps down her arms. Leaving them hanging at her elbows, he continued sliding his fingers down to her wrists. There, he merged his fingers with hers and pulled her forward to kiss first each hand then her lips. Pushing her erect again, he smiled so sweetly that her heart swelled fit to burst.

Reverently, he released her breasts from their lacy confinement, cupped them in his large hands, and began a loving assault on her nipples. They were already sensitive, and the buds were standing on end, begging for attention. His thumbs circled each, and she looked down in wonder to see how large they'd grown. She had never known her body could react like this.

Nicholas pulled her down, and freeing her breasts from the rest of the garment, closed his mouth first over one then the other, sharing his attention with each, leaving them wet and throbbing for more. Sammy's hands were busy also, tearing at his buttons until she finally felt the rippling hardness of his naked chest. Her fingers wandered in fascination over the smooth surface. When they encountered his hardened nipples, her thumbs teased in a repetition of his hands on her body.

He rolled and lifted her over onto her back. Kneeling at her side, he lowed his body to sit on his heels. His eyes traced his hands as they feathered across her chest and flattened to caress her pelvis. Loosening her belt, he bent to kiss her as his hand slid inside her waistband and hungry fingers searched beneath her tight curls. Pure pleasure escalated in tiny frissons. All at once, she felt hot and moist. When her shaking fingers undid his belt and she tried to reach for him, Mac groaned. In seconds he had removed her two pair of pants and her underwear. He kicked out of his clothes in a blink of an eye. When he laid his nakedness against hers, she gasped in shock as rolling waves of sensations raced through her senses. She wanted to touch him but was afraid. Her hands gripped his back and ached to inch closer to his private parts.

Mac felt just as lost as she appeared to be in the electric tension that vibrated between them. He stroked her so gently and yet so wantonly that he heard a catch in her breath. Slowly, he lowered his head and began to kiss a path around her wound. He wanted to show her how much he sympathized with her injury and how much he wanted to kiss away the pain. He carefully avoided direct contact with the most sensitive area of the burn. It had just begun to form a scab and he didn't want to disturb the healing.

"I wish the bullet had wounded me and not you. It tortures me to think of your pain."

Her heart threatened to burst. His words told her how much she must mean to him. She'd have gladly taken the pain from her mother. Could it be possible he loved her that much?

His lips rounded the top of the wound and that brought them to the underside of her breast. Like a homing pigeon, they took a straight path back to her hardened nipple. His hands wandered down her flank and belly. Soon his fingers gently parted her silken curls, then reached and found her bud of pleasure. She moaned deep in her throat. Jason had never touched her there. Nicholas began to stroke, rhythmically sliding his finger down and inside her, then up to flick that sensitive bud that seemed to swell and welcome his touch. She became wetter and wetter as he continued to stroke her, and she moaned in sweet pleasure. Totally forgetting her shyness, she spread her legs as far apart as she could get them, welcoming his touch. Her pelvis rose and moved to meet each thrust of his finger as it delved deeper and deeper into her body.

At one point, Mac thought he felt some resistance to his probe, but he dismissed it as she tightened her sheath around his finger. God! She was everything he'd dreamed of and more.

Her body responded to his like a fiddle to the stroking bow. Suddenly, Sammy's body arched.

She convulsed as the throbbing sensations seemed to careen in outward spirals from the center of her being to her extremities. He could feel the ripples as they entered her legs.

"Let go, Angel, let it happen." Mac licked at her ear and whispered as he rocked on top of her, keeping his fingers moving to the rhythm she set. As her body subsided, he kissed her deep and long. Slowly he lowered his head to her breast and began to nibble and suck.

Her breasts were so sensitive they responded immediately and in seconds he felt the crescendo starting again. Mac couldn't wait any longer. He positioned himself at her entrance, feeling so good there, he was almost afraid to move. She reached for his shaft, and it throbbed at the open invitation for him to fill her like his finger did, only deeper. She lifted her pelvis to accommodate his penetration, and he entered her slowly. He matched her movements sliding himself in and out of her hot, tight sheath, slipping just a little deeper with each thrust. This time he felt it again. There was definitely a barrier.

He tried to stop. *She can't be a virgin. She's been married.* Samantha continued her rocking, and Mac couldn't control himself any longer. He gave a final push, and she gasped in pain. "Sammy, Sammy, why didn't you tell me?" He lay with his head against her hair and tried to hold still.

"Tell you what?" she whispered in confusion. She was still twitching. "Please, Nicholas, don't stop moving now. Please..."

At her passionate pleading, Mac renewed his sweet assault on her body, his rhythm matching the bucking of her passion-filled body. This time, his body convulsed simultaneously with hers, and he was sure he saw stars. Mac collapsed on top of her, and rolling to his side, kept their bodies together as the waves of sensations gradually diminished.

As normality set in and Mac started to question her virginity again, he became aware of the salty taste of tears running into the corner of his mouth. He moved to kiss her eyes and found them streaming quietly. "I'm sorry, Angel. I didn't mean to hurt you. If I'd known you were a virgin, I... I don't know if I would have attempted to make love to you."

"I wasn't a virgin." Sammy jerked as if she had been slapped. "Jason made love to me on our wedding night."

"Sh-h-h," Mac whispered as he brushed his hands over her short, cropped hair and to the side of her face, wiping the tears away with his thumbs. His heart sank. He had alienated her!

"Anyway, I wasn't crying in pain. I was just thinking that was the most beautiful thing that I ever experienced. It wasn't like that when Jason did it. Then, I didn't feel anything but discomfort. I hated it, and I swore no man would ever touch me again. Now, here I am in your arms, and it felt so good. Why was it different?" Sammy asked her question in total innocence.

Mac's heart stopped, then pounded out a tattoo of happiness he could hardly contain. "I don't know what Jason did to you that night, Angel, but he never got far enough to break your maidenhead. Did you see any blood on the sheets the next morning?" He tried to keep his voice casual while his mind was screaming a thousand hurrahs.

"I didn't look. Jason was called away, and I got up and went to Sally's for my things. I never got back to the room." Sammy sounded astonished. Was this possible?

"When we get up, sweetheart, you will probably find blood. Don't let it scare you. It will never happen again, and it will never hurt like that again. From now on you will feel only pleasure when I touch you." Mac's heart pounded with happiness. Jason may have fumbled with her, but by God, he never got home. Mac couldn't believe the pleasure he felt knowing he was the first and would be the last and only man in her life. He hugged her tightly and laughed aloud in happiness.

Sammy shivered in a sudden chill. His amusement confused her, and she wondered if she had pleased him or if he was laughing at her inexperience. Then she remembered his words "from now on when I touch you." He meant to touch her again! The thought frightened her even more, and her body betrayed her with violent shaking.

"You're cold, Angel, let me get you warm again. Honey, I don't think I can ever be without you." Nicholas lovingly helped her back into her clothes and wrapped her in his arms. She knew then she had pleased him. He handled her so gently, almost reverently. He murmured words of love that finally penetrated enough for Sammy to relax. For the first time in months, she felt the peace of love settle over her.

Nicholas settled her in front of him, spoon fashion again. How did he know she felt so comfortable like that? He drew up the blanket, and she snuggled back against his body. A sigh escaped as he whispered, "Sweet dreams," in her ear. She held his arm tightly pressed to her body, just under her breasts. The band of steel felt like a lifeline that she never wanted to release. She wanted to lie awake and figure out the confusion of her thoughts. She tried to reason with herself about how she had allowed this to happen, but the languor she felt after that world-shattering experience soon lulled her into a deep sleep.

Twenty-three

As dawn broke the next morning, Sammy stirred and felt Nicholas waking at the same time. Everything seemed to be making a racket. The birds chirped, squirrels chattered, and the horses neighed. For the second day in a row, the sun had appeared, and the earth started waking up from a five-day sleep. The warmth had melted away the weight of snow, and everything had come to life again.

Sammy opened her eyes fully and stared into the deep blue of Nicholas' loving gaze. All of his feelings were shining out of those beautiful, dark-lashed eyes. His emotions lay bare for her to see.

He returned her stare and saw a reflection of his feelings shining in her hazel eyes. The green was predominate this morning, and he marveled how expressive her eyes were and how they changed color with her emotions. Mac saw her eyes ask an unspoken question and knew what happened had confused her. He gathered Sammy into his arms and tried to ease her mind with banter.

"Good morning, my lady! Are you up to cooking your servant some breakfast?"

"If, kind sir, you are my servant, then I believe it is you who should prepare my breakfast."

Mac felt so pleased with her rejoinder that he laughed aloud. Then he hugged her tightly. "Woman, you please me as no other ever has or ever will." The words spoken out loud sobered both of them, and looking deep into her eyes, Mac kissed her long and hard.

Sammy stiffened, shocked at the instant reaction of her body to his kiss. She'd thought last night a fluke, and now that it was out of her system, it would never happen again. How wrong she had been. Just a kiss and her body flamed to a burning torch. The heat from her inner core radiated throughout her body. Her heart hammered in her chest as she gasped for breath and control. Mac's eyes turned a smoky blue as he sighed.

"Ah, love. It feels so good. You turn me to butter, and I want to lather it all over you and lick it all off."

His words shocked her. He couldn't possibly mean that literally. Yet when he started licking her neck and continued down to her breasts, she practically came out of her skin as pleasure exploded wherever he touched.

No more words were spoken as he proceeded to shower her with love. Their joining was no less earth shattering than the previous night. This time, she experienced no pain, although she'd braced for it. She couldn't believe the difference. As Nicholas entered her, she felt the entire length of him strum every internal nerve. He'd left her on top of him, and she had control of her bucking body. Each time she sank to take him completely inside, she screamed in ecstasy. Then, she would bend forward to capture his lips as she lifted her body away from him until just the tip of his organ rested inside her entrance. Time and time again, she rose to arch her back, thrusting out her breasts for his grasping hands as she took him completely within her writhing body. Finally, the shuddering release spiraled in concentric circles, rippling through every nerve. She felt Nicholas explode inside her, and her sheath convulsed repeatedly as if to milk him dry. When she collapsed on top of him, their sweat-covered bodies melted together. She'd never imagined such heart-stopping passion.

Nicholas seemed just as stunned. His tenderness manifested itself as he helped her wash her body. Finally, she had to stop his ministrations. His slightest touch seemed to ignite her again.

Later, as they dressed, she felt shy and ashamed of her behavior. Her mother didn't raise her to be a loose woman. Her conscience bothered her because she'd let her emotions get out of hand. She still didn't understand why her body throbbed for Nicholas. Even now, after making love again, all she had to do was think of his hands working their magic on her, and her sheath tightened and throbbed in anticipation. She wondered if it could have ever been like this with Jason. She would never know now. The thought of him brought silent tears.

I'm sorry I never loved you, Jason, at least not enough, not as much as I know you loved me. I realize now that I loved you as my brother for your kindness, your gentleness, and your protection. We were married, yet I would have made you miserable because I could never have returned the intensity of your love. I'm so sorry, Jason. Sammy's line of reasoning jarred her from thoughts of Jason.

Was she in love with Nicholas? Is this what her parents shared? How could it happen so fast? Nicholas had whispered words of love, but never said, "I love you." What did he feel for her? She knew men didn't need to be in love to make love. Was it just the circumstances of their being stranded together for five days, or was it four days? Time had lost all meaning and perspective in the last few hours. She knew that from this moment on, her whole life had changed. If Nicholas left her, she would wither and die.

She realized now, she needed him as much as she needed the air to breathe. She knew she couldn't let him fathom her feelings. She would keep her own counsel on the emotions that struggled to escape until she was certain of his feelings. If she were just another roll in the hay, as she had overheard her brothers' laugh about, she would just have to mask her feelings and never let him know how deeply his departure would hurt her.

Mac preened in pleasure, with himself and with Sammy. He'd picked up on her shyness in the light of day, but he would give her time to adjust to having him around all the time. All of his convictions of bachelorhood were a thing of the past. He would track and find Tyler and his cohorts. Then he would settle his accounts with the army and settle down to a life of bliss. If Sammy were uncomfortable living at the scene of her family's massacre, he would take her further west, build her a dream house, and start a ranch. She would help with the horses until their children began taking up all her time. He visualized miniature Sammys and brave little Nicholases running circles around the pair of them, wrapped in a loving embrace. Laughter and love filling the air with the sounds of their joy, he saw them living in utopia.

They completed their breakfast in companionable silence. In less than an hour, Mac had the horses saddled and all their gear packed. Lowering the remaining deer carcass, he tied it on Renegade's rump. He again bundled Sammy into as many clothes as she could get on, then they were on their way.

"We're leaving none too soon, Sammy."

Sammy's heart jumped. Oh, Lord! He couldn't wait to be rid of her.

"I'm afraid both Sassy and Renegade have had a bad couple of days. There wasn't enough grass under all that snow for feed, and what little oats I had for Renegade wasn't quite enough for both horses. We'll have to take it easy and not push their strength. I'm sorry this will be an uncomfortably long ride for you, but I don't want to tax their energy."

Relief then anxiety for the horses caused Sammy's words to come out in a rush. "Nicholas, you know I don't mind. I would never do anything to risk Sassy's health. I can stand the discomfort. It won't be the first or the last time I'm sure."

"Good girl, I knew I could count on you. We should make it back to town before dark, but it will be a long cold day."

Sammy felt so relieved that Nicholas wasn't in a hurry to get rid of her that she would have ridden through a blizzard. As it was, the day had turned crisp and cold, but not uncomfortably so just yet. The wind remained calm and the sunshine bright as a summer day. The snow had melted quite a bit, and though it still covered the ground with several inches, it wasn't too difficult for the horses. The slow walk back to Charrette Village would be a pleasant day's outing until the sun set.

Hungry for every morsel of information she could learn about him, Sammy ventured a few more questions about Mac's family. They talked easily, discussing their pasts. The easy companionship spurred Sammy to find the courage to ask how he'd acquired the cloth he'd used as her bandages.

Mac hesitated before answering. He realized it was not the right time to explain the scene at the waterfall. Since she'd confessed her disguise as a boy, and he'd introduced himself at the waterfall, he couldn't play dumb anymore. He told her about seeing a boy at the falls, and why he'd doubled back. "I was troubled about leaving a young boy all alone, so I came back to try to reason with him. I found him gone, but I saw the buckboard and discovered where he'd hidden a cedar chest. That's where I found the cloth. I kept it because it was so pretty, and I didn't want it see it go to waste."

Sammy responded with awe. "Nicholas, isn't it amazing that the buckboard you found, the cedar chest, and this cloth belonged to me? I can't believe the coincidence that we met each other almost six months ago and now here we are. This cloth seems like an invisible bond that drew us together."

Wordlessly, Mac nodded. He still berated himself for indulging in voyeurism instead of investigating her actions more quickly. It would have saved him so much anguish and her so much sorrow and pain. "I'm only sorry I didn't insist on your joining me. I could have taken you to the fort, and maybe Commander Williams would have sent out some troops to investigate the fires."

He neglected telling her about digging up her hair. He still envisioned having her wrapped lovingly in his arms when he told the whole story from the very beginning. Only then would she learn that bringing her and that scrap of material together had been no coincidence.

"I've thought of that myself, Nicholas. But at that time, I couldn't be sure you weren't involved with the raiders."

Mac refused to spoil the pleasure of the day by bringing up the horror of Sammy's memories or the ways and means of bringing Morgan and Tyler to justice. His only thought was to get her to the safety of the village and to pursue the villains on his own. To distract her, he told a story about the time his stepmother found his medicine pouch and shrieked when she discovered the treasures he'd collected.

"My father explained to her the bits of bone, feathers, and colored stones were just things I collected because the nature of the object called to me. Did I tell you my mother wanted to name me after the red-tailed hawk? She saw one land on a tree branch next to the stream where she knelt to fill a water pouch. The hawk squawked and screeched so insistently that she rose and walked under the branch to see if he was injured. Just as she reached the tree, the hawk flew up and dove to the water's edge. When he rose to fly away, he had a snake in his talons. It had been right next to where she'd knelt only moments before." Mac looked at Sammy to see how she accepted his story. Green and yellow highlights sparkled in her hazel eyes. They glowed with avid interest, and he smiled.

"I was due to be born in the next moon, and she told my father that the hawk had protected her unborn child. She insisted the baby should be named for the hawk because without his protection, she would have been bitten, and she and the baby might have died."

"So, did your father honor her wishes?"

"Yes. He named me Brave Hawk. You see when the hawk flew away with the snake, a feather drifted down, and my mother saved it. It is one of the treasures in my medicine pouch. The hawk has always been my protector."

"You are a brave hawk. Look how you swooped down to snatch me out of the line of gunfire," Sammy teased.

"Don't let your imagination run away with you." Mac laughed at the picture her words drew. "I only did what anyone would have done given the opportunity."

Later, he thought, he'd tell her how his hawk spirit had protected her by coming to him in a dream.

Sammy smiled at him and scoffed at his humility. "There were plenty of men ducking behind doors and water troughs. None of them risked their hide to save me."

"Well, they just didn't think as fast as I did. Someone would have pulled you to safety sooner or later."

"Most likely, too much later." Sammy purposefully neglected to ask Nicholas about his plans for the future. She was afraid of what she would hear. Instead, she tried to enjoy this time alone with him. Once they reached Charrette Village, this interlude would be over.

Sammy noticed Nicholas as he kept a watchful eye on the horizon in each direction. She knew he thought that Tyler had to be out there somewhere, and he wasn't taking any chances on being ambushed. His caution and his act of nonchalance earned her admiration. But, she smiled to herself, he still didn't credit her trail knowledge. She also knew he had no idea she'd kept her own vigil. J.R. always taught her that two pair of eyes were better than one. It saved a lot of surprises.

The sun had set, leaving only the full moon to guide their steps when the town came into view. Tiny lights sparkled from scattered windows, winking in the darkness. The horses perked up their ears. They seemed to know food and shelter were ahead. Sammy could smell the tang of cook fires, and soon she caught a whiff of someone's supper. White columns of smoke rose from chimney tops against the beauty of the star studded sky. The temperature had dropped drastically in the last hour, and Sammy felt almost frozen to the saddle.

The horse's hooves made a slushy sound as they plodded down the deserted street. The snow here had lost its pristine whiteness. Daily traffic had turned the street into a quagmire. Ridges of frozen mud had formed where the wagon wheels had churned up dirt and snow into a batter of brown mush. Only the rooftops reflected the unspoiled beauty of nature.

"Careful here, Sammy. We don't want the horses to stumble now."

Nicholas' words were an irritation to Sammy. She of all people knew the danger of injury to a horse's delicate fetlocks. However, she tempered her annoyance because he'd only voiced his concern for her.

They had only stopped twice all day. Both times were to relieve the stress of riding so long and to quench their thirst. They ate while they rode, trying to make the best time. Sammy knew if he had been alone, he wouldn't have stopped. Appreciation for his thoughtfulness caused her to smile.

Two riders approached the livery stable just as Jack finished his nightly rounds. His shoulders sagged at the thought of another customer and more work. His feet dragged with emotional and physical exhaustion. He just wanted to go home to Sally's comforting arms. Jack waited patiently as the two strangers rode into the stable yard. He recognized Mac first, then Sassy, which caused him to jerk his head up and examine the second rider. Tears streamed down his cheeks and into his beard. He didn't care about the spectacle he made of himself as he yelled his welcome and rushed towards Samantha. By the time he lifted her from the saddle, he could no longer control his crying. He hugged her so hard he realized he had come close to crushing her when he heard her half grunt, half laugh.

Renegade had reacted to Jack's outburst, and Mac had his hands full trying to control the huge stallion. He finally dismounted and slapped Jack on the back to catch his attention. In quiet, soft words, he tried to calm the man. "Easy, man, she's been wounded. You'll reopen her side unless you let her go. She'll be okay. We're just both tired, cold, and hungry, and we need to feed and water our horses."

Jack gently set Sammy aside and stared at her. A sweet smile flooded her face. Jack returned the greeting and with a nod acknowledged that she was alive. Her injury couldn't be too bad since she seemed able to stand on her own.

Tucking her under his big arm in a sheltering hug, he half carried her in his haste to get her into the house so Sally could tend to her. He yelled for his wife before he reached the porch, and as they mounted the steps, she opened the door. The light spilled out catching Sammy in her bedraggled array of clothing, and Sally nearly swooned.

"Oh, Samantha! You look even worse than the first day you showed up on my doorstep."

With that Sammy laughed. “I hope I receive the same treatment. I need a hot bath, a good meal, and a nap, in just the same order as that day so many months ago.”

As much as Jack wanted to stay around to hear from Sammy what happened, he allowed Sally to shoo him out to fetch Miss Laura and Rebecca. When he returned with the two women and escorted them to the house, he had to content himself with getting the story from Mac.

The men stayed out in the stable, tending the two tired horses. Jack began cleaning the icy snow that had accumulated on Sassy’s hooves while Mac did the same for Renegade. As they worked together, Mac gave Jack a censored version of the last several days. Jack returned the favor by relating what had happened in town after the shoot out with the outlaws.

Mac couldn’t believe the good news that the posse Jack marshaled to follow the men shooting at Sammy had found a wounded man. Although his recovery was uncertain, Jack had the foresight to assemble some witnesses while Mr. Frank wrote down the man’s confession. Everyone present witnessed his X and left him in Doc’s care.

Jack explained how frantic with worry they all were about Samantha. “When Mr. Ruggers assured us that you were an honest man, and he would trust you with his most prized possession, Mrs. Ruggers, well, then I calmed down a little. Although no one knew why you had ridden off with Samantha, they all figured she was in good hands and safe.” Jack picked up a curry brush and started on Sassy’s coat.

“We buried Jason the first day after the big snow and then set out to find Samantha. Actually, we stumbled on Joshua’s body quite by accident. Someone noticed the top of a hat sticking out of the snow and reaching for it, uncovered his head. At first we thought he was dead, but the covering of snow must have saved him from being frozen. Doc said it apparently slowed down his system enough to keep him alive. He still isn't sure if he'll pull through, but at least we got a signed statement from him explaining why they shot Jason and why they were after Samantha. Personally, I think he's going to make it. If he was going to kick the bucket, he'd have done it before now." Jack paused, "You know, Mac, he's just a kid. I think that Tyler bullied him. His story pert' near shocked Mr. Frank, Mr. Ruggers, and Doc, but at least I was able to explain Samantha's past and why she was in hiding."

After Jack finished his lengthy story, Mac clapped him on the back. "I couldn't have done better myself, Jack. With the statement you have, I can now go to the commander at Fort Howard and have Morgan arrested and tried for murder. This is the proof I needed to hang that scoundrel. Once he's in the brig, Sammy can be free to be herself again and never have to worry about someone trying to kidnap, rape, or shoot her in the back. Come on, walk me to the barber. I want a hot bath, too. I can't wait to tell Sammy that her problems are just about over."

As they walked in companionable silence, Mac had a thought. "Jack, Sammy will want to go with me to Pinckney to arrest Morgan. I can't allow her to go. She needs to recover fully from her wound and the infection. She'll still be in danger until Morgan is behind bars and Tyler is apprehended. I don't think we should tell her about the confession or let on that I will be leaving for Pinckney as soon as Renegade's rested. Can I depend on you and Sally to keep her under wraps long enough for me to return with the news that she will be safe from Morgan?"

"Of course. Listen, Mac, I don't think Sally will let that girl out of her sight for one minute ever again. Samantha can stay with us as long as it takes. Do you think she will want to return to her ranch?"

"I don't know, Jack. I guess we won't find out until I get back. It could take me as long as a month. I'm hoping with that confession, though, I can get the commander to act a lot quicker. Before anyone else is killed."

~ * ~

The three women fussed over Samantha, making quick work of bringing in the water to heat for her bath and examining her wound. They agreed that it had healed nicely enough not to need Doc's attention, and while Rebecca and Miss Laura helped Samantha bathe and wash her hair, Sally retrieved one of her dresses and began pressing it.

Samantha refused to allow Laura and Rebecca to redye her hair. She would never again pretend to be someone she wasn't. She planned on revealing her identity and explaining why she had to be in disguise. The lies were over forever. If Tyler wanted to find her, he would. He knew who she was anyway. She saw no sense in continuing the charade. Jason was dead. She planned on taking her maiden name back. After all, she'd only been married less than twenty-four hours. Surely it didn't even count, especially since Jason had left her a virgin bride.

The women tried to reason with her to no avail. They must have realized that the strain of the last few days had begun to take its toll and together by silent looks and nods, agreed to let her have her way for now. Sammy saw the gestures and quiet communication passing between them, and she felt relieved that they were giving in on this. Somehow, she knew they would try to find other ways to protect her.

Most of the black dye had worn off her hair during her illness, and the rest washed out after several dousings of warm water. The natural brilliance of her vibrant chestnut still looked dulled, but it was better than the black. Laura assured her that it would return to its normal color after a few more washings. Sammy resigned herself to looking less than her best and realized her vanity stemmed from wanting to be beautiful for Nicholas.

After the women thoroughly washed, pressed, and primped her, Rebecca ran out to the stables to bring in the men. She returned alone.

"There's no one there. The place is locked up and dark," she announced.

"Well," Laura piped up, "if I know Mr. MacNamee, he probably headed over to wake up the barber for a bath himself. He's the cleanest man I've ever had in my bed." Rebecca tried hushing her, and Sally giggled at the implication.

Sammy felt the blood drain from her body and sat heavily on the nearest chair. Sally turned and noticed her pallor first. "Samantha, are you all right? Oh dear, it looks like she's going to pass out." As the three women fluttered around her in real concern, Sammy snapped out of her daze.

"Sorry, I guess I'm more tired than I thought. I really don't feel hungry at all anymore. I'll be fine after a good night's sleep. Would you mind if I bowed out of tonight's festivities? I really need to go to bed." Sammy had to get out before she started crying. She needed to analyze her feelings and understand what had happened to her. And, she didn't want any witnesses to her soul searching. "Thank you for all your care. You are all my dearest friends, and I love you."

Sammy choked on her suppressed tears and left the room. Before she mounted the stairs, she looked back down the hall into the kitchen. Laura had put her arm around the shaken Sally. "Don't worry," she soothed. "Think about what that poor child has been through these last few months. It's no wonder she's emotionally at the end of her tether. After a good night's sleep, I'm sure she'll be more like her old self."

Thankfully, Samantha realized none of the women imagined what had upset her. How she reached her room she would never know. The searing, hot tears refused to stop. They blinded her, and her heart felt broken in two. What was she so upset about? Was she jealous? Of course, she hated the thought of Nicholas being with any other woman the way he had been with her. She was so naïve! She should have realized that a man like Nicholas would never be without a woman for long. She just happened to be one of many, certainly not the first—as his expert kissing had taught her—and most certainly not the last. A man as good looking as Nicholas would never be alone.

Well, she had known there was no commitment between them when she allowed herself to be dazzled by his charm, so there was no reason for her to think that after making love to her, he would give up all his other women. *I wonder how many he has strung out along his various paths?* The thought brought renewed tears, and Sammy realized she had to get control of her emotions. Rather than think about Nicholas, she should channel her thoughts to how she would bring Mr. T.J. Morgan to justice.

Nicholas had probably already forgotten about her anyway. Since he had shared all of his knowledge about the slaughters and the culprit behind them, she couldn't wait to set her gun sights right between Mr. Morgan's eyes. Sammy fell into a fitful sleep, thinking about her revenge.

~ * ~

When the men returned to the house several hours later, it was to find Sally alone in the kitchen. The room showed no evidence of Sammy's bath, and the fire reflected wavering shadows over the table set with only three places. Mac looked around the darkened room, trying not to be obvious in his search for Sammy. Jack, not needing to be so casual, demanded loudly. "Where's my girl hiding?"

Sally hushed his booming voice and motioned for the men to sit. As she dished up their supper, she explained, "Sammy almost passed out from exhaustion, and right now, she's sleeping soundly."

Mac's concern was immediately evident, and he hastened to explain his bewilderment. "She ate well every day, and we took it easy coming back because the horses were weak. Her wound isn't infected again, is it?"

His concern for Samantha seemed to confuse Sally. "Why are you so worried about Samantha? I'm sure she's just exhausted from her ordeal. After all, she lost her husband, got wounded, and had to hide in a cave for five days. That's enough to topple a giant, let alone a mere child like Samantha."

Mac wasn't sure if they were talking about the same woman. His Sammy wouldn't be knocked flat by twice as much as she'd endured, least of all a little inconvenience of camping in a warm cave. "Are you sure she's okay? Sammy's pretty tough, and I don't think she would pass out just from exhaustion. What that woman has been through in the last week puts many a man I've ridden with to shame."

"She's not feverish. I'm sure she was just being brave for your benefit. She's so proud, she would never let anyone know if she was suffering." Sally didn't appear to like answering his questions, and her answers came out a little sharp. As Jack laid a hand over Sally's to calm her, Mac jumped up from his chair so fast it fell over on its back.

"I'll just go check on her real quick. Where's her room?"

"You'll do no such thing! You have no right to go into Samantha's room while she is in bed." Sally's loud, angry retort brought both herself and Jack to their feet also.

"I've slept with her every night for the last week, tended her wound, fed, and cared for her twenty-four hours a day, every day we were gone. What do you think I'll see that I haven't already seen?"

Mac was so upset he didn't realize he had been shouting until he looked up and saw Sammy standing in the doorway. Her pallor frightened him. He froze. He hadn't meant to get so demanding with his hosts. These were people whom Sammy loved, and he was a guest in their home. Seeing her stricken eyes shooting sparks of fire, he realized he'd overstepped his manners. His concern for her had overridden his awareness of how he sounded and, forgetting to apologize, he'd rushed to Sammy's side. His words dried in his throat as she stopped him dead in his tracks with the daggers flying out of her eyes like green darts.

"What are you doing here, Nicholas? I thought you would be all tucked in at Laura's by now." Damn! She hadn't meant to say that. What was wrong with her? Why couldn't she just bite her tongue for once?

"What? Laura's? Why would I be at Laura's? I was worried about you. Sally said you almost passed out and went to bed without eating. She said you were exhausted. I was afraid your wound had reopened and become infected again."

Sammy saw the confusion and the caring in his eyes, but she couldn't let go of her jealousy. It burned her stomach with acid fire. "I'm no longer your concern, Nicholas. All your shouting woke me, so I came down to see what all the commotion was about. My wound is healing nicely, but I feel quite exhausted by the trauma of the last week. You needn't stay on my account. I'm sure Sally and Jack will excuse you. You can pursue your own life now. I no longer need you to look after me. Thank you for saving me from Tyler. I do appreciate your rescuing me from being delivered into his hands." Sammy hesitated as Nicholas looked at her in stupefaction.

"Goodbye, Nicholas." Sammy held her hand out stiffly in front of her body. Her left hand clinched into a fist behind her back so hard, she could feel her nails digging into her palm.

"Goodbye, hell!" Who was this cold polite stranger speaking to him like a servant? Mac reacted like a man losing his own heart. He grabbed her in a steely embrace and with one arm around her back, held her chin firmly with his other hand and kissed her soundly.

Sally started screaming and pounding her fist on Mac's unfeeling back while Jack tried to contain his wife's flaying arms.

Jack finally managed to get Sally into a bear hug as Mac lifted his head and looked into Sammy's eyes. In the merest whisper, with the softest words, speaking from the depths of his love for this woman, Mac instructed her, "We will never say 'Goodbye'. We belong together as sure as God made Adam and Eve for each other. I'll leave you now to rest. But, my dear, I will be back for you. I have a room over at Mr. Rugger's hotel if you need me. I don't know how I will ever sleep tonight without you curled at my side. I know you can't accompany me to the hotel, but I don't intend to be without you for very long. I love you, Samantha Turner, and I want to spend the rest of my life with you." With that Mac turned on his heels and snatched his hat from the peg on the wall. He left in a swirl of cold air as the door slammed behind him.

As soon as Nicholas' lips had touched hers, Sammy had lost all control. If he hadn't been holding her in such an iron grip, she surely would have fallen to the floor. The doorjamb was all that supported her now as she woke to the fact that he had already left. Her hand remained clinched in a tight fist, and she had to force her fingers to obey the dictates of her brain to uncurl.

Although Nicholas had spoken softly to her, the Billings were uneasy witnesses to the passion that flared between the two of them. Jack had Sally's arms constrained and had stilled her raging in time to hear Mac's whispered words of love.

All three of them remained frozen in a shocked tableau. Jack was the first to break the uneasy silence. He kept his voice gentle. He remembered Mac's story and detected in his words more than had been related out in the stable.

"Are you okay, Samantha?" He was afraid to ask more, and he saw Sally, picking up on the pressure of his hand softly squeezing her waist, bite her tongue.

Nodding her head silently, Samantha turned and left the room as quietly as she had entered it.

Not able to contain herself any longer, Sally let fly a string of questions that kept Jack talking into most of the night. Unable to deny what they witnessed, they both concluded the same thing. Whatever happened in the last week between these two young people, they were in love with each other.

"Did you see Samantha's eyes, Jack? I could see the love as she looked up at Nicholas. Even her attempt at cool politeness didn't hide the emotion that simmered below the surface. I never saw Samantha look at Jason that way."

Jack nodded. Sally had a tendency to romanticize things, but he had to agree.

After hearing Jack's version of Mac's story, Sally said she understood his need to confirm for himself her well-being. His anger at being dismissed so casually now made sense.

"You know," Jack admitted, "if I were in Mac's shoes, I would have torn the house down to find Samantha. We're lucky he only turned over a chair and no damage done." As always, Jack had Sally laughing over theoretical scenarios. After peeking in to be sure Samantha slept soundly, they retired to their room to give their well-used bed another workout.

~ * ~

Sammy heard them come up the steps and quickly pretended to sleep. She knew Sally would check on her before retiring, and she didn't want to talk. She was still trying to sort out her feelings. Nicholas had touched her lips with a soft kiss that on contact reached into her very soul with his passion and she had melted on the spot. If his arm hadn't supported her, she knew she would have fallen to the floor. Then, he'd lifted his head and looked straight into her heart when he said, "I love you".

Tears sprang unbidden to her eyes as she repeated the scene over and over in her mind. She knew she loved him as she'd loved no other. It felt different than anything she'd ever experienced with her family, Dennis, or Jason. Her toes curled as she remembered last night and this morning in the cave. He had stimulated emotions and feelings in her mind and body that presented an unknown factor. She knew she'd reacted with unreasonable jealously over the women he'd known before, and she felt insecure enough to doubt his ability to be a one-woman man.

If he'd shared Laura's bed, it must mean glamorous women attracted him. Someone who had beautiful clothes and was well-groomed with long sensuous hair. That thought brought fresh tears for her shorn locks, lost forever. How could a man like Nicholas even look twice at a tomboy like her? He'd only seen her in men's clothes with her hair dyed this ugly black and cut so short it defied the curling iron. She looked skinny compared to Laura's voluptuousness and, next to her, totally inexperienced. Sammy continued listing her shortcomings and losing all sense of reality, cried herself to sleep.

~ * ~

Mac wasted no time on what-ifs. He returned to the hotel and, after speaking to the Ruggers, went to his room. He had a lot to plan, and he meant to start first thing in the morning. Renegade would respond quickly. After a good rest and plenty of oats, he should be ready to ride come sunup. Mac planned to leave at daybreak and take Joshua's signed confession to Fort Howard. In formulating his plans, he dismissed his hastily spoken words of, “I’ll be at the hotel if you need me”. The way she’d sent him off, she wouldn’t come looking for him anyway. He knew with the evidence he had and a confession he could see justice done. Then he could return to Sammy and marry her. The sooner he left, the sooner he could return.

He tossed a few minutes before he jumped out of bed and retrieved the treasure of Sammy’s hair, still wrapped in the same cloth as he’d rescued it. He inhaled the scent of her and snuggled his head on the sweet pillow her tresses made. *Some day, I’ll have the real thing again,* he thought as he fell into a deep slumber.

Twenty-four

Mac arose early the next morning. He had wanted to stay in Charrette Village to celebrate the New Year with Sammy. He had a fleeting thought that if he stayed another day or so, he could smooth her ruffled feathers. He couldn't imagine what had riled her. But no matter how many times he recalled their last day together, he couldn't put his finger on what put a burr under her saddle.

He realized that if he lingered any longer, she could foil his plans. He conferred with Jack and Mr. Ruggers before he decided to ride out that day. They knew his plans and approved. Jack had assured Mac he and Sally could keep Samantha safe until he returned, and as the sun poked its orange nose into the eastern sky, Mac started for Fort Howard.

Sammy overslept and woke to the loud grumbling of her stomach. At first, the bright sunlight streaming into the room through the curtained glass confused her. Then she remembered she no longer shared the cave with Nicholas. She lay in her room at Jack and Sally's house. A glance around the chamber showed her nothing had changed. It seemed as if she'd never left. The time between Christmas morning and now was only a nightmare. She lay still for several minutes. The time with

Nicholas hadn't been a nightmare, although at the moment she regretted her indiscretion.

As she contemplated the past week, a plan began forming in her active mind. She arose, quickly completed her morning wash, dressed, and went down to face the Billings. She dreaded the questions she'd left unanswered last night, and she knew they would try to stop her once they heard her plan. She would just have to brazen this one out. She hoped they were good enough friends that they would help rather than hinder her. Saying a quick prayer, she entered the kitchen.

"Mmmm, that smells wonderful. I didn't realize how much I missed fresh bread until I caught a whiff of your special recipe, Sally." Sammy sat at the table as Sally sliced the hot bread and slid the mound of fresh churned butter in front of Samantha. She tried to be as nonchalant as she could. Sooner or later she would have to explain last night, but at this point she couldn't even comprehend it herself.

Sally, determined to let Samantha set the mood, bit her tongue to keep from asking the questions that ran through her mind.

"You must be starved, Samantha. You didn't eat anything last night, and it is already noon."

"Are you serious?" Sammy gasped. "How could I have slept so long? You should have woke me earlier."

"I had strict orders from Jack to leave you catch up on your rest. Not that I needed any such orders from him. I know when a body has reached its limit." Sally bustled around the kitchen setting one dish after the other in front of Samantha.

"I have stew left over from last night, and here's some roasted chicken and mashed potatoes. I can open a jar of beans that I canned last summer, or would you rather I fry you up some bacon and eggs?"

"Sally, Nicholas provided for me quite well. We had plenty of food. We even brought the rest of the deer carcass for you." Shaking her head at the number of dishes Sally continued to bring to the table, she continued, "I assure you I couldn't possibly eat everything you're putting in front of me." Samantha chuckled as Sally tried to tempt her appetite with everything in her larder.

"It's just that you didn't eat anything last night, and I know you must have gone to bed hungry. You are getting too thin. You must nourish yourself, especially after being wounded and the ordeal of the last week."

Jack entered the kitchen as Sally continued to push forward one dish after the other to tempt Samantha. "Leave the child be, Sally. I'm sure she will eat her fill without you shoving it down her throat." With a hearty laugh and a hug, he softened his criticism as he whispered, "I love you," into Sally's ear.

"Well, Samantha my dear, have you finally slept your fill? I think Sally wore out the hinges on your door this morning just checking to see if you were still breathing."

Sammy saw Sally blush and grinned. Their love and concern warmed her down to her toes. "I'm sorry I worried you, truly I didn't mean to sleep so long. I have so much to do today."

"You should rest," Sally interjected. "You need to regain your strength."

"I don't need rest, Sally. I need to see about Jason's burial and so many other details that I am probably not even aware of yet." Catching the look between Jack and Sally, Samantha continued, "You might as well let me know what has happened now? I can see you have something painful to tell me."

Jack stuttered and Sally sat at the table and took Samantha's hand. "My dear, we buried Jason three days ago. We couldn't wait any longer. No one knew where you were, whether or not you were even alive, or if you would ever be back. We had to lay him to rest."

Tears started in Sammy's eyes. "Of course, Sally. How silly of me not to think of that. Perhaps I could visit his grave after lunch."

"Certainly, my dear, Jack and I will take you."

"No, Sally, I prefer to go alone. I will need to say goodbye, and I would like to do so in private. I'm sure you understand." They must have seen the look of determination in her eyes. Sammy saw Jack nod to Sally, and they agreed to honor her wishes in quiet acquiescence.

The day sped by so fast Sammy hardly noted the passage of time. She'd visited Jason's grave and cried for the waste of a life so young and only just beginning to enjoy the happiness of his future. She cried because she knew that she hadn't loved him as much as she should have. Remorse brought more recriminations because she should never have married him, and yet in doing so, she'd made his one wish come true. He would never know his devotion hadn't been reciprocated, nor that he'd left her a virgin widow. For that and because she hadn't caused him any emotional pain, she thanked God.

The effort of her graveside visit left Samantha quite exhausted. She could not understand her lack of energy until complaining to Sally after dinner. "Samantha, do you realize you are still recovering from a wound and a serious infection? You've always enjoyed good health. Now, admit the truth of my words and agree to go easy for a couple of days."

"You're right, Sally. I don't ever remember being sick. I didn't realize it would take so much out of me." No one mentioned Nicholas, and embarrassment kept Samantha from asking. Although it surprised her, she breathed a sigh of relief that the Billings did not bring up the scene they had witnessed in the kitchen the previous night. Nicholas hadn't come by all day, and his absence confused her. *After all*, she thought, *he declared himself to me last night. You'd think he would be anxious to see me again.* Samantha grew more withdrawn as the evening progressed, and by the time she could not delay going up to bed any longer, she felt quite despondent.

New Year's Eve, Samantha came down for breakfast in time to help Sally prepare the meal. She felt more like herself and looked forward to seeing Nicholas. If he didn't come to see her, she would go find him. He'd told her he had a room at Mr. Rugger's hotel, and she could reach him there if she needed him. She could admit to herself now that she did need him.

Her jealousy had waned when she'd admitted that Nicholas had only answered the same call of nature that most men responded to when the opportunity presented itself. If only she knew for sure he hadn't just used her to alleviate a discomfort. She needed to feast her eyes on him and reaffirm to herself that he didn't regret speaking the words he'd whispered two nights ago. He'd said, "I love you." He'd said, "I want to spend the rest of my life with you." What did he mean by that? He'd never mentioned marriage. The way her insides melted when he kissed her, she thought if he asked her, she might even go with him without the benefit of clergy. Then, she would see to it that he never needed the solace of Miss Laura or anyone else ever again!

How she managed to pass the day, she would never know. The hour hand on the mantle clock crawled around the face making each tick last an eternity. By three in the afternoon, her nerves were stretched to the limit. "Sally, I'm going out for a little walk. Do you need anything from the store?"

"The temperature seems to be dropping, and the sky doesn't look too friendly. Are you sure you feel up to going out?"

"Sally, I need some fresh air. If I don't get some exercise, I'll go crazy."

"Okay, Honey. Take my coat. There's no need to stop at the Frank's, I've got everything I need."

"Thanks, Sally, you're a dear."

Sammy briskly hurried down the boardwalk towards the hotel. Her progress temporarily slowed as several people stopped her to welcome her back and express sympathy for Jason's death. She accepted hugs and handshakes from people she hardly knew. They all seemed genuinely happy she had returned unharmed. For a moment, she chided herself for chasing after Nicholas just after these well-meaning friends reminded her she was newly widowed.

Sammy burst into the hotel lobby with a gust of wintry wind that pushed her through the door. Weak beams of winter sun rushed into the room then reluctantly retreated when she shouldered the entryway shut. *I have to see Nicholas now,* she thought as she forced her guilt aside.

She saw Daniel first as he came down the steps with an arm full of dirty laundry. He let out a whoop and jumped down the remaining steps, tossing the sheets over the rail. He swooped down on her with yells of delight and in his exuberance picked her up and twirled her around.

"Daniel," she laughed. "Put me down. Gracious you've grown a foot in the last week." Smiling she looked at her friend with affection. "You've become a young man overnight. All the young girls will be batting their eyelashes at you."

"They already are, Miss Samantha." Samantha turned to include Mr. and Mrs. Ruggers in her amused smile.

"We're mighty glad to have you back safe and sound, girl. I'll tell you, this whippersnapper didn't like it one bit when those varmints took out after you. The only thing that kept him sane was the fact that Mac snatched you up, and we knew he'd keep you safe."

"Thank you, Mr. Ruggers. I really appreciate all the concern you good people had for me. And you were right, Daniel. Mr. MacNamee looked after me very well. In fact, I've come to thank him formally. Is he in?"

"Samantha," Daniel said in surprise, "Mac left here at sun up yesterday morning."

For a moment, Sammy couldn't find her voice. Then with a quiver that she hated, she asked, "Did he leave a message for me or say where he was going? When he would return?"

Daniel looked at his grandparents. He didn't understand the pain he saw in Sammy's eyes. Mr. Ruggers kept his silence. Daniel answered when he realized his grandparents would not.

"No, not that I know of. Grandpa?" With only a silent shake of his head, Mr. Ruggers turned his back and led his wife from the room.

Ignoring Daniel's cry of protest, Sammy swung on her heels and in a half run returned to her room at the Billings. She spent the afternoon fueling the anger that built into a blinding hate in her heart. His words were empty. "Never say goodbye!" Ha! What a joke. He'd only been after her body, and she had allowed him complete freedom to her person. How could she be so naive? Never again would she let a man best her. No matter how much her body might betray her, she would never mistake lust for love again. She hoped she would never find out if Nicholas had spent his last night at Laura's.

Now, she would put her plans into immediate action. She had to assuage her hate before she thought about Nicholas again. She decided to ride to Pinckney and kill J.T. Morgan if it was the last thing she ever did. She wouldn't join in the celebrations of the village. Her bereavement provided a convenient excuse.

“Maybe it’s best to let her rest, Jack.” Sally looked worried, but Samantha assured them she didn’t need company.

“You two go on and have some fun. I’ll be fine after a good night’s sleep.” Thankfully, the Billings did not insist on her accompanying them.

That night she made repairs to her clothes and gathered what she would need to disguise herself again. With the house empty, it afforded a perfect opportunity to collect all of her belongings in preparation for her trip.

~ * ~

Mac reached Fort Howard on the evening of New Year’s Day. It frustrated him that he had to wait for two more days for the Commander to return with his family from a visit to St. Louis. By the time a private finally ushered him into Commander Williams’ office, he couldn’t control his temper.

“Where in the hell have you been? I need a troop of men right now. Look at this.” His anger had exploded before he could marshal his thoughts. He slammed down the written confession and leaned over the Commander’s desk with his weight supported by his flattened palms bracketing the paper.

“Mr. MacNamee, if you persist in this insubordination, you will spend some time in the brig for your insolence.”

“I don’t have time for the brig. I need your help, and I need it now.”

Commander Williams casually leaned back in his chair and reached for a cheroot. “Perhaps you’d better simmer down and tell me your problem.”

Mac stood and paced. He needed his iron control. Smacking his fist into his open palm he turned to face the commander. Taking a deep breath, he calmed himself down enough to explain the urgency needed in issuing a warrant for T.J. Morgan's arrest and the necessity of sending a troop of solders to execute it. After an hour of beseeching, arguing, and defending his position, Commander Williams finally agreed to examine all the evidence Mac had revealed. Faced with the unvarnished truth of Morgan's duplicity and Mac's narration of the chain of events, he had no choice but to grant Mac's request for a warrant and the help to bring Morgan back to the fort for justice.

"Commander Williams," Mac apologized, "I'm sorry I came in here and lost my temper. Usually, I exhibit much more patience than I've shown you today. However, I'm sure you understand the anxiety I have regarding my future wife. I could never forgive myself if something happened to her because I was unable to enlist your help. We both desperately need to see Morgan apprehended."

William's stopped Mac before he could complete his apologizes. "Mac, I've known your father for a long time, and I know you as an excellent scout and an honorable man. I should have listened to you to begin with. But your attitude and actions didn't match the Nicholas MacNamee I know so well. At first, I wasn't sure just whom I was dealing with. Actually, young man, I thought you might be drunk or even worse, you'd totally lost your mind." He laughed at the look on Mac's face as he slapped him on the back in friendly fashion.

Bundling up in their winter coats, they opened the outer door. They both struggled to fight the wind that wrapped its cold fingers around their exposed skin and threatened to peel it right off. "Looks like a blizzard headed this way," Mac yelled. "Do you think we could head out before it hits?"

"Let's check with the Quartermaster to see if we have the equipment necessary for a foray into this weather. I also want to see if enough of my men have returned from their holiday leave. I know you're anxious, and I know why. I would be, too, but I won't send anyone out on a suicide mission."

The force of the wind made even shouting impossible and, saving their breath, the men hurried into the shelter of the stables before they continued their conversation. To Mac's utter frustration, they found out that the Quartermaster had taken advantage of the holiday season to send many of the tents off for repair.

"Normally, we only used the tents for summer deployment. Winter, you keep the troops close to the fort." Turning to Mac in apology, he continued, "Commander Williams usually doesn't send his troops out for long this time of year. I also have a lot of the tack at the saddle maker's for repair," he explained.

To top off that disappointment, at least ten men hadn't returned from their Christmas leave, and Commander Williams was reluctant to deplete his fort of the manpower he would need to defend it from any potential Indian attack. No amount of arguing could change his mind.

"Be sensible, Mac. Look at the weather. No one in his right mind would be out in this. We are in for another blizzard, and this time it will be worse than last week. You can feel how much the temperature has dropped, and neither you nor my men could survive exposure to this wind and snow without shelter. I won't allow it. You can be sure a man like Morgan won't be far from his fireplace, and I'm sure the type of bullies he hires will be holed up, too."

Mac had to acknowledge the wisdom of the commander's decision, but he didn't have to like it. It was fortunate that the commander was sympathetic to Mac's position, or he would have found himself under house arrest. Mac knew he shouldn't have taken his anger at the weather out on the commander, but he felt so helpless. His fear for Sammy's life held him in an icy cage and refused to release its grip on his heart.

~ * ~

January second found Sammy a prisoner of the weather again. Only this time, she chafed at the delay. This was no idyllic space out of time, spent with a stranger to whom she'd lost her heart and her virtue. This became pure torture. Every day she sat and watched the weather turn from raging blizzard to temperatures dropping to the lowest on record. The harsh winds made even the trip to the stable an excruciatingly painful dash. It seemed that even a roaring fire, burning twenty-four hours a day, did little to dispel the cold that penetrated every nook and cranny of the Billings sturdy home.

As the days turned to weeks, Sammy's brooding did not go unnoticed by Jack and Sally. They were both very concerned for her, but neither of them could reach her. Day by day, she sat staring out of the patch in her window that she kept rubbed clean of frost. What she saw, what she looked for, they never knew.

"I'm sure it's because Mac left her without a word. Damn," Jack cursed. "I wish I'd never promised to keep Mac's destination from Samantha."

"I think she's mourning for Jason, and it's best to let her come to terms with the change in her status."

"Well, whatever it is, we can't let her go on like this."

"You're right, Jack. We've got to do something."

~ * ~

Sammy lost track of the time she spent at her window. Her mind tossed in constant confusion over her feelings. She mourned for Jason, berated herself for not loving him more. Guilt, for betraying his love by giving herself to Nicholas, ate at her soul. But mostly, she mentally prepared to ride to Pinckney. She needed to find Morgan, the man who'd hatched the scheme to kill her family and all her friends. She kept an eye on the weather day in and day out, trying to gauge when she would be able to disguise herself and sneak away. There was never a doubt that she would do it. The only question was when and how long would it take for the weather to break.

Each day brought renewed torture, renewed remorse, and more despair. Day after day, she totally relived the time in the cave with Nicholas. She constantly tried to find a reason for her uncharacteristic actions. Her parents had raised her to know better than to allow her feelings to overcome good judgment. Yes, she was impetuous. Yes, she sometimes regretted her actions, but never had she behaved so carelessly. She had let her heart and her instincts guide her. They had failed her miserably. Again, she had trusted her heart and her mind when they whispered that Nicholas was everything she had ever dreamt of, everything she ever wanted. He'd made her believe in him. He'd even said, "I love you," yet he left without a word. "Come to me if you need me." Yet he had disappeared. No message. No explanation. Nothing.

With the dawn of each new day, she resolved to take care of herself in the future. Never again would she trust another. Her battles were her own. She could take care of herself and her own problems. She didn't need or want any help. She knew what she had to do and she would do it.

Her heart pounded in relief when her normal monthly began. *Thank you, God. I couldn't bear being with child, now,* she thought. If worse had come to worse, she'd even considered passing the child off as Jason's. Thank God that would not be necessary, especially if the baby had been born with a shock of dark hair like Nicholas. The picture brought more tears. She would have loved giving him a son, and she fantasized about the idyllic family they could have had.

Quickly, she banished that line of thought. It did no good to dwell on the impossible. She would never see him again, and she'd better get used to the idea.

Sammy was at least realistic enough to realize how foolish it would be to start her journey during this terrible weather. She knew her limits and realized that she could be dead of exposure in a very short time if she left now, but the wait almost killed her.

She lost weight and except for Sally's prodding, would have forgotten to eat at all. She even had to be tempted away from her window for a bath, something Sally had never had to do before Nicholas disappeared. Now, Sally took to preparing Sammy's bath and gently knocking at her door to tell her the water was cooling, and she better hurry. That usually received an apathetic reply and finally a grudging assent.

One afternoon towards the end of January, Sammy realized she felt so weak she could barely walk down the steps to the kitchen for her bath without holding on to the banister. She knew then that she'd better overcome her turmoil or she would be too fragile to ride once the weather broke. Valiantly, she struggled through her bath and, without coaching from Sally, ate a decent meal for the first time in almost a month.

Sammy saw Sally look at Jack and only by a silent nod did he indicate he'd noticed. She was only too happy to relieve their anxiety. The next few days she showed them a marked improvement in her behavior. She left her room for longer periods of time and began to help Sally around the house, gradually building her strength. A week later, she insisted on accompanying Jack to the stable.

She wanted to see Sassy anyway, and she knew she should begin to accustom her body to physical labor again. She realized she only resembled a silent ghost of herself, but her strength had begun to return. *The resilience of youth,* she thought with a smile. *A miracle of healing.* Sammy felt thankful she was basically a healthy young woman. Her physical wounds had healed, leaving only a puckered scar no one could see. Her emotional wounds were so deep they would never heal, but they too would leave scars invisible to the naked eye.

On occasion, Jack had to leave the stable to fetch feed or supplies from the store. During those times, Sammy did strenuous exercise. She'd hoisted herself up on a barrel and did chin-ups on the rafter beams. Daily, she repeatedly climbed up and down the ladder to the loft. One afternoon, she actually laughed aloud at the commotion she'd caused among the horses with her antics when she ran the length of the stable and back.

Jack returned to find her soothing each animal and in minutes the horses were peaceful and quiet. "What's the problem, Samantha?" Jack boomed as he did a double take, looking at Samantha's flushed face. "I never have trouble with the horses when you're with them."

"Nothing, Jack. I wanted to see how fast I could run from one end of the stable to the other, and I guess the horses felt like they wanted to join me. I think I was beginning to go stir crazy not exercising for a month. Besides, I got cold and I thought if I ran awhile it would warm me up." *There,* she thought, *close enough to the truth.*

Jack smiled his understanding and tucked her under his massive arm to escort her through the wind to the house. Once in the warm kitchen, he looked at her as she removed her wrap. "It's good to see you come alive again, Samantha. Welcome back." The words were spoken quietly with love.

Tears immediately sprang to Samantha's eyes for the pain she had caused these lovely people. They had taken her in, given her a home and love, and she had shut them out totally. She felt terrible, but Samantha realized they would never understand her need for revenge or her sense of guilt over her conduct. Most of all, they didn't know how deeply Nicholas had hurt her.

"I'm sorry I've isolated myself this past month, Jack. I've just had so much to think about, and the weather has been so depressing. I hope you can forgive me."

"There's nothing to forgive, child. You've just been through a terrible time in you life, and you wouldn't be normal if you didn't have some doubts as to why life is the way it is. It just gives me pleasure to see you are beginning to bounce back. Sally and I have been very worried, but we knew you needed time to heal. Just because we have been keeping out of your way is no indication that we don't care. We love you like the daughter we never had, and we only want you to be happy. Things will work out, Samantha. Just give it time. Be patient, child, you'll see. By spring, everything will seem like a bad dream, and you'll wake like the earth to a new life."

"What a beautiful thought, Jack. Thank you for your reassurance. I just hope I never cause you and Sally any disappointment. I love you both."

Sammy looked up to see Sally standing quietly in the kitchen doorway. "Lordy, Samantha, you could never disappoint us. We love you. The last few days have given us so much hope for you. We are both so happy you are beginning to heal. Come on, you two. Wash up, supper's on, and I even made dessert to tempt Samantha's budding appetite."

That evening marked a turning point for Sammy. She started talking again but never about the time she'd spent with

Nicholas. She kept her conversations general, just daily observations of the weather, the horses, or discourse she'd had with any of the townspeople who happened by the stables.

By the middle of February, the weather suddenly broke. Sammy woke to sun streaming into her room, and she blinked at the unaccustomed bright light. Her first thought was that she had overslept. She hadn't done that since the first morning back from the cave. Her dash to the window caused her heart to soar. The street bustled with activity. People seemed to be walking at a normal pace and not hunched over to avoid the blistering wind. She washed and dressed faster than she ever had before and bounded down the steps like an adolescent.

Sally stopped and watched her. Samantha almost bowled her over by her exuberance as she stood at the bottom of the steps. "Sally! The sun! It really is still there! Why didn't you wake me!"

"You still need your rest, whether you realize it or not. I think this last week has been the first time since you came home that you slept through the night without nightmares. I was determined to let you sleep round the clock if need be. I don't think you know, but I look in on you every night and it broke my heart to see you tossing and turning." Sally hesitated as if reluctant to continue. "Most of the time with tears streaking your face. Oh, Samantha. I'm so happy you are finally getting better." Taking Sammy by the arm and tucking it under hers, Sally led her to the warm kitchen.

"Come on, it's only eight o'clock. I've kept breakfast for you, but if you'd rather, Jack will be coming in for a snack, and you can have some stew with him." Releasing her at the table, Sally looked deeply into Sammy's eyes. "Anytime you want to talk about what's troubling you my dear, I'm here."

Nothing could make Sammy sad or introspective today. The sun was shining! With a shy smile she acknowledged Sally's invitation. "Thanks, Sally. I will need to talk to you some time, but not now, not yet. There are still things I need to figure out and do. Right now, I'm so hungry I could eat breakfast and lunch. Bring it on!"

It was a day of renewed hope for Sammy. She'd watched and listened and planned. This was what she'd been waiting for so impatiently. This break in the weather revitalized her spirits. She could smell spring in the air. Everyone knew that winter wasn't over, not by a long shot, but finally, this was the respite that gave hope.

Twenty-five

All day long, Samantha listened to the old-timers give their weather predictions. The best educated guesses were that this would last at least a week. She hoped they were right. She needed two good days to make it to Pinckney. She had the money she'd saved from the stash her father left her and what she'd earned at the stable. It would be enough for her to get a hotel room and find Morgan. She figured she only needed one shot, and she could disappear before anyone even suspected a young boy of the crime.

She planned to travel as a boy, but change into her dress outside of town. She would ride in boldly and book a room at the hotel. If anyone remembered Samantha Turner, she wouldn't deny her identity. Her explanation would be that she had been away visiting relatives since last August.

Counting on the fact that people assumed Samantha Turner had died in the raids, she hoped they would only imagine she resembled that Turner girl. She would check in under her married name, no first name, just Mrs. Sudholt. That way, if the question came up, she could acknowledge her identity and explain that she had married on her trip west. Unless someone made inquires about her family, Sammy would reveal nothing. She had better expect questions if she had to stay longer than a day. But, if her plans worked out, she could be on her way back to Charrette Village in twenty-four hours—just long enough to kill Morgan and return before any questions were asked.

The next morning, Sammy awoke just before dawn. Her waking thoughts were that she would again cause the Billings worry, but it had to be done. She could tell by the cloudless sky that today would be beautiful. It felt like the temperature would climb to at least forty degrees.

Before she changed her mind, she hastily wrote a note for the Billings, explaining that she cared for them very deeply but felt that she had to leave. She told them she planned to head west to look for her uncle. Promising to keep in touch, she would let them know how she was and what she was doing. She asked them to forgive her for leaving so suddenly, but with her decision made, she wanted to avoid causing them additional pain by having to refuse their entreaties to stay.

Having completed the note to her satisfaction, Sammy dressed in her brother's clothes and packed carefully. She left the Billing's home on silent feet. Sassy greeted her with a neigh, and in minutes Sammy had her saddled and ready to go. Before the sun broke over the horizon, she had already traveled a good distance from Charrette Village. This time, Sammy had planned well. She'd packed food, warm clothes, and her weapons. Just for good measure, she'd taken one of Jack's guns and tucked it into her waistband.

Since the snow had melted off the road, and the ground maintained a hard crust from the deep freeze, she made good time. As darkness settled, she found an isolated farmhouse and begged shelter in the barn in exchange for mucking out the stalls. The farmer and his wife readily agreed since they saw the young boy alone. The woman even provided an extra blanket and a warm meal.

The next morning, the farmer found his barn cleaner than when he first bought the place. "If you're ever back this way and need a job, I'll hire you. I've never seen the place so clean. You've earned your keep, boy."

"Thanks, but I don't think I'll be back." Sammy chuckled to herself as she supplemented the biscuits the farmer's wife provided with a chicken leg from Sally's kitchen. After her quick meal, Sammy left the farmer and set off for Pinckney. About three in the afternoon, she stopped in a grove of trees outside of the town. She dismounted and fed Sassy a hand full of oats and poured some water from her canteen into her hat for the weary horse. Once she'd seen to Sassy, she unpacked her saddlebags and draped her clothes over the saddle. She completed her transformation swiftly. After she finished dressing, she combed out her hair and tried to fluff it around her face. Then, she repacked her saddlebags, wrapped her shawl around her head and shoulders, and boldly rode into town.

Her first thought was to get Sassy to the livery stable. She'd pushed her unmercifully, and the hand full of oats weren't near enough. Sammy smiled, elated to see the stagecoach rumble off the ferry and up the main street just as she started down the road. She followed the stage and mingled with the passengers as they disembarked. Dismounting, she led her horse right up to the livery stable. The blacksmith was busy so Sammy handed her reins to the stable boy.

"I'll pay you double if you give my horse a good rub down and extra feed. She's had a rough trip. Please see to her hooves. There might be some ice built up around her shoes."

"Yes'um, I'll do it right now."

The boy seemed so eager for the extra money, Sammy felt confident he'd do a good job on Sassy. After giving her mare a hug, she sauntered down the street. So far, so good. The stage passengers caused so much commotion, the clerk at the hotel barely looked up from his register. No one seemed to notice that she wasn't one of the original travelers. Sammy couldn't believe her good fortune. She checked into the hotel without comment.

Now, all she had to do was wait until dusk, walk to the bank, and linger inconspicuously until she observed the bank clerk leave. She wanted to confront Morgan there. She wanted him to know he was going to die, just as her mother knew. She also wanted him to know who she was and why she was going to pull the trigger.

~ * ~

Mac and Commander Williams made their preparations carefully. The bad weather turned into an advantage as it forced them to spend hours forming their plan of action. The five weeks of enforced isolation was worth the effort when the weather finally broke.

First, they headed out to Morgan's ranch. There, they spoke to the cowhands, and finding four of Morgan's men still unaccounted for, they began a systematic search of all the cattle on the ranch. They separated out the ones they discovered with altered brands. The design looked very clever, and only by careful examination were they able to identify the rustled livestock. A small herd of horses, as well as the stolen cows, were rounded up with the help of Morgan's men. Williams easily persuaded them that cooperation would be better than jail time. With sworn affidavits from the ranch hands on the particulars of when the extra livestock began to show up, they were able to build a solid case of evidence that pointed to Morgan's involvement in the murder of all five families and the ultimate destruction of their farms.

Armed with everything they needed, they rode into Pinckney. The troops drew little attention and quietly dispersed through the town. Mac wanted no warning of Morgan's impending arrest to leak out prematurely.

~ * ~

The bright February sunshine ushered a stranger into Charrette Village. He rode directly to the hotel to get a room and clean up from his long trek. This had been the hardest trip he had ever made, six weeks of pushing through deep snows and howling winds. The storms always moved ahead of him as he followed their paralyzing influence across the plains. He never wavered from his easterly course. He had to reach the eastern edge of Missouri as soon as he could.

Twenty miles west of Charrette Village, on the Booneslick Road, he had come across the body of a white man. Obviously, he had been dead for weeks. The last blizzard must have buried the man so deep that no animals had yet discovered the body. The partially melting snow of the last day or so finally yielded up its gruesome hoard.

He couldn't leave the body there, but he hated the delay it would take to reach his destination if he took it. Sighing in resignation, he had lifted the dead man across the back of his horse and tied him securely. He thanked his lucky stars that the frozen state of the corpse had prevented its deterioration and continued his journey, the grisly burden slowing him more than he'd wanted.

As he dismounted, he thought for once in his life he would be grateful to be indoors. He'd never felt so weary. This was the end of the line. He'd finally made it. His priorities were a hot bath and shave, clean clothes, and as soon as he saw Samantha, bed.

But first, he had to turn the body over to someone in charge. He found the town without a sheriff, but the proprietor directed him to the barber who doubled as the town mortician. After relinquishing the body and giving his statement, he tried to dismiss the event from his mind. He needed to proceed with his own agenda.

However, he continued to shake his head in wonder. It seemed the body he'd brought in belonged to a man by the name of Tyler, the man thought to be responsible for the raids on all those farms in the bottoms, the man who had most likely killed his brother and his whole family with the exception of Sammy. It seemed ironic that he would be the one to find him. Considering the condition of Tyler's body, the men in town readily believed his tale of discovery. All agreed it was no loss to human society for the man to be found dead, but no one could fathom the cause of death.

Finally, Padraig Turner checked into the hotel. He asked the whereabouts of Samantha Turner, his niece. He was a little taken a back by the third degree Mr. Ruggers put him through before he accepted Padraig's story. The man eventually told him Samantha was staying with the Billings over by the livery stable. Padraig felt so relieved to have finally found his niece that he relaxed enough to order a meal and inquire about a hot bath. He didn't want to arrive on Samantha's doorstep looking the way he did.

Mrs. Ruggers took over in her motherly fashion and sent him to his room with hot water and food close on his heels. "We are so relieved that Samantha has some family that cares about her. Everyone loves her, but with Jason's death and all the poor child has been through, we're glad you cared enough to come to her aid." Mrs. Ruggers directed Daniel to empty the hot water in the wash bowl while she uncovered a tempting array of food for Padraig.

"Mrs. Ruggers, the smell of that fried chicken is enough to make a grown man cry. Bless you woman, you are a life saver."

Mrs. Ruggers waved off his blarney, but a smile of acceptance lit her face as she turned to leave. "You just eat up,

Mr. Turner. There's more where that came from. Just call down for Daniel when you're done, and he'll fetch the tray."

"Thank you, madam. Your hospitality renews my faith in the human race." When Mrs. Ruggers left, Padraig flipped a two-bit piece to Daniel. "Do you think you can find me another bucket of that hot water lad?"

"Yes, sir." Daniel deftly caught the quarter and smiling, left the room.

It was only a matter of a short hour before Padraig felt recovered enough to leave the hotel. He stepped out the door into the brilliant sunlight and decided to walk to the end of the street. His thoughts were all on Samantha's letter, and he shook his head in disbelief again. His brother and sister-in-law dead, all his nephews! Only Sammy was left, by some miracle of circumstances.

If she wanted to keep the farm and stay here, he would make a home for her. At thirty-five, he should have the wanderlust out of his system. Trapping had earned him enough to grubstake his desire to search for gold. His Irish luck had brought Padraig success, and he had left a good producing mine in capable hands. He had also started a banking business for the less fortunate, and now his income far exceeded his needs. For a poor Irish immigrant, he couldn't complain. His business sense had borne the fruit of his wise investments, and he was thankful he could offer Sammy financial stability.

Her letter had pleaded for help to find her family's murderer, but he had sensed between the lines that she also pleaded for rescue. He only regretted it had taken him so long to get his business in order and make the trip. Her letter had reached him in November and here it was almost the middle of February. He hoped she'd received his missive that he was on his way, but with the weather he had a feeling his haste in reaching her far had outstripped the mail. He quickened his stride. His thoughts were on seeing Samantha once again and just folding her into his embrace.

Engrossed in thoughts of his niece, he didn't see the young lady who whirled out of the general store just as he approached.

Ashley had sashayed to the door in all her New Year finery, intent on showing off her new clothes. The weather had forced her to remain indoors for too long, and today she intended to get out. She hated being cooped up inside where she couldn't be seen and admired.

As Ashley pulled the door closed and swung around, she landed herself square up against the chest of the handsomest man she'd ever seen. In her mind, the image of Jason and that man Mac paled. For the first time in her life, Ashley lost the ability to speak. She stared into his eyes and couldn't utter a word. All she could do was to clutch at his coat lapels to keep herself upright.

Padraig stared, mesmerized. A whirl of blue velvet wrapped itself around his legs and flung back. He grabbed the young lady to keep her on her feet, then couldn't let go. He wasn't sure if it was the months of celibacy or the impact of her gaze, but for the few seconds it lasted, it seemed like time stood still.

They both began stuttering an apology simultaneously then looked directly into each other's eyes. A delightful giggle bubbled out of the woman's pert mouth, and he couldn't resist grinning in return. Padraig reluctantly withdrew his arms from around her and took one step back to doff his hat and apologize.

"Padraig Turner at your service, Mrs..." he tentatively questioned.

"Miss Ashley Frank, sir." Ashley answered with emphasis on the "Miss".

The smile that broke across Padraig's face lit the shadows from the porch overhang. Ashley felt her eyes reflect the light, and she dipped her head at the introduction. It took a second or two for the name to register before Ashley looked at Padraig with curiosity.

"Are you related to Miss Samantha Turner? I mean Mrs. Sudholt?"

Padraig looked shocked. Then, blurted, "Mrs. Sudholt? When did that happen?" His eyes had narrowed, turning dark and angry.

Oh no! Ashley thought to herself. I've upset him. What if Samantha had already married this man before she married Jason? Oh Lord! Why were all the best-looking men attracted to her? Tears welled into her eyes but she blinked them back and cleared her throat of the lump that had lodged, threatening to make her incapable of speech.

Padraig became instantly aware of the distress she tried to hide. He felt attuned to her, as he never had been with anyone else in his life. "I'm sorry", he explained, "the letter I had from her was written back in October. She's my niece. Her father was my brother. I'm on my way to see her now." Why he felt he had to explain his purpose to this woman he didn't know. He just seemed to be babbling on, unable to stop the stream of words pouring out of his senseless mouth.

"I'm sure you are anxious to see Samantha after your long journey, Mr. Turner. I won't detain you any longer. Samantha will be able to explain everything to you when you see her, and I know you'll be proud of her for the way she endured this horrible experience." Ashley felt so relieved, for the first time in her life she didn't respond in her normal arrogant manner.

"Thank you, Miss Frank, I am anxious to see her. If I may be so bold, may I call on you later? I'm sure I will be in town for a while helping Samantha, and I would like to see you under different circumstances."

"Please do, Mr. Turner, I would enjoy hearing about your travels." Ashley kept her eyes downcast, she felt so shy with this man, and she didn't understand the pulsing of her body. For once in her life, she forgot her haughty manner and dipped her head in acceptance.

At six-feet tall with dark hair and roguish mustache, he appeared just better than average looking. It wasn't until one came close the she could see the twinkle in his piercing brown eyes staring out from under heavy brows. The square jaw, slash of a cleft in his chin, and the straight Roman nose combined to make Padraig's looks outstanding. He had the bearing of command. His walk seemed measured and smooth. He carried himself with an air of confidence that made heads turn.

Ashley watched his retreating back and abruptly turned and reentered the store. She lost the inclination to strut about town. She wanted to sit quietly in her room and remember every word, every gesture, every facet of Padraig Turner.

Padraig had returned his hat to his head and, bowing one last time, set off at a brisk pace and a happy whistle. This wasn't going to be so bad after all. There was a woman he wanted to get to know much, much better. Once he saw Sammy and caught up with her news, he just might take a walk back to the general store.

The woman who answered his knock at the Billing's door wore a worried expression and a startled look. Clearly she looked for someone else by the disappointed, "OH!" that escaped from her so unexpectedly.

"Good Afternoon! Mrs. Billings?" At her nod, Padraig continued, "My name is Padraig Turner, and I am looking for my niece, Samantha Turner. I understand she has been under your care." To Padraig's utter astonishment, the woman lost all self-control at that point. Her composure broke, and she began to sob hysterically.

A man, obviously her husband, heard her cry and appeared at her side in seconds. He took his wife in his arms. "What's going on? What did you say to her?" He looked at Padraig as if he were ready to kill him.

Padraig stammered. He twisted his hat in his hand and felt so befuddled he wasn't sure how to proceed. He decided to try again. "Mr. Billings?" At Jack's nod, he continued, "My name is Padraig Turner. I'm sorry I upset your wife, I've just inquired about my niece, Samantha Turner. I understand she is staying with you."

Jack's relief was evident as he practically jerked Padraig into the house with one huge fist, while he kept his other arm wrapped protectively around his wife. "Come in, man. I'm so glad you're here." It took more than a few minutes for Jack to calm Sally and, over hot coffee in the cozy kitchen, they finally related their story.

Sally had found Samantha missing that morning. Her horse had disappeared from the stable, and after a careful search, they could find no trace of her in the house or in town. Sally had summoned Jack. He'd ridden out to the cemetery, checked in town, and not finding her returned to tell his wife Samantha had disappeared. They were still discussing where she might have gone when Padraig knocked on the door.

An hour sped by while the Billings appraised Padraig of Sammy's marriage, the death of her bridegroom, her rescue by Mac, her return, wounded but healing, her despondency, and her gradual return to normal. Their search showed her mount, saddlebags, and some food gone.

Padraig asked to see her room, hoping to find a clue in the way she lived. As Sally opened the door, he spied a flutter of white float under the bed in the draft. They'd found more than a clue. They'd found a small miracle. In a flurry of excitement, they read Sammy's note. Gone to find her uncle! Padraig's hopes turned to puzzlement.

"I just came in on Booneslick Road. It's the only road to the west, and with the weather, she wouldn't have left the path. Travel through the forest is too dangerous even for Sammy's wild nature. I didn't pass a soul."

Then Jack voiced what he feared most. "I think she felt no one was doing anything about the death of her family. Mac swore me to secrecy, depending on us to keep her here out of harm's way. He went to Pinckney to apprehend the man responsible. I thought it wrong at the time. He should have trusted Samantha enough to explain how dangerous it was for her to accompany him. I think she would have understood his concern for her safety, and I feel she would have let him get Morgan. The way he handled it, she probably thought he deserted her, too, and she was on her own again with no one to rely on to help her."

Padraig ran his hands through his long hair in frustration. His fingers laced through his thick thatch, massaging his scalp, trying to comprehend all that had happened to the poor child in the last six months of her life. "So you think she is headed back to Pinckney? To go after Morgan herself?!"

"That'd be my guess. She seemed hell bent on revenge," was Jack's simple answer as Sally again broke down in quiet sobs.

"How long a ride?" Padraig asked.

"One day. A half if you push. I reckon you'll be pushing yourself and your mount to the limits."

"She only has a half-a-day start ahead of me." Padraig spoke his thoughts aloud. Then, turning directly to Jack, he asked, "Do you have a good mount that would take a punishing ride? My horse has only had about three hours rest. I don't think I can push him that hard."

Jack had already jumped to his feet. "You can take my personal horse. He's used to carrying about two stone more than you weigh, so he will feel like he's running without a rider." With a clap to Padraig's back Jack led him to the stable. "Don't worry, man! Mac has been gone since January first. I'm sure that Samantha will find Morgan behind bars by the time she gets there."

Jack led a large bay with a black mane and tail from the first stall. "He's big, and he's strong. Don't worry about pushing him." He gave the horse a pat on the rump. "Sally and I figure she left early this morning, which means she won't get there until late tonight the earliest. You'll be able to reach her in time. I must warn you, if Samantha disguised herself as a boy again, you may not recognize her. Keep a sharp eye out. I'd go with you, but I'd only slow you down, and I'm worried about Sally. She loves that girl, and this is really hitting her hard. That's why I haven't left her to start the search myself. Until you showed up, I really didn't know where to start."

"Thanks for your help, Jack, but I travel better alone. Besides, I know you're needed here. Could you just do me a favor? I left my horse at the hotel and..."

"I'll take care of everything. I'll get your horse and explain to Mr. Ruggers where you went and what happened today. Be careful. Morgan is bound to be desperate with everything closing in on him, and unless Mac has him in custody, I fear for what he might do."

"Don't worry, Jack, I'll find Sammy. She won't ever be alone in the world again." With a hot meal and extra food packed by Sally, Padraig left by mid afternoon. With any luck he'd be in Pinckney before dark tomorrow.

Twenty-six

Mac and Commander Williams watched the bank from across the street. They stood in the shadows of the dry goods store that had already closed for the evening. As near as they could tell, only one clerk and Morgan remained inside the bank. They planned to wait for the clerk to leave and then to confront Morgan. They didn't want to take any chances of innocent people getting hurt. If he left first, they would follow him to his house. They would arrest him before he entered and endangered the housekeeper.

If Mac hadn't been as alert as he was, he would have missed the furtive shadow sneaking along the boardwalk across the street. He had to stare hard to be sure his eyes weren't deceiving him. *Bank robber* was the first thought that flashed through his mind, but he instantly dismissed it. No horse. No accomplices waiting to help with a quick get away. No bandana covering his face.

There was no time for further speculation. At that point, the clerk left, calling out a goodnight to Morgan as he closed the door. Behind his back, the door cracked open to admit the shadowy figure.

"Who the hell is that!" Williams barked in a harsh whisper.

"I don't know, sir," Mac answered. "Maybe one of his people coming in to report on our being at the ranch."

"Damn!" Williams exploded. "Now we won't have the element of surprise. I thought the men at the ranch were cooperating!"

"It could be someone else, sir," Mac responded. "Let's give it a minute or two." Mac tried to puzzle out the queer feeling of fear that gripped his belly. He couldn't understand the sensation and wondered what had caused it.

Just at that moment, they were all distracted by a lone rider barreling into town on a lathered horse. He galloped the animal down the street and went directly to the sheriff's office.

"Trouble," Mac whispered. "Let's move now while the sheriff is busy. I still don't know whose pocket he's in."

As soon as the stranger slammed the door of the jailhouse, Commander Williams gave the signal and the troops surrounded the bank. Mac crept to the door and cracked it open to listen. He could hear conversation in Morgan's office, and it sounded intense. Then Mac's blood froze in his veins. His heart stopped beating for a second then thundered through his brain like a stampede.

"Sammy!" What was she doing here? He motioned for Williams to wait with one whispered word, her name! Williams cursed under his breath.

"The girl will be killed for sure," the commander muttered. "I won't jeopardize her chances. You better take over, Mac."

Mac eased into the bank and closed the door. He tiptoed across the lobby, his moccasin covered feet silent. The door to Morgan's office was open, and he could hear Sammy telling Morgan who she was and how much she knew.

The little fool. Morgan will squash her like a bug and never think twice! Mac's heart hammered in his ears. He thought the noise would betray his position. With his back plastered to the wall next to the doorframe and his gun drawn, the sweat poured down his temples, despite the cold in the room. He looked at his hand and saw the gun tremble. *God,* he prayed, *let me get control of myself. I have to save her!* Taking a deep breath, he turned into the open door and began to shake harder at the sight that met his astonished eyes.

Sammy had Morgan backed inside the large room-size safe. Mac could see her profile with the drawn gun. Her back was plastered to the door of the safe. *Smart girl,* he thought, *she's protecting her back.*

"You are a dead man, Mr. Morgan." Sammy spoke with quiet intensity. "I plan on shooting you right through your black heart. You will die alone like my mother. I will lock you in your precious safe with all your stolen money, and you will rot here and in hell for the crimes you have committed against innocent people. Eventually they'll find your body, but not before I am long gone. How does it feel, Mr. Morgan, to look down the barrel of a gun and know it will be the last thing you see? Think how my mother felt, Mr. Morgan." Each "Mr. Morgan" she uttered cracked like a whip with sarcastic emphasis.

"Your thug raped her unmercifully. She lost the baby she was carrying, then he shot her right through her beautiful, loving heart. I know my mother is with the angels in heaven, but you, you piece of slime, will rot in hell for all eternity."

Mac advanced into the room as she spoke. The venom pouring out of her alarmed him. So did the fact that she hadn't even taken into consideration how she would feel taking a life in revenge and hatred in cold blood. He knew she wasn't thinking beyond her need to have Morgan pay for his crime.

Though she focused on Morgan, Sammy became aware of another presence in the room. At that moment she was glad she'd snatched Jack's handgun from the barn before she left.

She had both pistols drawn and now she kept one trained on Morgan and swung the other towards the intruder. From the corner of her eye she recognized him instantly. *Nicholas!* She couldn't believe her eyes. *What is he doing here?!* Her eyes only flicked away from Morgan a moment. He'd never moved. Coward through and through, he shook so badly she thought he'd disgrace himself before she shot him.

"Hi, Sammy love, need any help?" Nicholas gave her a tentative half smile.

Not taking her eyes from Morgan she barked back. "Don't call me, "Sammy, love," and no, I don't need help. Get out of here, Nicholas."

"Ah, Angel! I can't let you have all the fun! Come on, let me help you turn this scum bag over to the authorities."

Mac froze. He could see his attempt at humor had infuriated her, and he backed off, afraid of what she would do if pressured.

"Nicholas MacNamee, I've listened to your lies long enough. I don't intend to listen to any more. You can leave quietly now, or you can join *Mr. Morgan* in this safe!" Mac stood frozen. Then he lowered his gun and forced his stance to appear relaxed but alert. Her next words shocked him. "If you don't intend to leave, I suggest you drop your weapon and get over here with Mr. Morgan. Let me assure you, Nicholas, I am as proficient with a gun in my left hand as I am with my right."

Remembering her accuracy, Mac didn't doubt her for a moment. "Sammy, please! Let justice take care of Morgan. If you kill him in cold blood, you'll be no better than him. You will always be a hunted criminal, and even if you escape detection, you will never escape your conscience. I know you, Sammy. In time you'll hate yourself. Your grief over your family will ease with time, but your grief over killing a man in cold blood will never leave you. It will eat your soul and destroy the goodness in you."

Nicholas' words, as well as the caring she heard in his voice, finally penetrated Sammy's vengeance clouded mind. She could question why he left her later. Should she let him help her? More important, could she trust him? "How do I know I can trust you, Nicholas? You've lied to me before. How can I believe you now?"

"Sammy, I've never lied to you. I told you I would get Morgan for you, and that's what I've been trying to do. We needed an airtight case against him. It just took longer than I thought, and with the weather, we couldn't move till now. Come on, Sammy, don't do something you'll always regret."

Sammy couldn't deny the weather. After all, that is what had held her up, too. She wanted to believe him. She wanted to believe he'd only left her to get Morgan, but she shuddered, afraid to let herself trust again. Her brows furrowed. What had he said? They needed an airtight case against him?

"You mean you have proof of his conspiracy and didn't tell me?" She knew her voice quivered with the pain of his omission. His lack of trust in her hurt more than anything, but it also left her with a sense of defeat.

"I tried to protect you, Angel. I didn't want to see you get hurt, and I wanted to spare you the horror of Morgan's arrest and punishment." Sensing her hesitation, Mac pressed his point.

"Sammy, I'm here now. Let me help you bring him to justice without losing your soul."

"I can't, Nicholas. I swore on my mother's grave I'd get the man responsible. I have to keep my oath."

"You have kept it, Angel. He's right here. All you have to do is turn him over to the authorities. You honored your oath. If you hadn't been so persistent in finding him, no one would have ever investigated his actions. Now, it's time to let the law take care of his punishment."

The quiet pleading in his voice tempted her. After all, he was here now. If she could believe him, everything he'd done seemed to be for her benefit. Maybe she would let him help her. But, if he betrayed her, no matter how much she loved him, he'd live to regret it.

~ * ~

Outside, Commander Williams had a hard time containing the wild man who had ridden into town and came charging down the street with the sheriff in tow. In a stringent whisper he quieted the two and explained the events that had led to the bank being surrounded by federal troops. The sheriff seemed totally shocked that he had been taken in by Morgan and quickly offered his help.

Padraig didn't want to wait outside while his niece was inside with a killer, but Williams finally convinced him to have patience and give Mac a few more minutes. He spread word to the troops to hold their fire and use their guns only if Morgan attempted an escape. They all knew Mac, and Williams gave a description of Sammy's disguise. Morgan would be the easiest to distinguish from the two. His dandified clothes and solitary exit would identify him if things backfired on Mac and Sammy. Commander Williams stayed close to the bank door, and with guns drawn, the rest of the men backed off a few paces.

~ * ~

A sigh escaped from Sammy as she allowed her body to relax. "Okay, Nicholas. What now? How do we bring Morgan to justice?" She stepped away from the safe door and turned her attention to Nicholas. Her guns sagged and her posture slumped.

Desperate, Morgan must have seen a window of opportunity. He lunged for Sammy, jerking her left arm up behind her back, causing her to drop one pistol. The other hand he forced up to her temple, his grip tight over her fist, his finger over hers on the trigger. "Nicholas, drop your gun, or Miss Turner will die right here."

"Shoot him, Nicholas," Sammy yelled. "Kill him. I don't care what happens to me. He has to be stopped."

"You're right, Sammy. He has to be stopped, but even if he kills both of us, he'll have a hard time escaping the federal troops that surround this building."

When Mac saw Morgan stiffen and furtively glance toward the window, he pressed his point. "I told you we needed an airtight case against the illustrious Mr. Morgan, didn't I, Sammy? Well the commandant has in his possession a signed statement from one Joshua Preston. It says that Mr. Morgan hired him and three other men to raid the farms and kill off all the people so that he could assume ownership of the land. He planned to sell it to the railroad for a handsome profit."

Mac saw the haunted look harden Thaddeus' eyes as he tightened his grip on the pistol. The man looked insane, and he wasn't sure if his instincts were right in pushing him. With no other option in mind he continued to hope he could stall Morgan from the inevitable. Sweat trickled down the side of his face. He had to save Sammy, even if it meant his death. "Commander Williams and I just returned from Morgan's ranch, The Free Spirit. Sammy, you'd be surprised at how many horses and cattle he has that wear an altered brand."

"That's enough, Nicholas. Start moving into the safe. Miss Turner, turn around real slow and follow lover boy."

Mac saw Sammy twitch as Morgan wrenched her arm further up her back to force her to move. Rage built to a boiling point. He couldn't allow the man to hurt Sammy. She'd dug in her heels and refused to move. Words seemed his only defense at this point. Morgan looked ready to pull the trigger. "How do you think you're going to get out of here alive, Morgan?" Mac tried to keep his voice as nonchalant as he could. "Do you think I came here by myself? At this moment, Commander Williams and ten federal solders have the bank surrounded. You'll never walk out that door alive unless you unhand Samantha and surrender now."

"That's the oldest trick in the book, Nicholas. Why should I believe you? Now, drop your gun and move or Miss Turner dies."

Sammy'd had enough. This brute could kill her, but she'd be damned if she'd ever let him get away to kill another innocent person. As she watched Nicholas, she realized her love for him transcended anything she'd ever felt. She couldn't let him die. Somehow, someway, she had to save him, even if it meant Morgan would escape, even if it meant she would be the one to die. She'd just have to stop shaking and do something. Gradually, she stopped resisting his efforts to man-handle her. She let her body relax to the point of almost going limp. As soon as she stopped fighting him, Morgan loosened his grip.

Sammy bent at the waist, taking advantage of his momentary lapse, and kicked backwards with the heel of her boot connecting with his shin. She hoped Mac would use the opportunity, or she'd never get another chance. Time seemed to stand still before she heard the report of Mac's shot. She felt the impact of his bullet hit Morgan, and she continued her downward motion somersaulting out of the way. Morgan staggered but recovered enough to raise his weapon with the help of his left hand. She saw blood stain his right shoulder. Mac had aimed high, probably to avoid hitting her.

She scrambled around looking for the gun Morgan had forced from her left hand. He couldn't be allowed to escape and kill anyone else, especially Nicholas. She had to save Nicholas.

Before she could reach the gun that Morgan had kicked into the corner, the door burst open and federal troops poured into the bank. Morgan squeezed off a shot, and Sammy saw Nicholas duck. An officer behind Nicholas caught the bullet in his left shoulder. When the man fell to the floor, Morgan bolted out the door onto the boardwalk. Just as she reached her gun, a volley of shots erupted.

Nicholas holstered his smoking gun and tried to help Sammy to her feet. “Let me go. Don’t let him escape. Go after him. How can you let him get away?” She beat his hands away, hampering his attempt to help her to her feet. She seemed unable to control her pounding fists and screaming rage. Her action had saved Nicholas, but Morgan had run away. Before Nicholas could utter a word, they were surrounded by federal troops, a man with a badge, and a strange man bellowing her name.

Sammy stared at the man as recognition dawned. She wrenched herself from Nicholas’ grip, ran, and took a flying leap right into Uncle Paddy’s arms. The storm within her broke. Padraig held on and rocked her. All her emotions vied for release. Nicholas had come back. Uncle Paddy had arrived. The federal troops and the sheriff all seemed to have answered her need for help at the same time. She could never have killed Morgan. Nicholas had been right. She realized now that she was incapable of a cold-blooded execution. With these good people, she had all the help she would ever need.

Mac watched in awe and pain. Who was this handsome man? It had to be someone Sammy loved very much. She seemed to have forgotten him in her joy at seeing this stranger. He felt his heart break. She’d never greeted him with such abandon. Jealousy tore his gut and left him weak. He turned away from the painful scene. Sammy and the stranger had their heads buried in each other’s shoulders. Both of them cried, whether in grief or joy he didn't know. He should have known she would never have allowed herself to marry a half-breed. Despondent, he went outside to see what happened to Morgan.

Sammy and her uncle released the grief pent up from the loss of their family. "Uncle Paddy, I can't believe you found me. You can't know how happy I am to see you. You look wonderful."

"It's happy I am, too, lass. You've grown, Sammy girl. Let's see a smile. We still have each other, you ken?"

With Padraig's words, they stood back, looked at each other, and burst out laughing. Their shirts were wet with the tears of the other, and Sammy knew she looked a sight with red-rimmed eyes.

"You never looked better to me, lass. I feared I'd get here too late."

"Never too late, Uncle Paddy. You are a sight for sore eyes." Sammy turned to introduce Padraig to Nicholas, but he had disappeared, again! Puzzled, she looked around the empty room. Padraig took her arm, apparently unaware of her turmoil, and led her from the room.

"Come on, luv. Let's go to the hotel and get cleaned up. We'll have a good meal, then it's bed for both of us. I'm exhausted, and I know you must be, too. We'll take care of everything else tomorrow, when we're both thinking straight."

Mac stood outside and heard the endearment, then the plans the stranger made for Sammy. Before they stepped out on to the boardwalk, he slipped around the corner. He couldn't bear to see her with her lover. He'd been jealous enough of her dead husband lying with her and touching her body intimately, but Jason had never tasted the fruit of her love.

Mac had taken her virginity, and with it he thought he had the promise of her love for all time. In just six weeks of absence, she'd found a new protector. Her venomous words came hauntingly back to him. "Don't call me your love!"

God! Why did I leave her with Jack and Sally? Why didn't I just bring her with me? Once he got here, he could have hog tied her and put her in the brig until he'd finished this business with Morgan? Mac couldn't stop himself from peeking around the corner as he heard them walk off towards the hotel. The big man had his arm around Sammy's shoulders, and she had both her arms wrapped around his waist even though it made walking difficult. It seemed like she'd attached herself to his hip and would never let go. He should have never looked. Despair hit Mac so hard he felt sick to his stomach.

A hand clapped down on his shoulder, causing Mac to flinch. The sheriff turned the clasp into a gentle pat. "Come on, man. I know death is an ugly sight. Commander Williams is over at the doctor's, and he'd like a word with you. If you're up to it?" He added the last in a sympathetic voice that made Mac get a grip on his emotions. He shook off the sheriff's touch, pulled off his bandanna, and wiped the sweat from his face. It wasn't Morgan's death that had made him sick. Not one to confide in strangers, he couldn't tell the sheriff it was his own emotional death that churned his stomach. Mac wished Morgan's bullet had found his heart. It couldn't have hurt any worse. He tried to push his despair below the surface as he followed the sheriff down the street.

~ * ~

Padraig escorted Samantha to her door then went to his room to clean up for dinner. His eyes burned and his head throbbed. He'd been without sleep for more than twenty-four hours. Jack had lent him a good horse. He'd arrived in time. For that, he'd be forever grateful. He knew one of the bullets that slammed into Morgan's body was from his well-directed shot. The thought gave him a sense of satisfaction. He still hadn't heard from Samantha what had transpired in the bank or the identity of the man with her. He thought to question her over supper, but as he splashed water on his face to refresh himself, he realized explanations would have to wait till morning. For now, Padraig only wanted to feast his eyes on Samantha, replenish his flagging energy with some good food, and sleep in a soft bed for at least ten hours.

~ * ~

Sammy entered her room in a haze of unreality. Could it really be all over? Morgan lay dead, Uncle Padraig had come, and Nicholas reappeared. But then he'd disappeared so fast. Where'd he go? One minute she'd been beating on him and screaming in frustration over Morgan's escape, and the next she'd been wrapped in Uncle Paddy's strong arms. Nicholas had evaporated into thin air. Just like the last time. She had gone to bed at Sally's wrapped in the knowledge of Nicholas' love, and the next morning found he had deserted her. She began to suspect her sanity. Would she ever understand Nicholas' behavior?

~ * ~

Mac found Commander Williams being treated by the doctor and, in spite of his wound, thoroughly pleased with the events of the evening. "Mac, my boy! Tell me what happened in the bank! That scoundrel shocked the hell out of me. We heard the gunshot and thought you'd taken care of him. It's a good thing I dodged when I did or there would be two corpses laid out tonight. Pure reflex action, I assure you." He hesitated, his jovial speech turned serious. "What is it, man? You're as pale as a ghost."

Coming to his senses, Mac shook his head. "Everything just happened too fast, Commander. I had to distract Sammy to keep her from killing Morgan in cold blood. That's when he jumped her and held a gun to her head. He threatened to kill her if I didn't throw down my weapon. I'm still shaking. He could have killed her when he grabbed her gun." Mac grew quiet. The picture of her held in that madman's grasp would haunt him forever.

"Well, what happened then? Don't keep me in suspense, man."

Mac shook his head. He looked at Williams and knew he had to control the sadness that crippled him. "Sammy suddenly lunged forward and gave me a clear shot. Her arms have to be aching from the way her movement twisted them." Mac rubbed his shoulder. It hurt him just thinking about the way she had wrenched her body.

"Go on."

"Well, when I shot him, he released her and she rolled out of the way. He raised his gun to shoot at me, and you know the rest. By the way," Mac grinned, "should I thank you for taking the bullet that had my name on it?"

"Yeah. Well, lucky for both of us his aim wasn't that good," Williams laughed.

Mac couldn't think about the real reason that he felt so sick. The pain of seeing her in another man's arms had been enough to kill him.

"Well, no matter. All's well that ends well. Huh!" Commander Williams watched the doctor attending his arm and missed Mac's sardonic countenance. Looking up, he continued his pondering, "Did you meet Padraig Turner? I had a hell of a time containing him. He wanted to charge right in there and rescue his niece. It took me and two men to hold him back until he would listen to reason and understand that with you in there, Sammy would be safe. The poor man has been traveling for over a month, and guess what? He found Tyler's body on the Booneslick Trail. That accounts for the last of the culprits.

Anyway, when he finally arrived in Charrette Village, it was only to find Samantha had already left. He rode hell bent for leather to reach Pinckney before she did something disastrous. The man has been in the saddle for more than twenty-four hours without rest. I couldn't believe both of you got off the first volley. You both hit your mark dead center, too. Even if no one else had pulled a trigger, Morgan would be just as dead."

As Commander William's words "Padraig Turner…niece" penetrated Mac's numbed mind, the rest of his rambling became a jumble of words. Mac felt his pallor replaced by the flush of red as his blood surged through his body. Almost before the commander finished speaking, Mac headed toward the door.

"Hey, Mac! Where you going so fast?"

"I gotta see my lady, Commander. I haven't had time to even give her a kiss yet."

"Well, you give her one for me, too. That's one-quick-thinking young miss you have on your hands. I hope you can keep up with her."

"Me, too, sir. Me, too. I'll talk to you later." Mac closed the door on William's hearty laugh, and ran.

Uncle Padraig! The man's name became a litany as he sang its refrain over and over through his mind. He raced down the boardwalk. He needed to see Sammy. Mac skidded to a halt outside the hotel door. Doubt and confusion reentered his mind. All the what-ifs came back to haunt him. For the first time in his life, he lost his confidence. It took all his courage to gulp down his hesitation and enter the building.

Twenty-seven

First, Mac poked his head into the dining room. The room yielded no familiar face. They weren't down yet. He walked over to the desk, not sure how she would have registered. Finally, at the desk clerk's quizzical stare, he asked for Miss Samantha Turner.

"We do not have a Miss Turner registered, sir. However, there is a Mr. Padraig Turner in room 202."

Mac had to think a minute to remember Jason's last name. "Has a Mrs. Sudholt checked in?"

"Yes, sir. She is in room 204. Do you wish me to send up a bellboy for you?"

"No, I'll just wait here for her to come down. Thank you." Nicholas didn't want to do anything to harm her reputation, but he'd be darned if he would wait another minute to see her. He nonchalantly strolled towards the staircase. He took a seat on a green velvet sofa at the bottom of the stairs. The elegance of the room intimidated him. He'd feel more comfortable sitting on a bale of hay than he did perched on this fancy furniture.

Nervously, he twisted his hat between his hands. He waited until another customer distracted the desk clerk then bolted up the steps. Her room was midway down the hall next to 202. He would have to keep his voice lowered. Uncle Padraig was right next door. At his soft tentative knock, he heard her breathless, "Come in."

She clearly wasn't expecting him as the shock on her face revealed when he opened the door. "Nicholas! I thought you were Uncle Paddy." The relief in her voice changed to censure. "Where did you disappear to? I looked for you, but you left so fast."

"Did you? Did you look for me?" His voice held a quiet wonder.

"Yes!" His attitude puzzled Sammy. "I wanted to introduce you to my uncle and to thank you." Suddenly she didn't know what to say next. She looked down, not meeting the blaze of his eyes. He still had a lot of questions to answer, but she could see the love pouring out of his cobalt gaze, and it made her shy. The fire that started burning inside her at the sight of him standing in her room seemed to consume her.

"Sammy, I was so afraid I'd lost you. Don't ever do that to me again!" His voice was a desperate plea.

"Do what?" she whispered, confused.

"Come here." He held his arms open wide, and his voice cracked as he whispered back a command from his heart.

Sammy flew across the room and launched herself into his arms hard enough for him to stagger under her assault. "Nicholas, it's still not over. Tyler is out there, and he's probably looking for me." Her voice cracked with unshed tears.

"No, Angel, your Uncle Padraig found Tyler's body on the way to Charrette Village. You're free. Free from your oath. Free to be yourself, and free to be with me." He muffled her surprised exclamation with his mouth.

Their frantic kisses had made them oblivious as the heat of their passion began to boil, when a "Humph" announced a witness to their embrace.

Sammy broke away from Nicholas but retained a grip on his hand. He knew by the strength of her handclasp she felt as shaken as he. He wrapped his free arm around her shoulder and turned to meet the man he now knew to be her uncle.

The couple looked so flustered at being caught, Padraig took pity on them. "This must be the eminent Mr. MacNamee that Commander Williams told me about."

Samantha recovered herself to continue the introduction, all the while maintaining the blush that stained her face a rosy glow.

Nicholas acknowledged the overture with a nod, turned to Samantha, took both of her hands, and looked into her eyes as he spoke, addressing Padraig. "As Samantha's only living relative, sir, I would like to request the honor of asking for Samantha's hand in marriage."

Samantha's mouth gaped open, and her complexion turned from red to white, then back to red.

Padraig cleared his throat and seeing how it appeared between them, answered in his most serious manner. "That, Mr. MacNamee, will depend entirely on Samantha's answer to your question. If she wants you, I see no reason to deny your request. However, if not, don't you ever come near her again." He'd purposely hardened his voice for the last part to make sure Nicholas knew he meant business.

Padraig had a hard time keeping his visage sober. If what he witnessed a few minutes ago was any indication, he knew beforehand what Samantha's answer would be. Still and all, he was unprepared for Samantha's reaction.

She'd immediately burst into the most heartbreaking sobs either had apparently ever heard. Padraig's startled eyes sought Nicholas's. If he'd hurt her, Padraig would kill him. His gaze met a completely incredulous look in the man's blue eyes.

Looking at each other in perplexity, both tried to console her and both only succeeded in causing more tears.

"I think you'd better leave, Mr. MacNamee. You can see your intentions clearly distressed my niece."

"I'm sorry, I can't do that. I'm sure you'll understand our need for a little privacy, Mr. Turner. Sammy and I have some things we need to discuss that should be said in private."

"I don't want to intrude on your privacy, but from here on you will have no chance to be alone with Samantha. Please leave. You can see you are upsetting her." Padraig's hand went to his gun and found his hip bare. Damn! He'd left his sidearm in his room. He'd never imagined he'd need it just to take his niece to dinner.

At length, Samantha got her emotions under control. "Uncle Padraig," she hiccuped. "Thank you. Thank you for coming. Thank you for caring. Thank you for giving us your blessings."

Padraig looked at Nicholas and saw the man let out his breath. He felt much the same. Relief warred with confusion. What had upset the girl so much that she cried like her heart had just broken in two?

Samantha took a deep breath herself and seemed to square her shoulders as she continued, "Nicholas has a lot of questions to answer before I accept his offer, but I think we can come to an understanding. I can't say yes or no now, but after we have time to talk I will have an answer for both of you."

Padraig saw Nicholas gaze at her in astonishment. The only thing that seemed to keep him from exploding in anger had to be the ironclad grip Samantha had on his hand. She had never released her hold on the man.

Padraig bit the inside of his cheek to keep from smiling. He could tell she seemed loath to let loose, and Nicholas in turn didn't seem to want her to.

"In that case, let's go get something to eat, and we can talk over dinner. If you two think I'm going to leave you alone, by God, you are both crazy." Ushering the two in front of him, Padraig closed Samantha's door and with a mischievous grin, followed the lovers downstairs.

Dinner started out a solemn affair. It took Sammy a long time to fill Uncle Paddy in on the last six months. Nicholas helped complete the gaps by describing his investigations into Professor Morgan's affairs. By the time the young girl cleared the table, Sammy's uncle had a hard time suppressing his yawns.

"Samantha, lass, you'll have to forgive me, but I'm afraid the last twenty-four hours have caught up with me. I suggest we get an early night's sleep and head back to Charrette Village first thing in the morning. I'm sure Mr. and Mrs. Billings are anxious to hear about your safety."

"That sounds good, Uncle Paddy. I had hoped my note would relieve them of any anxiety, but from what you told me, I guess I didn't fool anyone with my story."

"Least of all me, lass." Padraig smiled at Sammy with such tenderness she felt tears pool in her eyes again. Nicholas saw her reaction and took her hand to offer what comfort he could. She squeezed back to let him know she was fine.

"Sorry I'm so weepy tonight. I can't imagine what's come over me." She tried to laugh but the sound couldn't get past the lump in her throat.

Nicholas scooted his chair closer to her in order to put his arm around her shoulder. "Don't worry, Sammy. We understand." He glanced across the table to Padraig before he continued. Sammy didn't know if he wordlessly asked permission to go on or if he had challenged her uncle for the right to reassure her. "I think you are finally allowing yourself to accept what happened. Maybe now, you can get on with your life."

"Yes, Sammy," Padraig interrupted. "You have some decisions to make now. But as I said before, it's getting late, and tomorrow is time enough to talk about what you want to do."

Uncle Paddy pushed back his chair to stand. He offered his arm to Sammy and spoke to Nicholas. "Mr. MacNamee, may we have the pleasure of your company for breakfast in the morning? Shall we say six o'clock?"

Sammy didn't know what to do. She wanted to talk to Nicholas, but her uncle gave her no option. Nicholas scowled. He certainly didn't look too happy that Uncle Paddy had dismissed him.

"Six sounds fine. If you don't mind, I'd like to accompany you and Samantha back to Charrette Village. Sammy and I still have some issues to settle."

"Certainly, my boy. We'll see you in the morning."

Paddy led Sammy from the dining room and started up the steps. She couldn't leave Nicholas like this. Her heart burst with the need to speak to him. She glanced at her uncle from the corner of her eye and watched him try to stifle a huge yawn. Taking a chance she turned to catch Nicholas watching her as he stood in the lobby. She had sensed him waiting for her to look at him. His fist came up, and he opened his hand to flash her five raised fingers. *Five minutes.* She heard him say in her mind. *Five minutes.*

Mac watched a grin break across Sammy's weary face, and she ducked her head to acknowledge his message. She'd heard him and understood. His spirits soared. He walked to the desk, got a room, and ordered a hipbath sent up immediately with extra hot water.

Tonight, he intended to pamper Sammy and indulge in his own fantasies at the same time. He figured the best way to answer her questions would be to show her how he felt about her from the first day at the waterfall.

Mac took the steps two at a time. He'd asked for a room at the end of the hall, far enough away from Padraig's door to muffle Sammy's cries of pleasure. He planned on giving her all the love he'd withheld in the cave. Not that he'd kept much from her, but this time they would have a soft warm bed instead of a cold hard ground.

Mac entered his room and immediately knelt in front of the fireplace to add another log to the low blaze. He turned down the bed, and before he could do more, he heard a discreet knock. He opened the door to admit a maid with big white towels over one arm and a bucket of steaming water in her other hand. Two boys followed her with the tub. He was pleasantly surprised at the speed of his request and, smiling, took the bucket from the girl.

"The boys will bring two more buckets each. That should be enough to fill the tub, sir."

"Thank you. That will be plenty." Mac handed the girl a small coin, and she dipped a curtsy as she left the room. Minutes later, the boys returned with more water. Mac tipped them also then watched as they ran down the hall and bounded down the steps.

Now, he could go for Sammy. He removed his boots and had to smile. They felt so good, that he sometimes forgot he had them on. He sure was glad he had them back. Mac left his door ajar by a couple of inches. Slowly, he tiptoed to Sammy's room. He put his hand on the knob and softly scraped a fingernail on the wood. The door opened so swiftly, it almost yanked him into the room.

Sammy stood uncertainly as Nicholas practically fell into her room. He smiled at her and reached out to caress her cheek. She felt her pulse thunder as another blasted flush heated her skin. Nicholas placed his finger against her lips then his own, in a gesture of silence. He walked over to her dresser and extinguished the light, then took her hand and led her from the room.

He stopped suddenly and she almost bumped into his strong back. Bending down, he lifted one foot then the other to remove her shoes. She never even questioned him. She trusted him completely and allowed him to lead her. Signaling her to remain quiet, he again took her hand and silently closed her door.

Sammy had to stifle a giggle that threatened to erupt. Nicholas took large exaggerated steps. He lifted his knees high and lowered his stockinged foot toes first in a ridiculous tiptoed fashion. Clamping a hand over her mouth to contain her mirth, she followed.

When they reached a room at the end of the hall, furthest from the steps, he pushed open the door and pulled her into the room. Closing the door softly, he turned and just grinned.

"Nicholas. What do you think you're doing? What if Uncle Paddy comes looking for me?"

"Sh-h-h. Don't worry about Uncle Paddy. The man's so tired he could hardly make it up the steps. We needed to talk, and we couldn't do it in your room." Nicholas' blue eyes gazed at her with such love, Sammy felt her knees begin to shake. He seemed to hesitate then advanced slowly until he reached out and caressed her cheek. The instant his hand made contact with her skin, she struggled to catch her breath. Heat spread from her toes to the top of her head. *Lordy*, she thought. *That's just his hand on my face. What will happen when he kisses me?*

"You scared ten years off my life, woman. Why did you tell your uncle you couldn't make up your mind yet?"

His voice pleaded for an explanation, and she didn't know how to bring up her worries. "Nicholas," Sammy stammered. "You have a life of your own. I wasn't sure what your plans were. And," shyly, she dipped her head, "You were so against my vengeance. I didn't think you'd want to be tied to a woman who could hate so strongly. Besides, I had no idea you wanted to *marry* me."

"What about your vengeance, Sammy? Is it satisfied?" He seemed to ignore her other concerns.

"Yes. I'm sorry Morgan died the way he did, but I'm not sorry he's no longer a threat to the other settlers. Actually, I'm more relieved that Tyler isn't around to abuse any more women. He's the one I really hated. He's the one that hurt my mother. Morgan may have ordered the raids, but he surely didn't tell Tyler to rape the women." Silent tears pooled then spilled over as the memory filled her vision.

"Ahh, Sammy. Let it out. It's okay to cry. You'll never have to worry about anyone trying to kill you again. You'll never have to worry about Tyler touching you."

Nicholas folded her into his strong embrace, and Sammy finally felt at peace. His gentle touch wiped away her tears. Her worries were over. Now, she could think about her future.

"What do you plan to do, Nicholas? Are you going to go back to scouting?"

"Most of what I do depends on you, Sammy. Do you want to return to your family farm? Is that something you'd like to do?"

"No. I really don't want to live there. It holds too many memories. It would be really hard for me to forget how I saw it last. Uncle Paddy said maybe he could help me sell it."

"In that case, how do you feel about a place a little farther west? I've always wanted to raise horses. You know enough to help. The army would buy as many as I could saddle break."

"Nicholas. You *really* want to marry me? And, you'd give up scouting?"

"Yes, I want to marry you. You're all I've thought about for the last six months. And, I'm ready to stop wandering around. Before I met you, I had been thinking I needed to do something different. I just hadn't decided what that would be."

"What about your degree? Have you ever thought of doing something with that?"

"Actually, my father wanted me to get into politics. I just couldn't stand Juliana's mockery about a half-breed lawyer. Anyway, that was my father's dream, not mine. Mr. Ruggers did ask if I might consider taking Jason's old job for a while. Would you mind staying in Charrette Village until we can find a place of our own? It would just be temporary, Sammy. I don't want to live in town."

"Oh, Nicholas. I don't care where we live as long as we're together."

"Is that a definite yes, Angel?"

Sammy looked up into Nicholas' eyes. They smoldered with blue fire. He looked so expectant she had to laugh. "Yes, it's a definite yes.

The air whooshed out of Nicholas' lungs, and he collapsed on the bed, dragging Sammy with him. She struggled to remove herself from his prone body, but he held her firm.

"I've missed you like this, Angel. It feels so good to have you back. But look. Look what I had brought up for you."

Nicholas gestured toward the fireplace. With her back to the room Sammy had neglected to notice anything but Nicholas. He had left the room in darkness, and the only light came from the flickering flames dancing in the fireplace. There in the glow sat a copper bathtub with vapors rising from the water. She looked from the tub to Nicholas, a question forming on her lips. Before she could speak, Nicholas took her hand and helped her off the bed.

"Come on, Angel. I know you're longing for a bath, and I'm longing to tell you a story."

He raised her up and helped her out of her clothes. At first Sammy felt embarrassed, then remembered how he'd cared for her in the cave. *Well,* she thought, *he's done this before.*

As he gave her a hand into the water, she felt her skin heat. Yes, he'd bathed her before, but not like this. His hand dipped into the warm water and brought up a sponge that he lathered with a sweet smelling soap. The sensuous feel of his hands moving over her back and around to her front made her catch her breath. She was afraid to look at him. If he could see the desire spiraling through her, he'd think she had no morals. She let her body sink further into the water to hide the rosy glow of her skin.

Nicholas seemed entranced, then he began to talk. "From the first time I saw you, I wanted to do this. I wanted to bathe you from the tips of your tiny toes to the top of your head." He picked up a bucket and told her to bend her head back while he poured water over her hair. Picking up the soap, he started washing her hair while he told her about what he'd witnessed at the waterfall.

Sammy sat up in shock. He'd seen her? Just then more water sloshed over her head. She sputtered and gasped. "You watched me at the waterfall? You knew I was a woman?"

"Well, you were so intent on disguising yourself, I didn't want to disappoint you. It was when you took that Bowie knife to your beautiful hair that I screamed out loud in protest."

Sammy felt dumbfounded. She didn't know what to say.

"Just a minute." Nicholas rose to his feet and walked over to his saddlebags. He reached inside and brought out a bundle that looked suspiciously familiar. When he returned to her side, she recognized the material. He opened the cloth and revealed her shorn hair.

"I let you ride away, then I crossed the creek and dug up your belongings. That's how I ended up with the material you buried and this. It's been my pillow for the last six months. Tonight I want the real thing to be my pillow."

Sammy felt totally overwhelmed. She couldn't believe Nicholas had loved her for so long and she never knew. Oh, how foolish she'd been. She'd wasted so much precious time.

Nicholas set the bundle of sheared tresses on a chair and reached for a towel warming by the fire.

"My turn. Let's get you dry and tucked in."

"Nicholas, I can't spend the night with you. What if someone finds out?"

"Angel, I've been married to you in my heart since we were stranded in that cave. I really don't care what anyone thinks. You've accepted my proposal, and as far as I'm concerned, we're already married. And don't worry about Padraig. If I had a guess, he's probably dreaming about Ashley Frank right about now."

"Nicholas!"

"Don't deny it. Did you ever hear so many questions about one particular woman before? I think he's smitten."

Sammy couldn't help the giggle that bubbled out uncontrollably. She toweled herself off with Nicholas' help. Her skin burst into flames wherever he touched. Her breasts felt heavy, and the nipples stood at attention. Ripples of sensation ran down to her belly and curled into a ball of throbbing need.

"I'll never get my bath if you keep looking at me like that, Angel. Be a good girl and climb under the covers. I'll hurry." Nicholas sat in the tub and started his own toilette.

Sammy watched for a moment and grinned. In a second, she hopped back out of bed and crossed to the tub. His copper skin glowed in the firelight. Slick and shiny from the bath water, she couldn't resist the need to stroke him.

"I think turn about is fair play," she whispered as she took the sponge from his hand and began a loving massage down his powerful chest.

Don't miss

DOUBLE DESTINY,

Rosina LaFata's sequel to

AVENGING ANGEL

Coming in August, 2003

DOUBLE DESTINY, is the story of the O'Brien twins stolen by Swift Arrow. The twin boys, raised by the Indians, grow to manhood believing their white family never wanted them. When they find and capture Nicholas and Sammy's daughter they are forced to acknowledge their white heritage and make some tough decisions.

DOUBLE DESTINY is a historical romance available from Wings Press, Inc.

Meet Rosina LaFata

Rosina is a member of RWA and the Missouri Chapter MORWA. She has been writing for 5 years having finished her first book 3 years ago. Since that time she retired to write full time and has 3 completed novels and has 3 more started. AVENGING ANGEL is the first book she wrote, but the second to be published. Rosina loves to travel, has lived abroad in both Ireland and Japan, and recently visited Italy. In addition to writing, dancing is another of her passions. She loves to garden and takes extreme pleasure in her country home where she enjoys the peace and serenity of 11 acres of woods.